TONKO HOUSE
AND
FIRST SECOND

PRESENT

the

DAM KEEPER

BOOK THREE

by

ROBERT KONDO
DAISUKE "DICE" TSUTSUMI

producer / agent

KANE LEE

art lead

YOSHIHIRO NAGASUNA

art

REBECCA CHAN
JJ JAEHEE SONG
LAURA SWALLEY

additional art

RYO MURATA   TOSHIHIRO NAKAMURA
TOMO OKUBO   SERGIO PÁEZ

production

GISELLE GRIMALDO
COURTNEY LOCKWOOD
DAISUKE "ZEN" MIYAKE

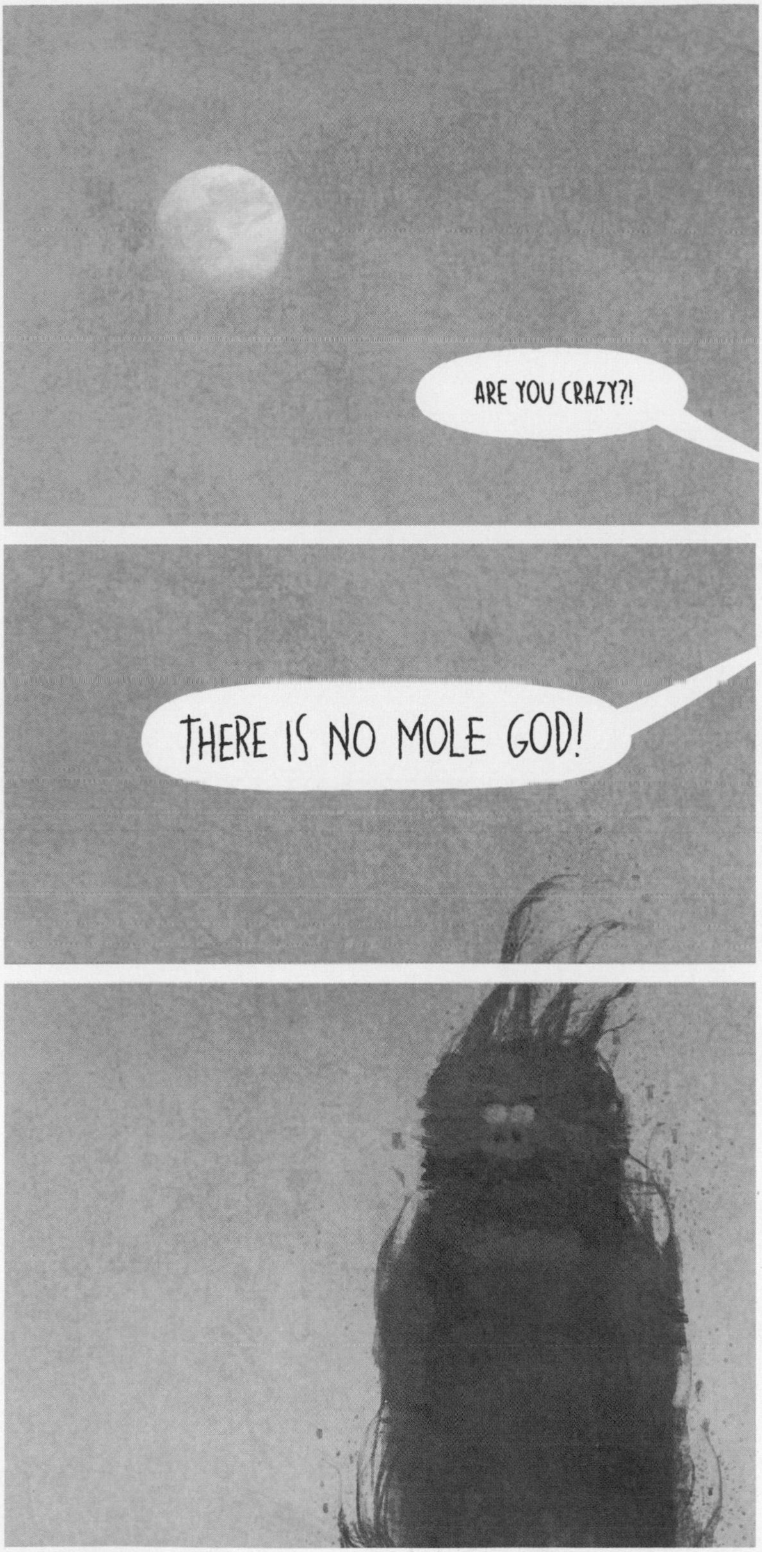
ARE YOU CRAZY?!
THERE IS NO MOLE GOD!

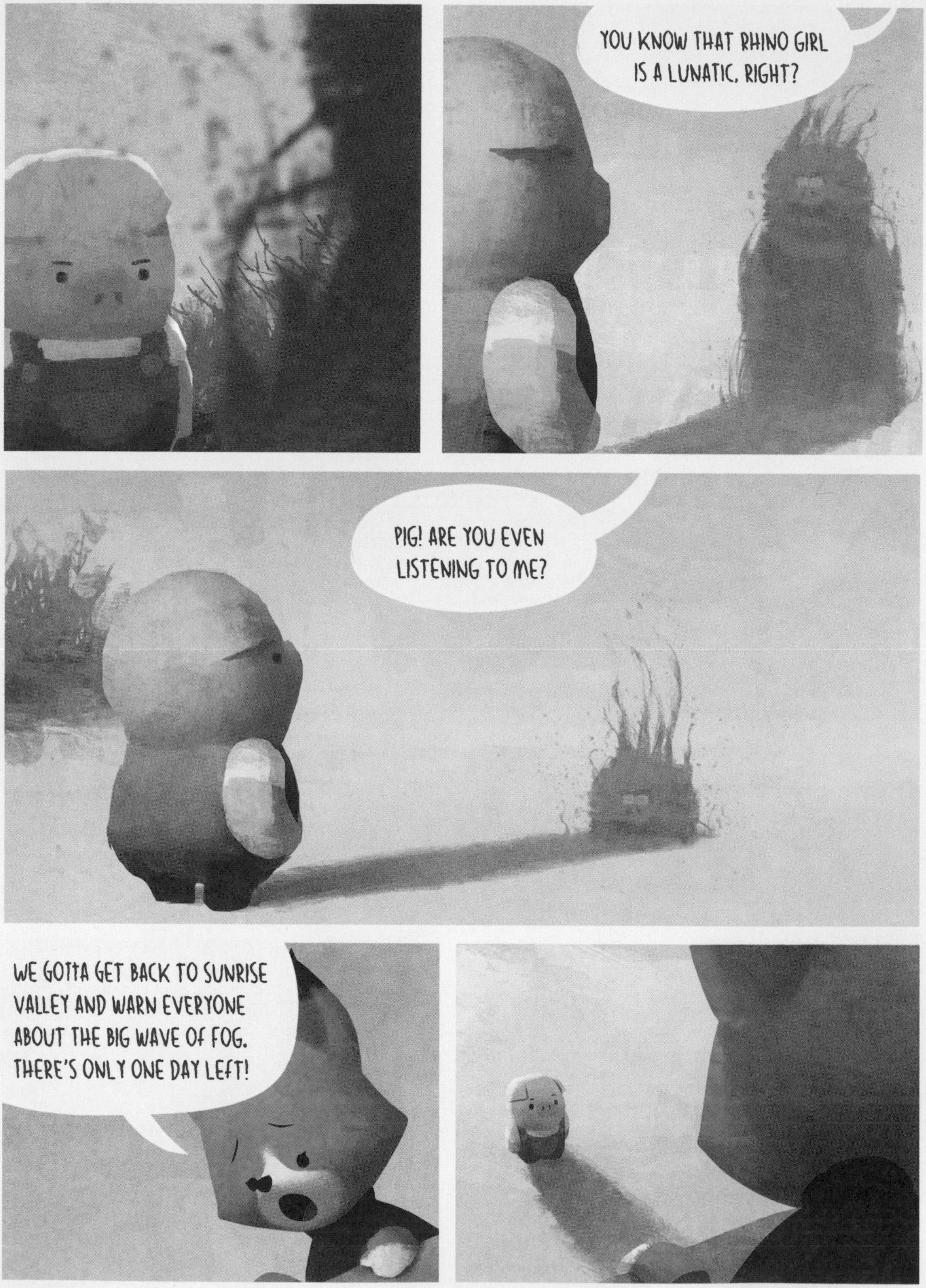
YOU KNOW THAT RHINO GIRL IS A LUNATIC, RIGHT?
PIG! ARE YOU EVEN LISTENING TO ME?
WE GOTTA GET BACK TO SUNRISE VALLEY AND WARN EVERYONE ABOUT THE BIG WAVE OF FOG. THERE'S ONLY ONE DAY LEFT!

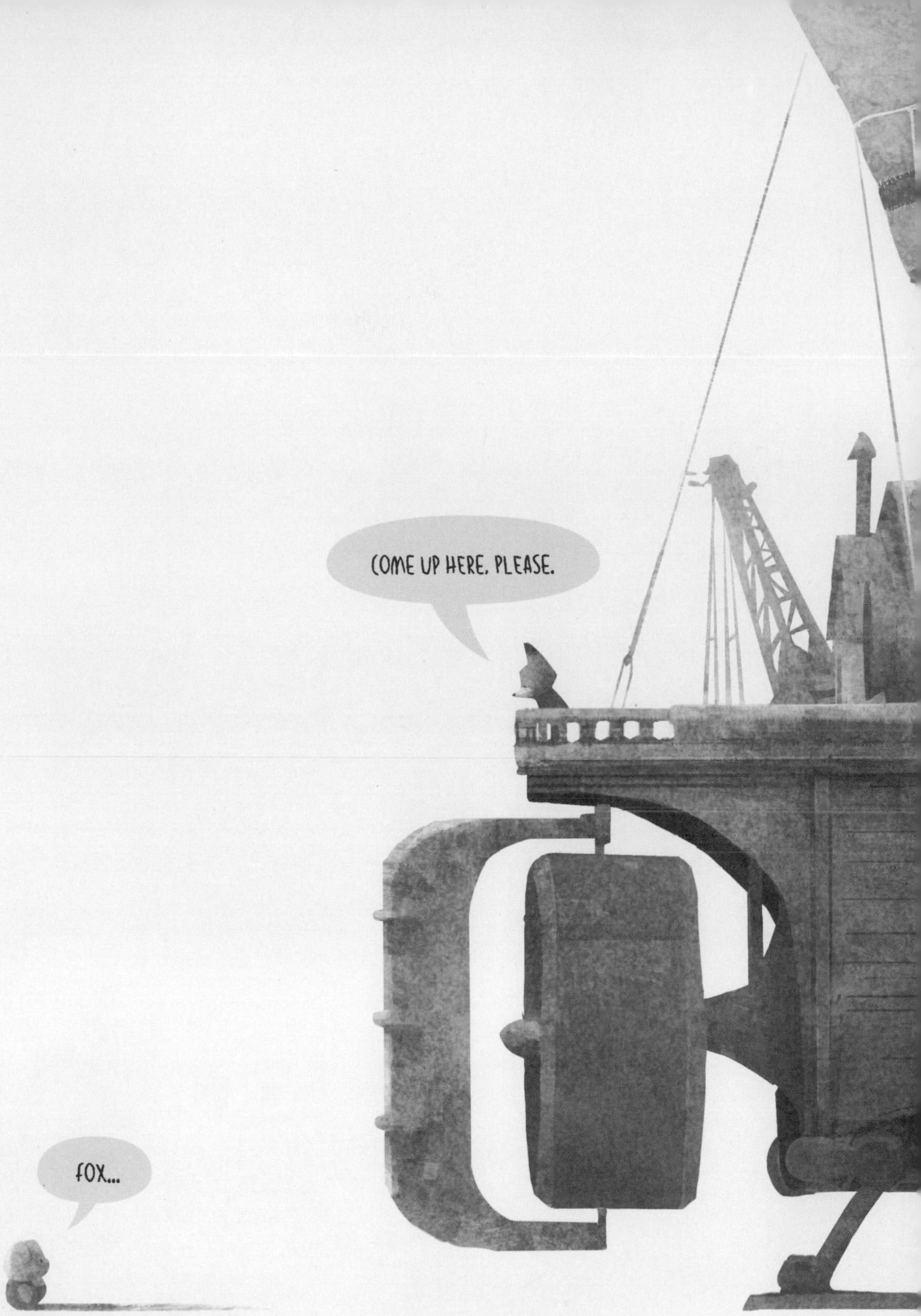
COME UP HERE, PLEASE.
FOX...

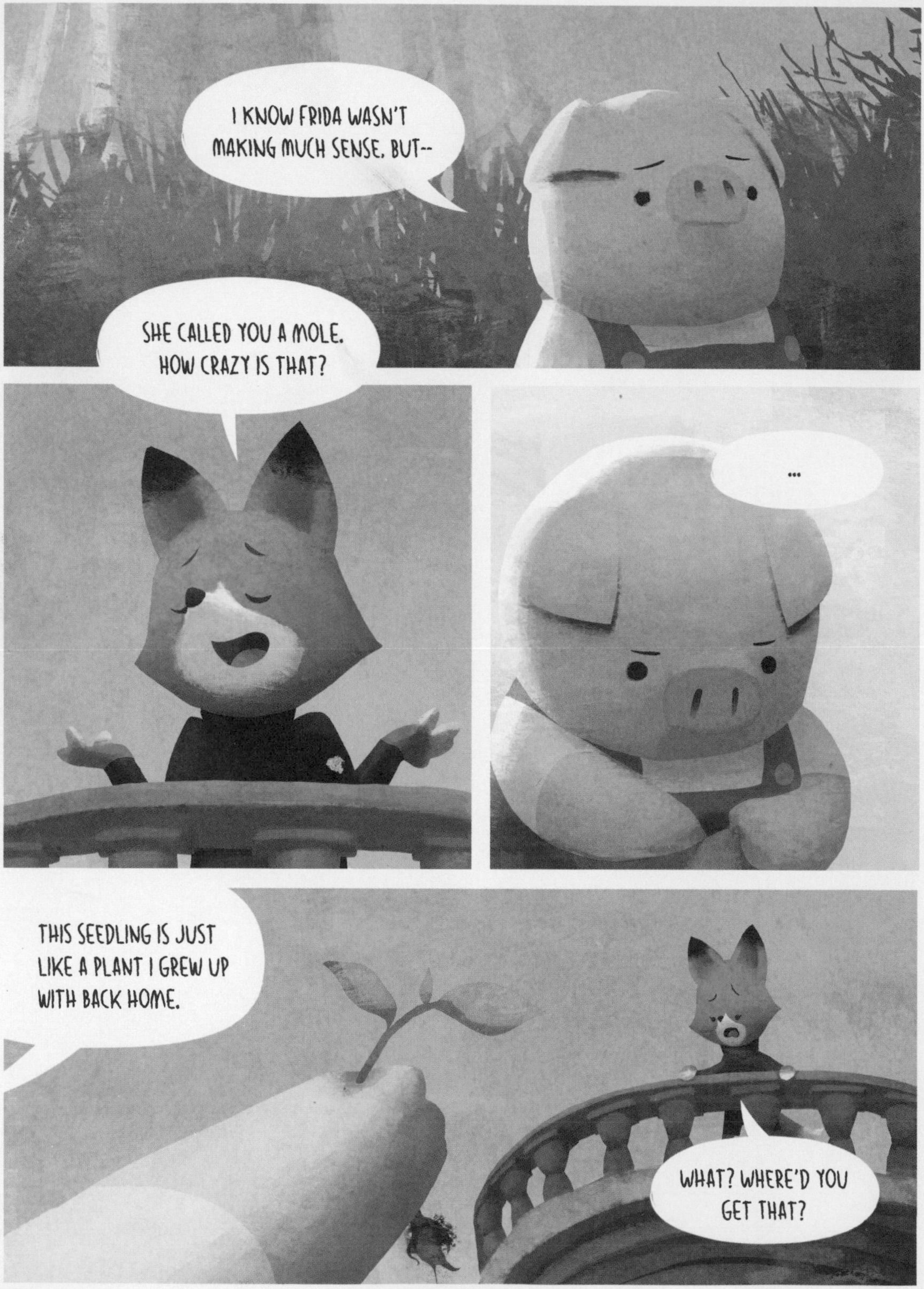
I KNOW FRIDA WASN'T MAKING MUCH SENSE. BUT--
SHE CALLED YOU A MOLE. HOW CRAZY IS THAT?
...
THIS SEEDLING IS JUST LIKE A PLANT I GREW UP WITH BACK HOME.
WHAT? WHERE'D YOU GET THAT?

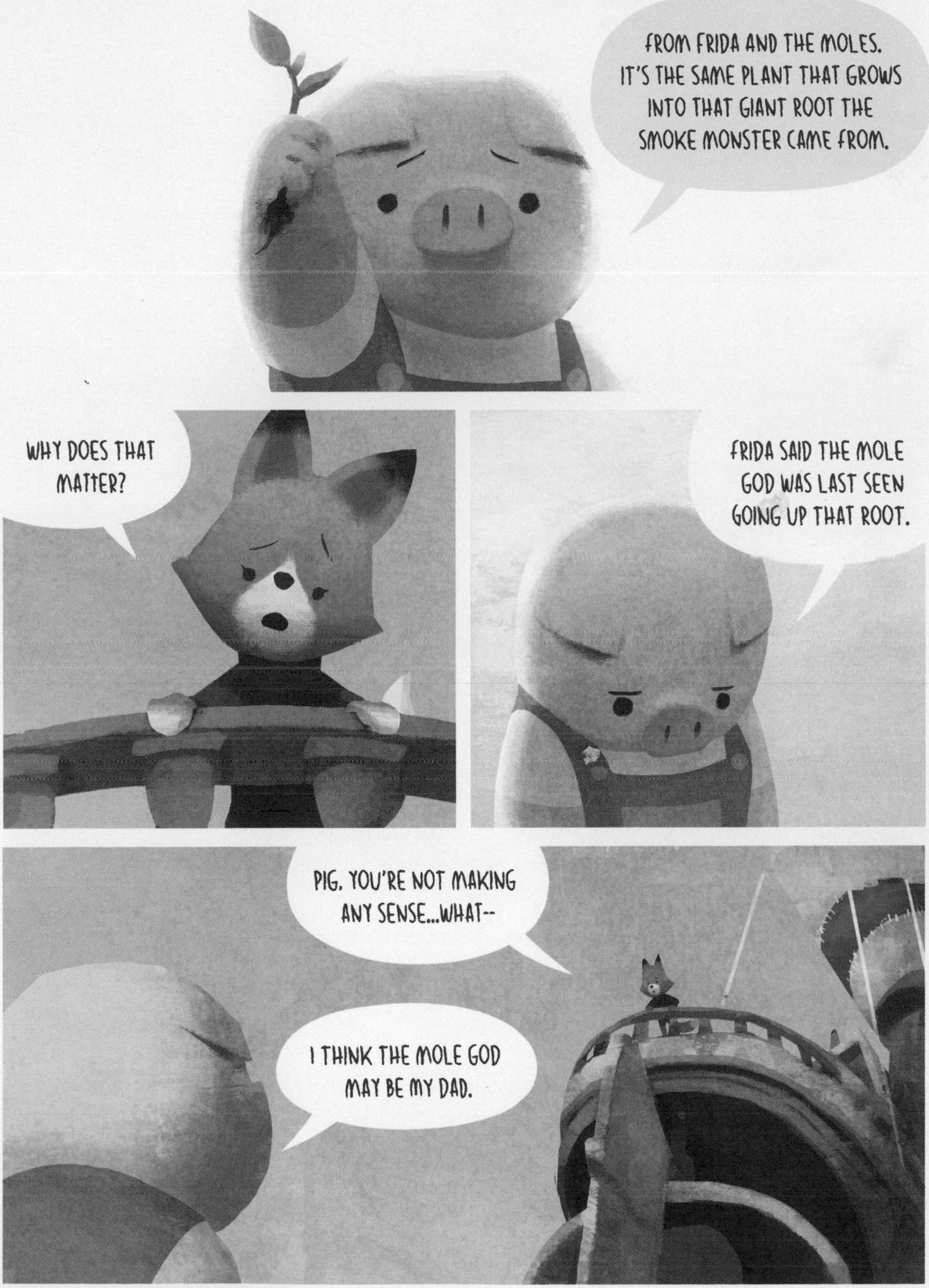
FROM FRIDA AND THE MOLES. IT'S THE SAME PLANT THAT GROWS INTO THAT GIANT ROOT THE SMOKE MONSTER CAME FROM.
WHY DOES THAT MATTER?
FRIDA SAID THE MOLE GOD WAS LAST SEEN GOING UP THAT ROOT.
PIG, YOU'RE NOT MAKING ANY SENSE...WHAT--
I THINK THE MOLE GOD MAY BE MY DAD.

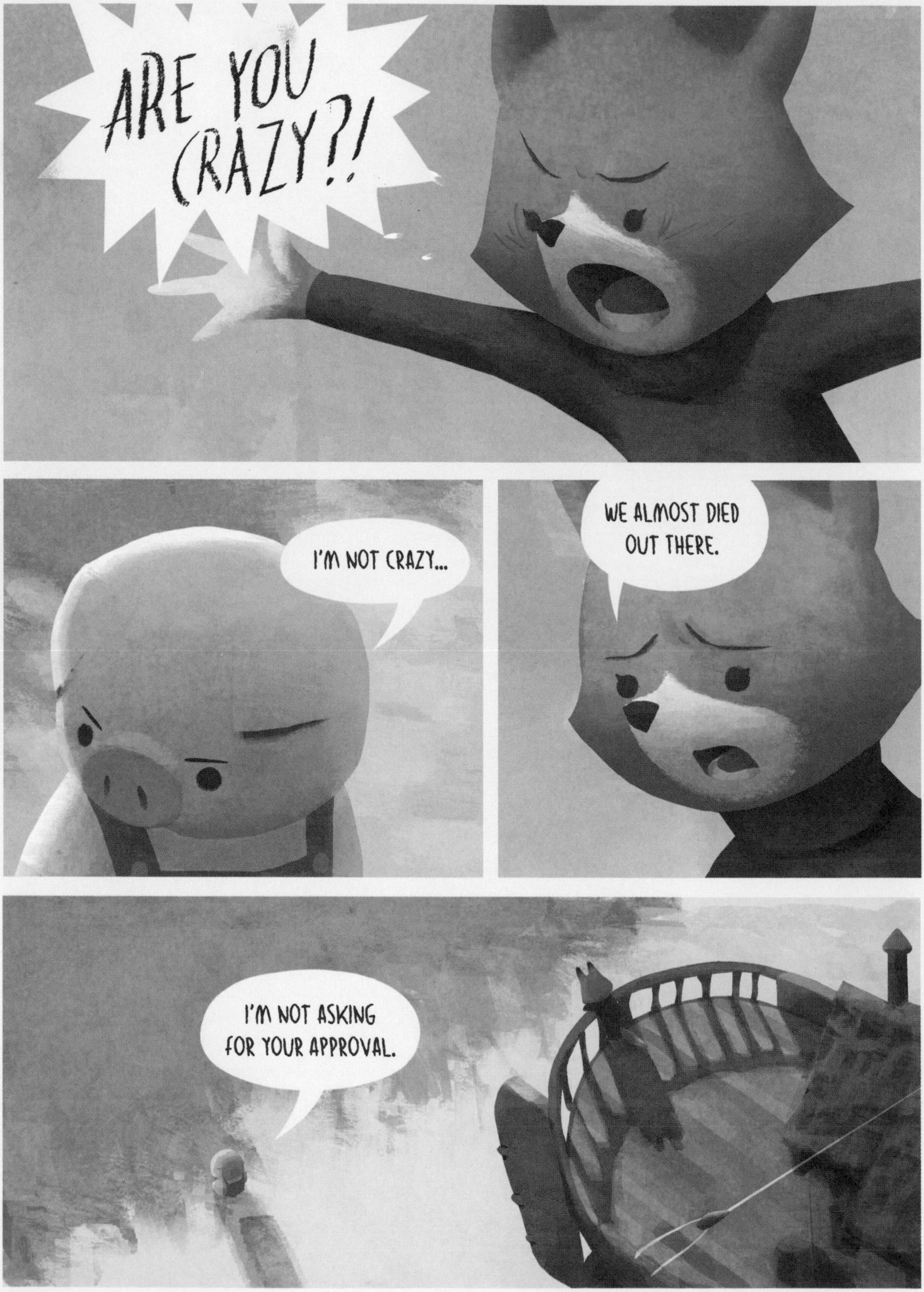
ARE YOU CRAZY?!
I'M NOT CRAZY...
WE ALMOST DIED OUT THERE.
I'M NOT ASKING FOR YOUR APPROVAL.

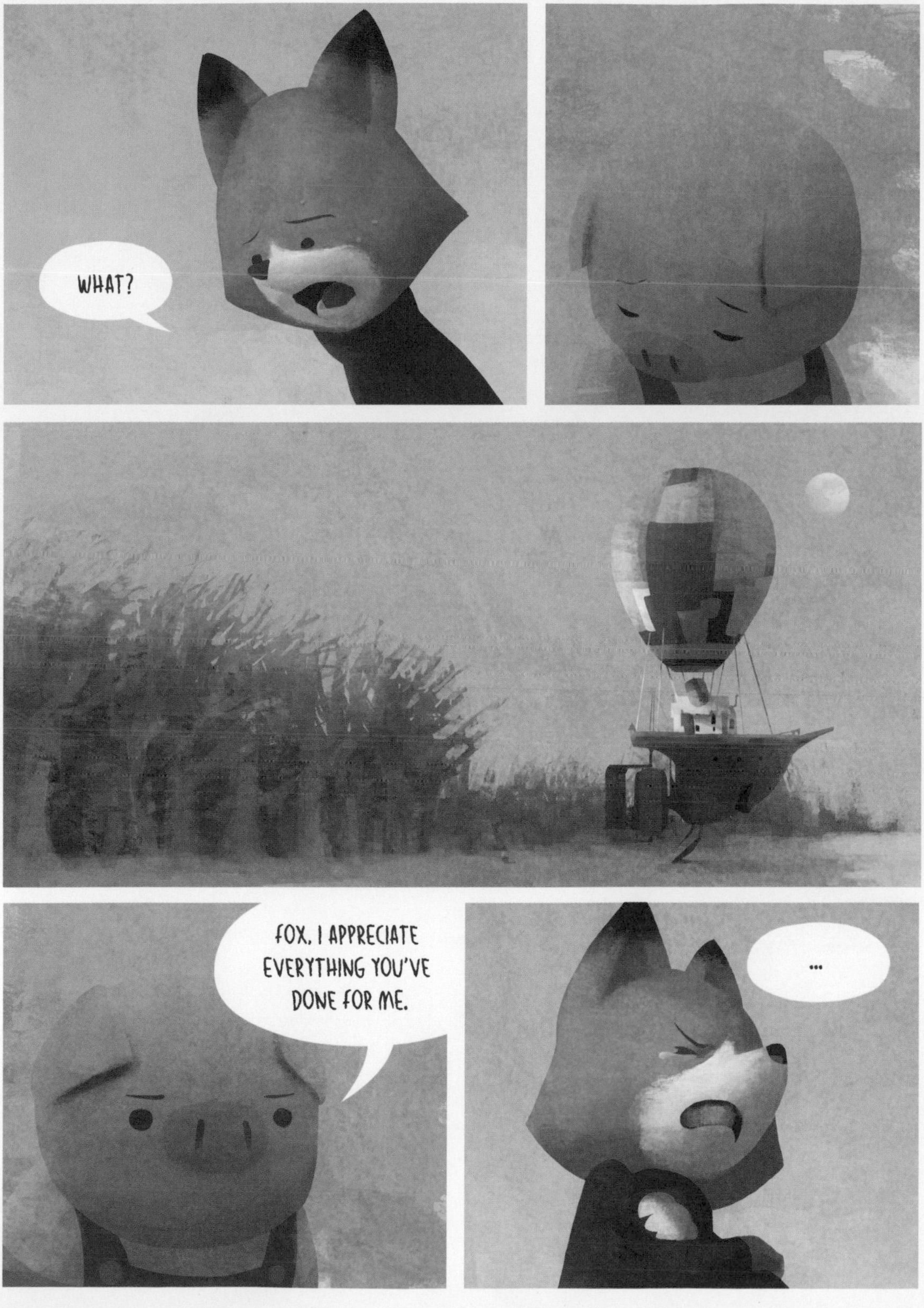
WHAT?
FOX, I APPRECIATE EVERYTHING YOU'VE DONE FOR ME.
...

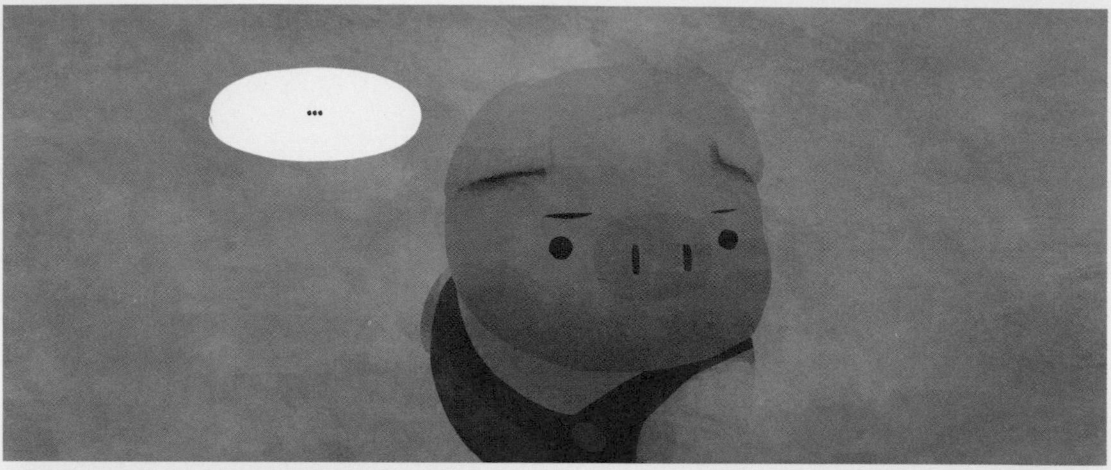
...

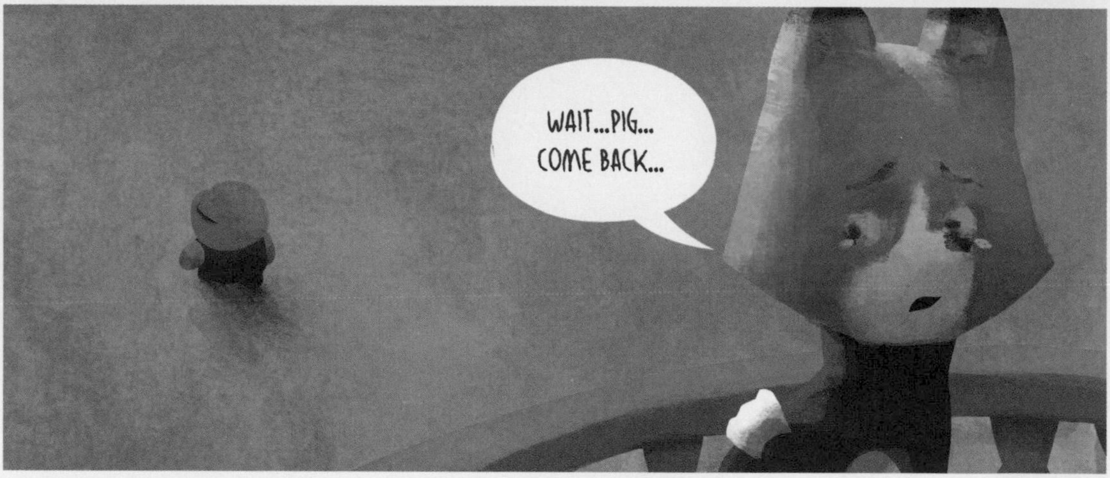
WAIT...PIG... COME BACK...

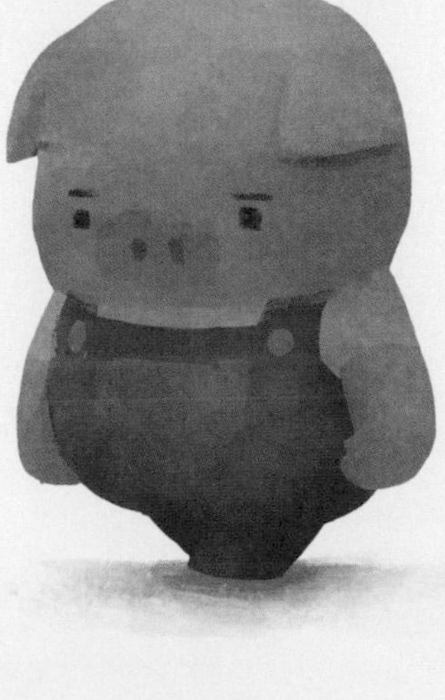

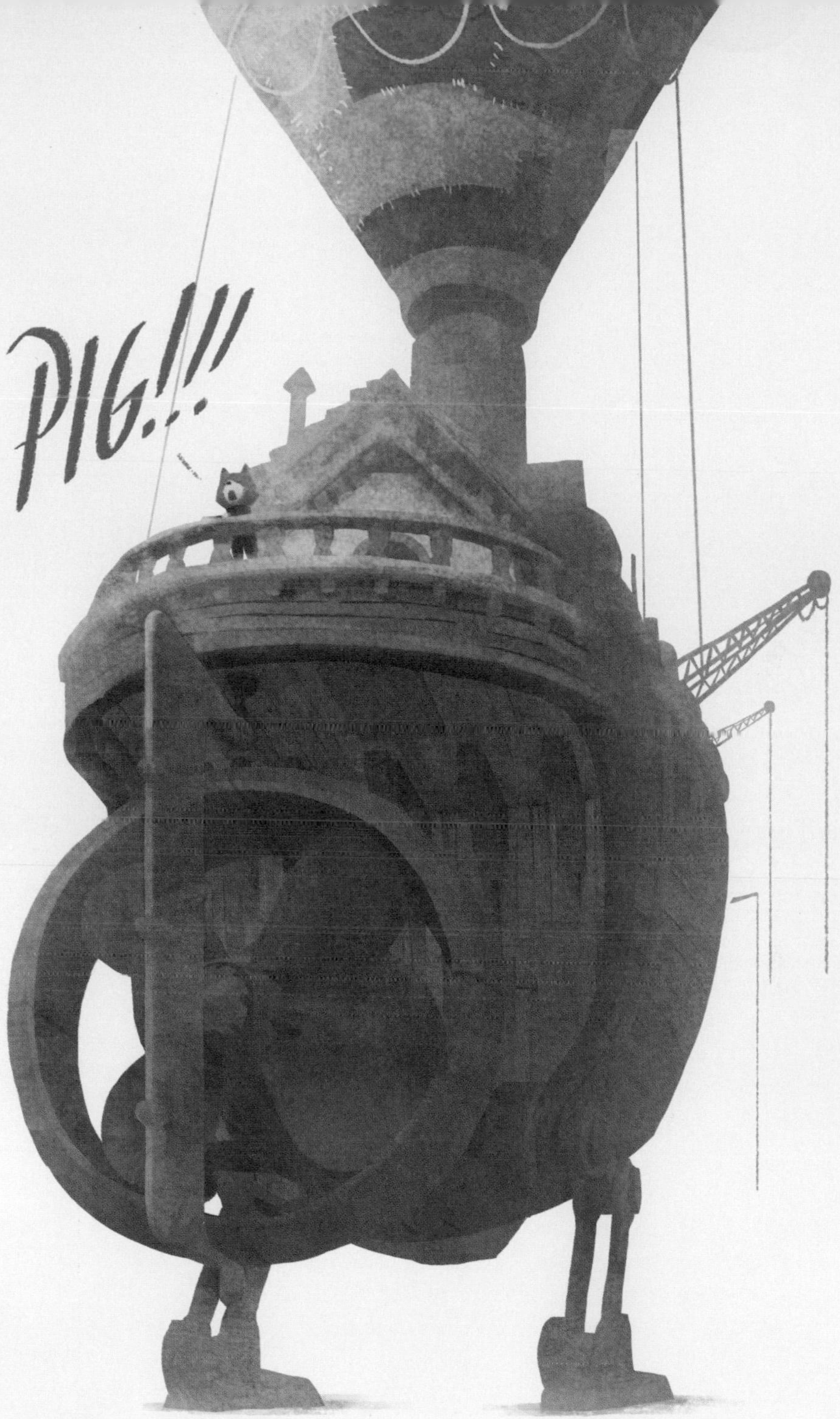
PIG!!!

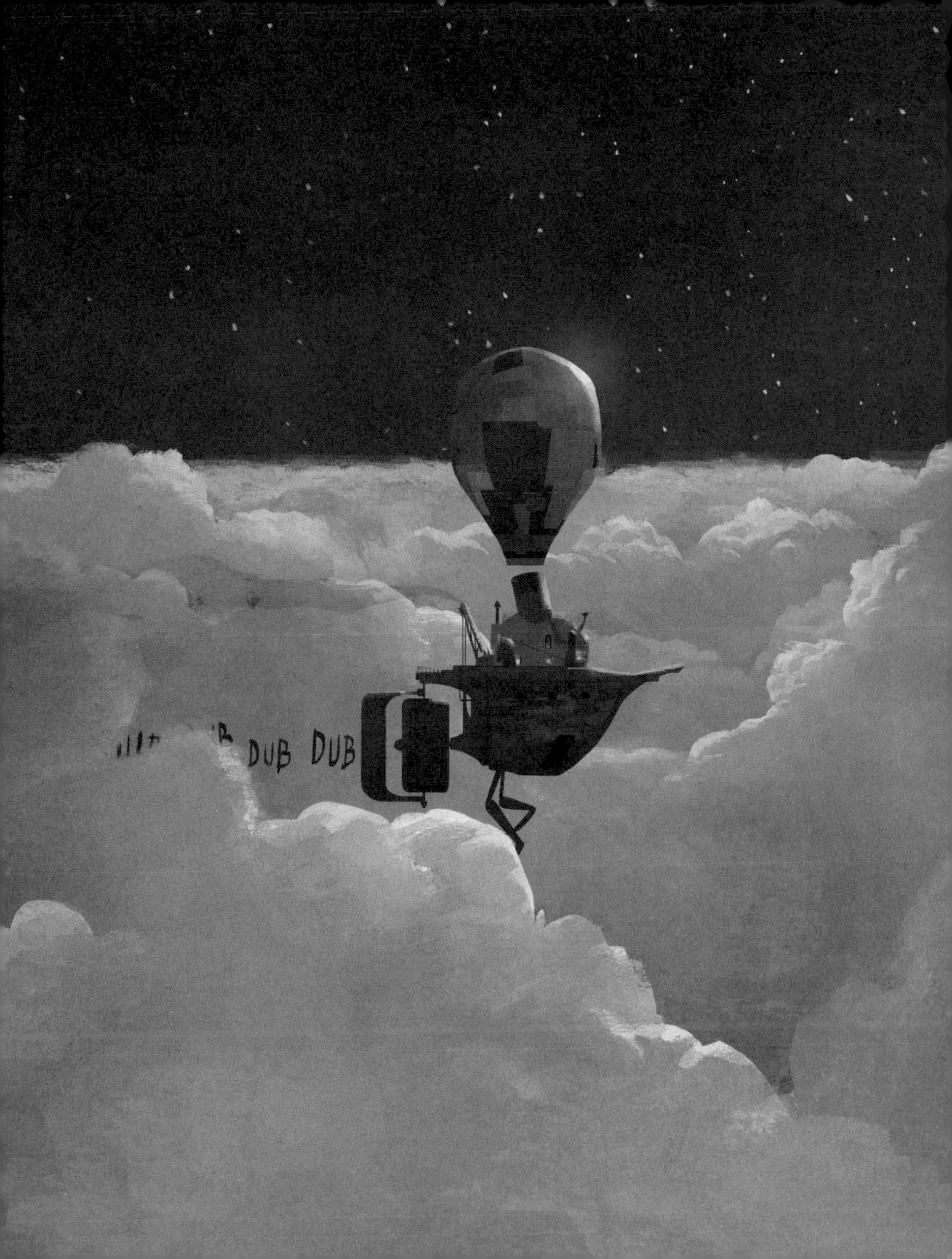
DUB DUB

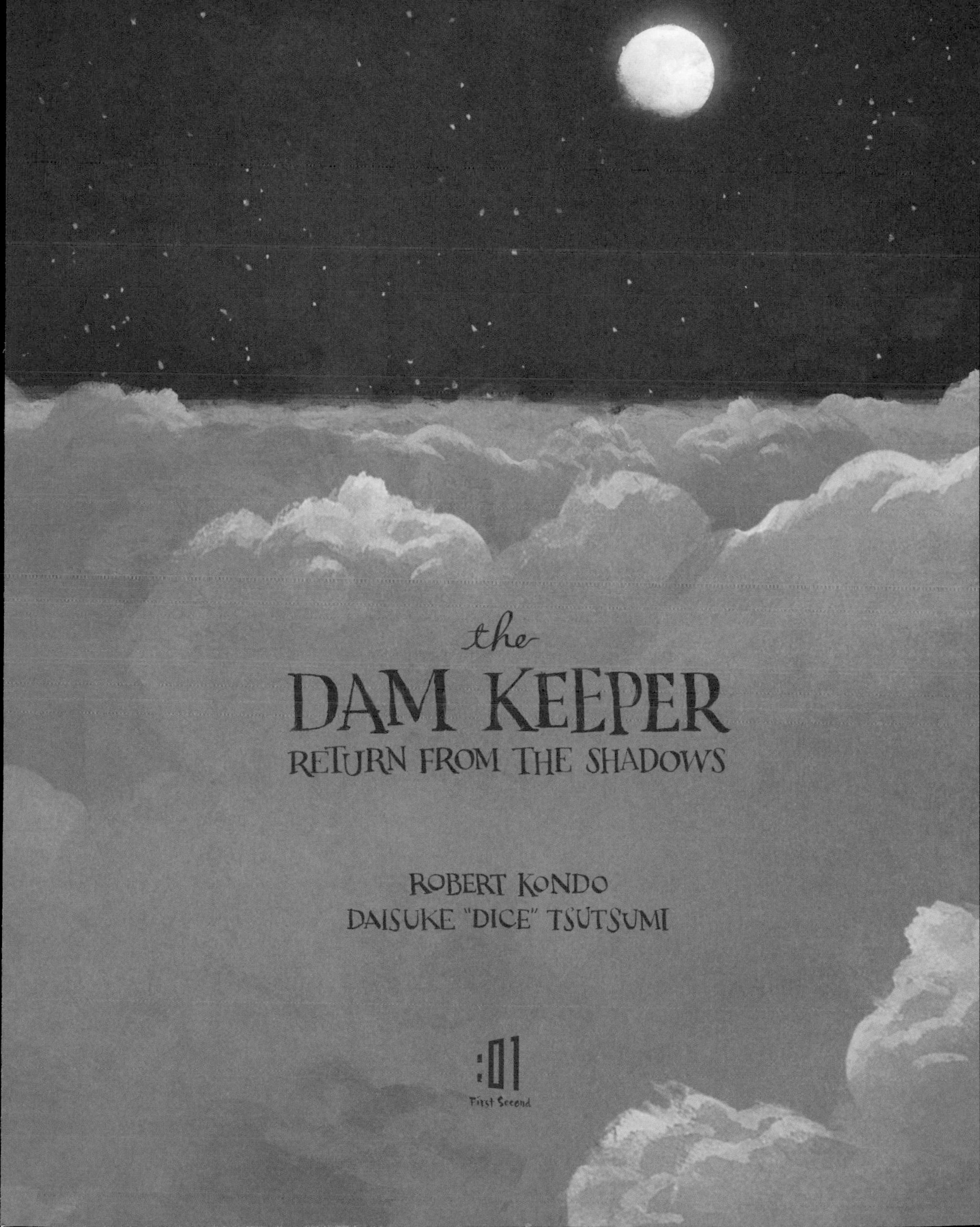

the DAM KEEPER

RETURN FROM THE SHADOWS

ROBERT KONDO

DAISUKE "DICE" TSUTSUMI

:01 First Second

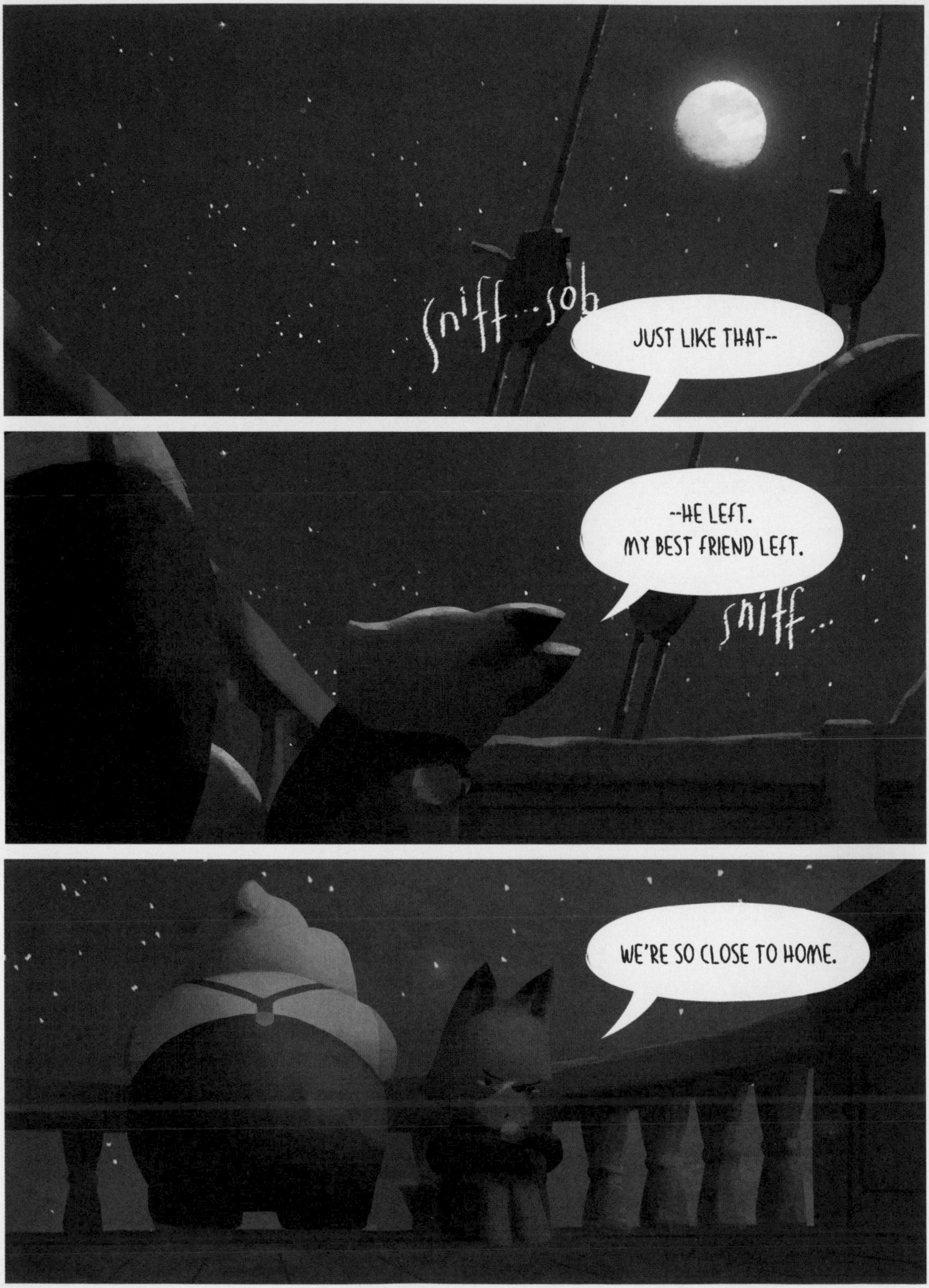
sniff...sob
JUST LIKE THAT--
--HE LEFT.
MY BEST FRIEND LEFT.
sniff...
WE'RE SO CLOSE TO HOME.

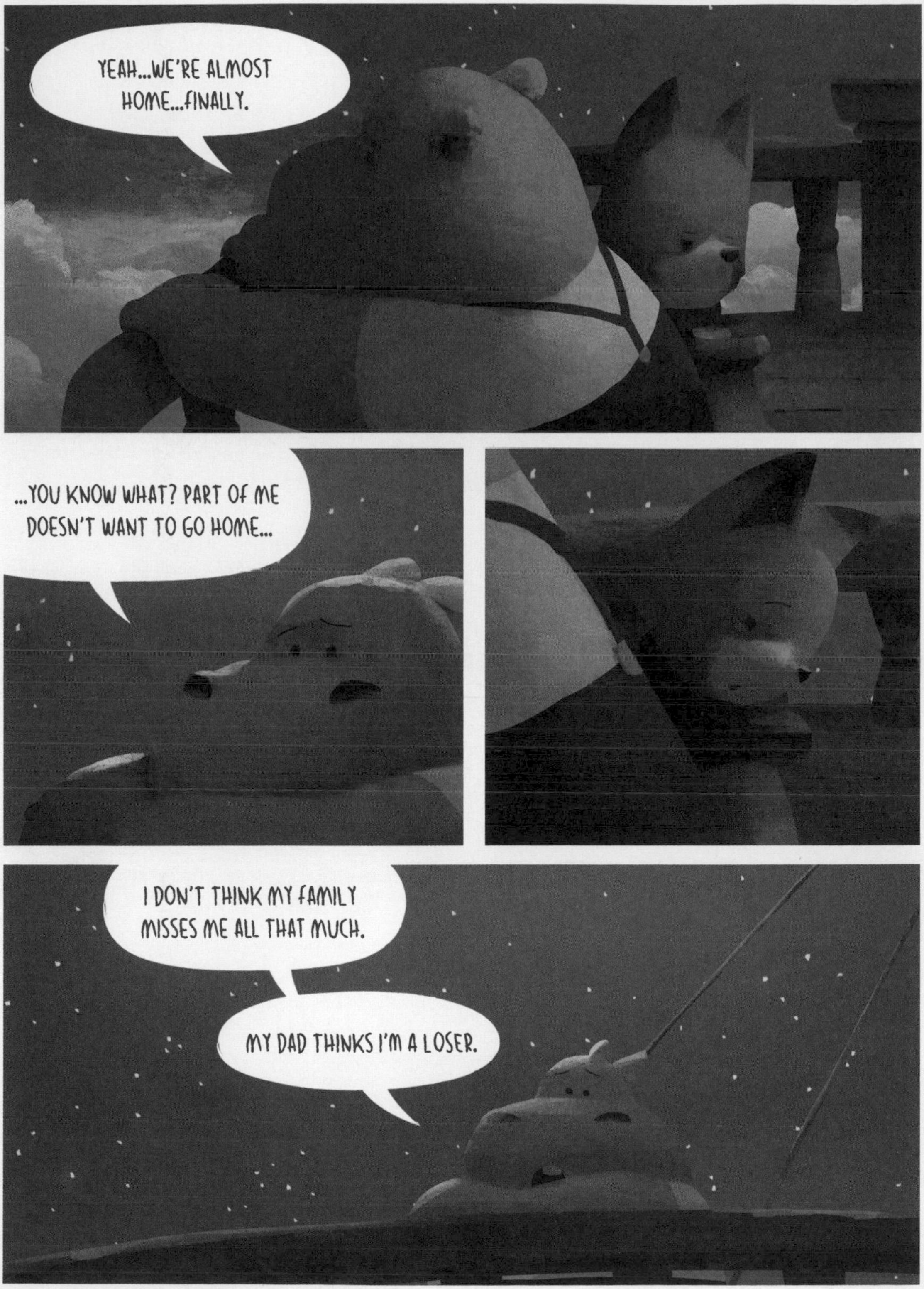
YEAH...WE'RE ALMOST HOME...FINALLY.
...YOU KNOW WHAT? PART OF ME DOESN'T WANT TO GO HOME...
I DON'T THINK MY FAMILY MISSES ME ALL THAT MUCH.
MY DAD THINKS I'M A LOSER.

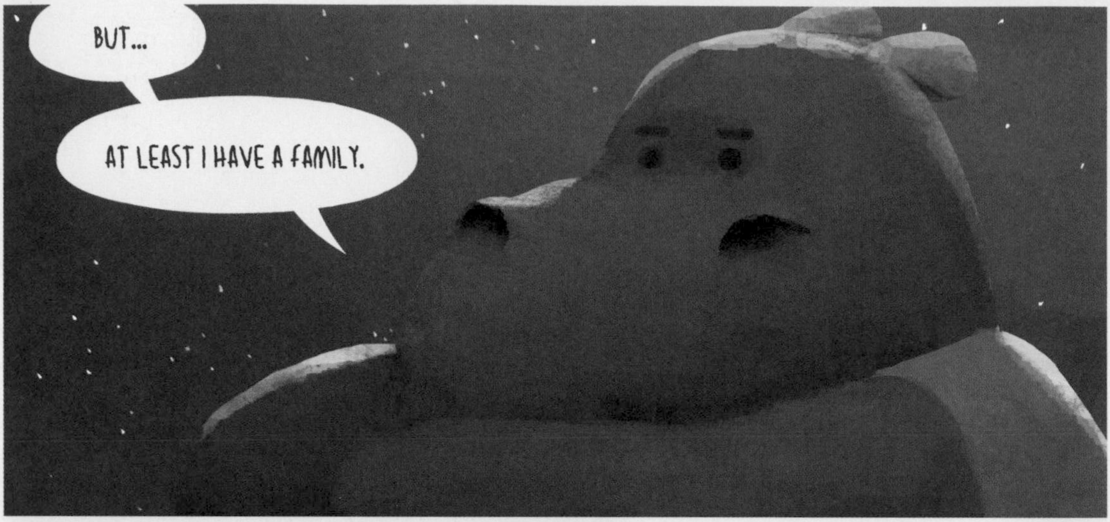
BUT...
AT LEAST I HAVE A FAMILY.

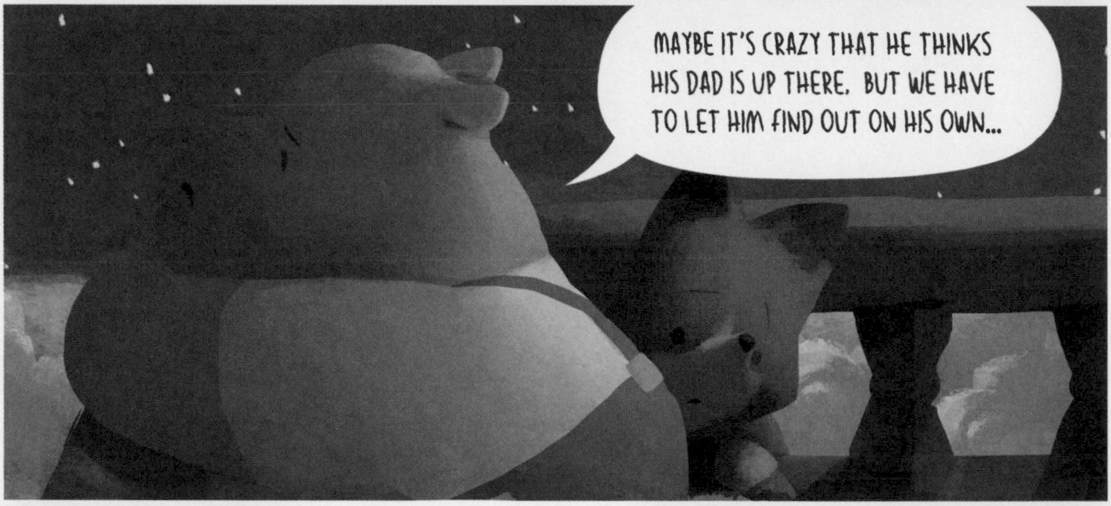
MAYBE IT'S CRAZY THAT HE THINKS HIS DAD IS UP THERE. BUT WE HAVE TO LET HIM FIND OUT ON HIS OWN...

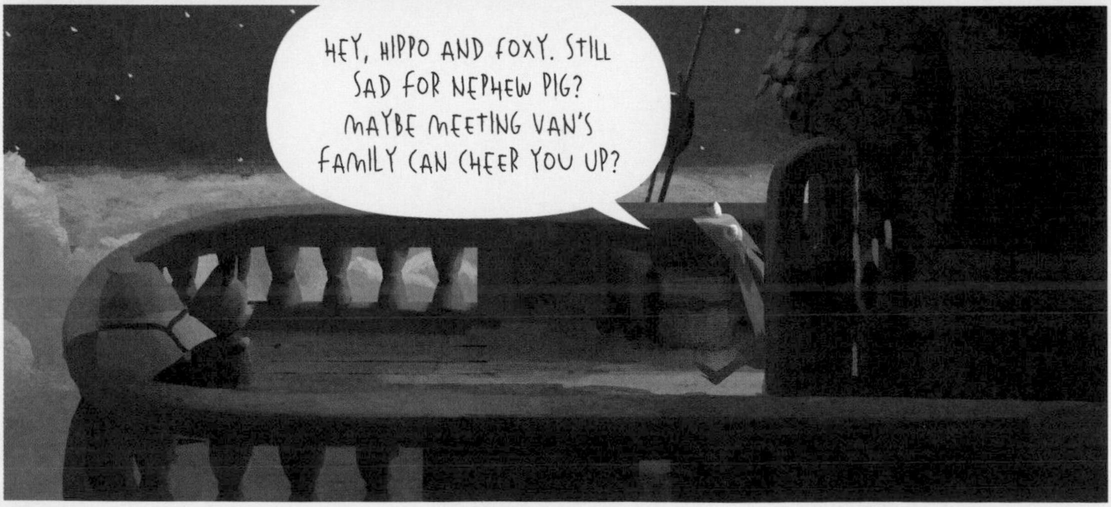
HEY, HIPPO AND FOXY. STILL SAD FOR NEPHEW PIG? MAYBE MEETING VAN'S FAMILY CAN CHEER YOU UP?

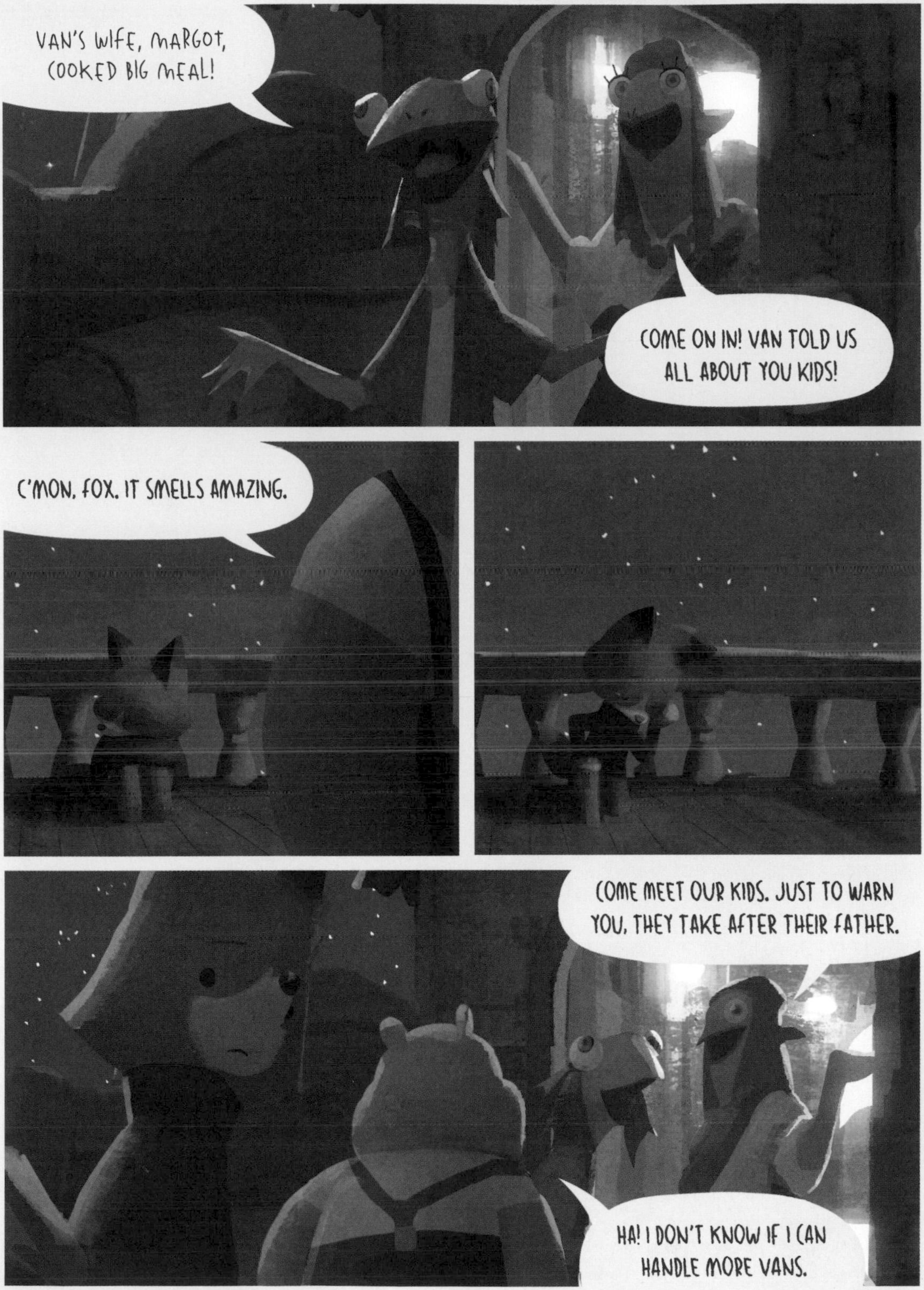
VAN'S WIFE, MARGOT, COOKED BIG MEAL!
COME ON IN! VAN TOLD US ALL ABOUT YOU KIDS!
C'MON, FOX. IT SMELLS AMAZING.
COME MEET OUR KIDS. JUST TO WARN YOU, THEY TAKE AFTER THEIR FATHER.
HA! I DON'T KNOW IF I CAN HANDLE MORE VANS.

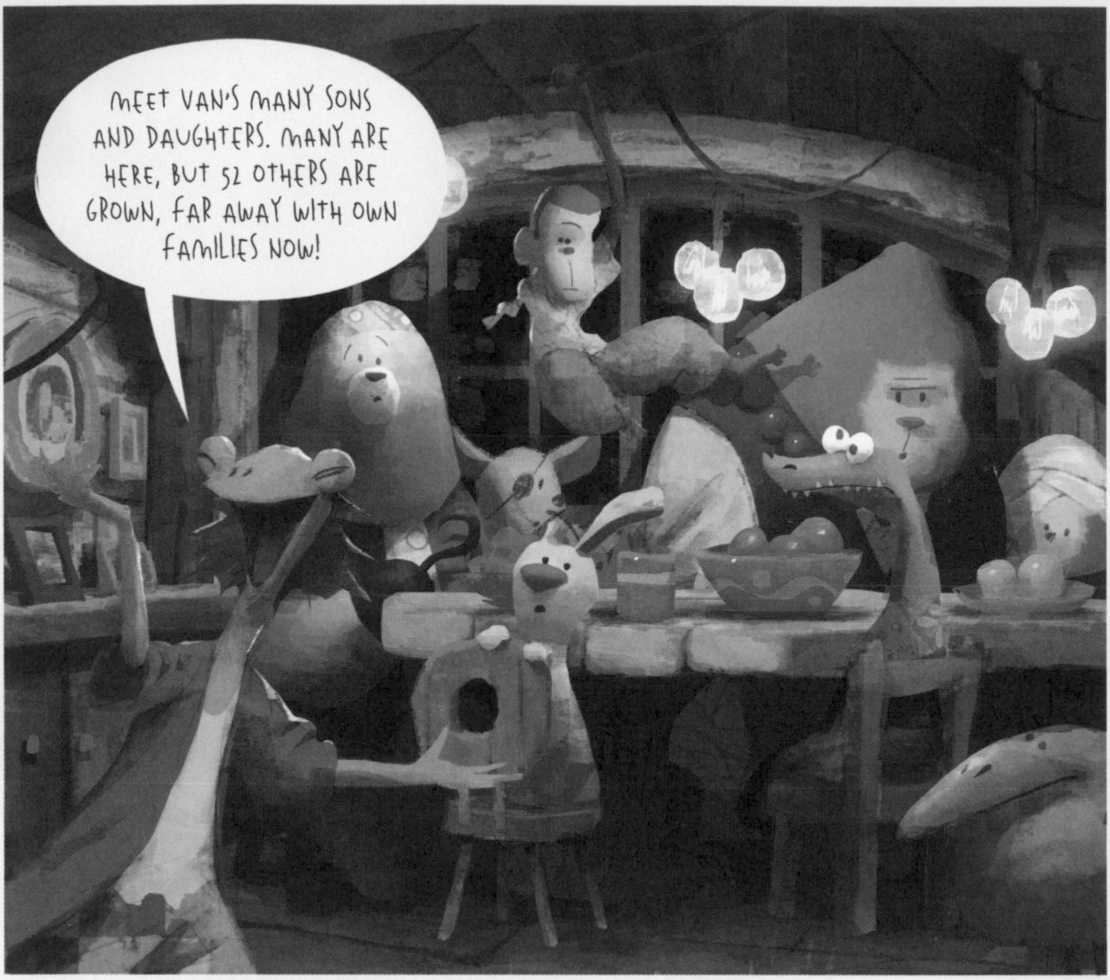
MEET VAN'S MANY SONS AND DAUGHTERS. MANY ARE HERE, BUT 52 OTHERS ARE GROWN, FAR AWAY WITH OWN FAMILIES NOW!

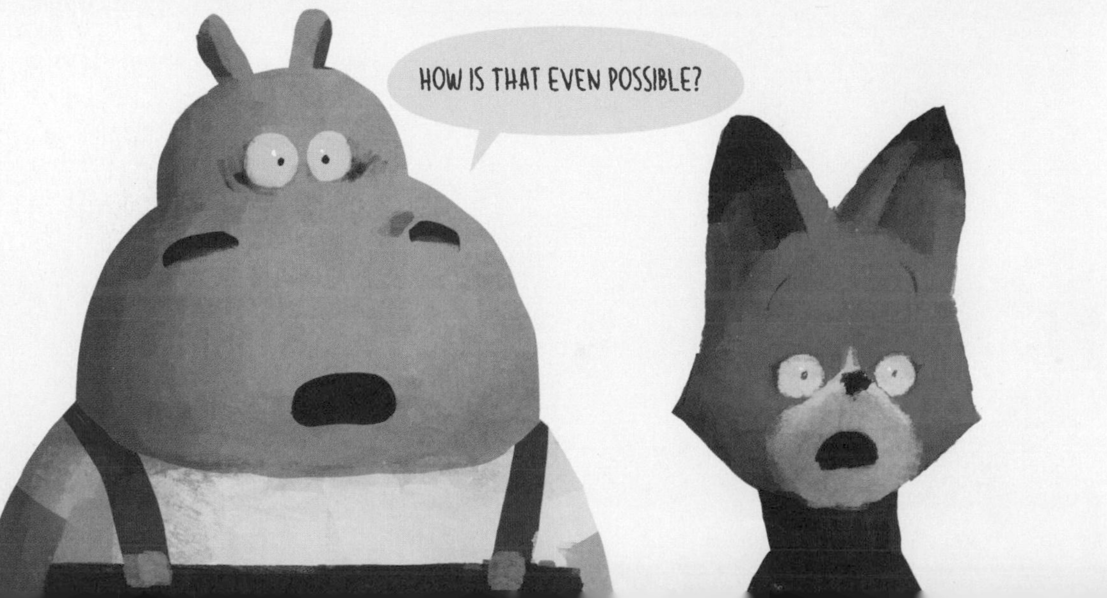
HOW IS THAT EVEN POSSIBLE?

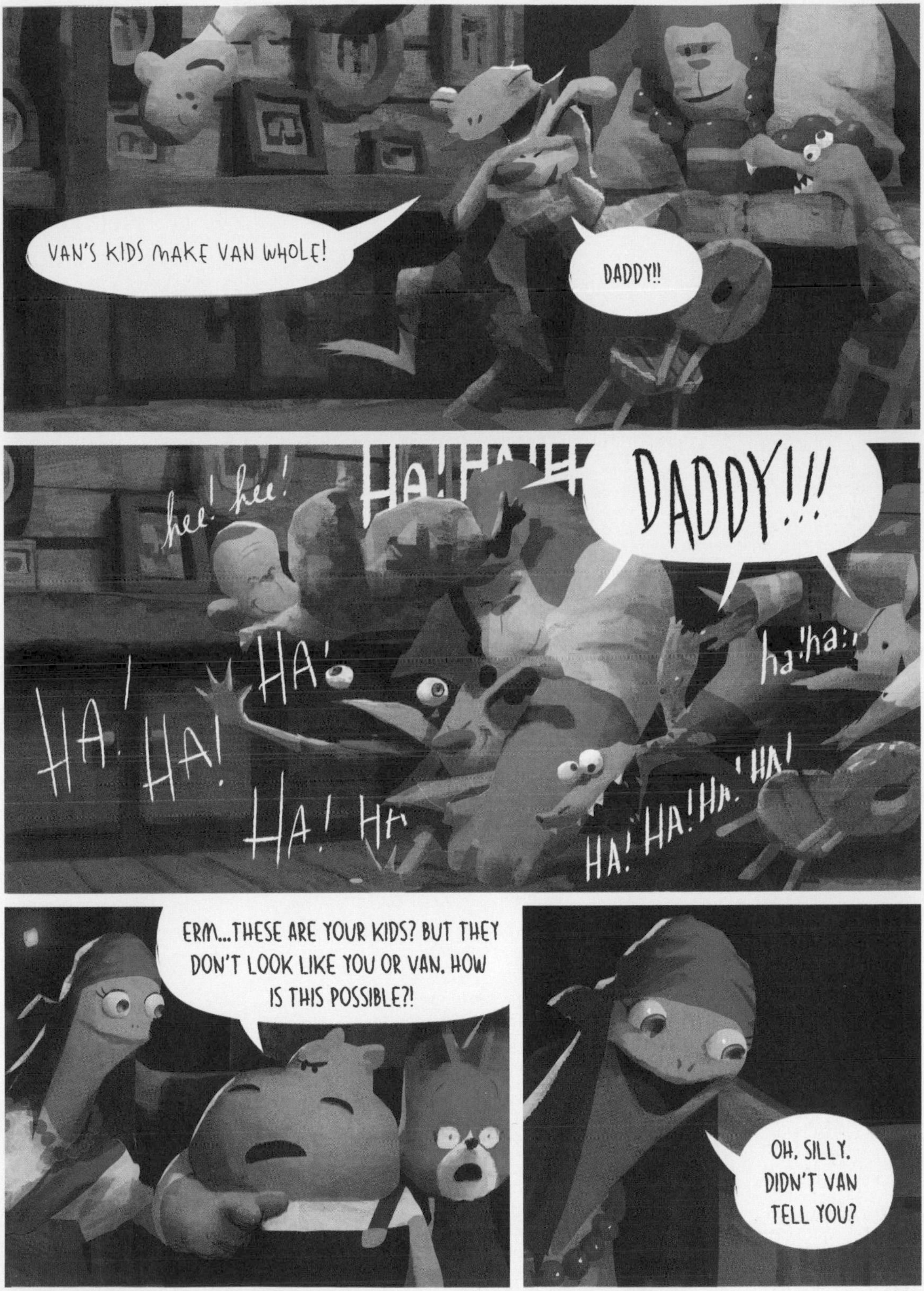
VAN'S KIDS MAKE VAN WHOLE!
DADDY!!
DADDY!!!
hee! hee!
HA! HA!
HA!
HA!
ha!ha!!
HA! HA!
ERM...THESE ARE YOUR KIDS? BUT THEY DON'T LOOK LIKE YOU OR VAN. HOW IS THIS POSSIBLE?!
OH, SILLY. DIDN'T VAN TELL YOU?

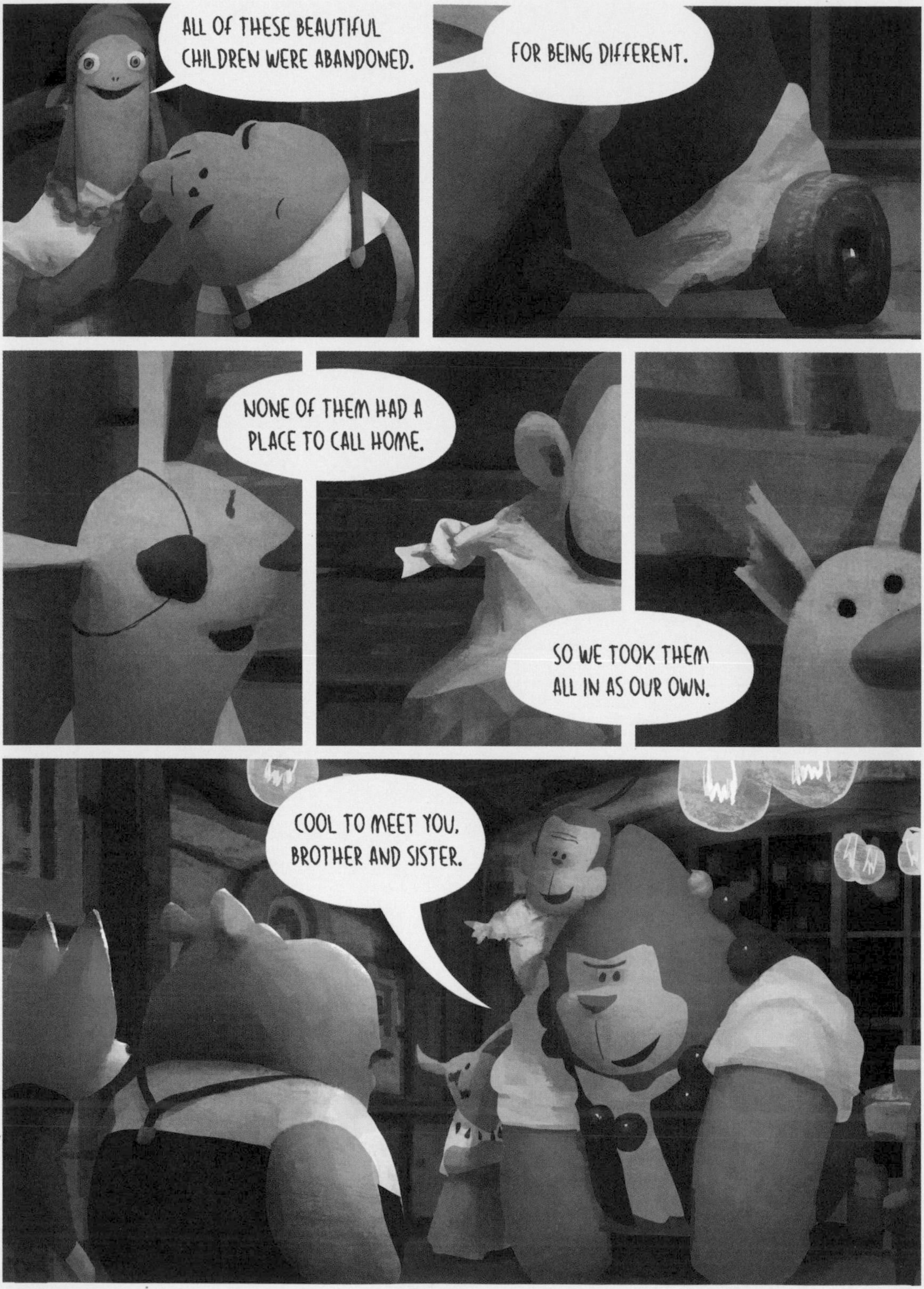
ALL OF THESE BEAUTIFUL CHILDREN WERE ABANDONED.
FOR BEING DIFFERENT.
NONE OF THEM HAD A PLACE TO CALL HOME.
SO WE TOOK THEM ALL IN AS OUR OWN.
COOL TO MEET YOU, BROTHER AND SISTER.

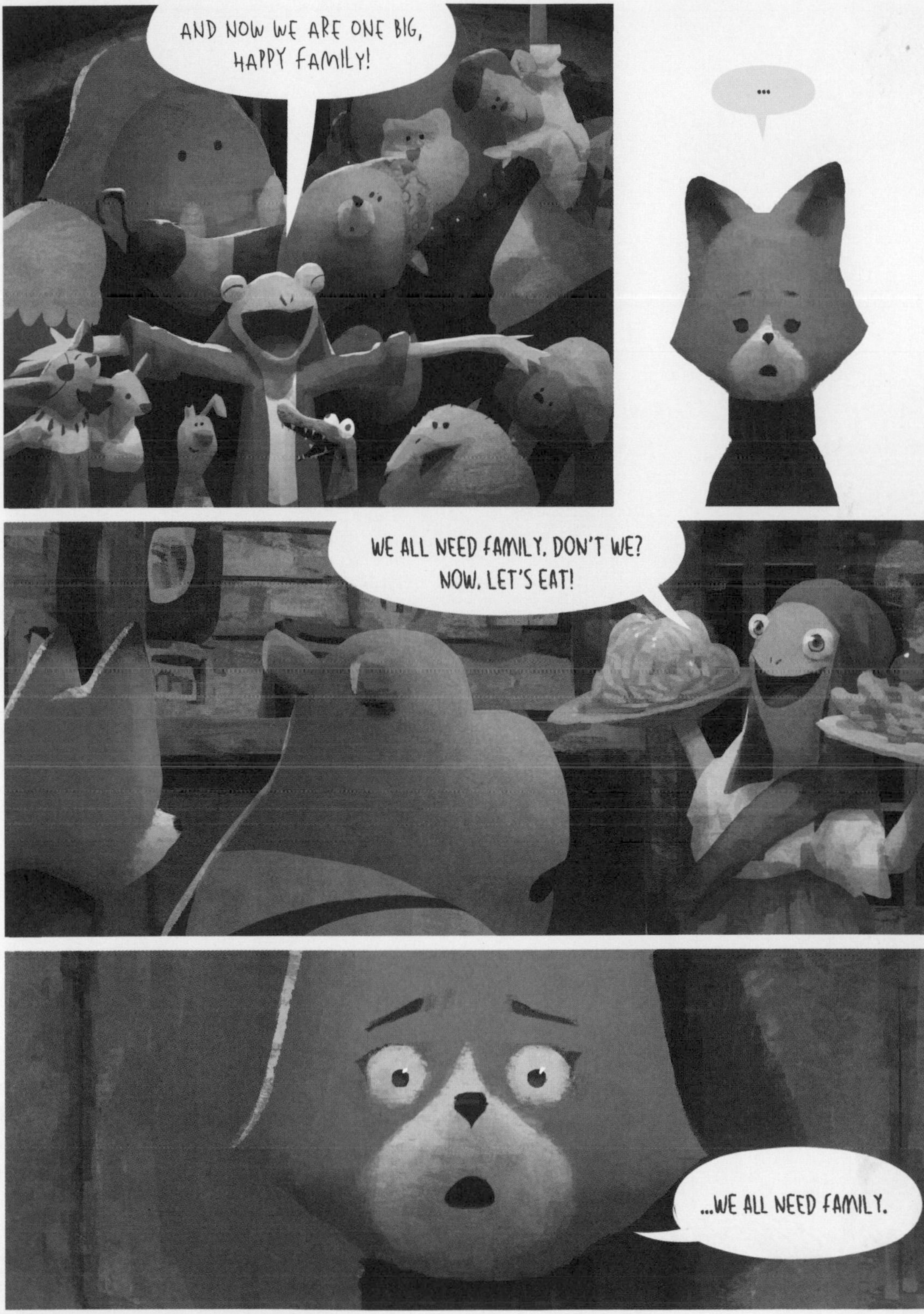
AND NOW WE ARE ONE BIG, HAPPY FAMILY!
...
WE ALL NEED FAMILY, DON'T WE? NOW, LET'S EAT!
...WE ALL NEED FAMILY.

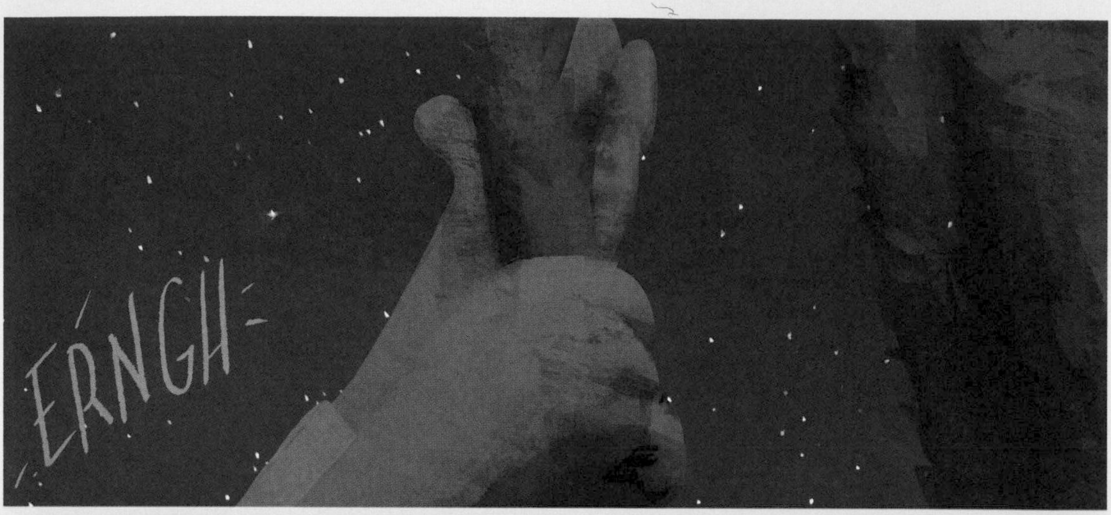
ERNGH

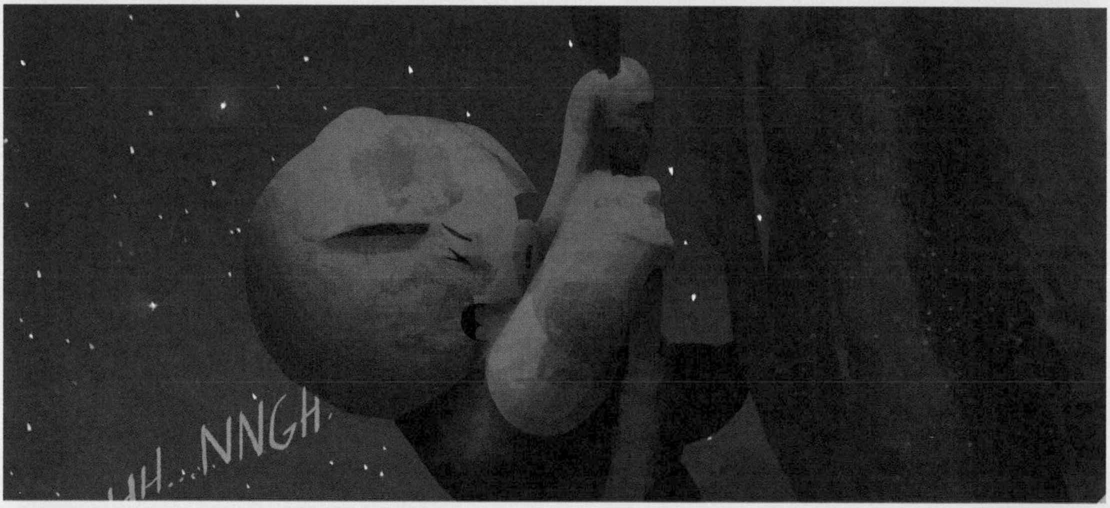
NNGH

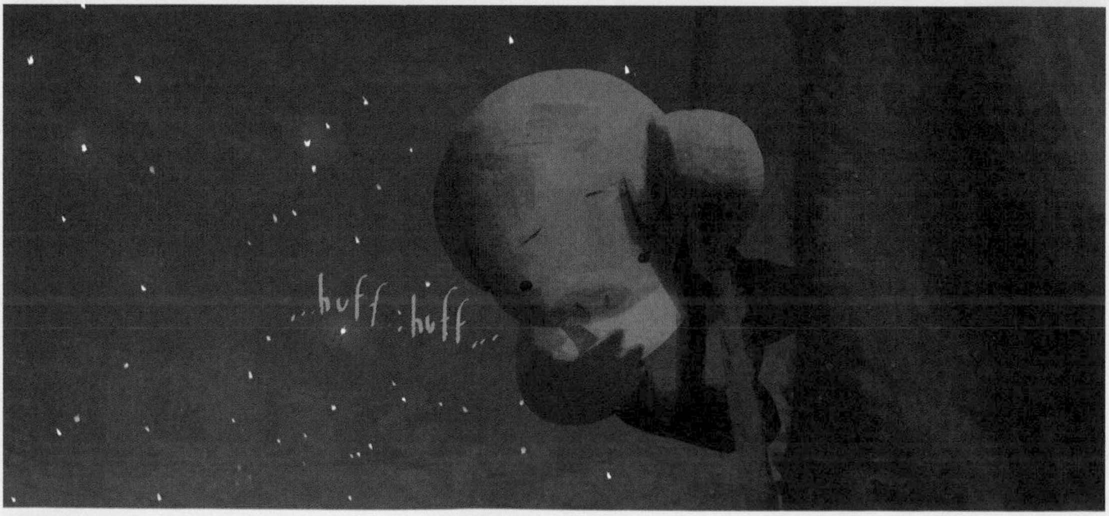
huff huff

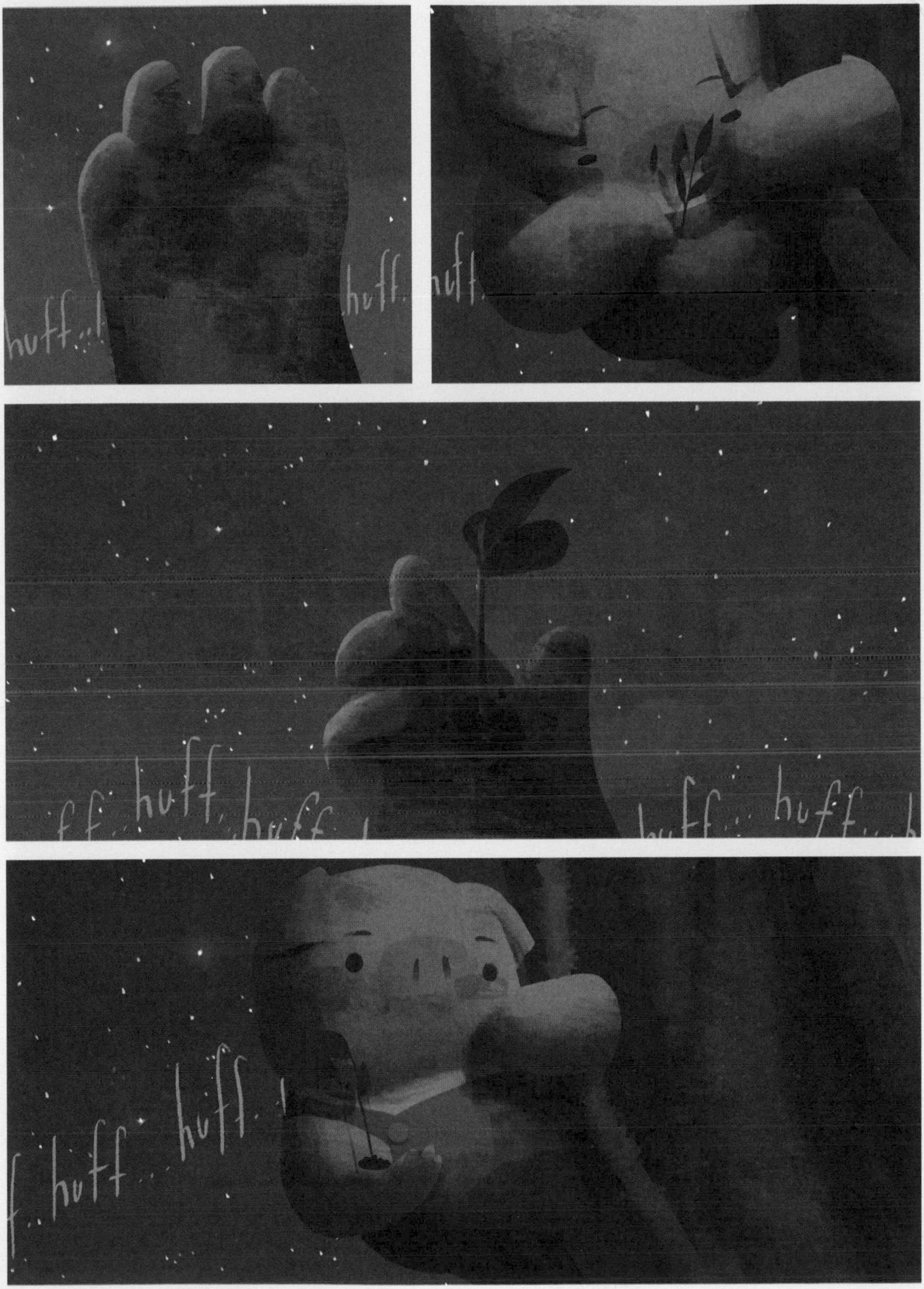
huff...!
huff...
huff...
ff... huff, huff...
huff... huff...
f... huff huff...!

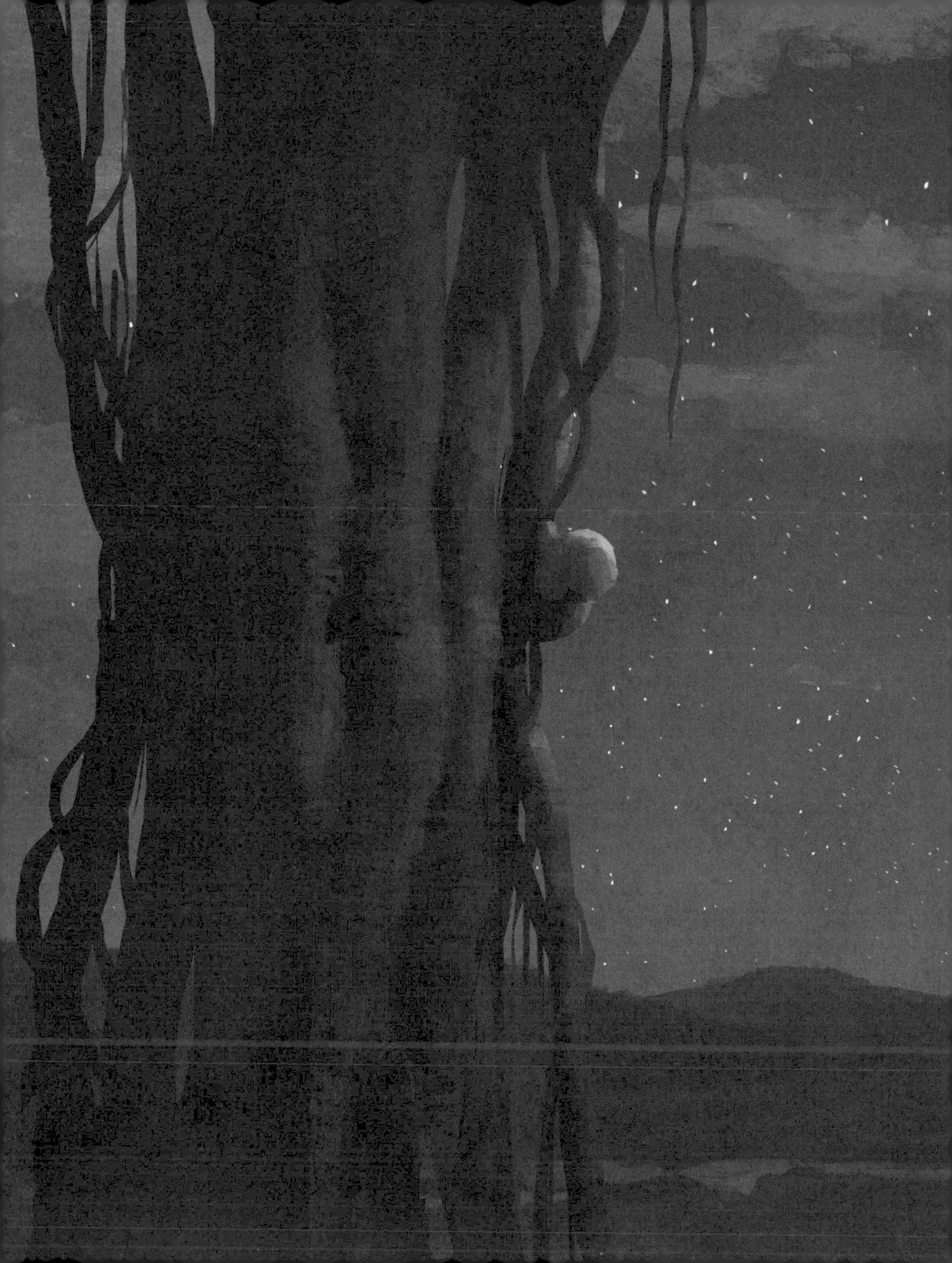

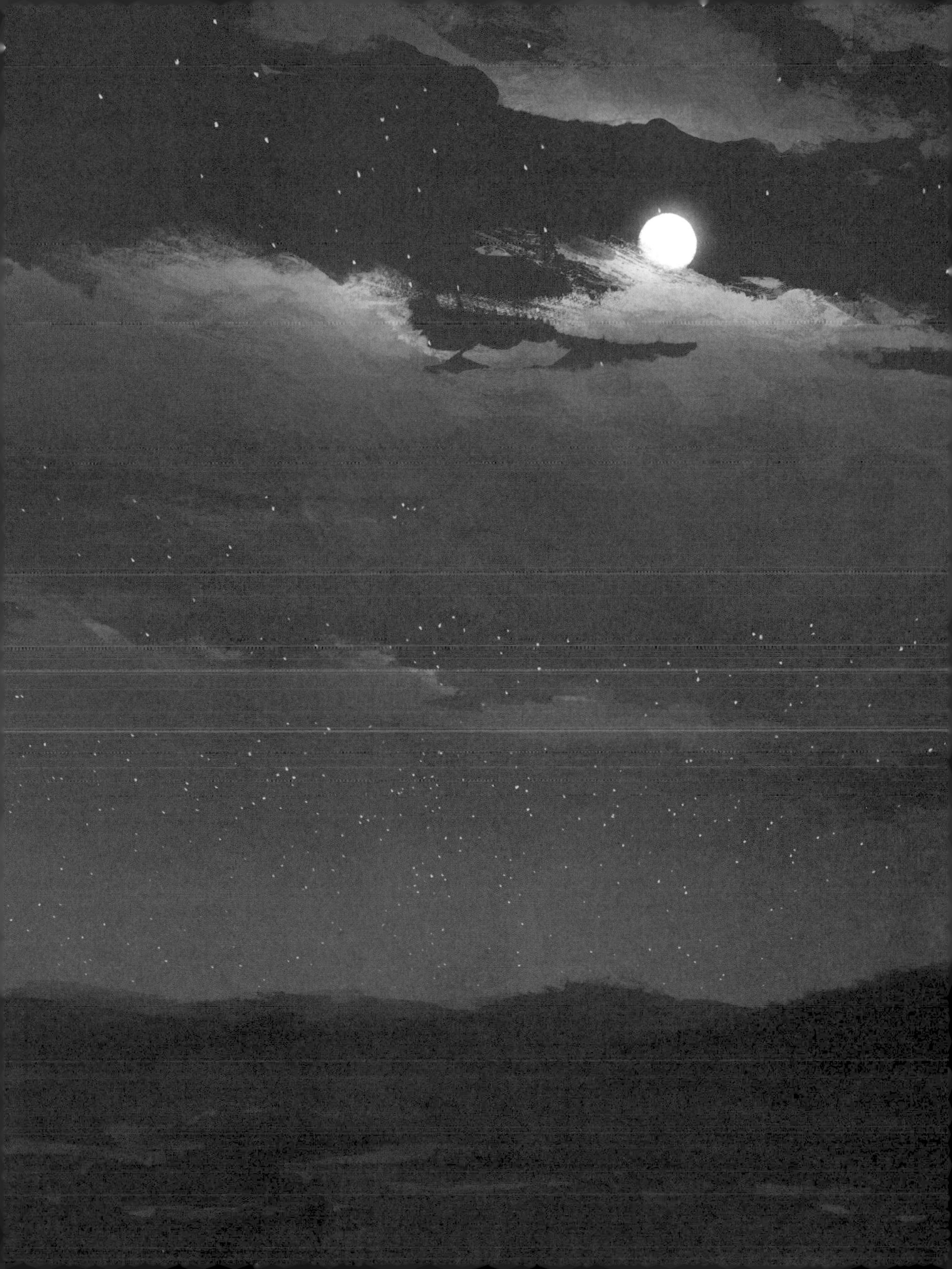

KRANCH
KRACK
SNAP
AAAAUUGHHHH

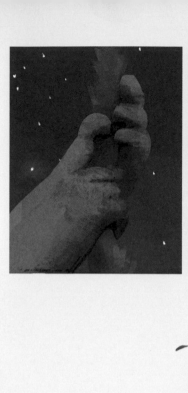

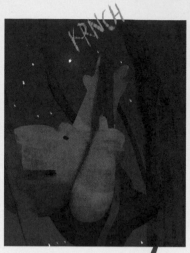

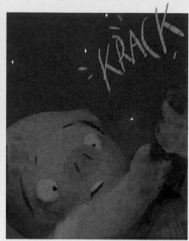

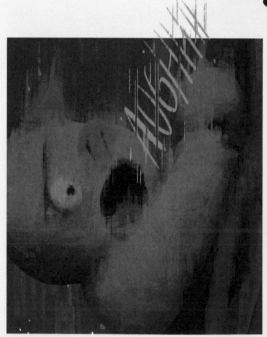

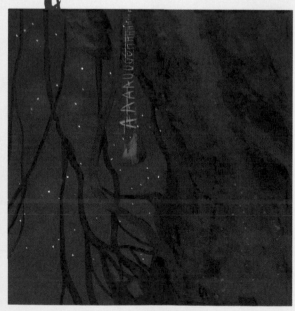

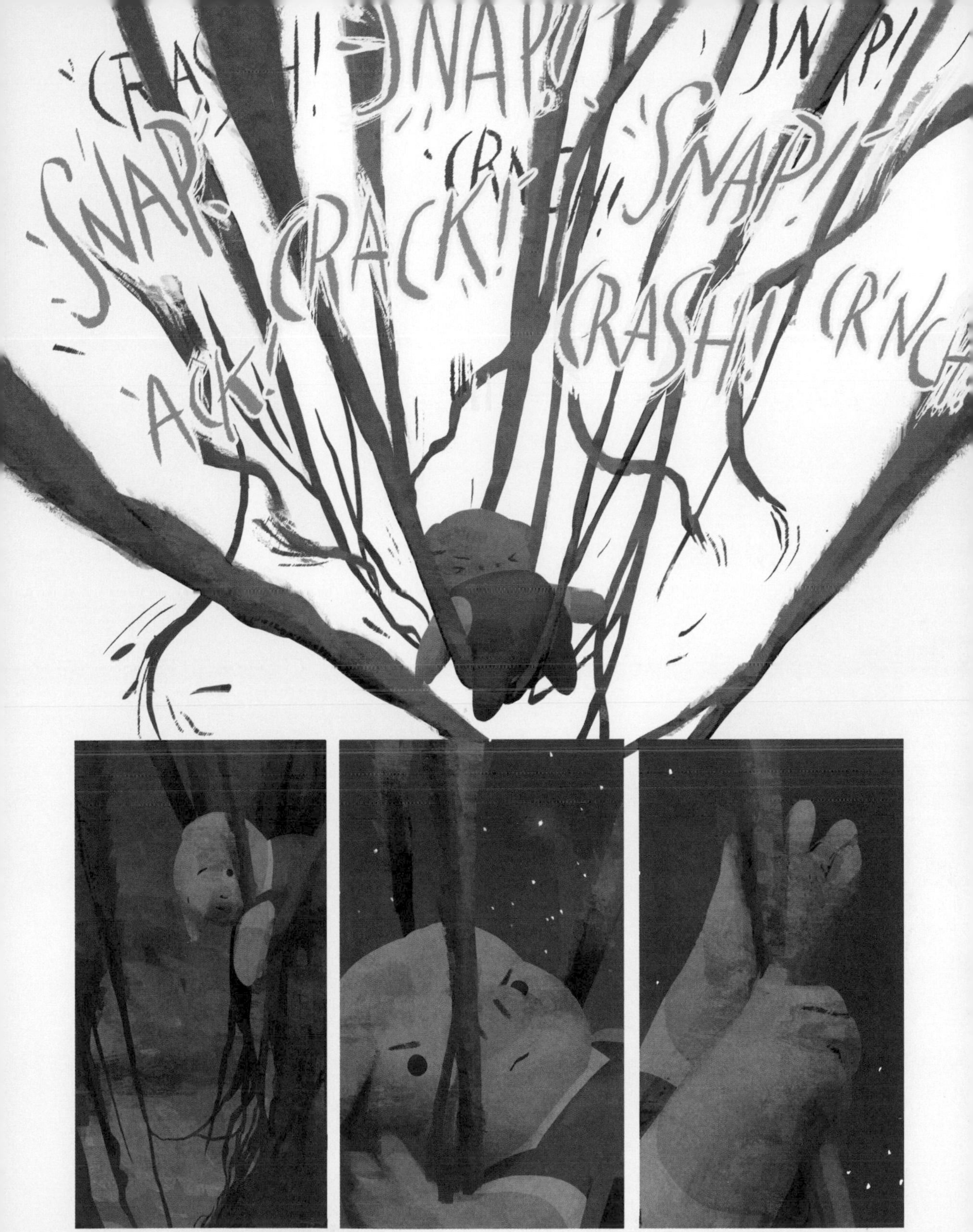
SNAP!
CRACK!
SNAP!
CRASH!
CR'NCH

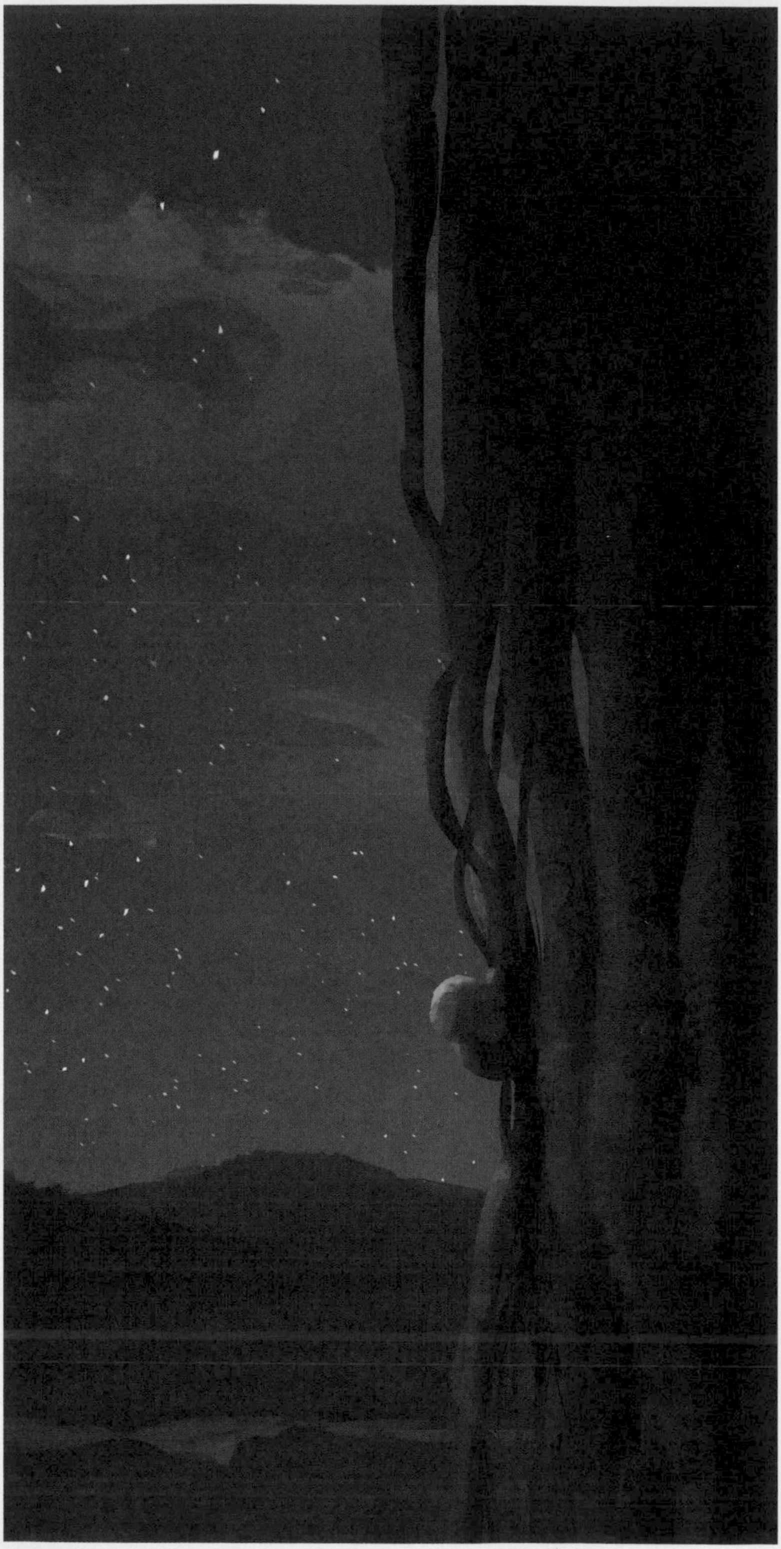

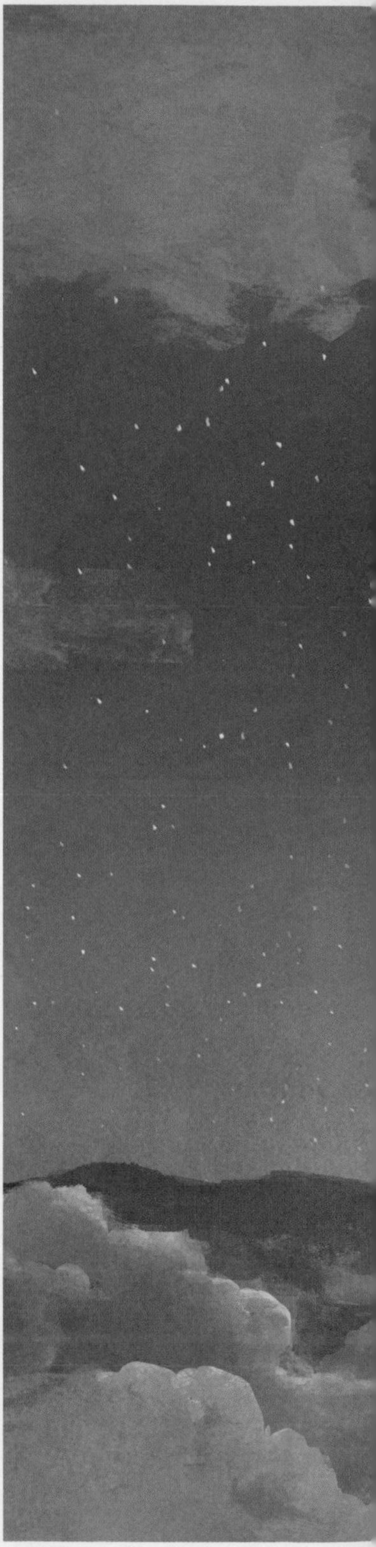

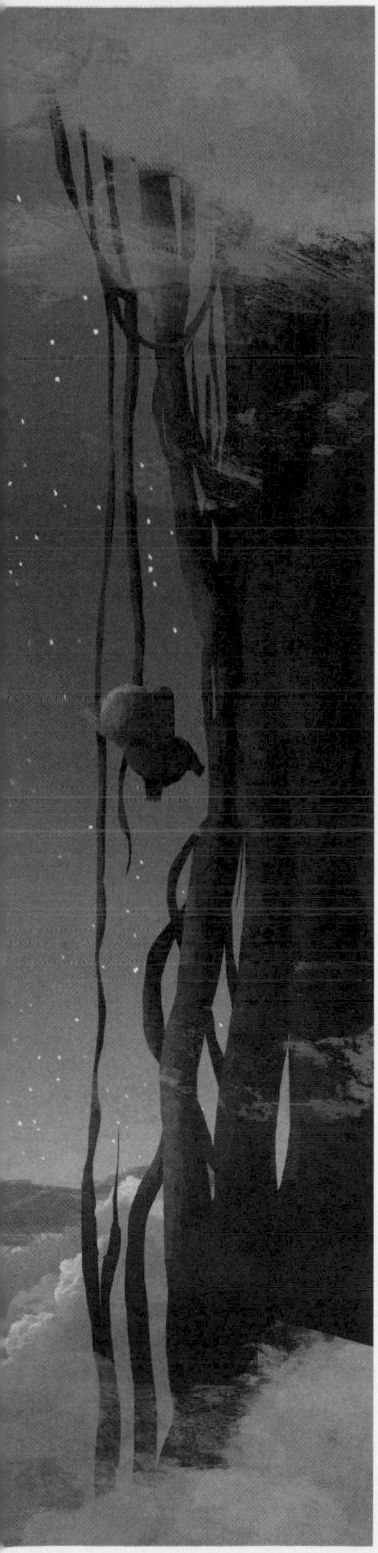

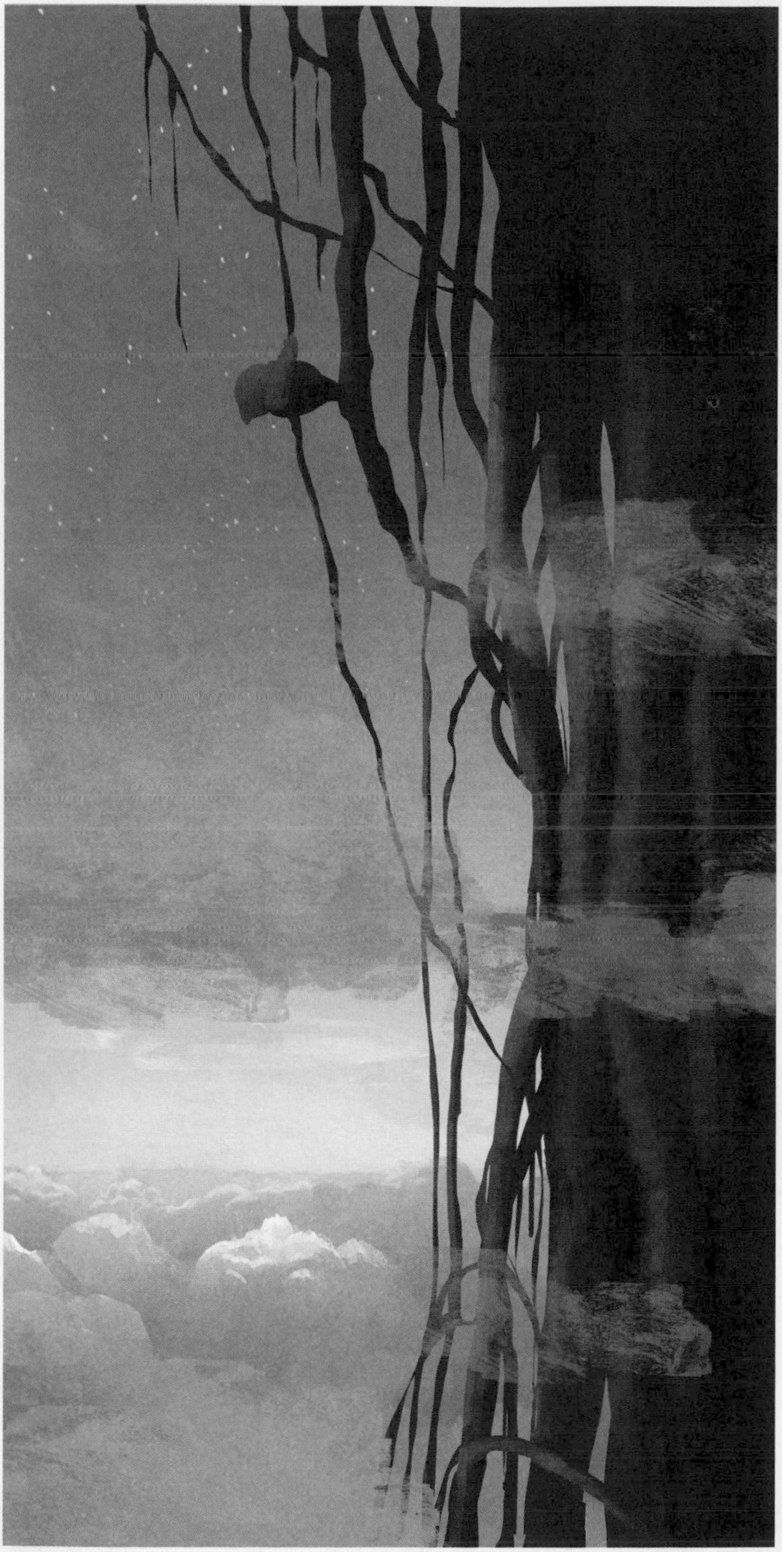

SEVERAL HOURS LATER...

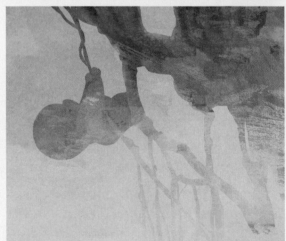

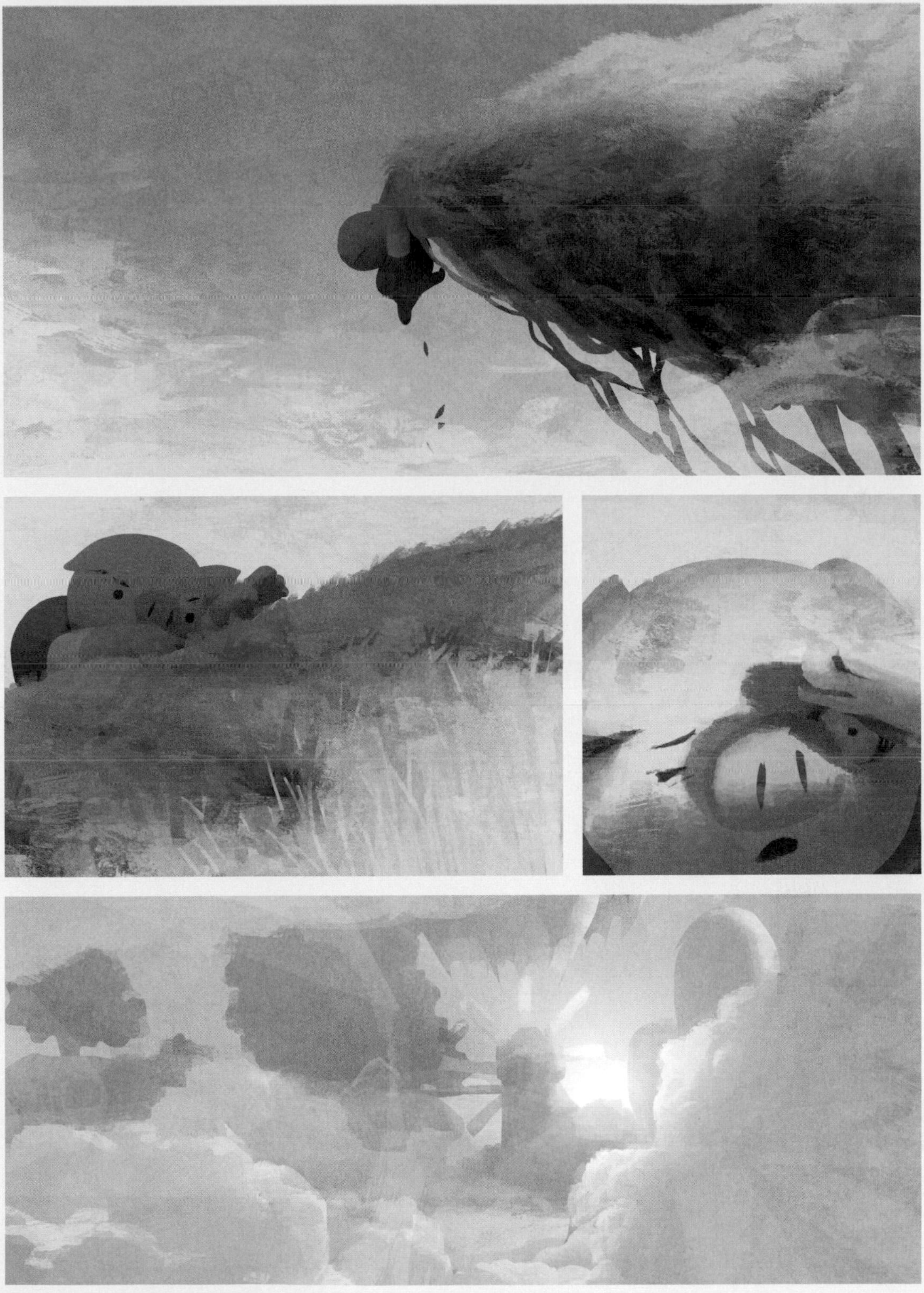

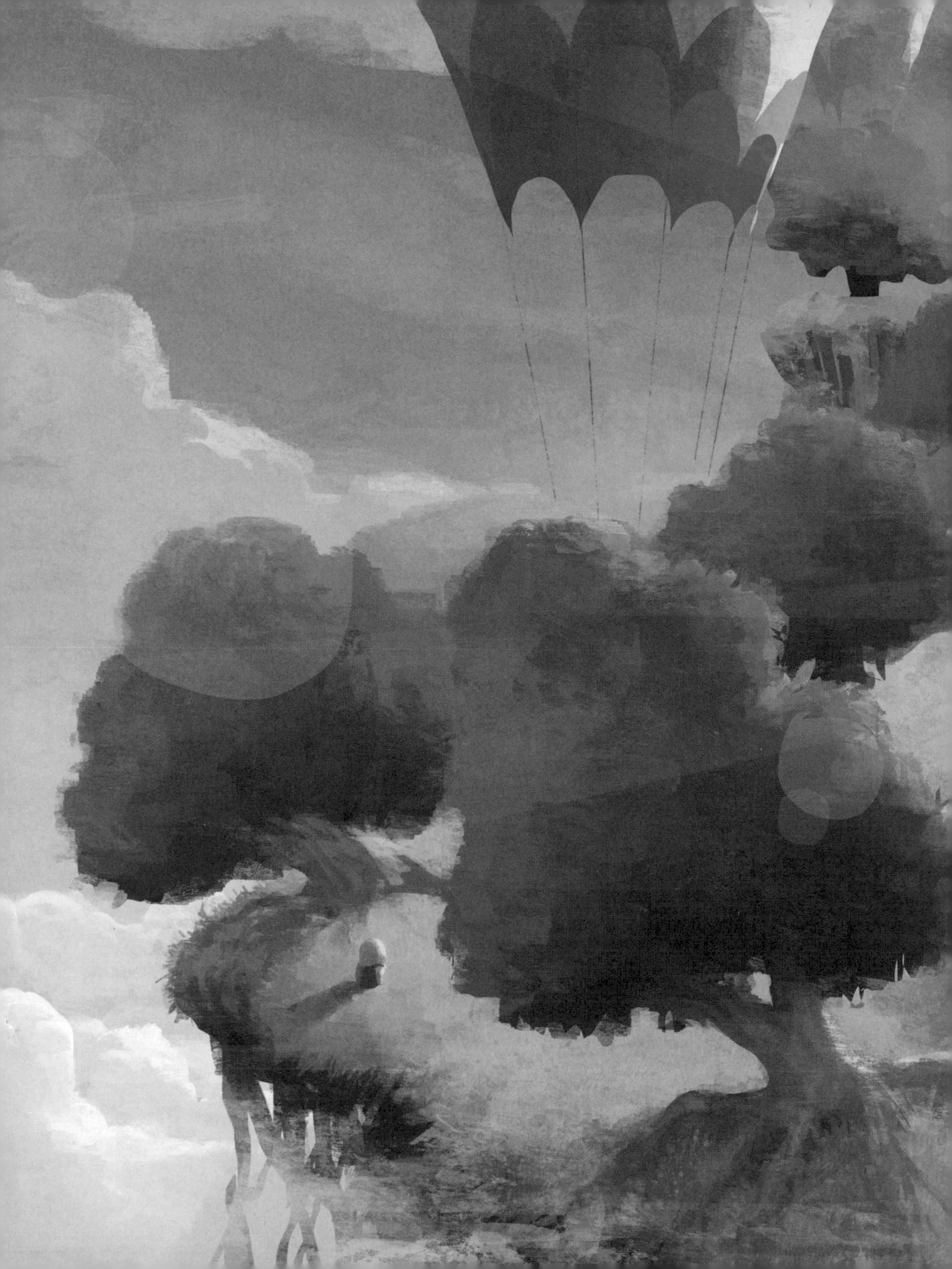

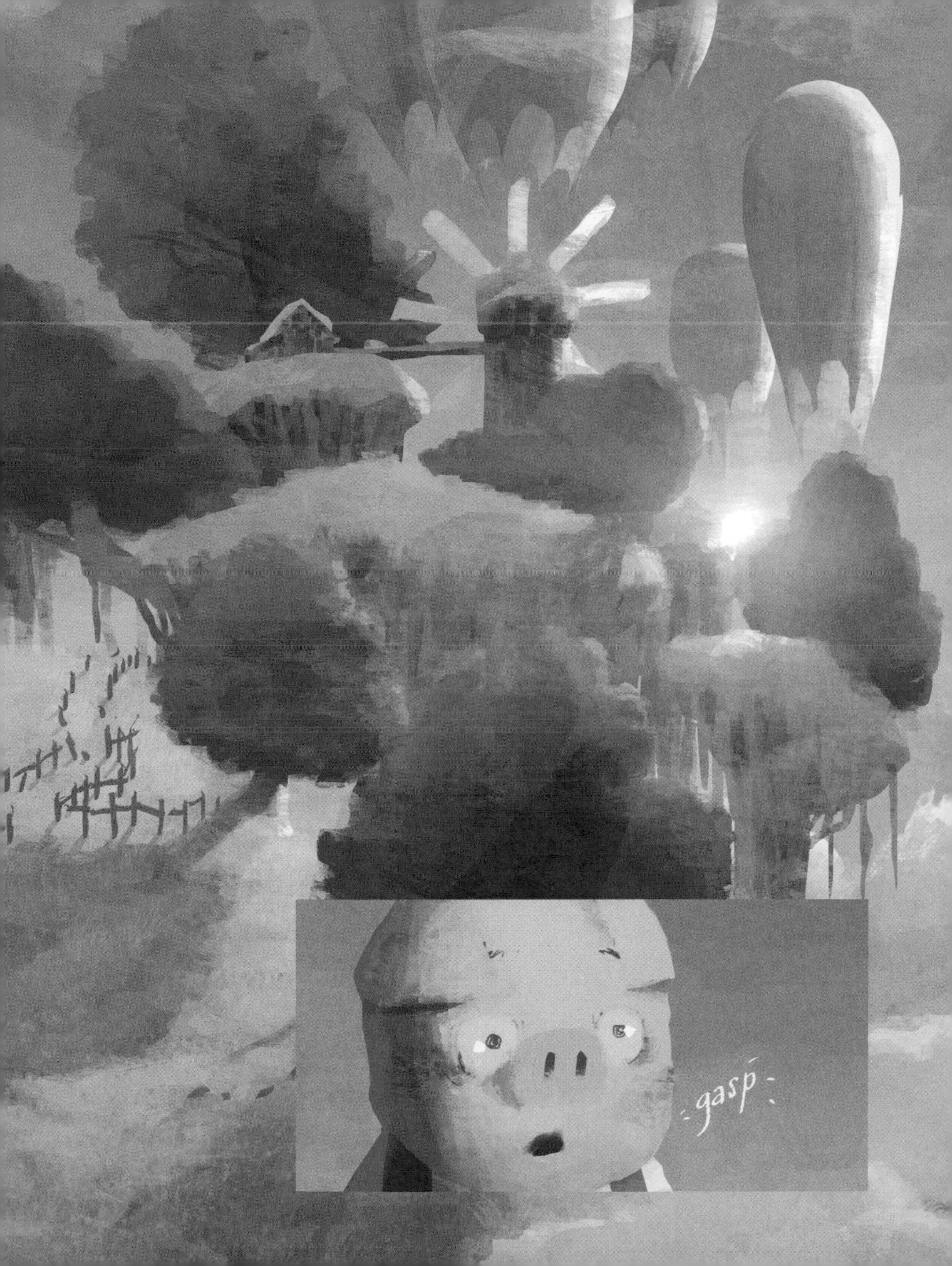
gasp

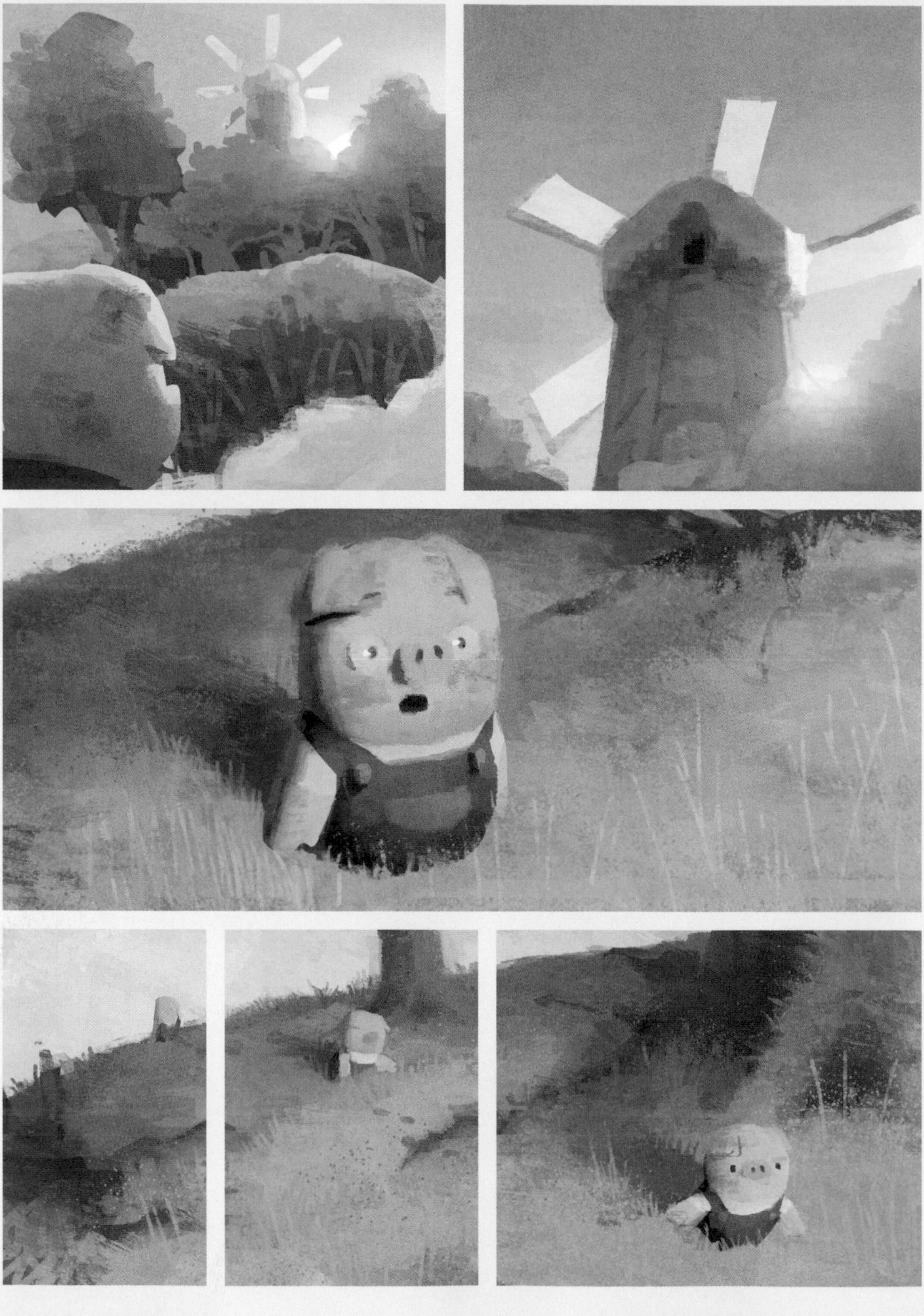

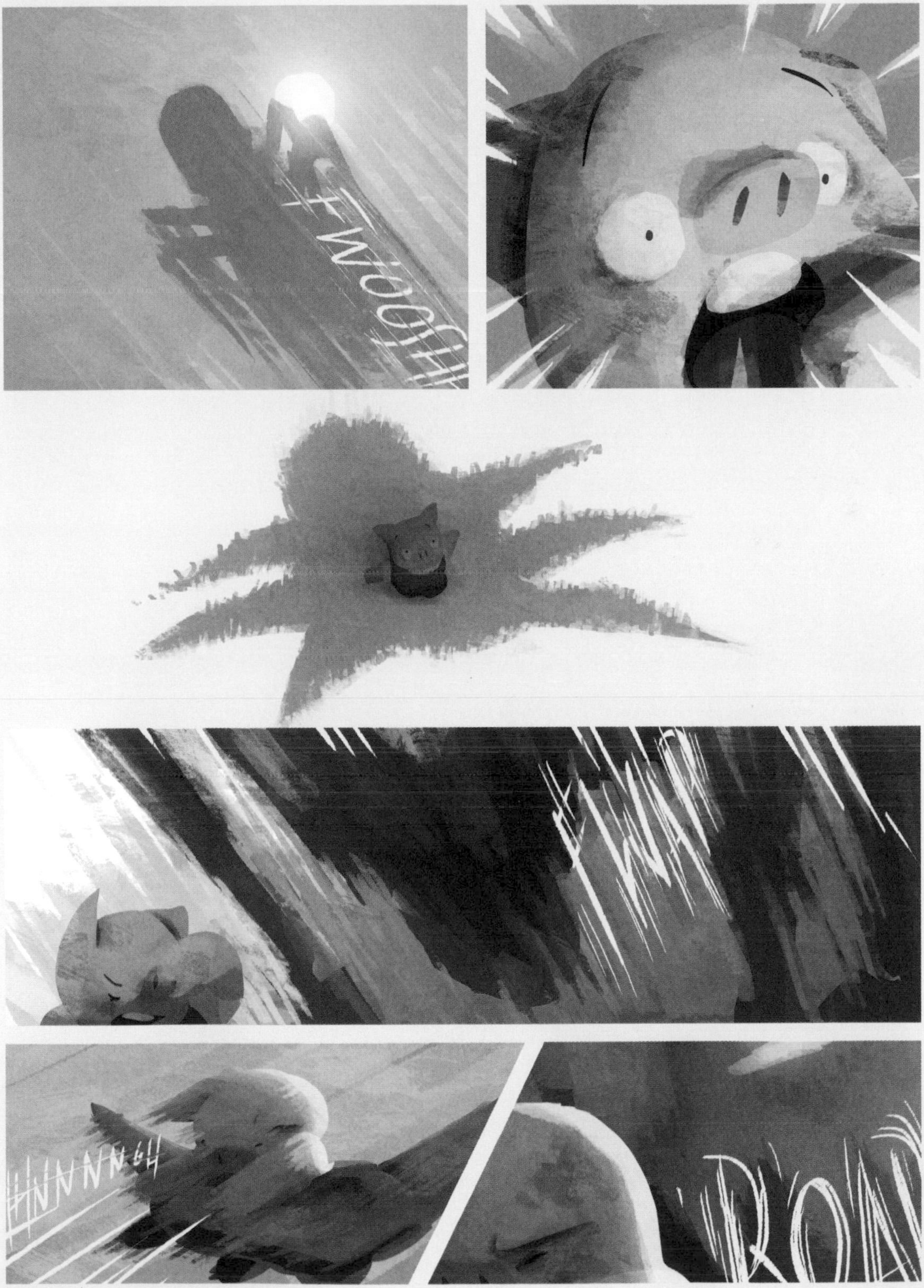
FWOOSH
HNNNNGH
ROA

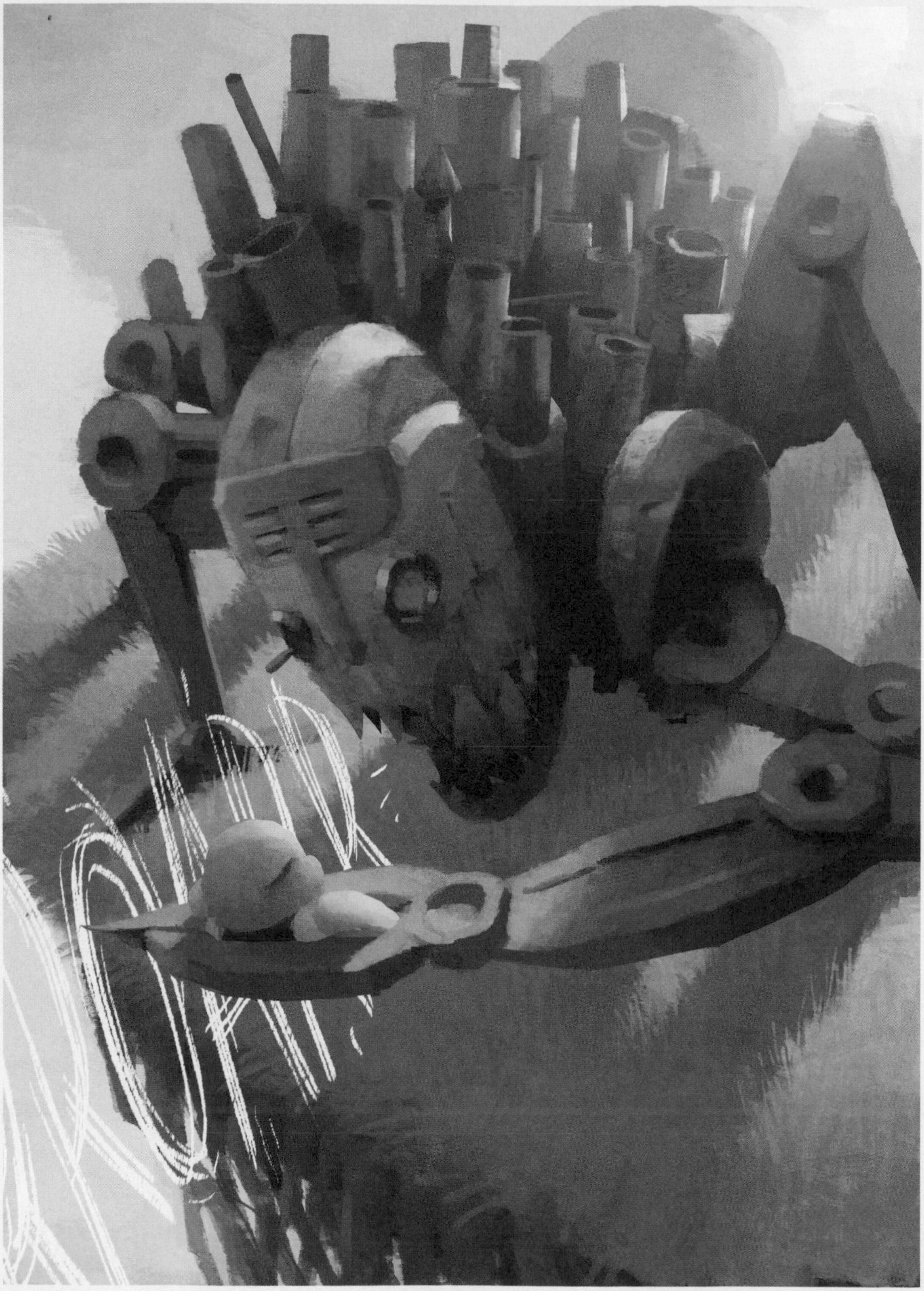

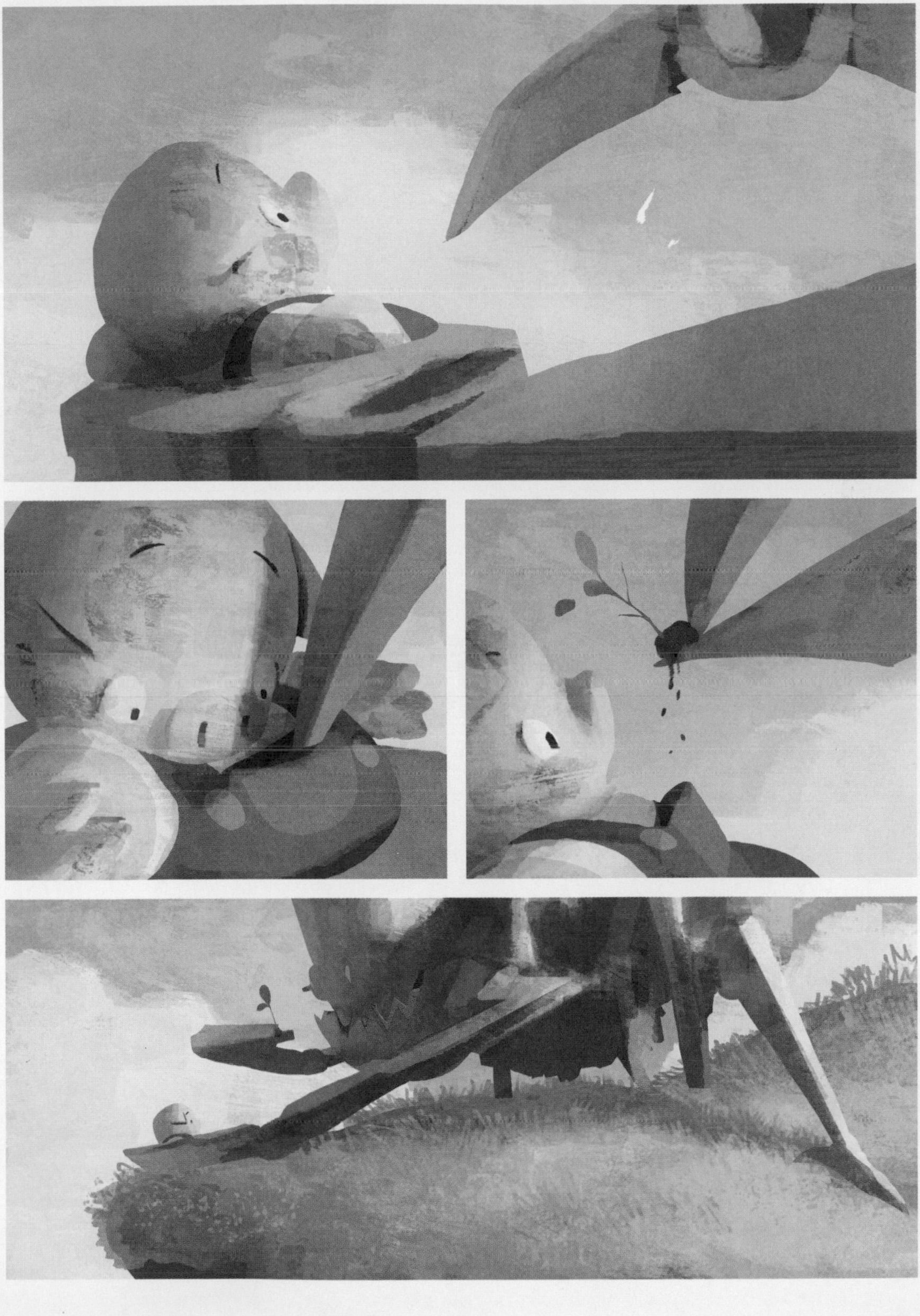

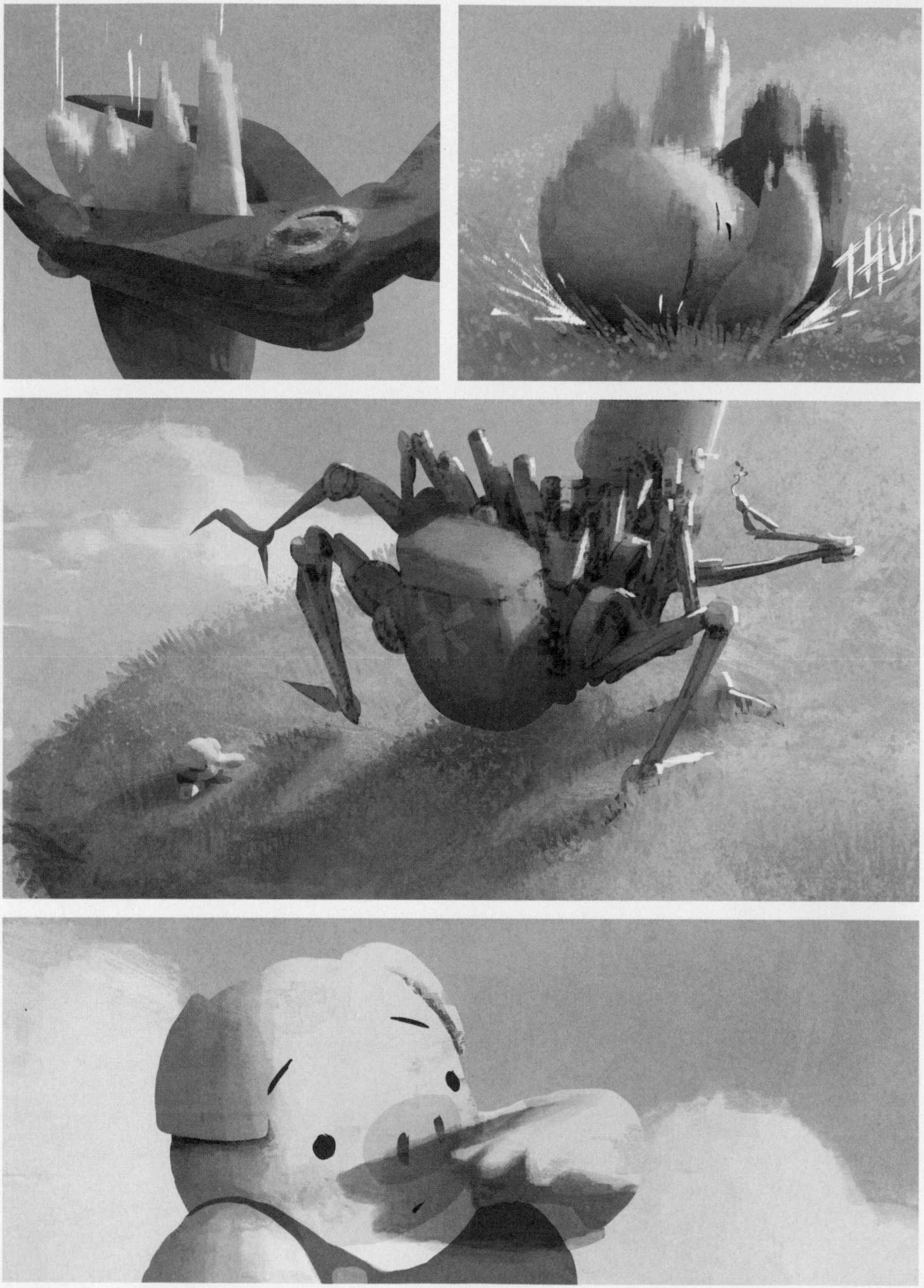
THU

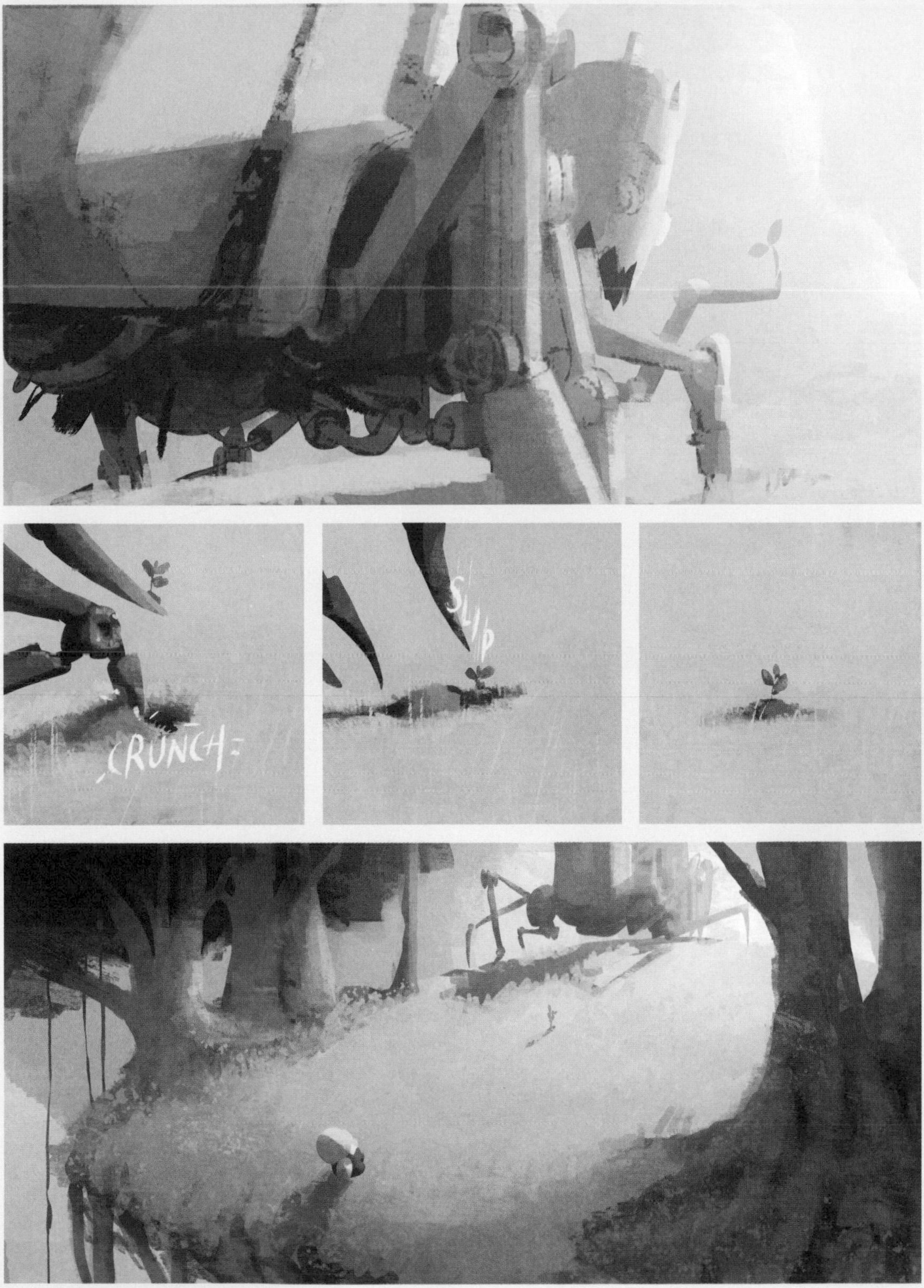
CRUNCH
SLIP

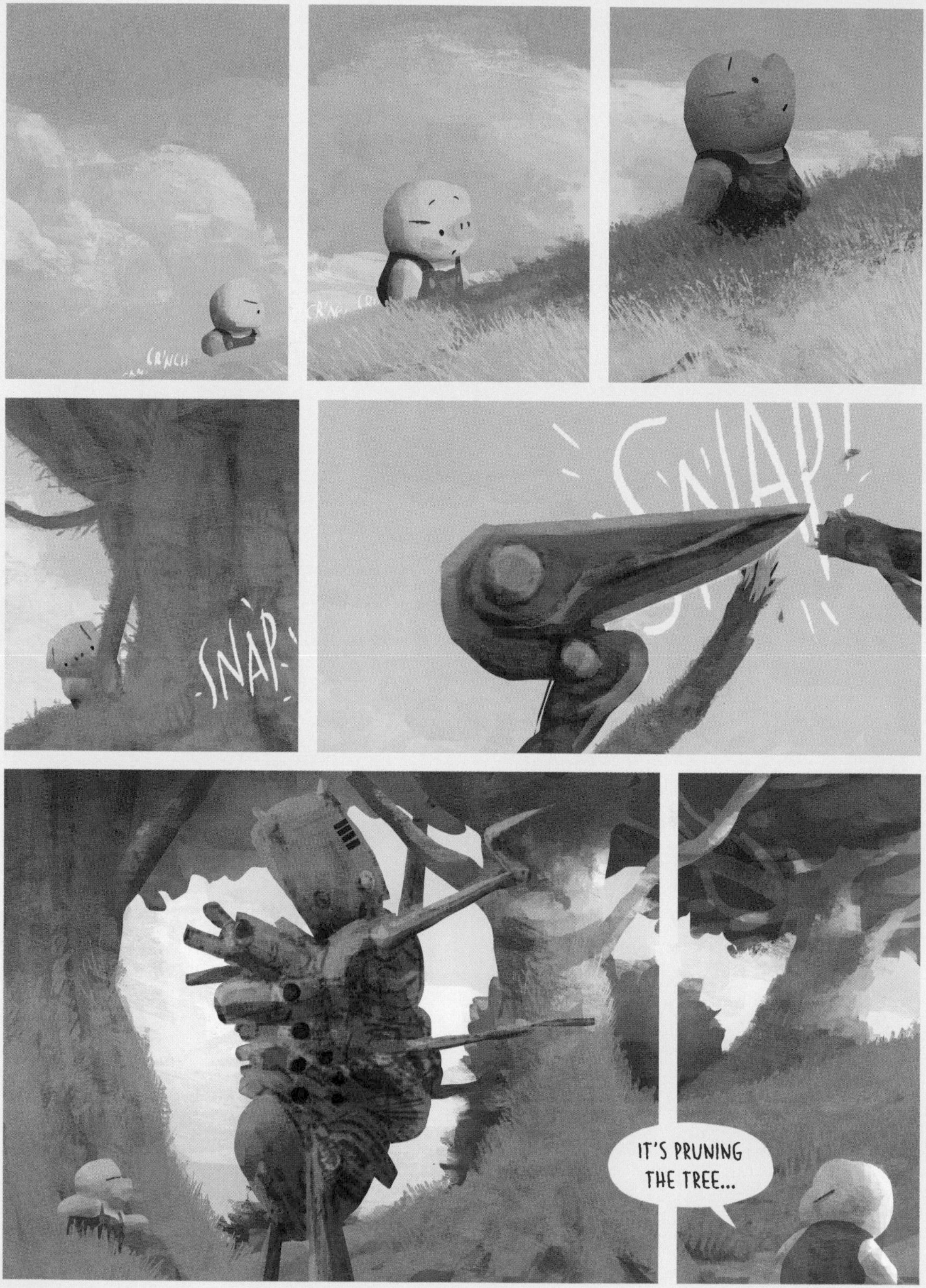
CR'NCH
CR'NCH CR'
SNAP!
SNAP!
IT'S PRUNING THE TREE...

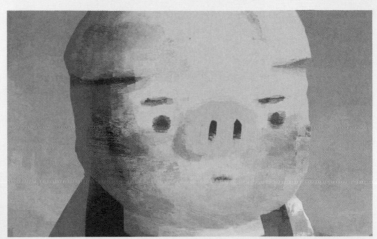

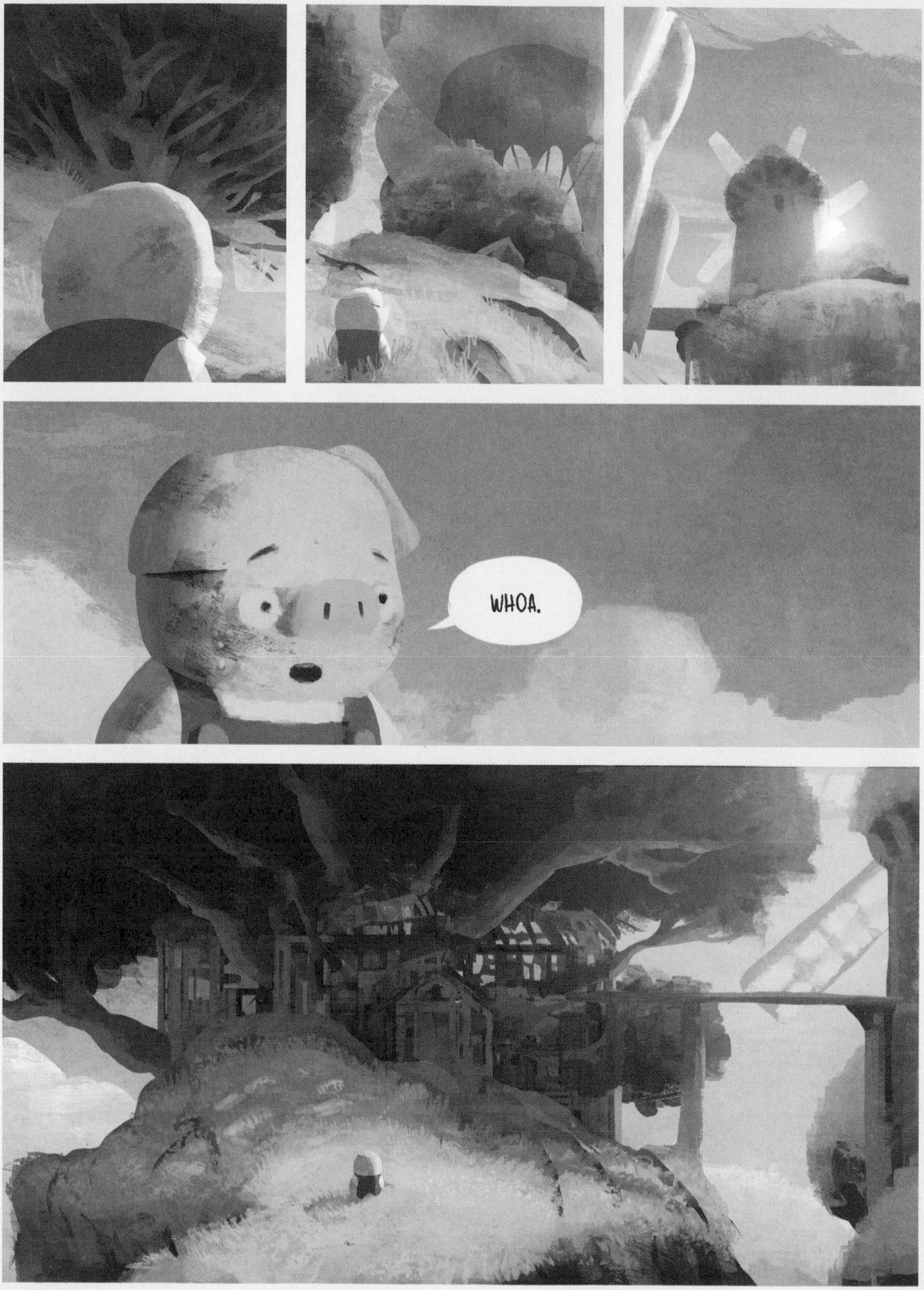
WHOA.

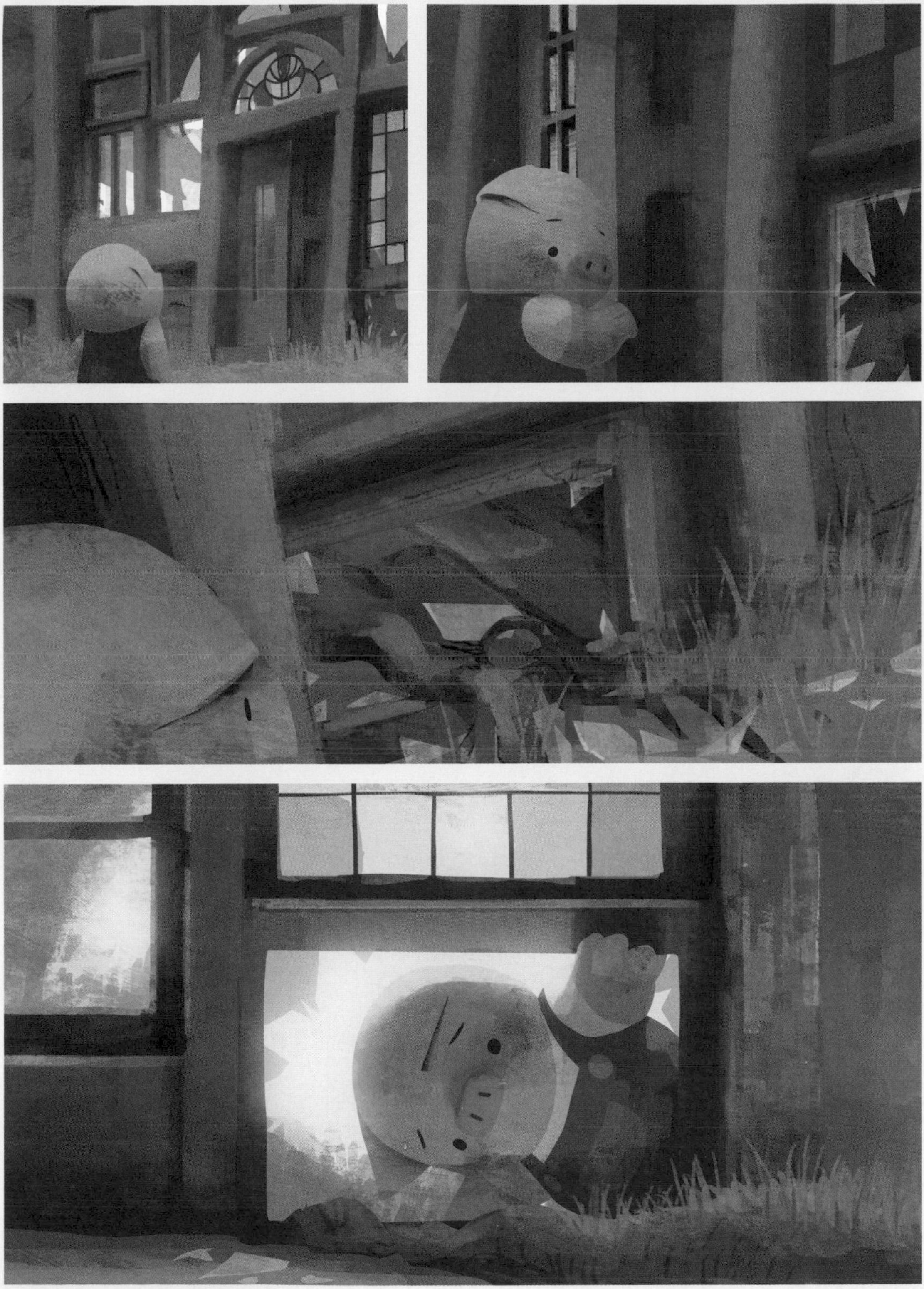

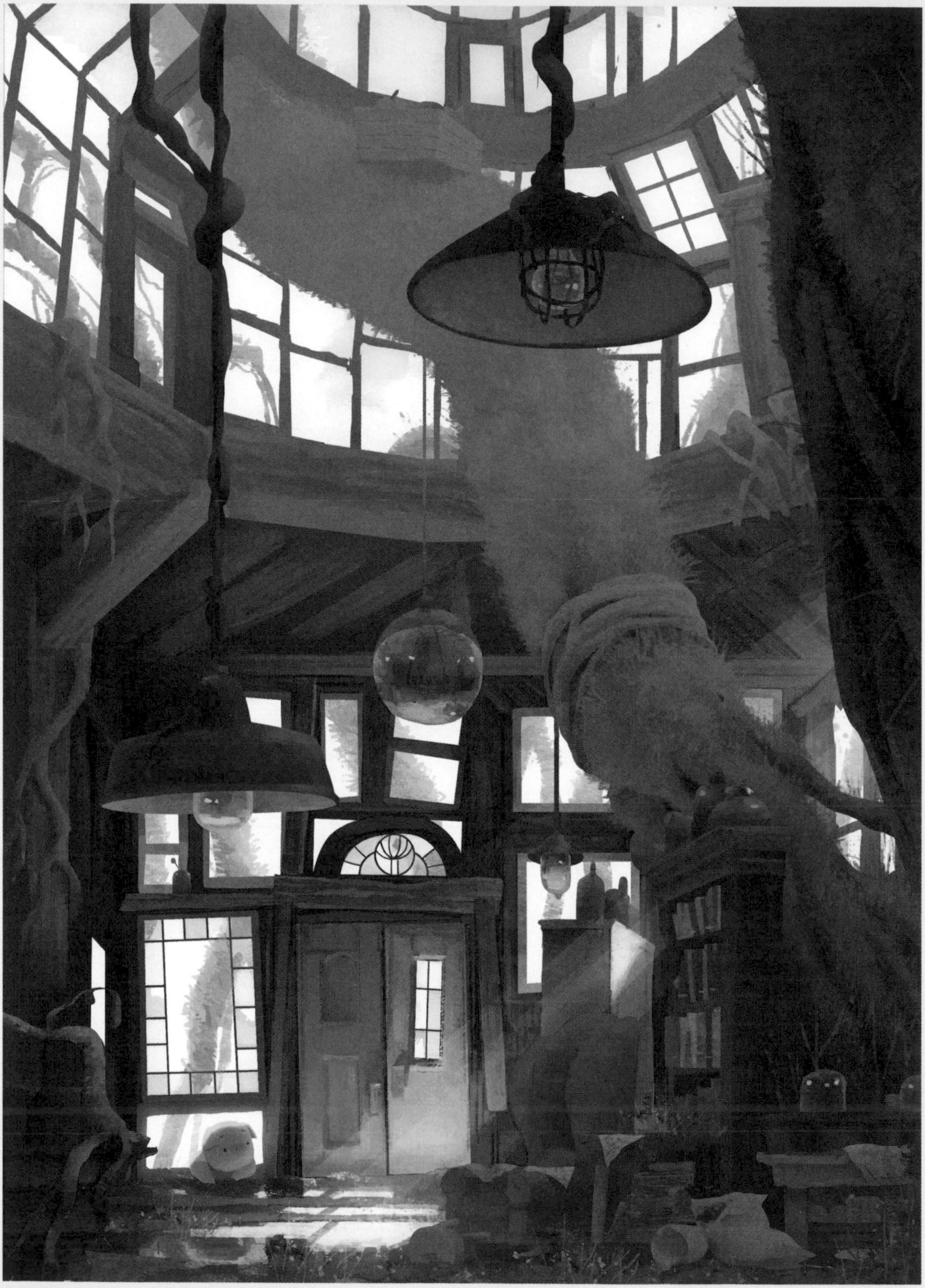

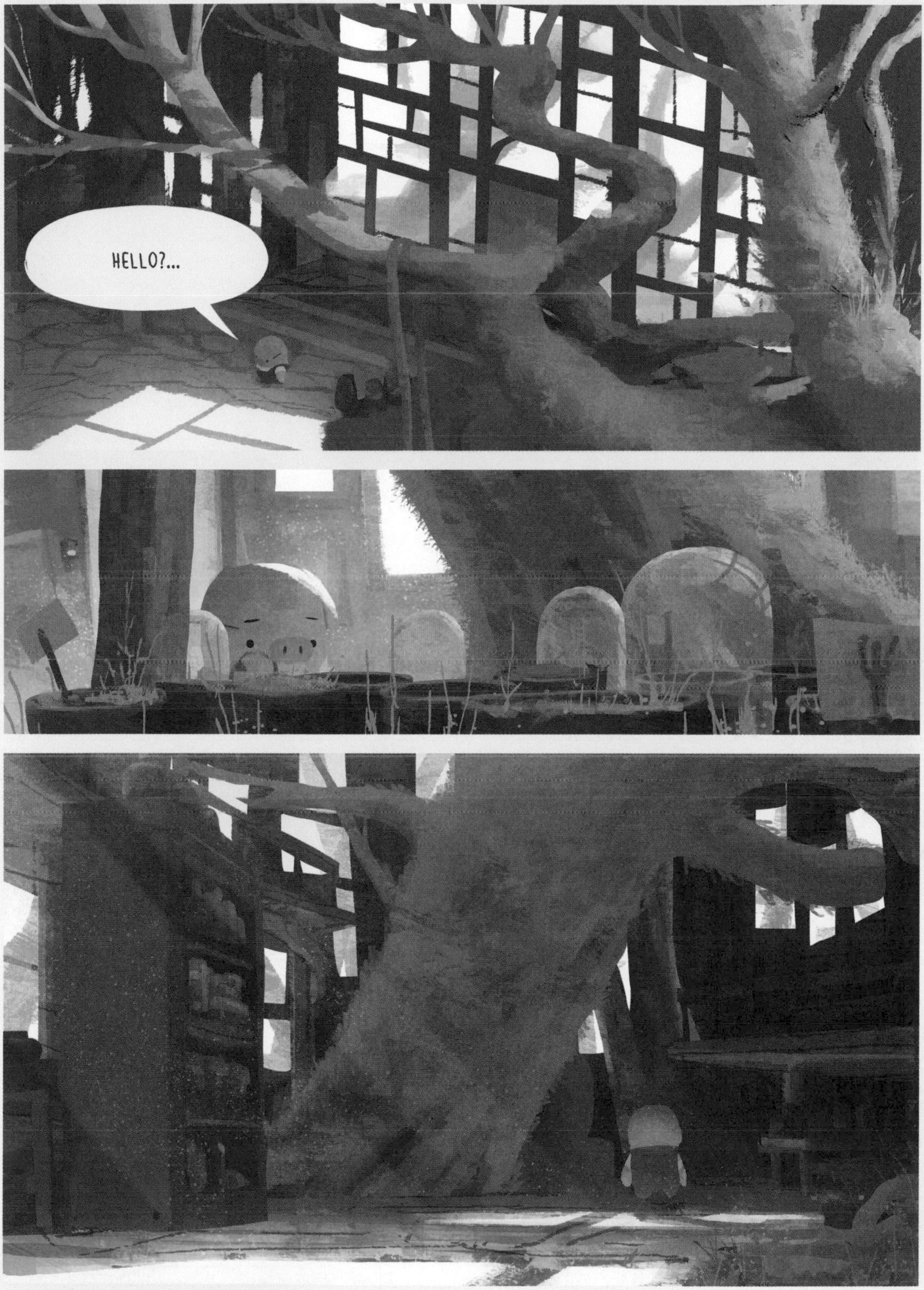
HELLO?...

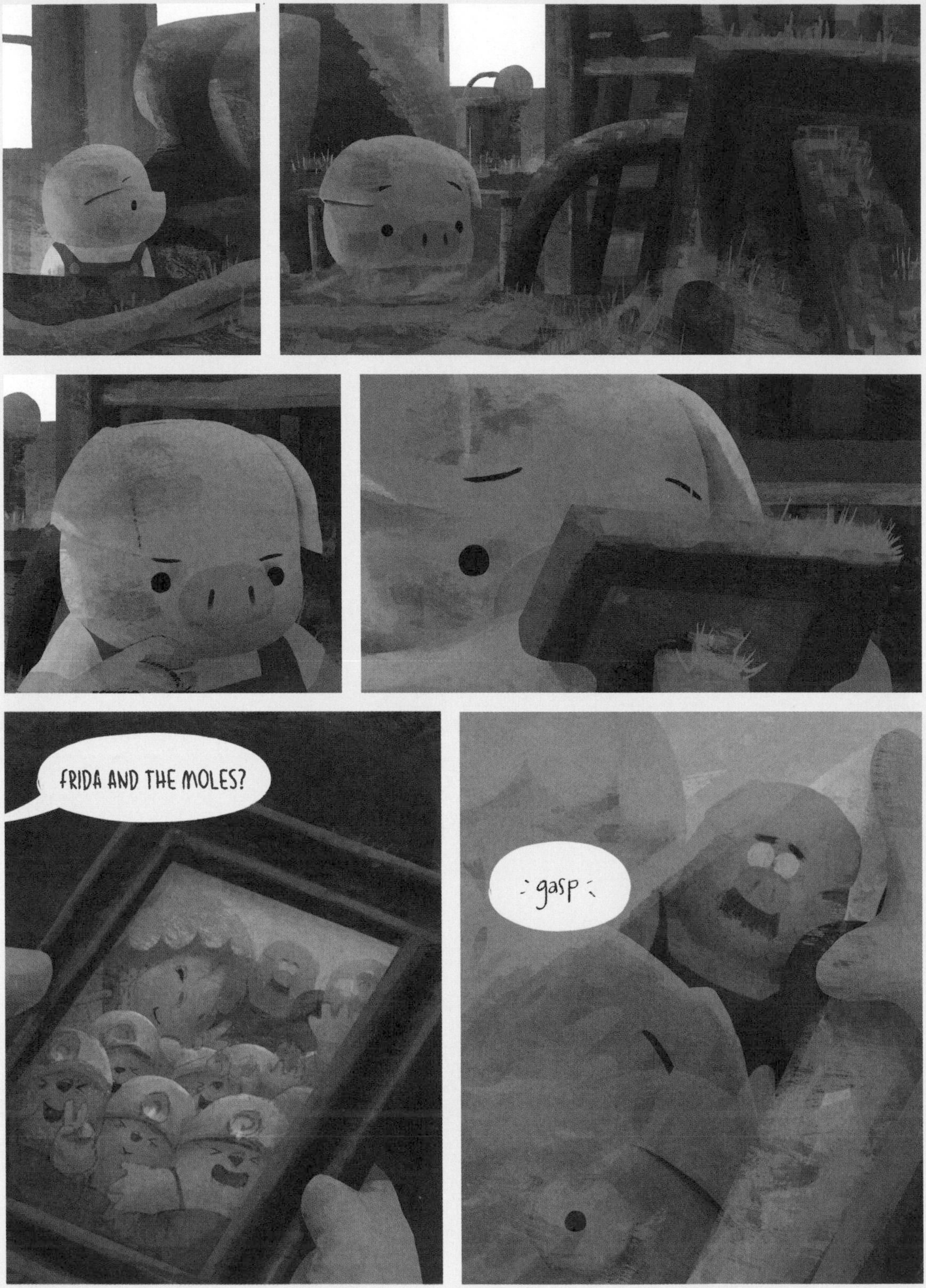
FRIDA AND THE MOLES?
gasp

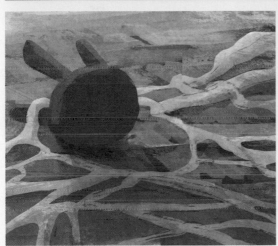

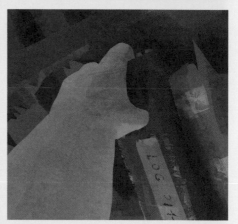

HIS JOURNAL?

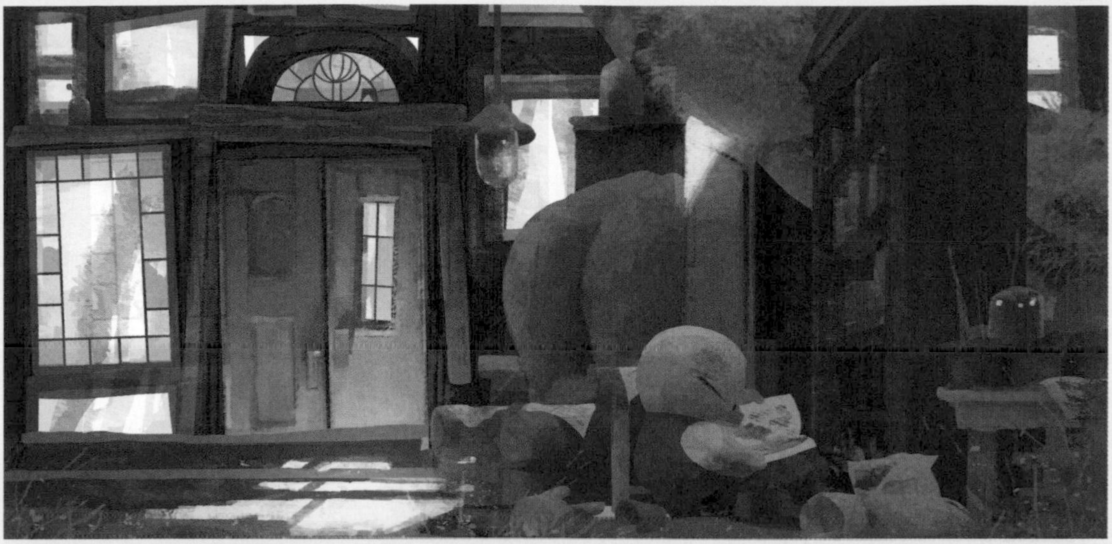

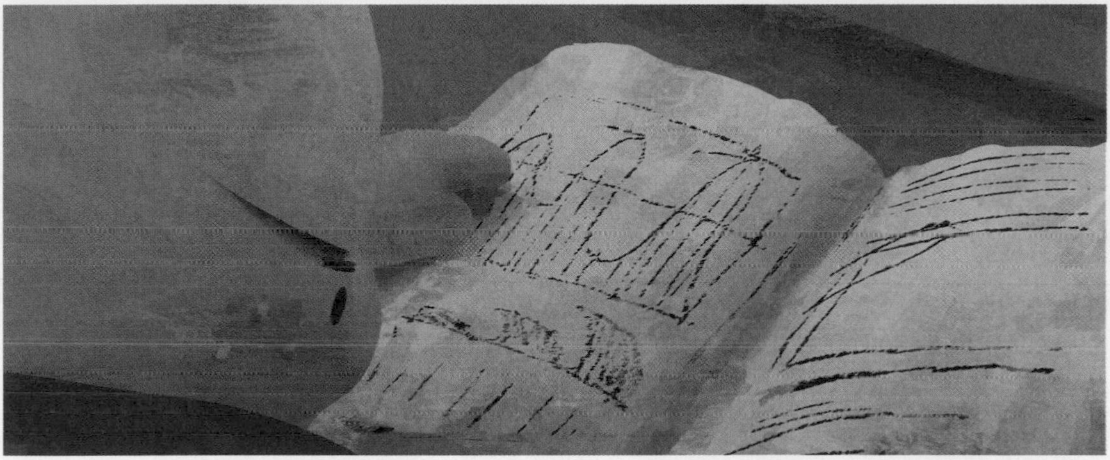

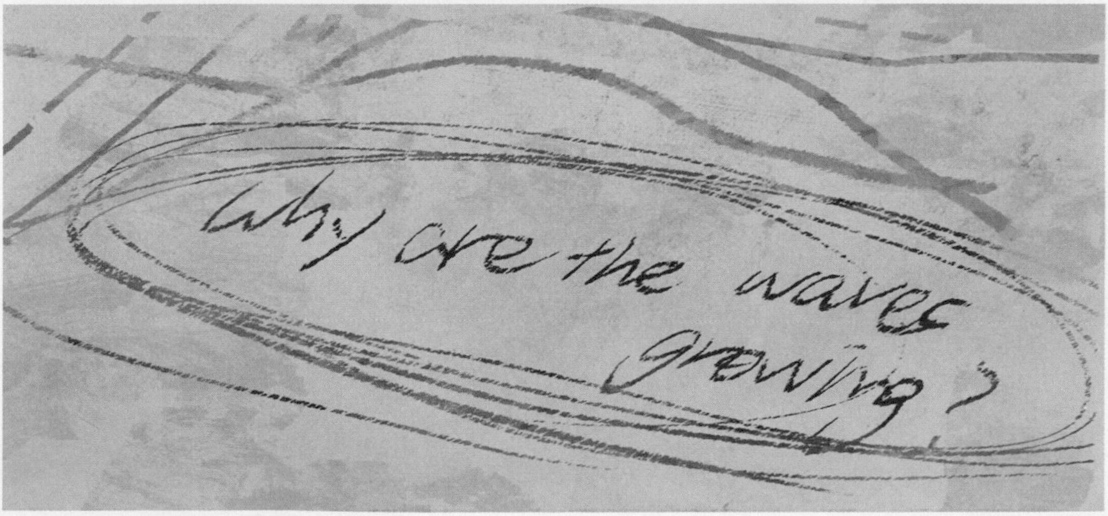
Why are the waves growing?

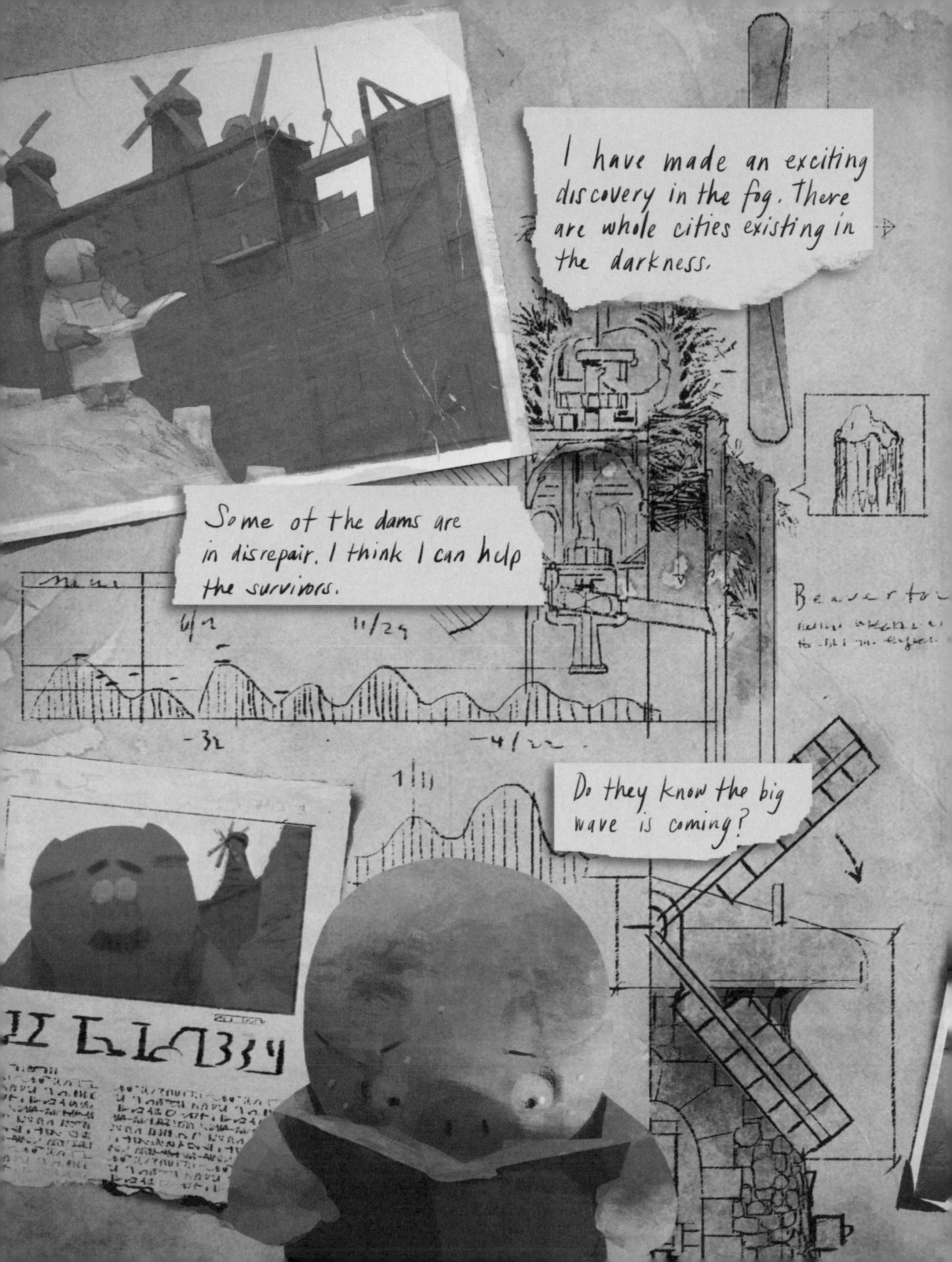
I have made an exciting discovery in the fog. There are whole cities existing in the darkness.
Some of the dams are in disrepair. I think I can help the survivors.
Do they know the big wave is coming?

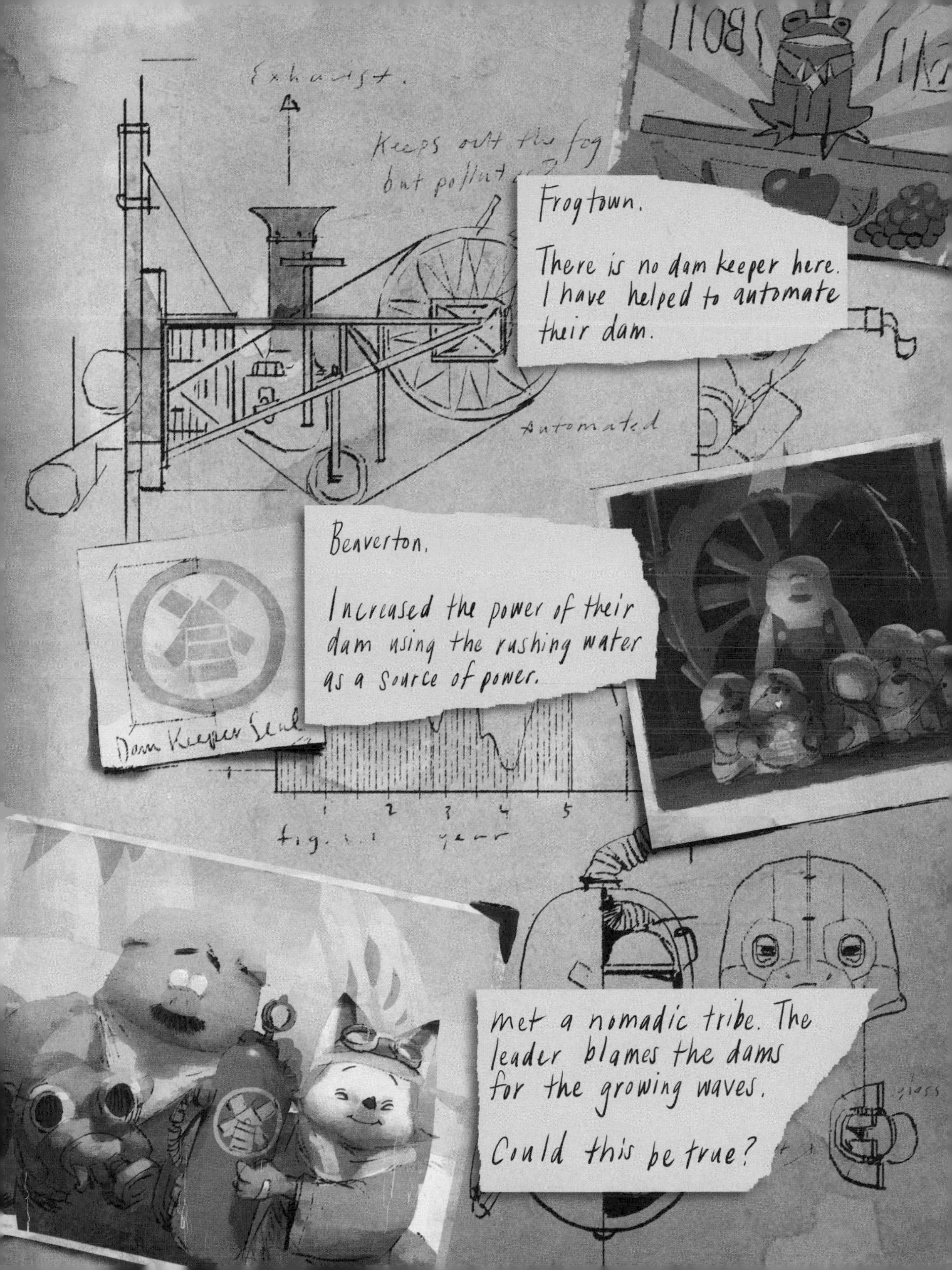
Exhaust.
Keeps out the fog
Frogtown.
There is no dam keeper here. I have helped to automate their dam.
automated
Beaverton.
Increased the power of their dam using the rushing water as a source of power.
Dam Keeper Seal
1 2 3 4 5
year
met a nomadic tribe. The leader blames the dams for the growing waves.
Could this be true?
glass

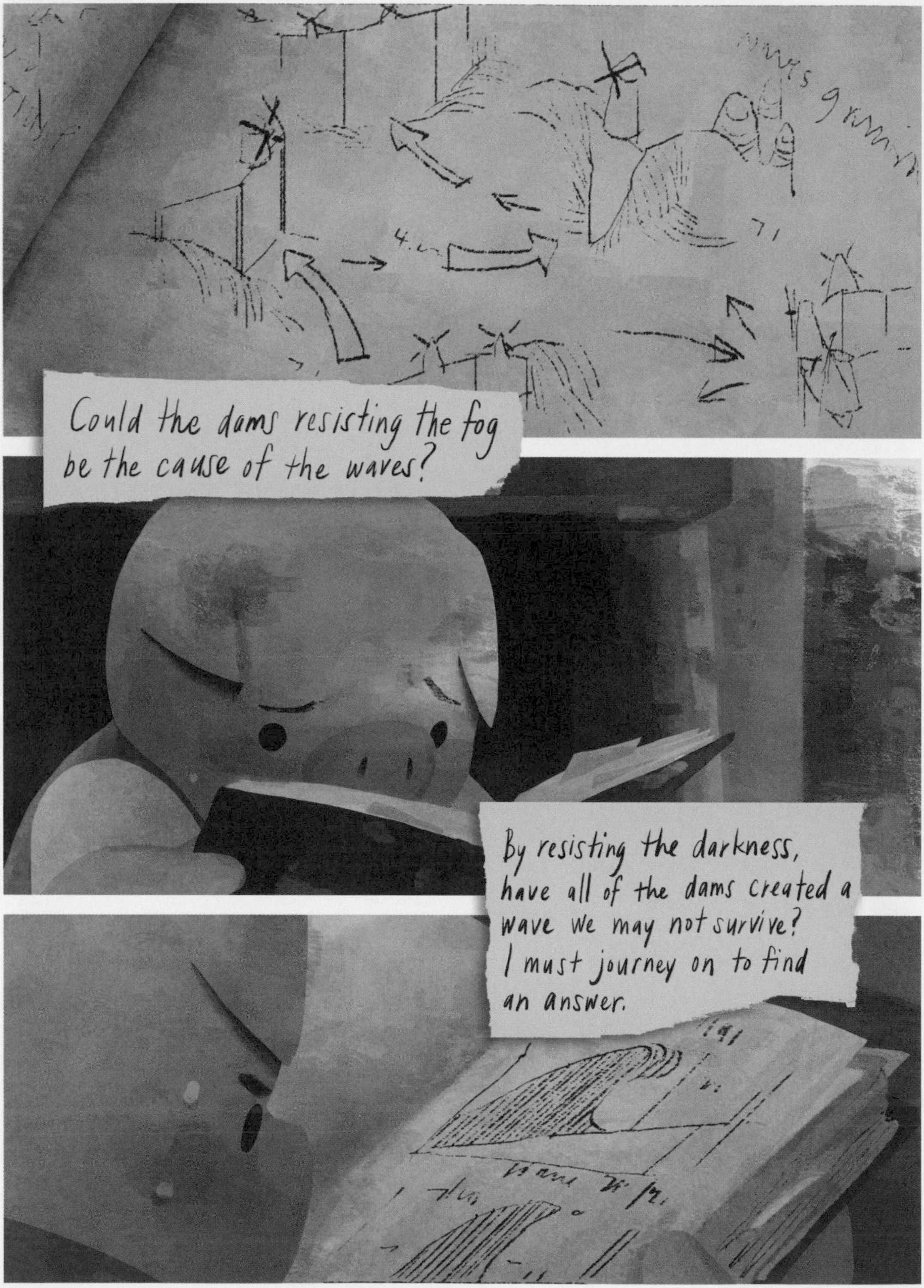
Could the dams resisting the fog be the cause of the waves?
By resisting the darkness, have all of the dams created a wave we may not survive? I must journey on to find an answer.

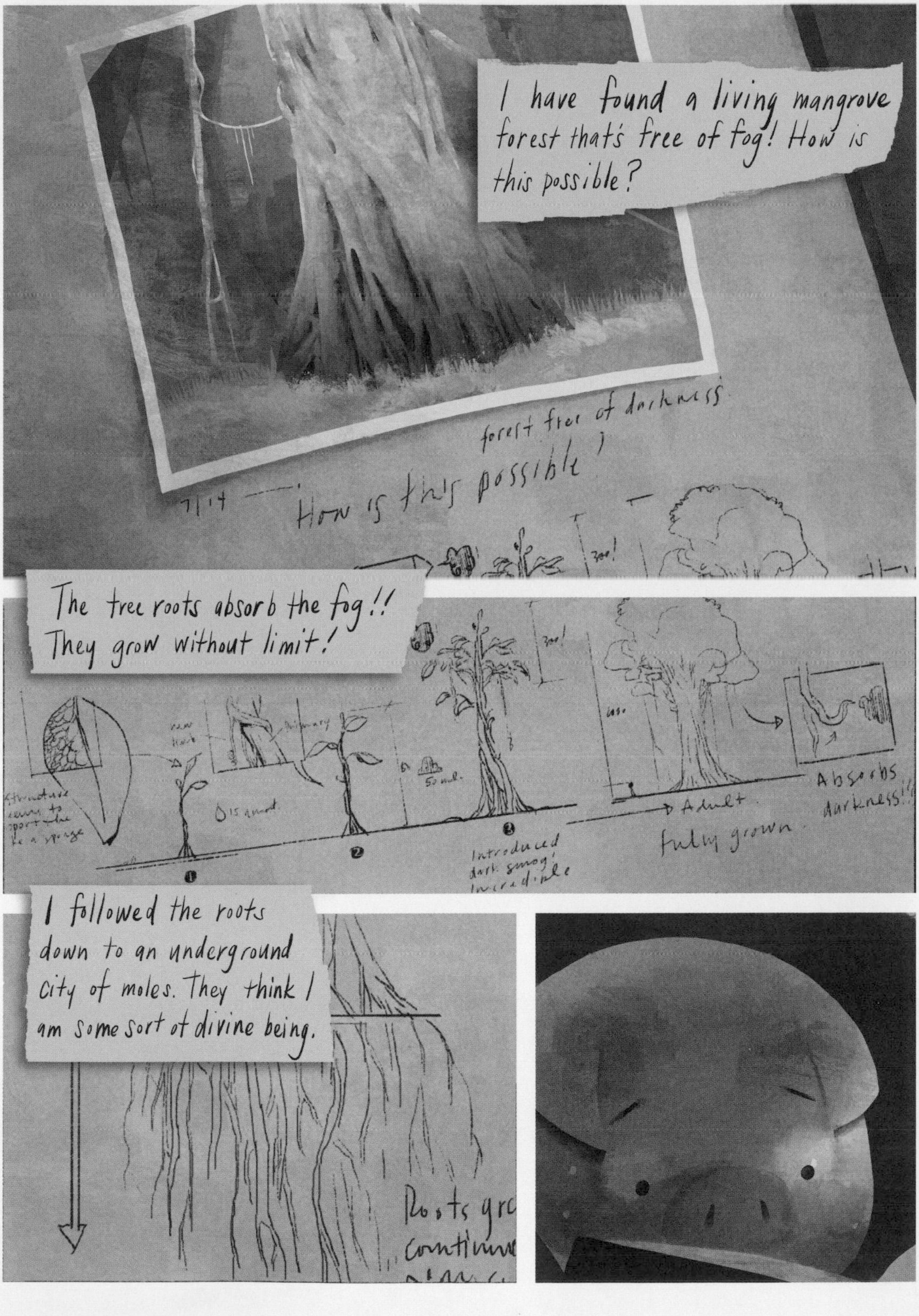
I have found a living mangrove forest that's free of fog! How is this possible?
forest free of darkness.
How is this possible!
7/14
The tree roots absorb the fog!! They grow without limit!
Adult
fully grown.
Absorbs darkness!!
I followed the roots down to an underground city of moles. They think I am some sort of divine being.

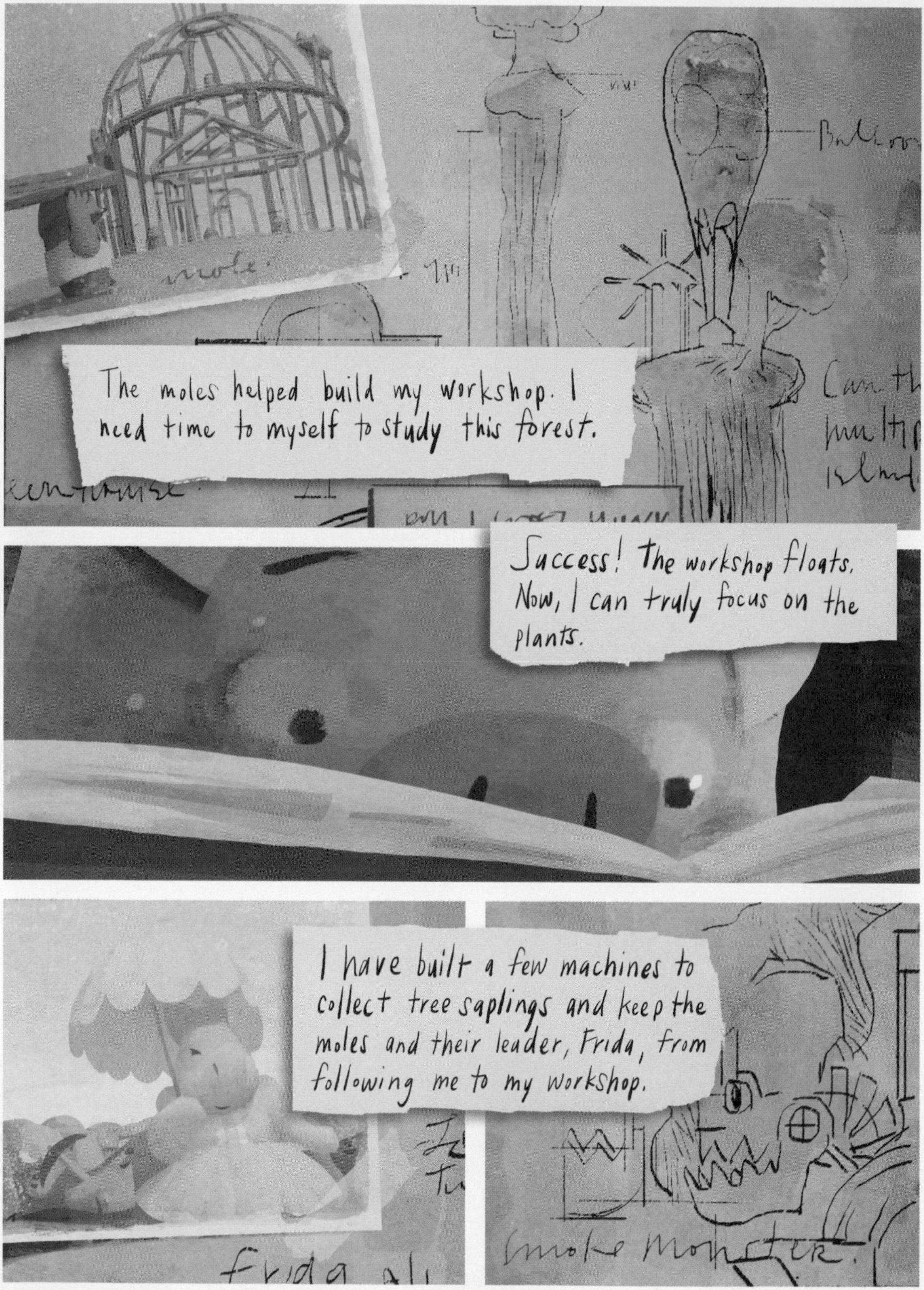
mole
The moles helped build my workshop. I need time to myself to study this forest.
Success! The workshop floats. Now, I can truly focus on the plants.
I have built a few machines to collect tree saplings and keep the moles and their leader, Frida, from following me to my workshop.
Smoke Monster.

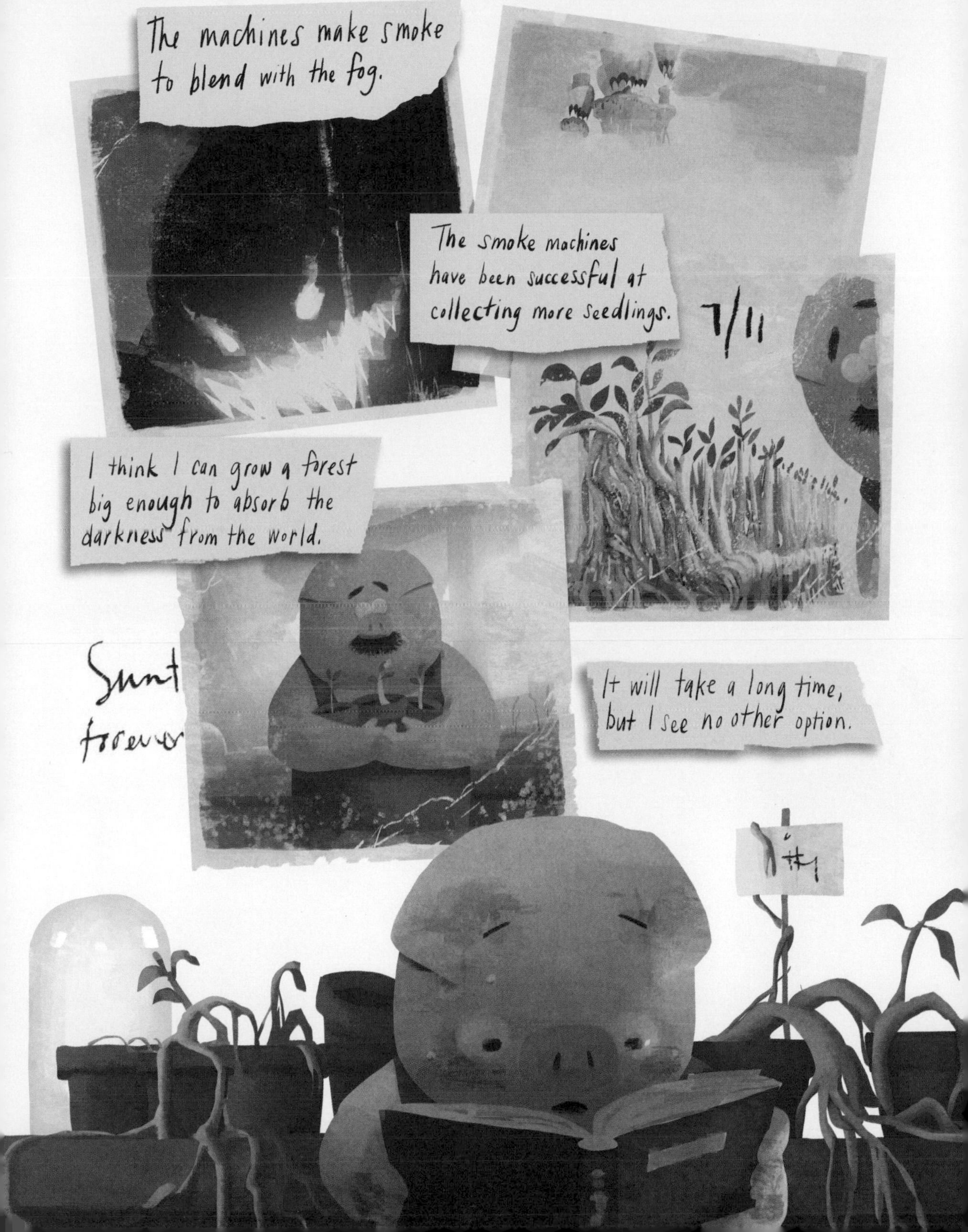
The machines make smoke to blend with the fog.
The smoke machines have been successful at collecting more seedlings.
7/11
I think I can grow a forest big enough to absorb the darkness from the world.
It will take a long time, but I see no other option.

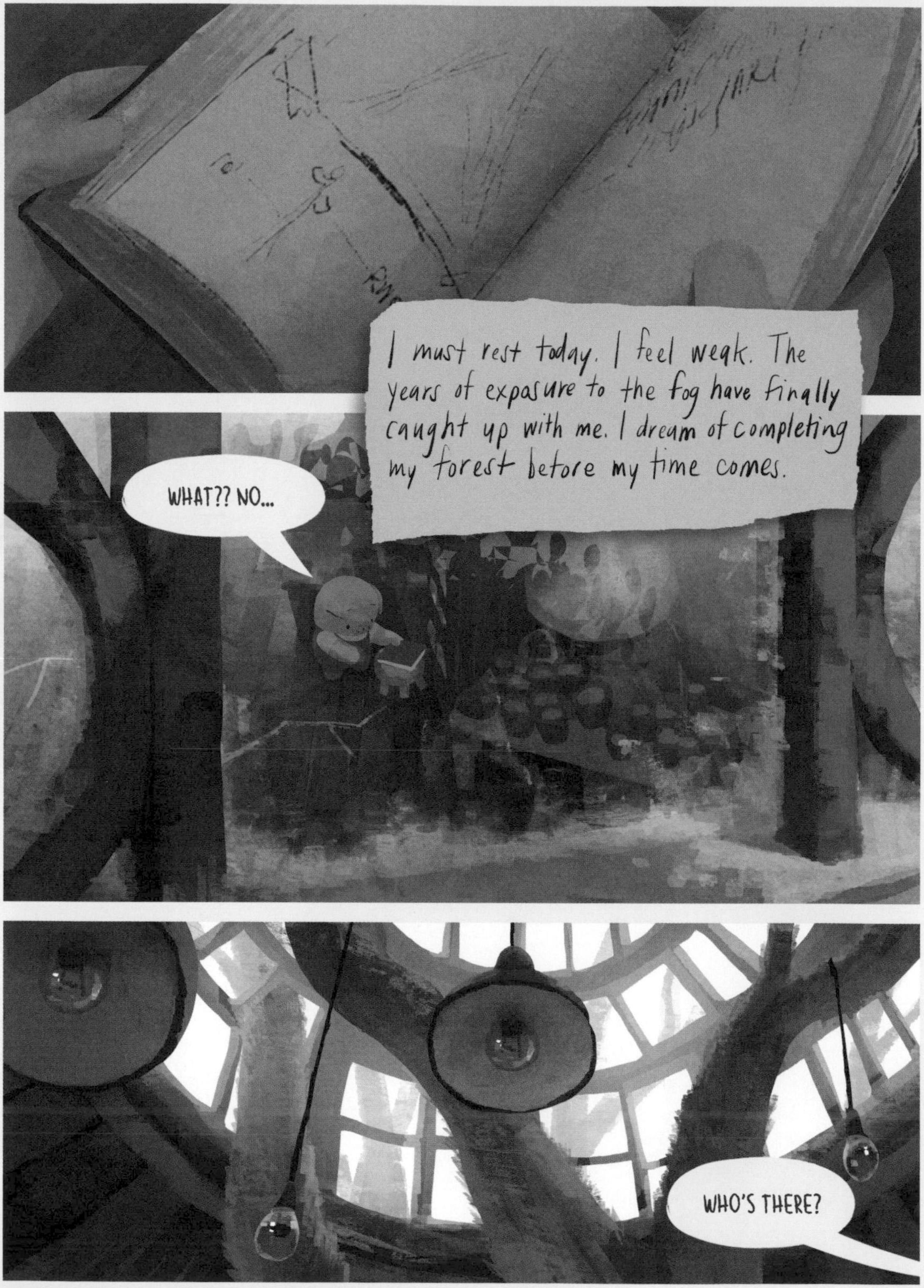
I must rest today. I feel weak. The years of expasure to the fog have finally caught up with me. I dream of completing my forest before my time comes.
WHAT?? NO...
WHO'S THERE?

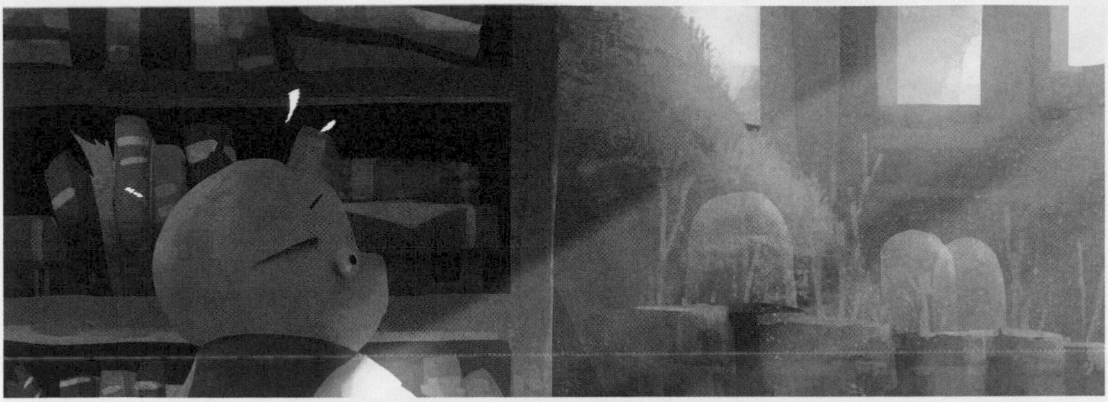

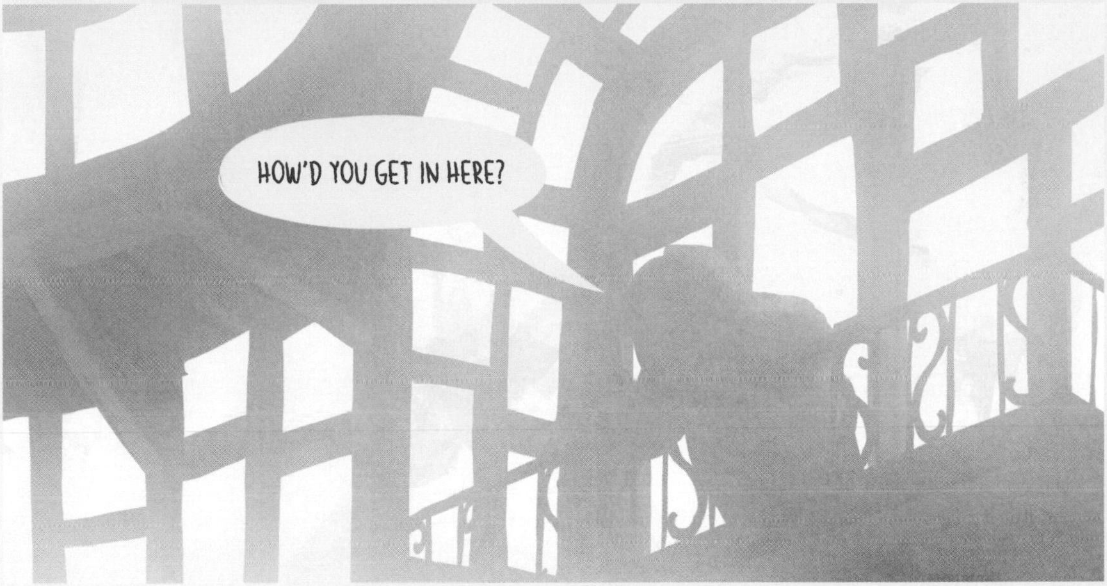
HOW'D YOU GET IN HERE?

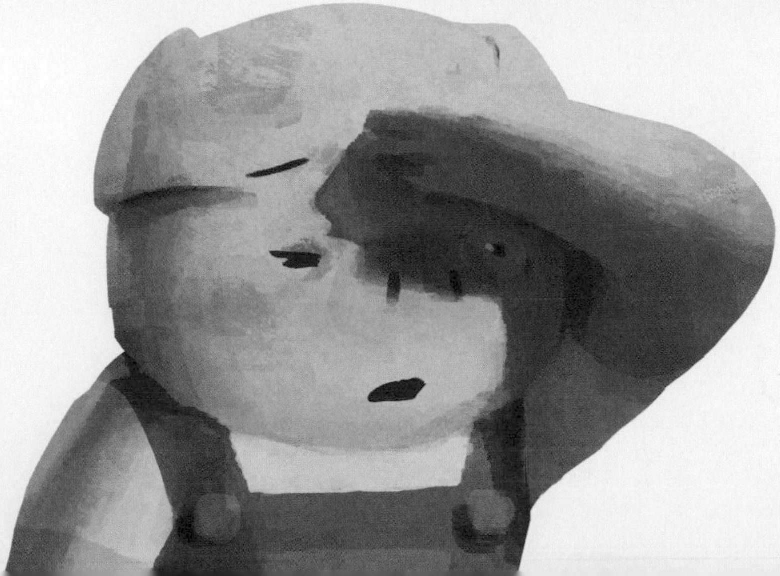

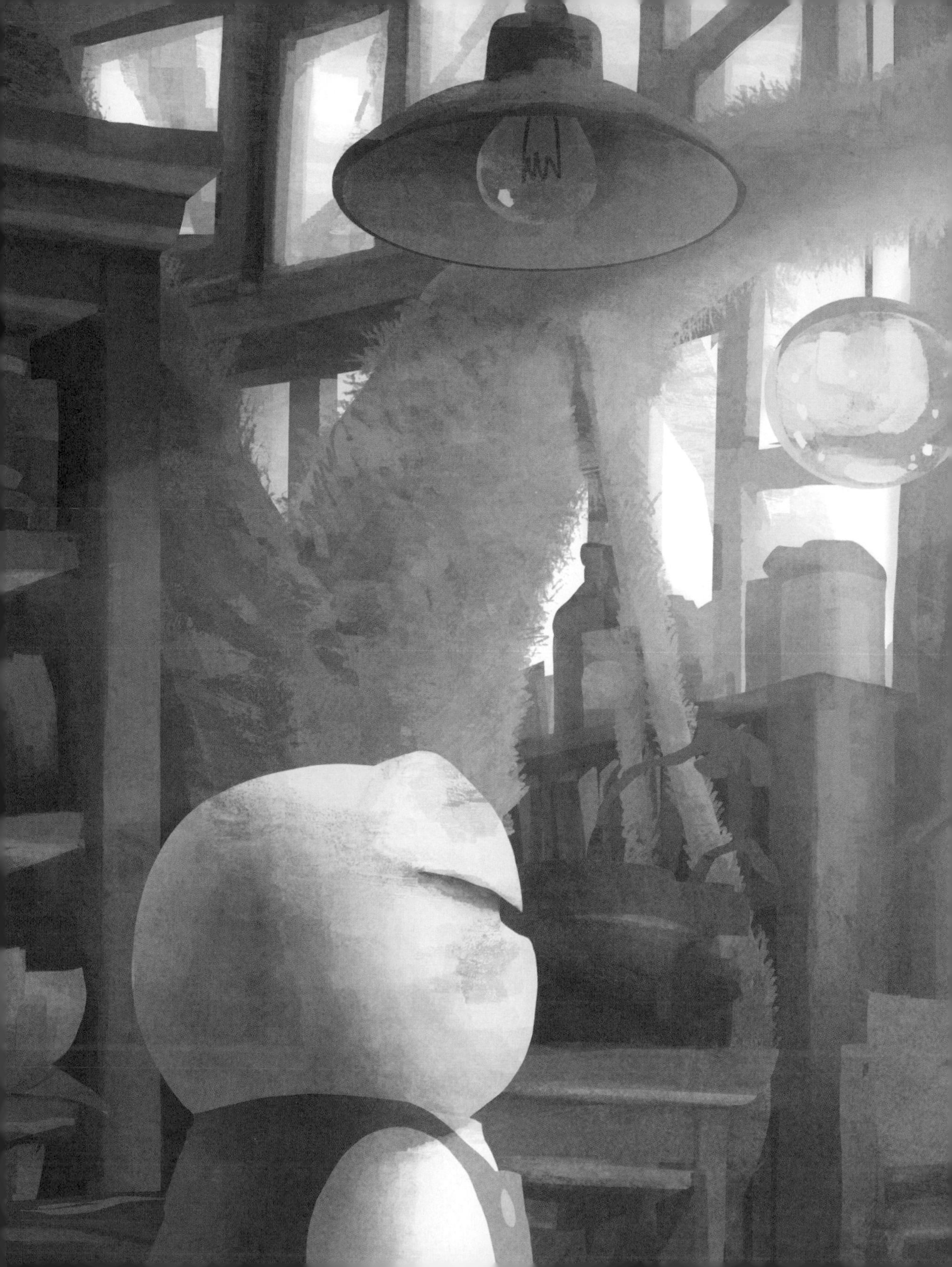

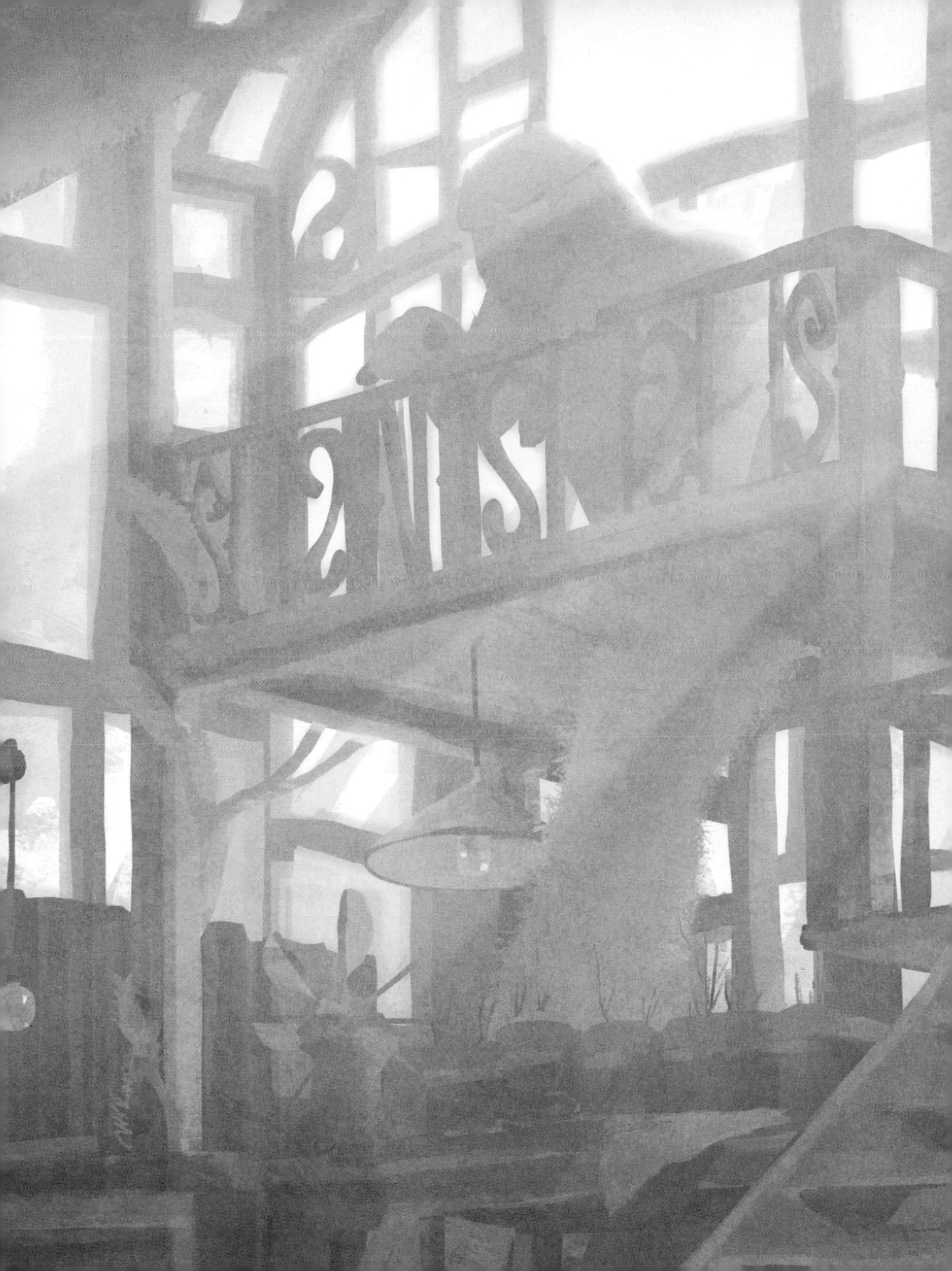

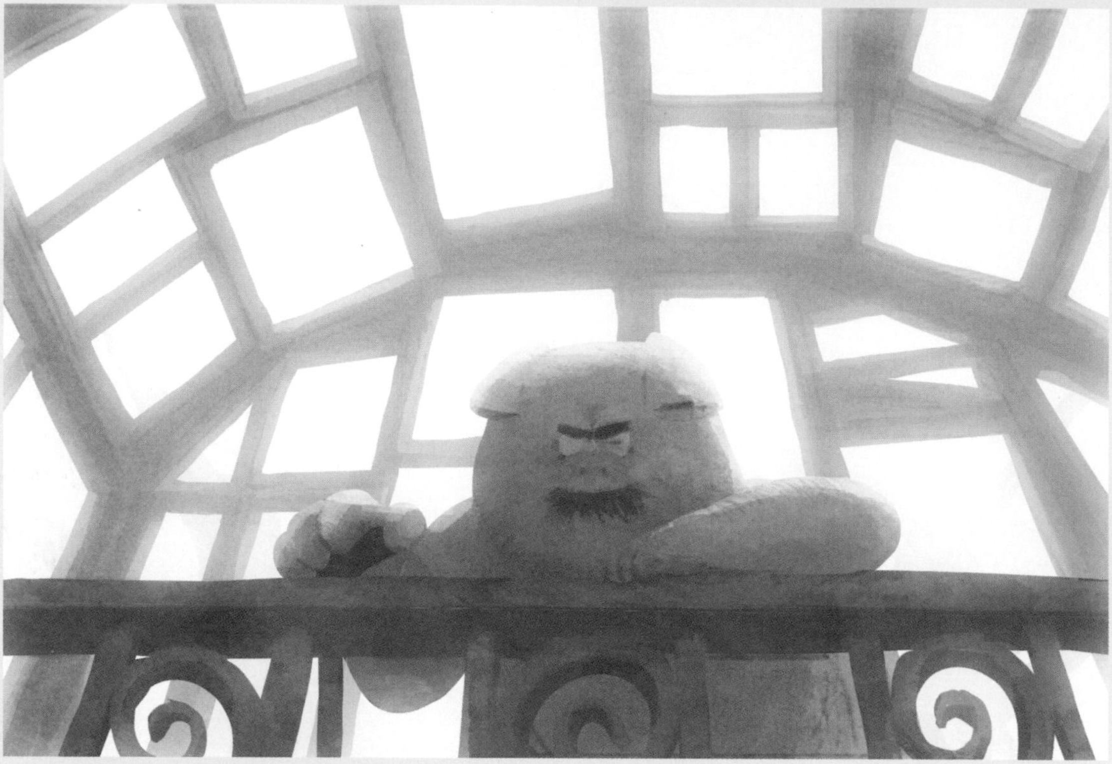

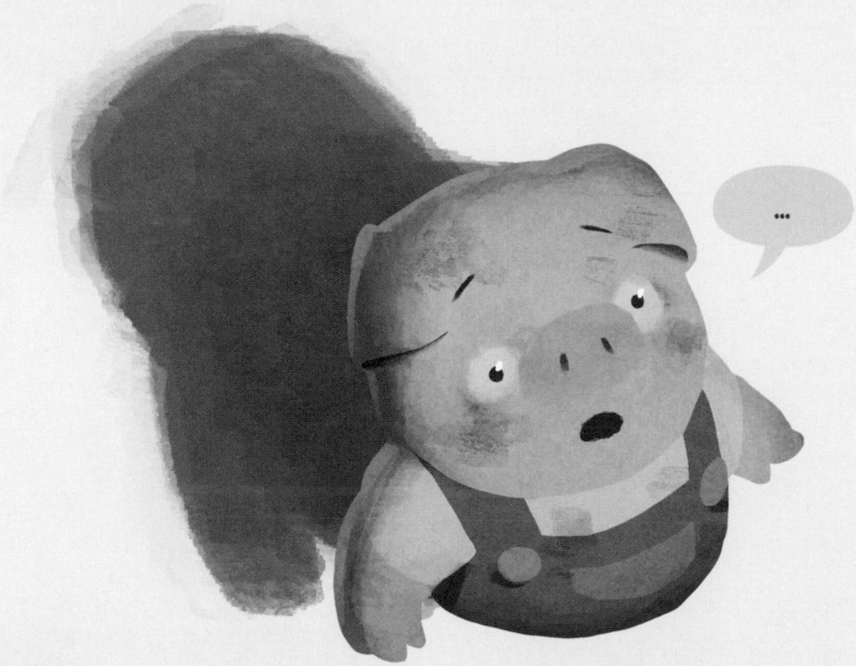
...

...SON?
...DAD...
...IS...IS THAT REALLY YOU?

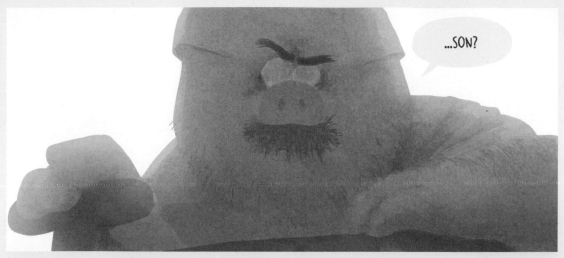

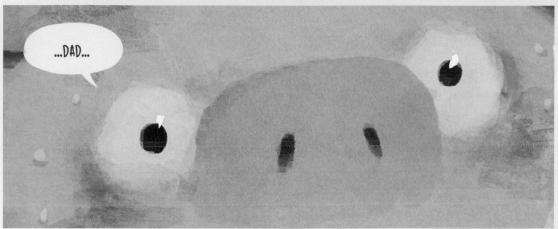

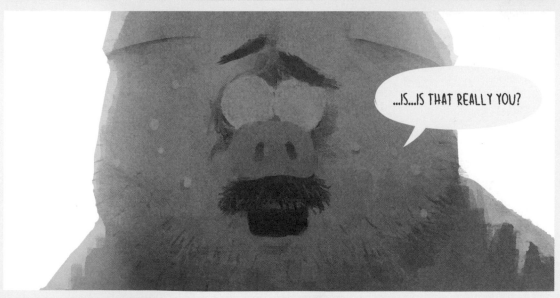

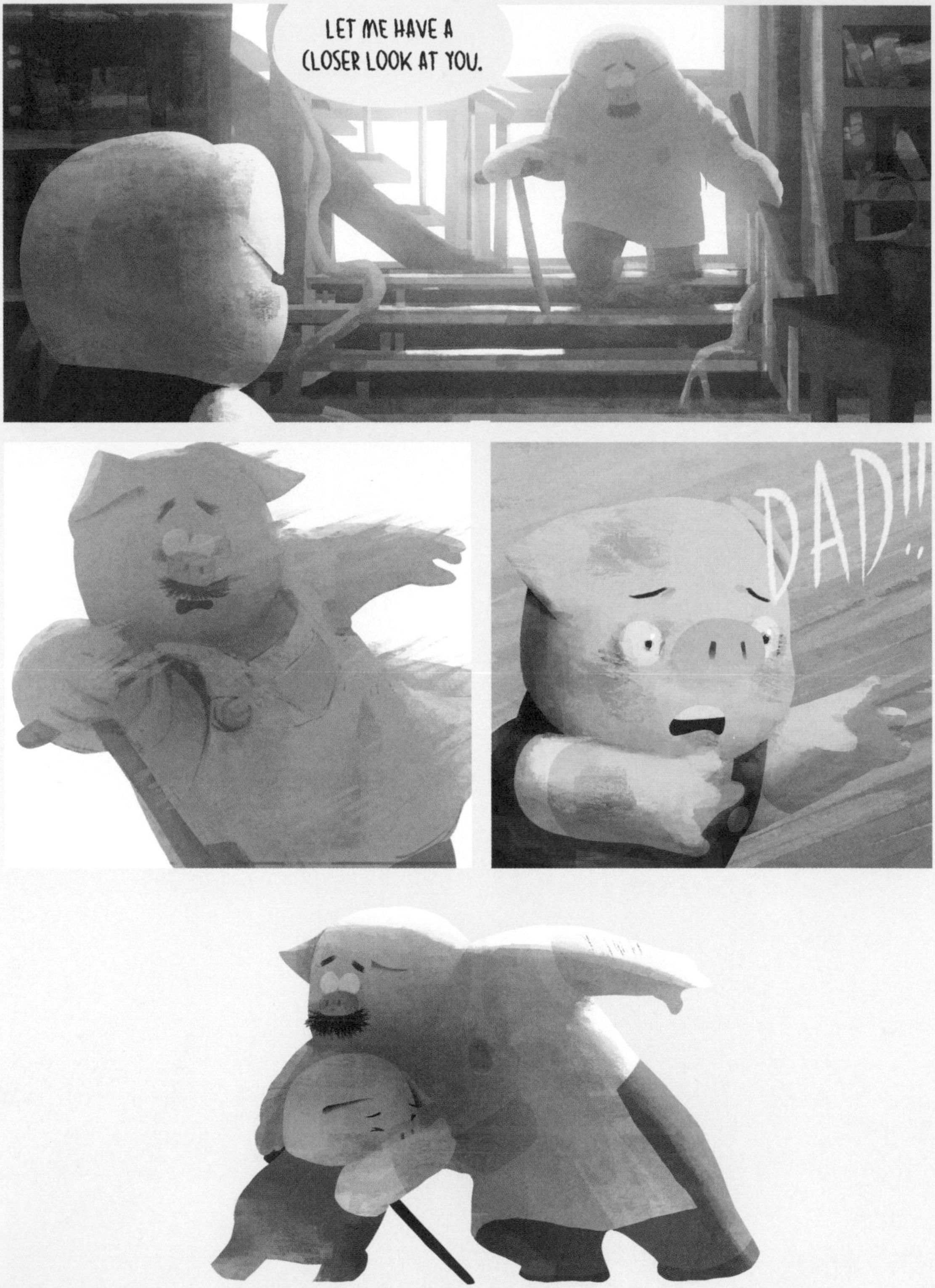
LET ME HAVE A CLOSER LOOK AT YOU.
DAD!!

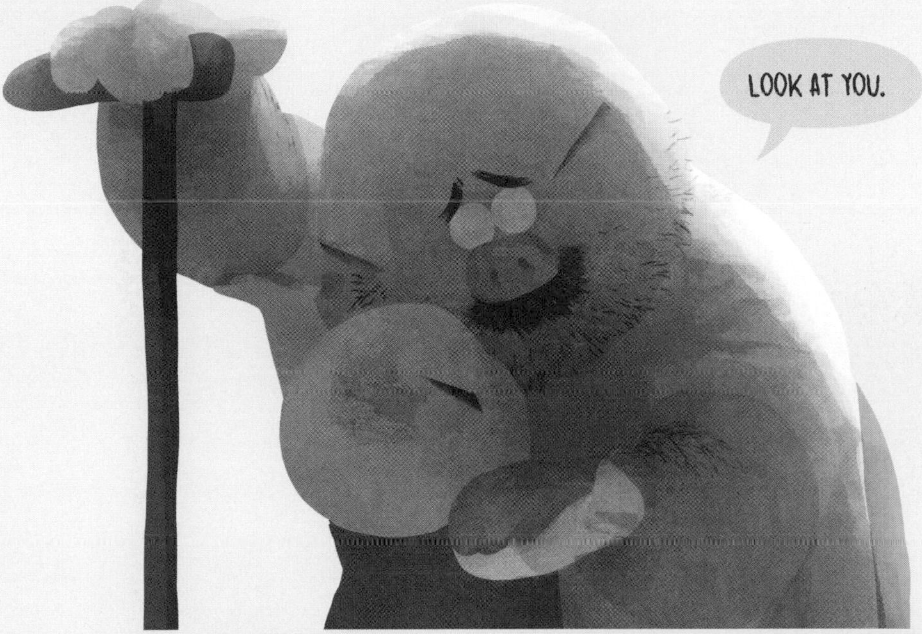
LOOK AT YOU.

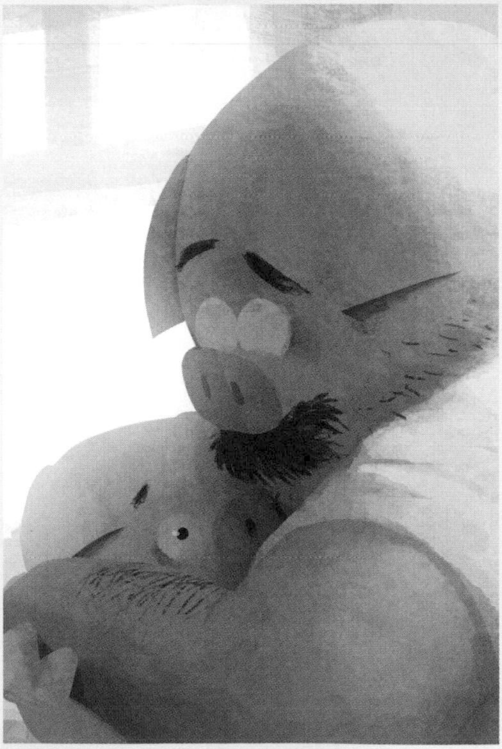

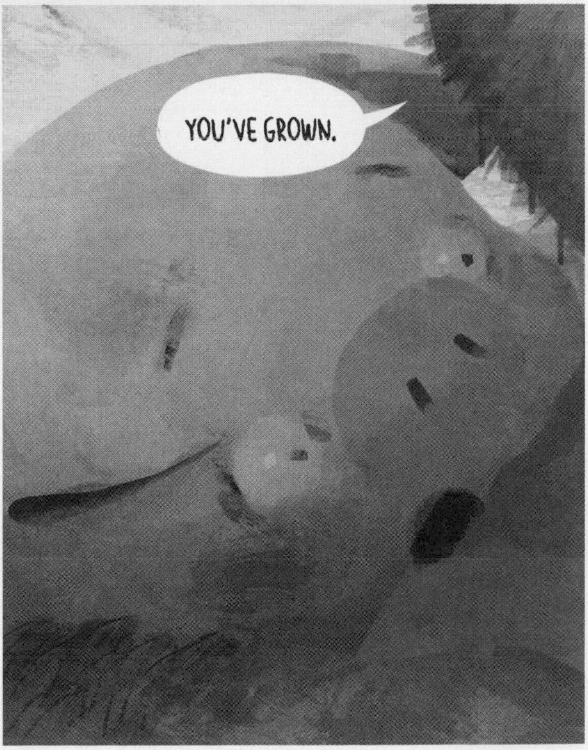
YOU'VE GROWN.

IT'S REALLY YOU.

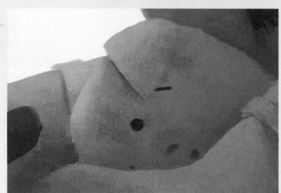

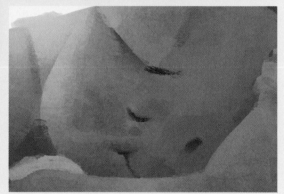

SO TELL ME...

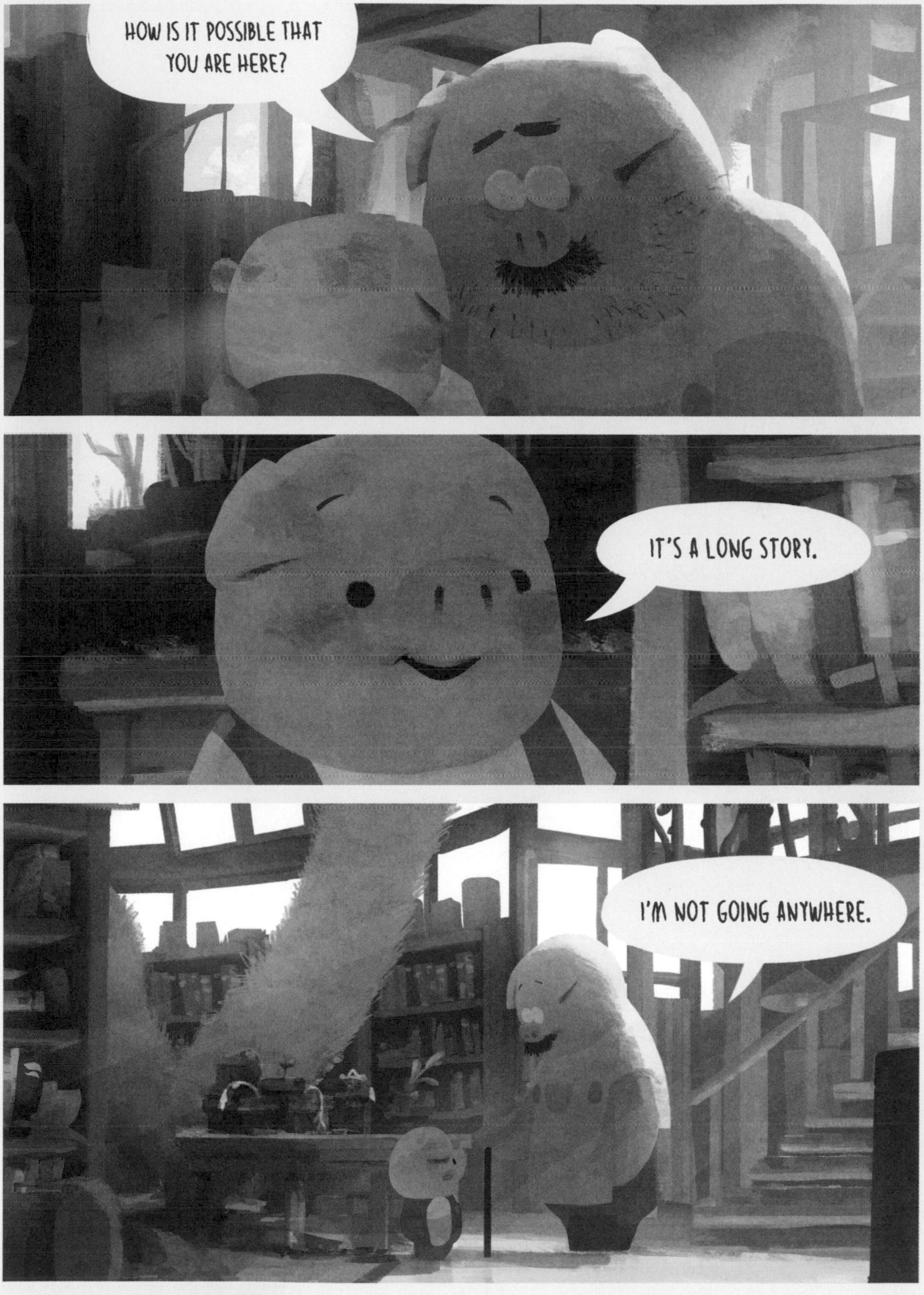
HOW IS IT POSSIBLE THAT YOU ARE HERE?
IT'S A LONG STORY.
I'M NOT GOING ANYWHERE.

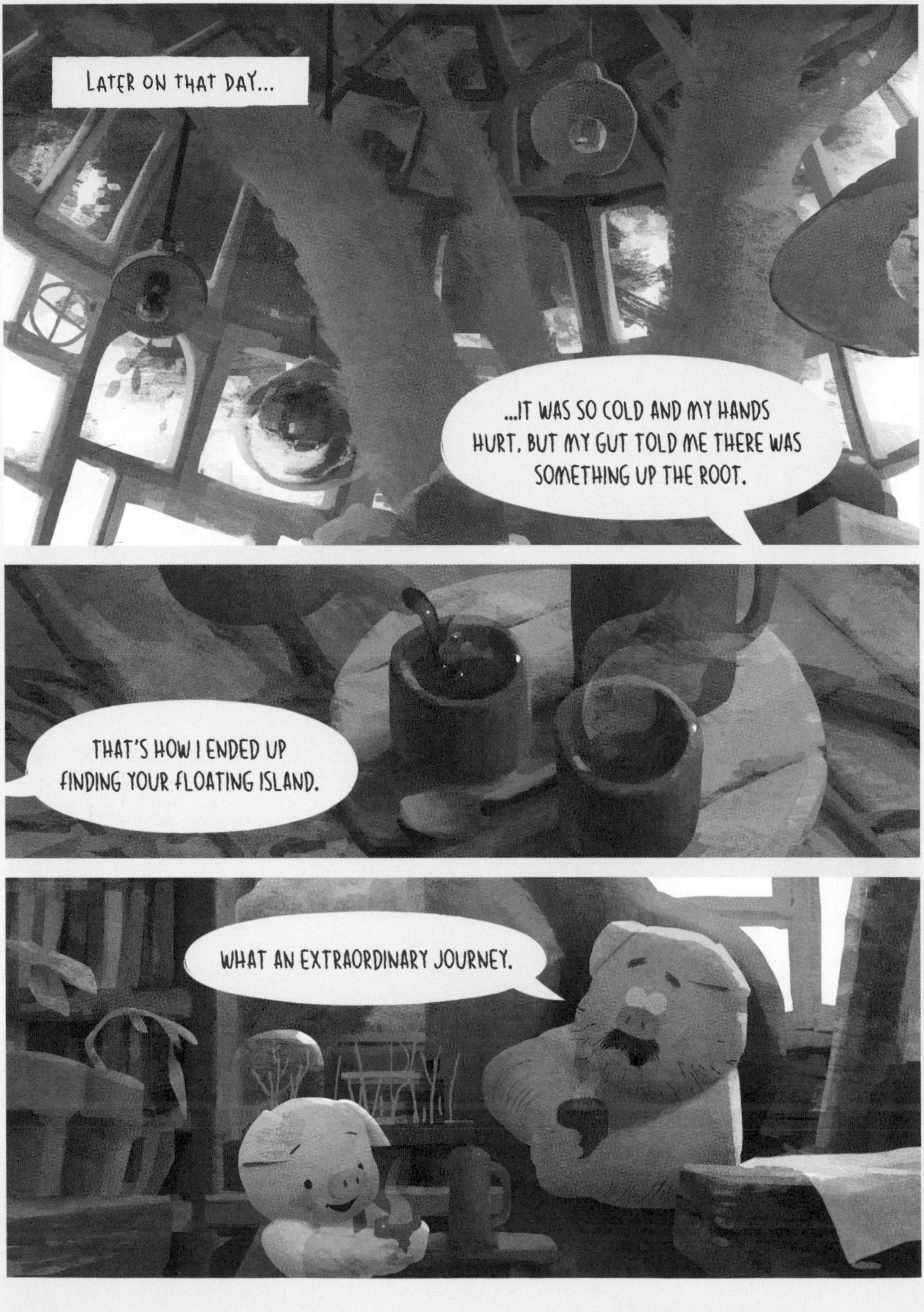
LATER ON THAT DAY...
...IT WAS SO COLD AND MY HANDS HURT, BUT MY GUT TOLD ME THERE WAS SOMETHING UP THE ROOT.
THAT'S HOW I ENDED UP FINDING YOUR FLOATING ISLAND.
WHAT AN EXTRAORDINARY JOURNEY.

I READ ABOUT THE FOREST PROJECT IN YOUR JOURNAL. IT'S INCREDIBLE.

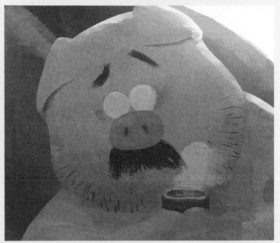

A FOREST THAT ABSORBS THE FOG. IT SOUNDS CRAZY, BUT YOU HAVE TO SEE IT WITH YOUR OWN EYES. THE TREES COME TO LIFE TO DRINK THE FOG--

I HAVE SEEN IT! DO YOU THINK THE TREES WILL BE ABLE TO STOP THE BIG WAVE THAT'S COMING?

NO. IT'S NOT READY YET.

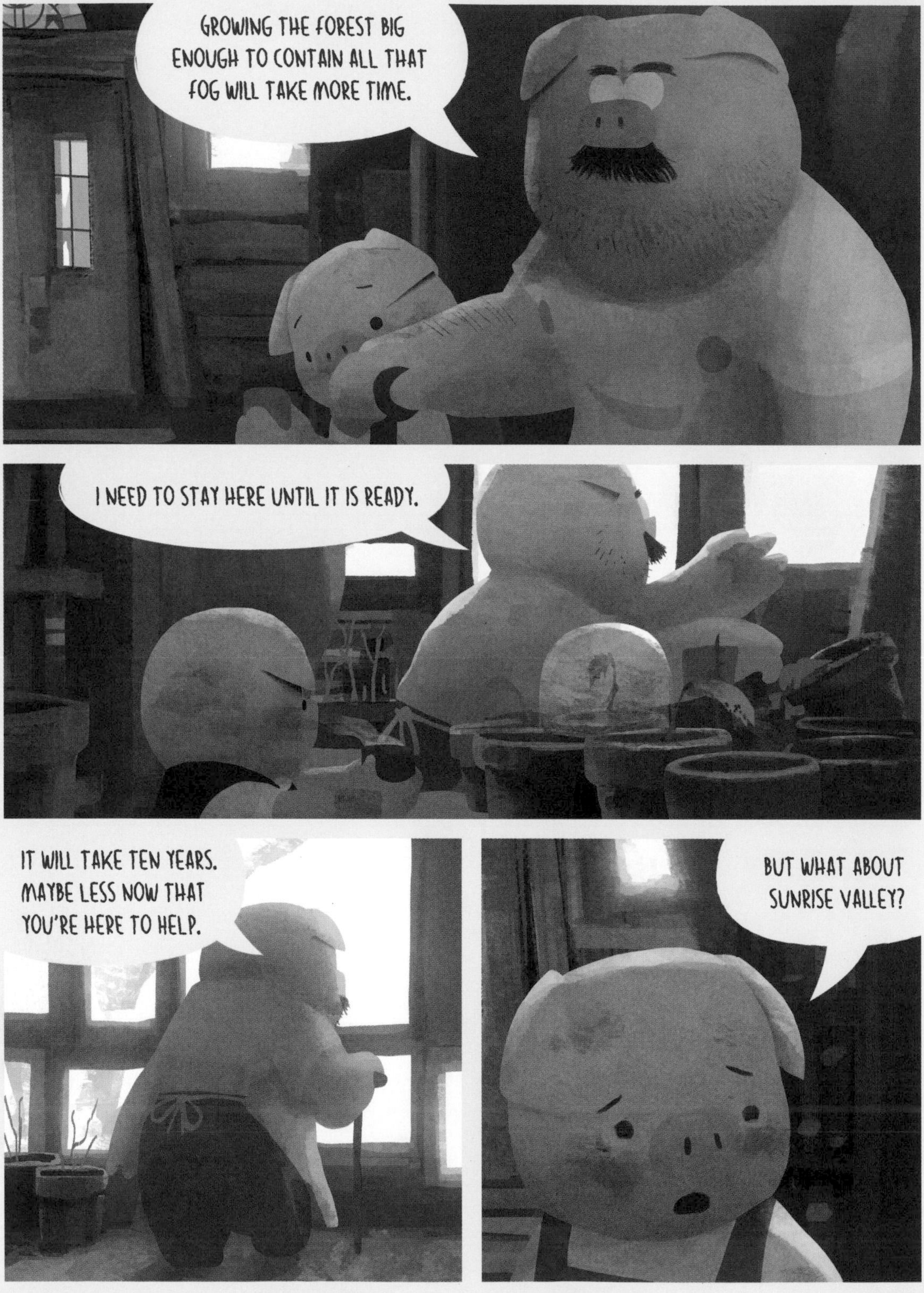
GROWING THE FOREST BIG ENOUGH TO CONTAIN ALL THAT FOG WILL TAKE MORE TIME.
I NEED TO STAY HERE UNTIL IT IS READY.
IT WILL TAKE TEN YEARS. MAYBE LESS NOW THAT YOU'RE HERE TO HELP.
BUT WHAT ABOUT SUNRISE VALLEY?

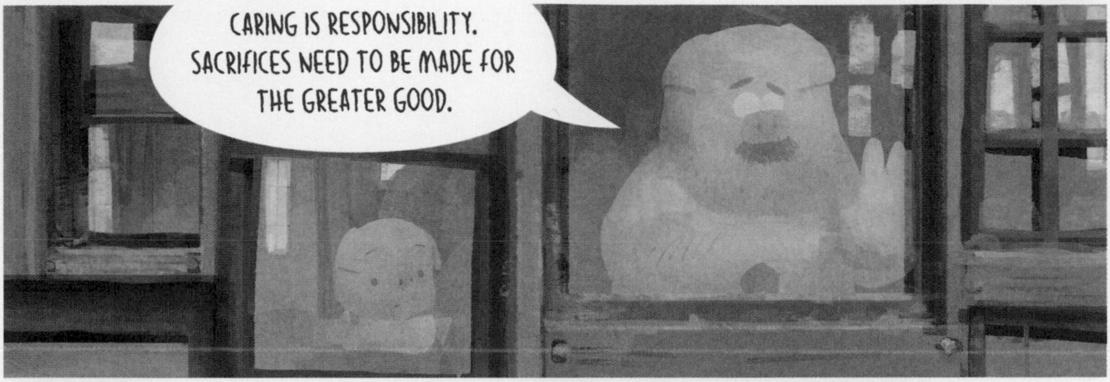
CARING IS RESPONSIBILITY. SACRIFICES NEED TO BE MADE FOR THE GREATER GOOD.

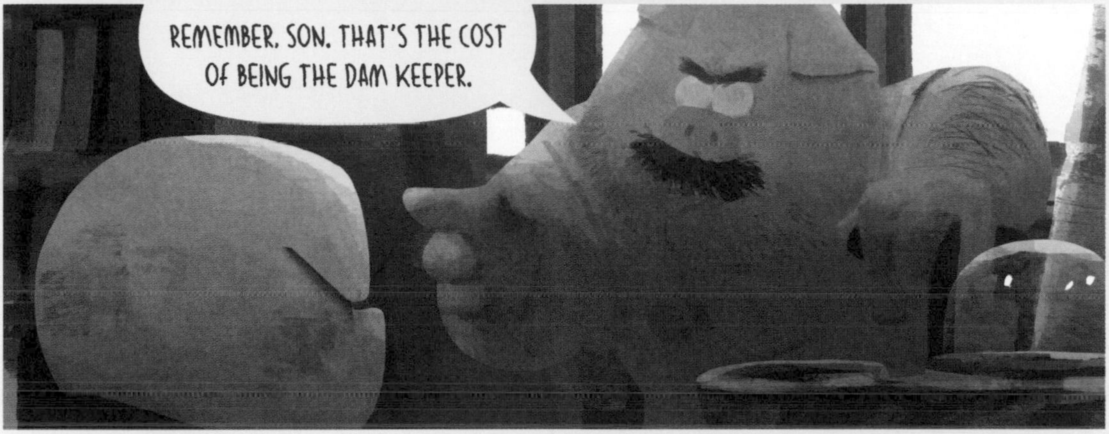
REMEMBER, SON. THAT'S THE COST OF BEING THE DAM KEEPER.

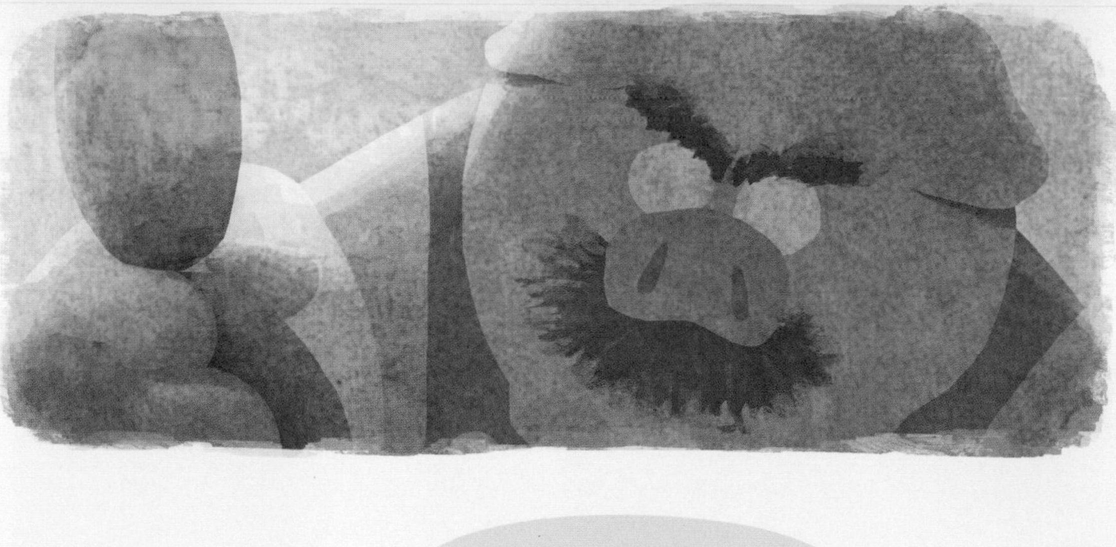

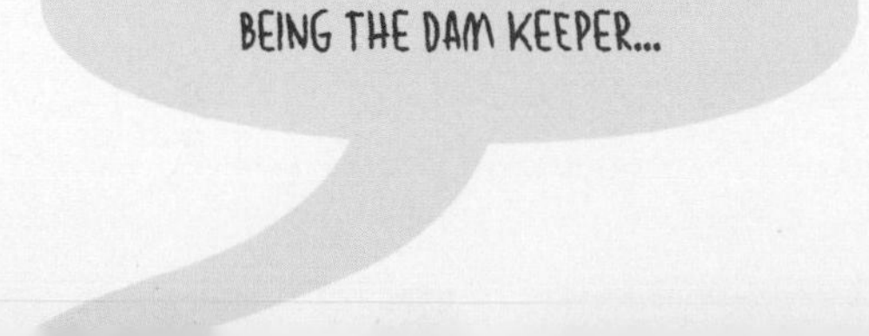
DAD, I THINK I KNOW THE COST OF BEING THE DAM KEEPER...

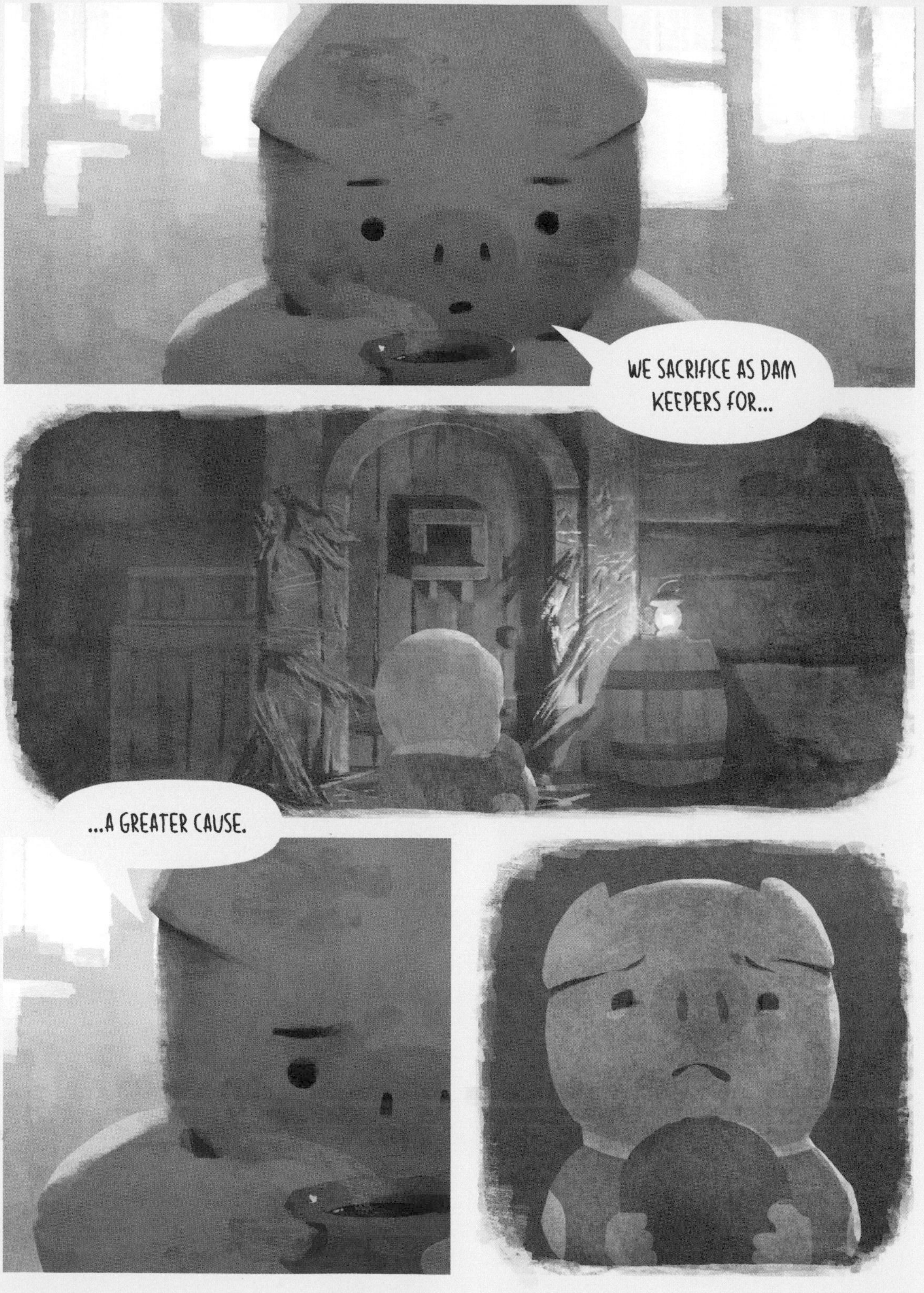
WE SACRIFICE AS DAM KEEPERS FOR...
...A GREATER CAUSE.

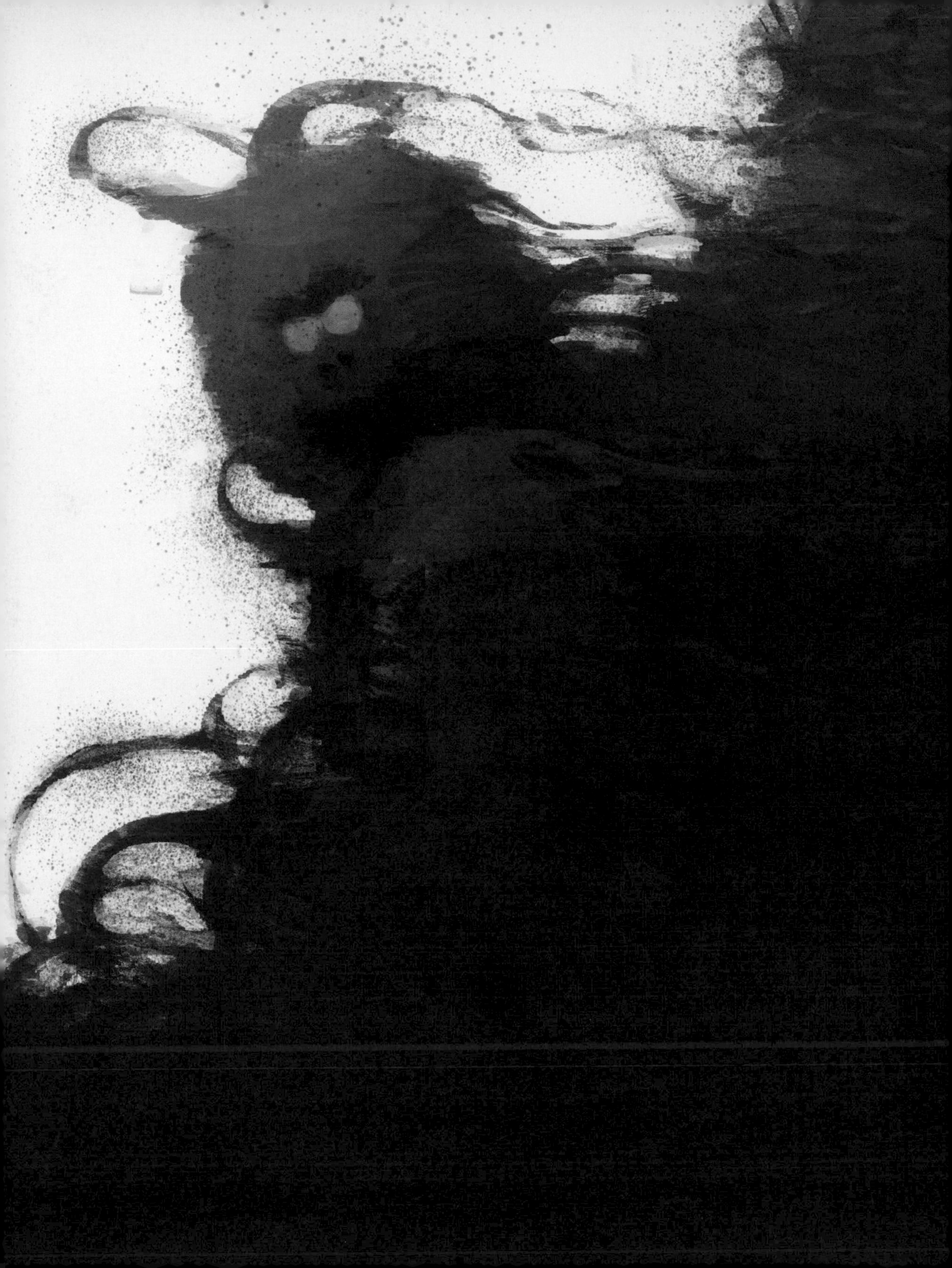

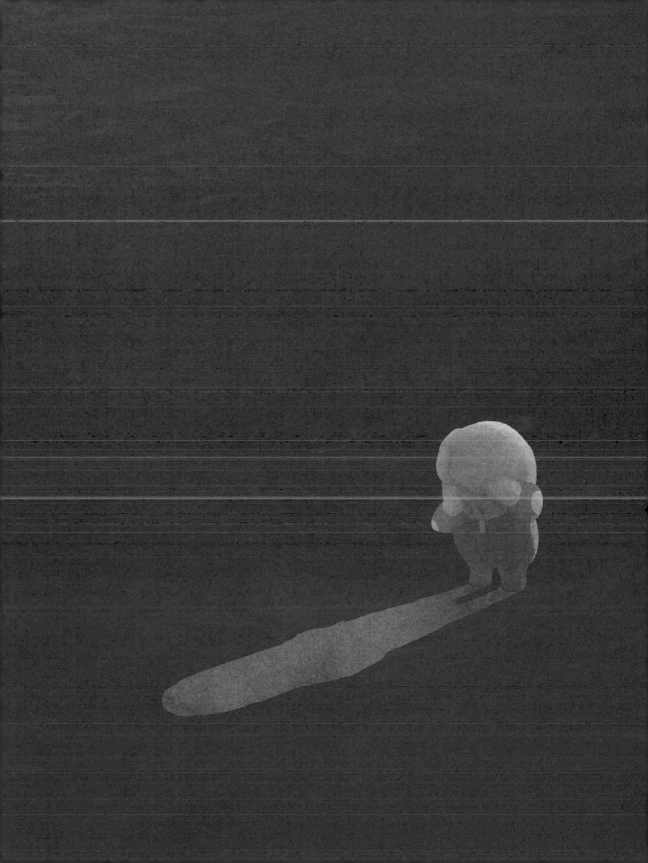

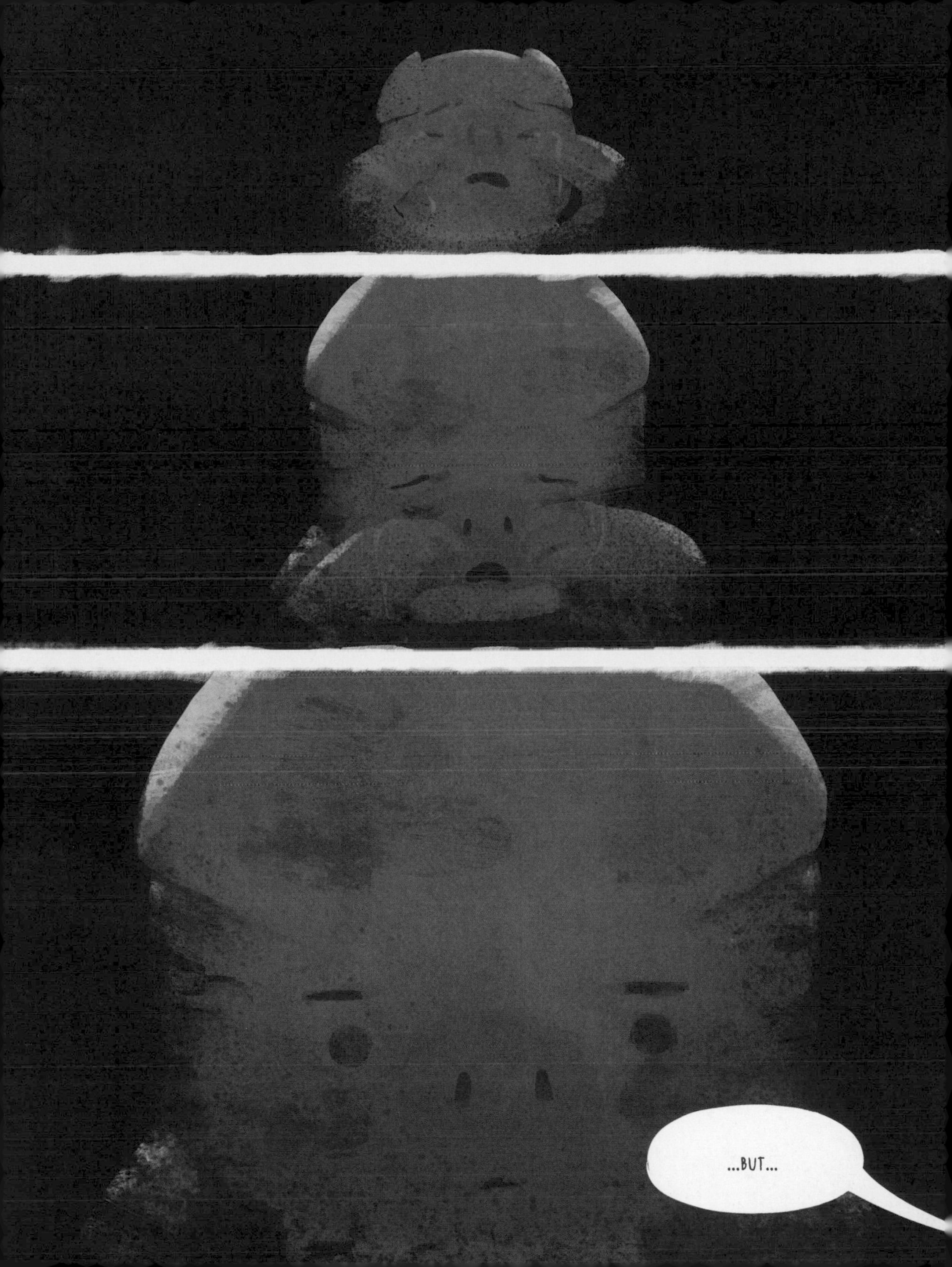
...BUT...

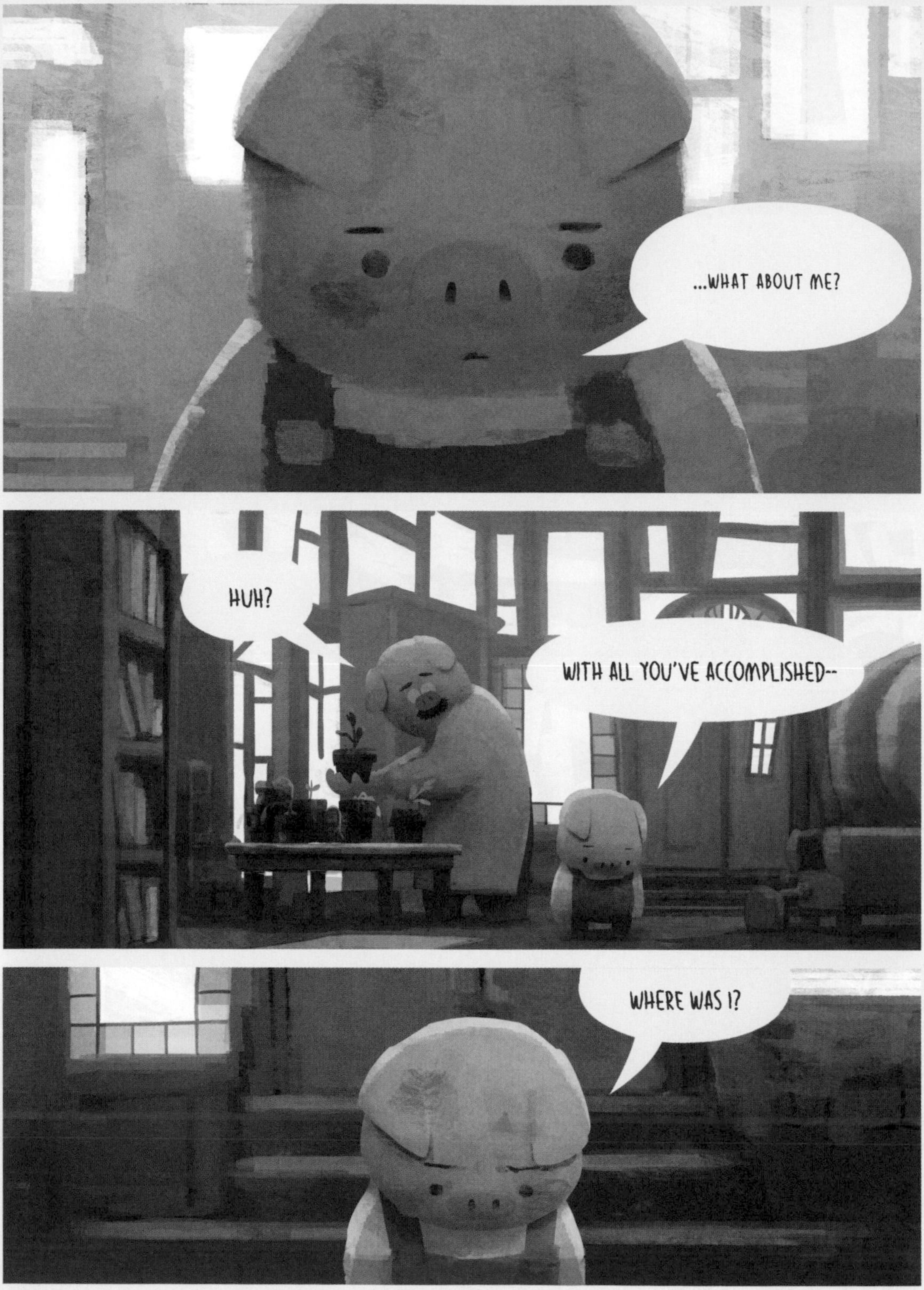
...WHAT ABOUT ME?
HUH?
WITH ALL YOU'VE ACCOMPLISHED--
WHERE WAS I?

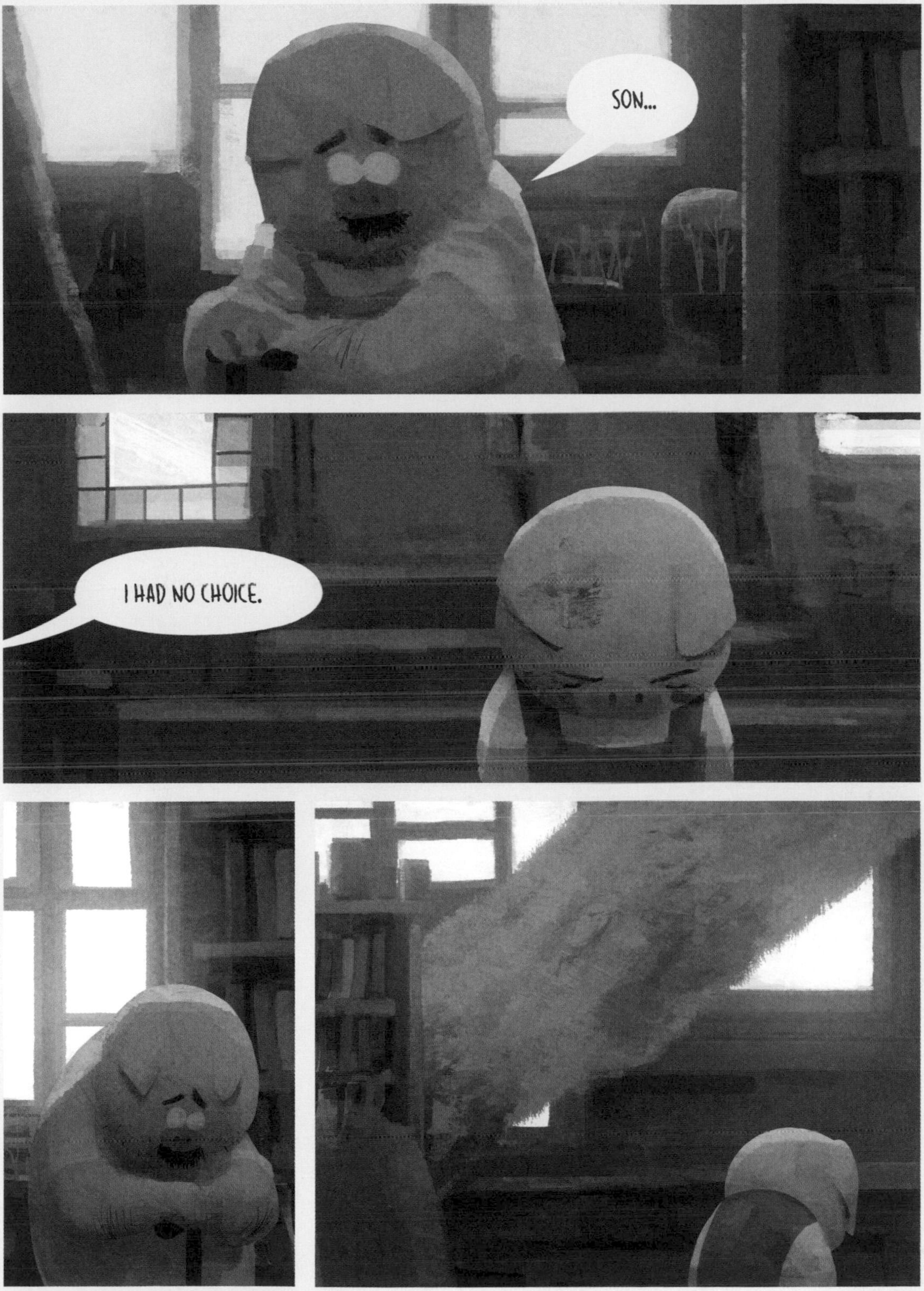
SON...
I HAD NO CHOICE.

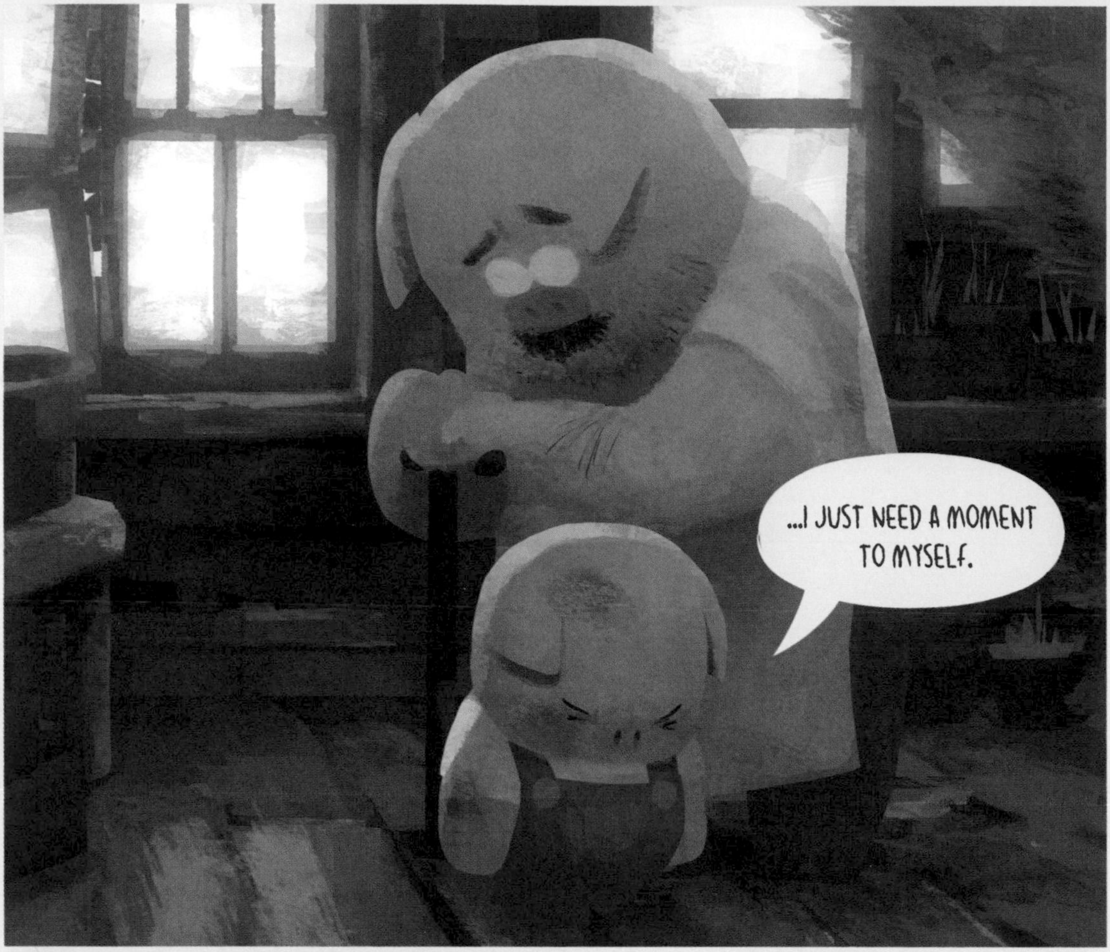
...I JUST NEED A MOMENT TO MYSELF.

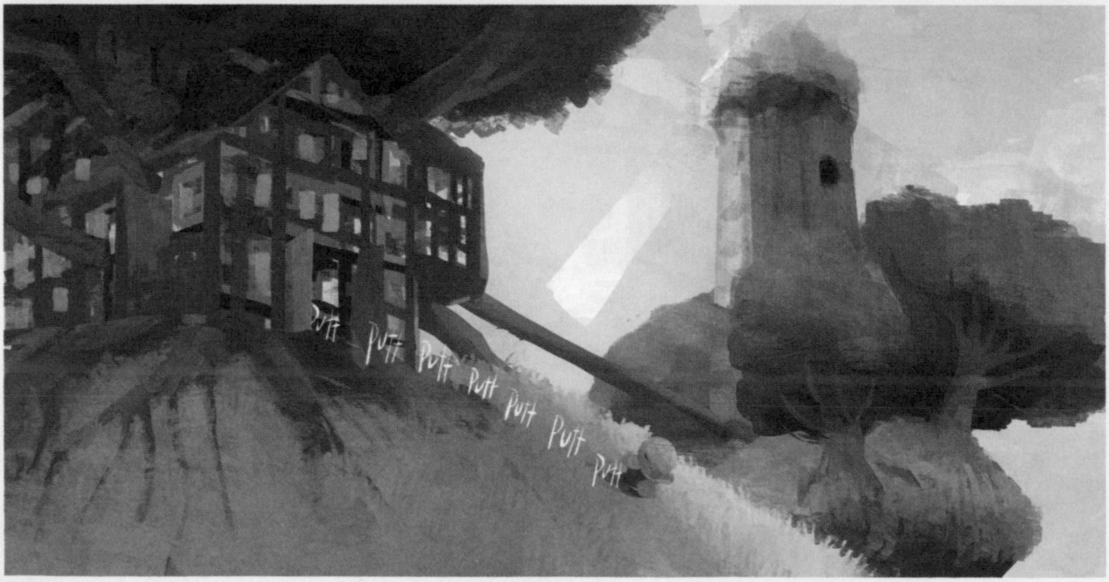
PUFF PUFF PUFF PUFF PUFF PUFF PUFF

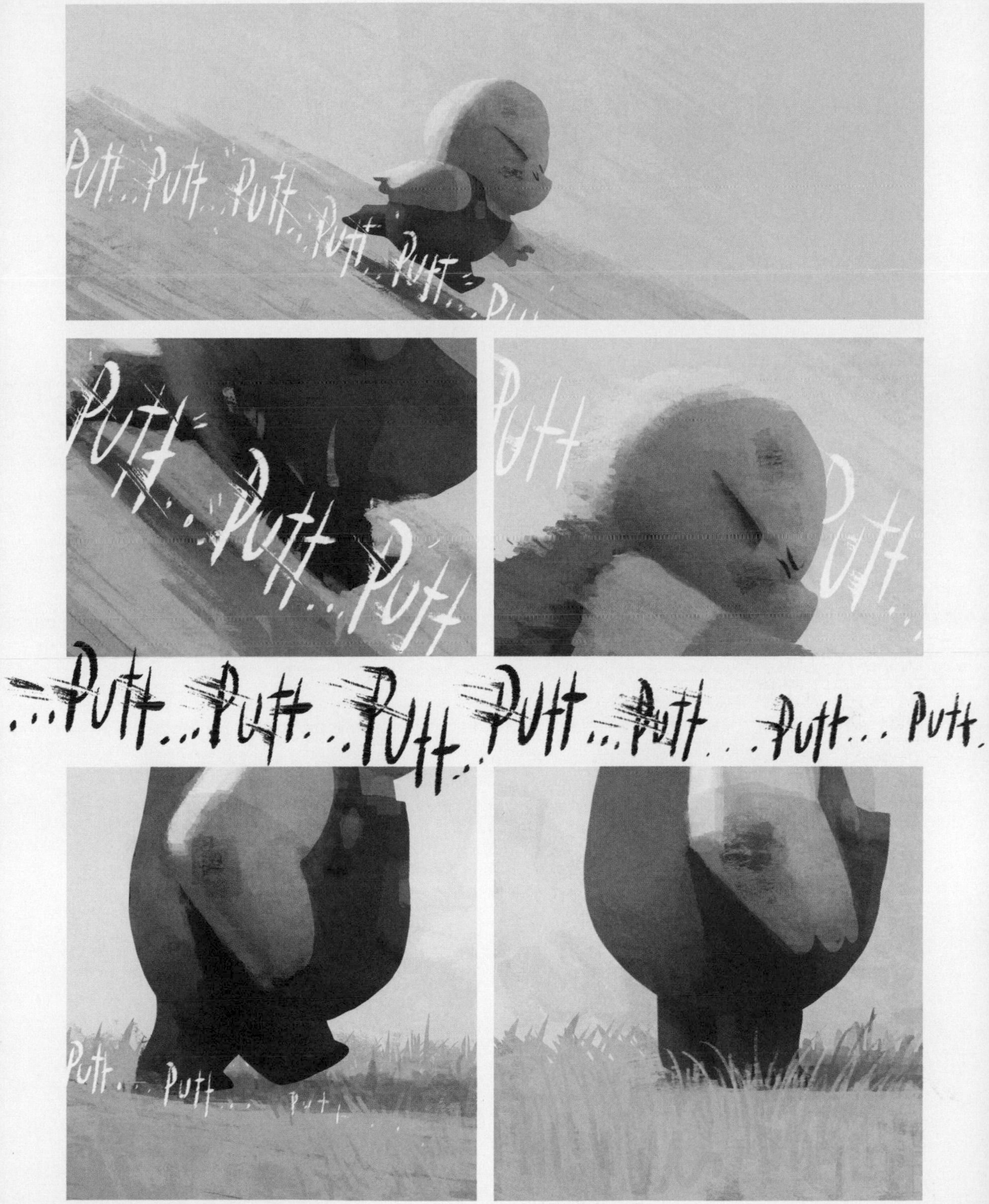
Putt...Putt...Putt...Putt...Putt...Putt
Putt...Putt...Putt
Putt...Putt
...Putt...Putt...Putt...Putt...Putt...Putt...Putt.
Putt...Putt...Putt

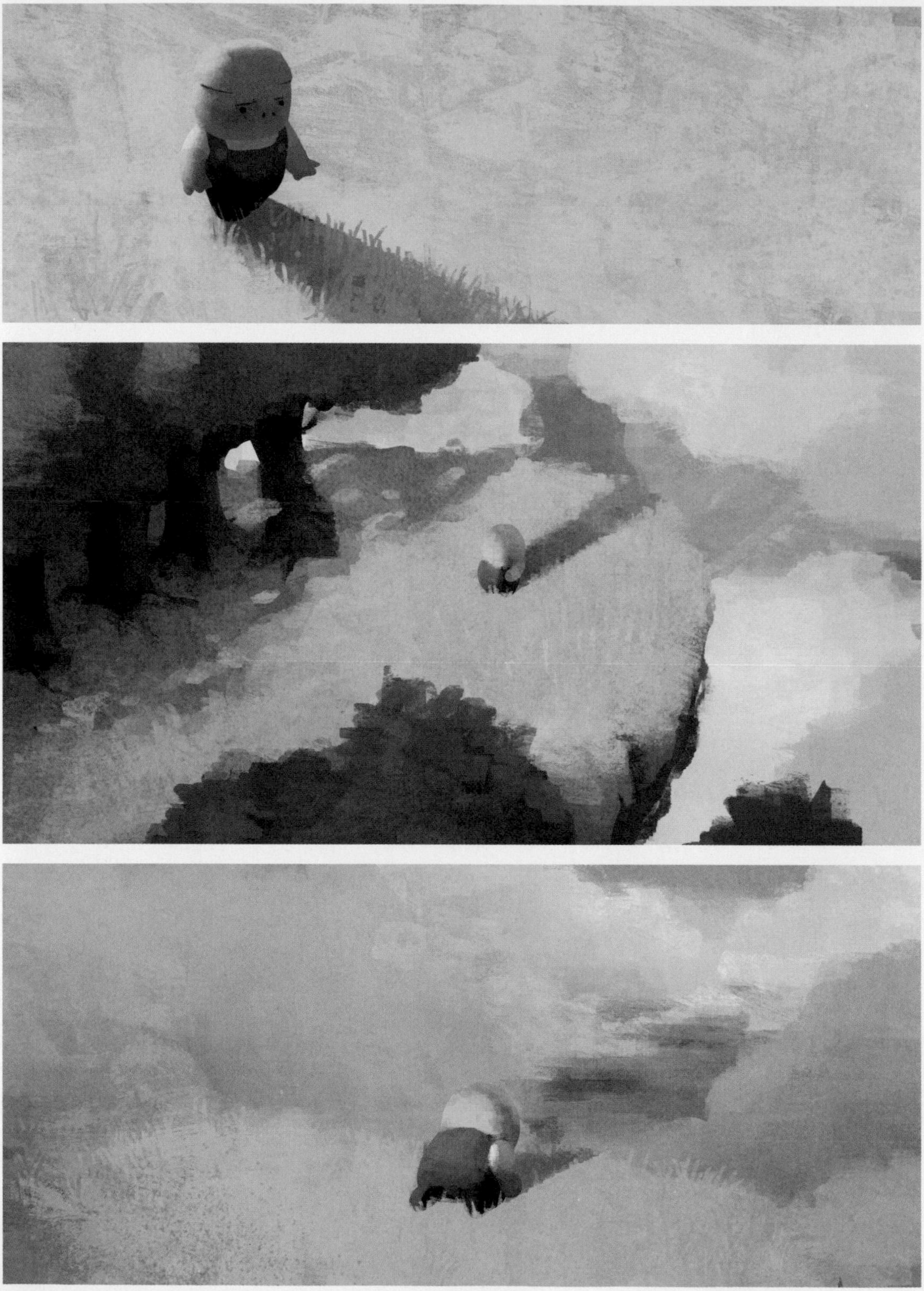

PLOP...

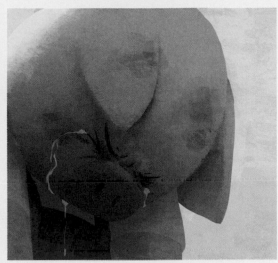

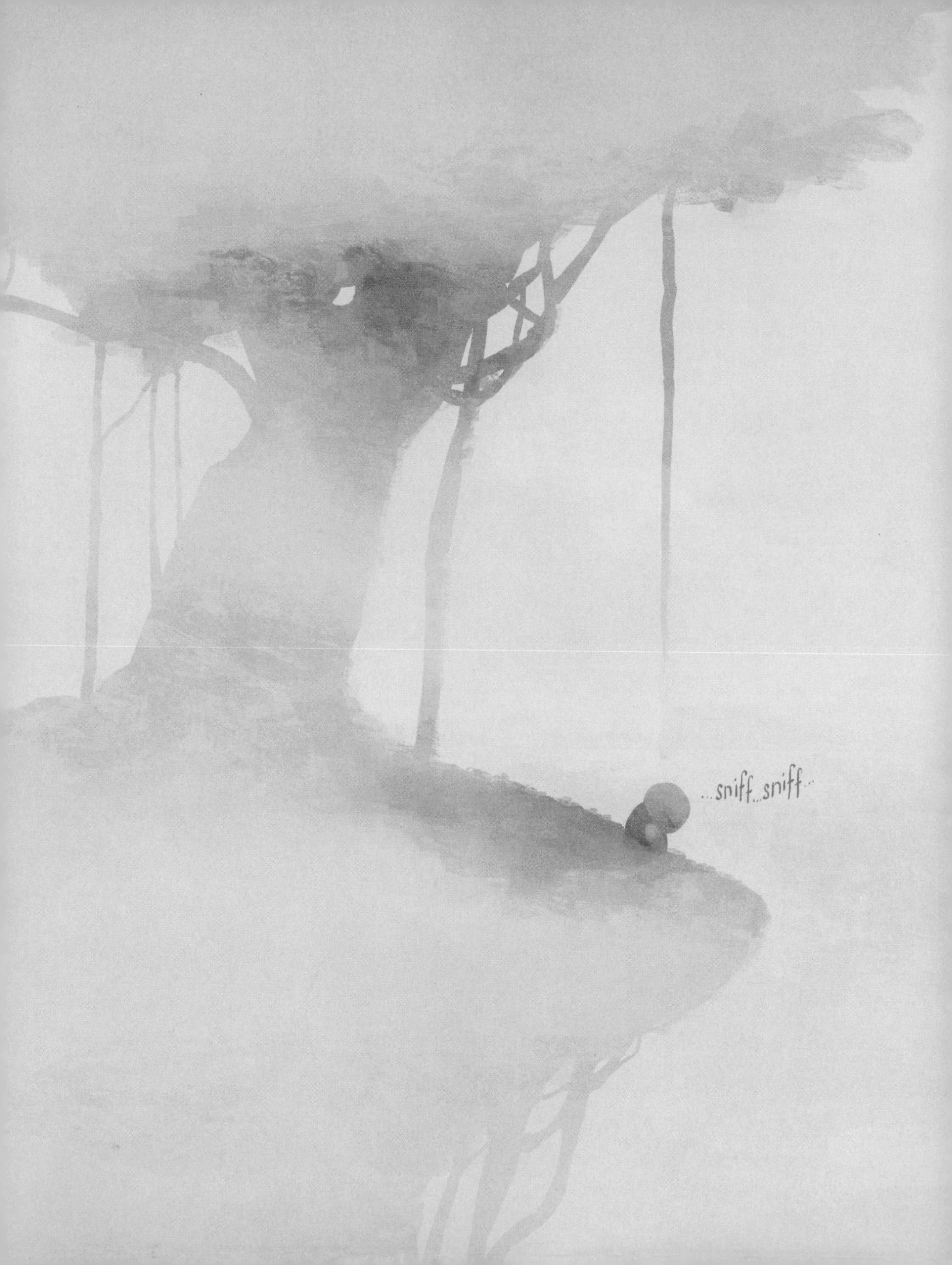
...sniff...sniff...

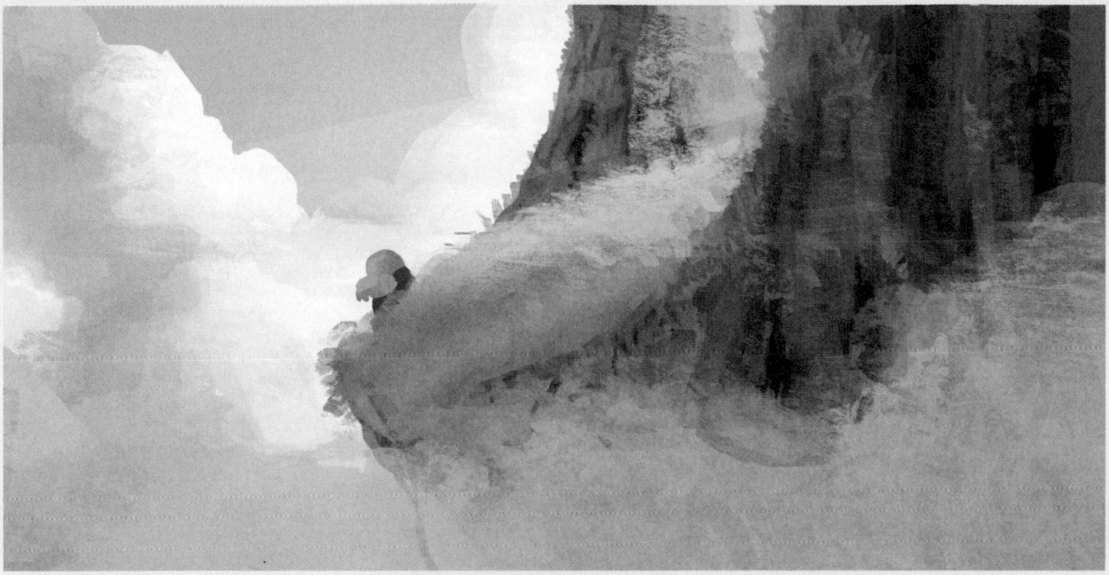

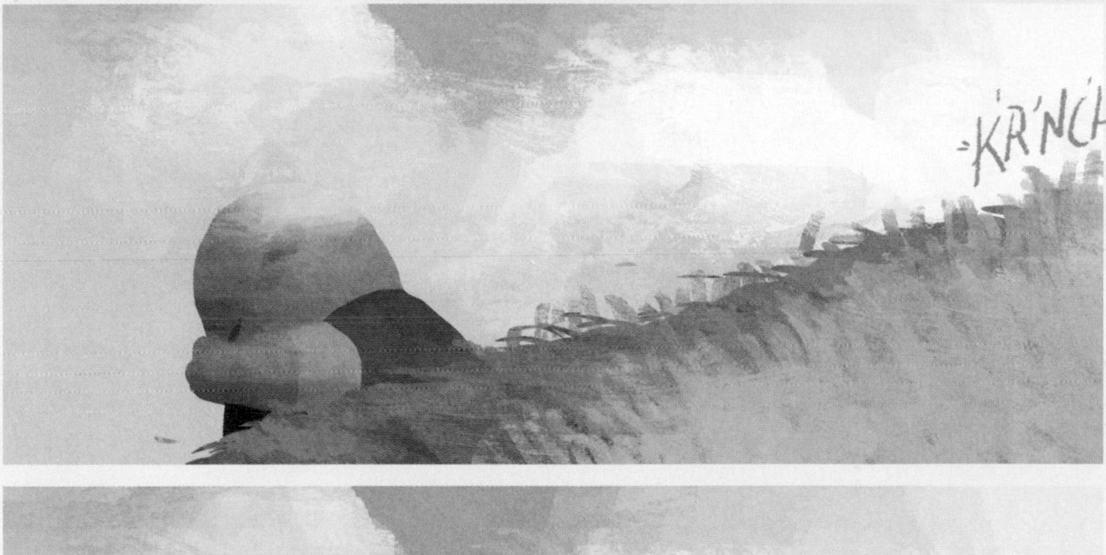
KR'NCH

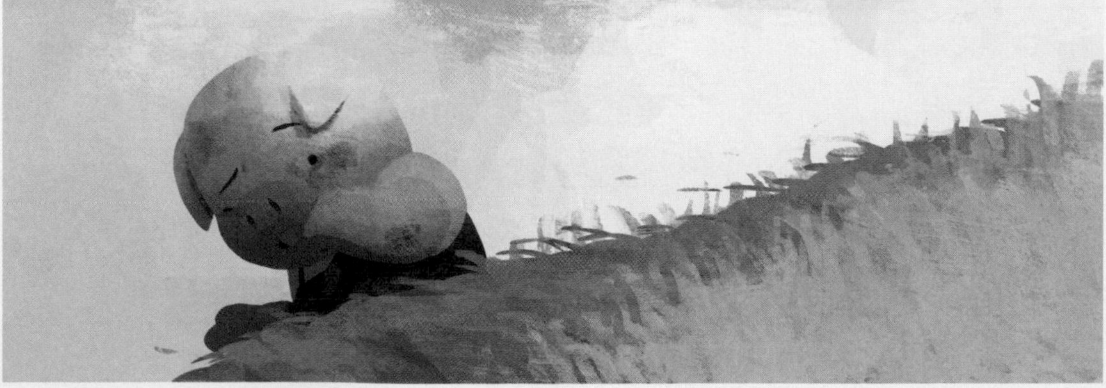

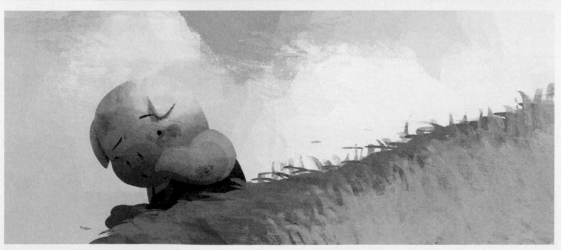

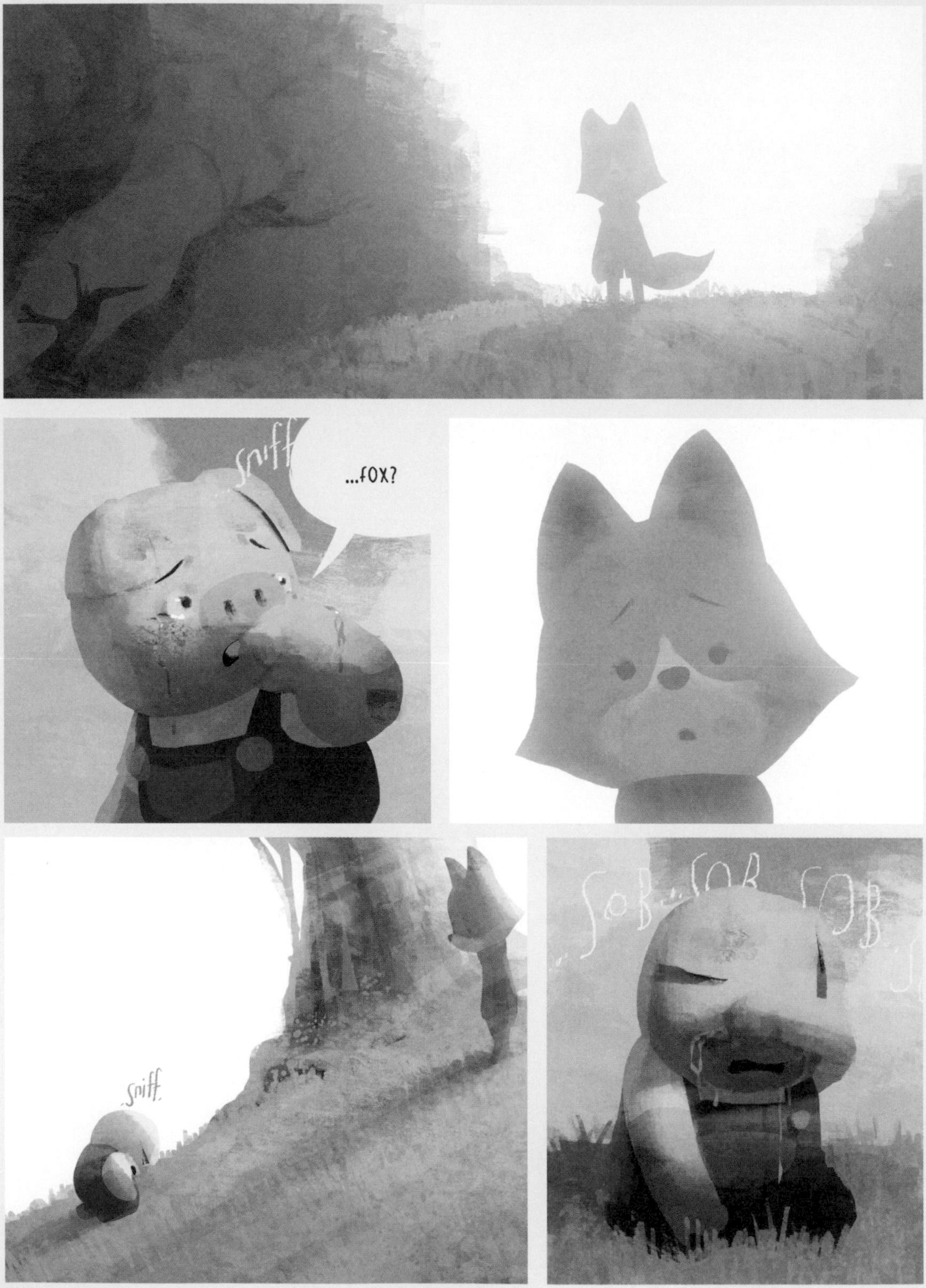
Sniff
...FOX?
Sniff
SOB SOB SOB

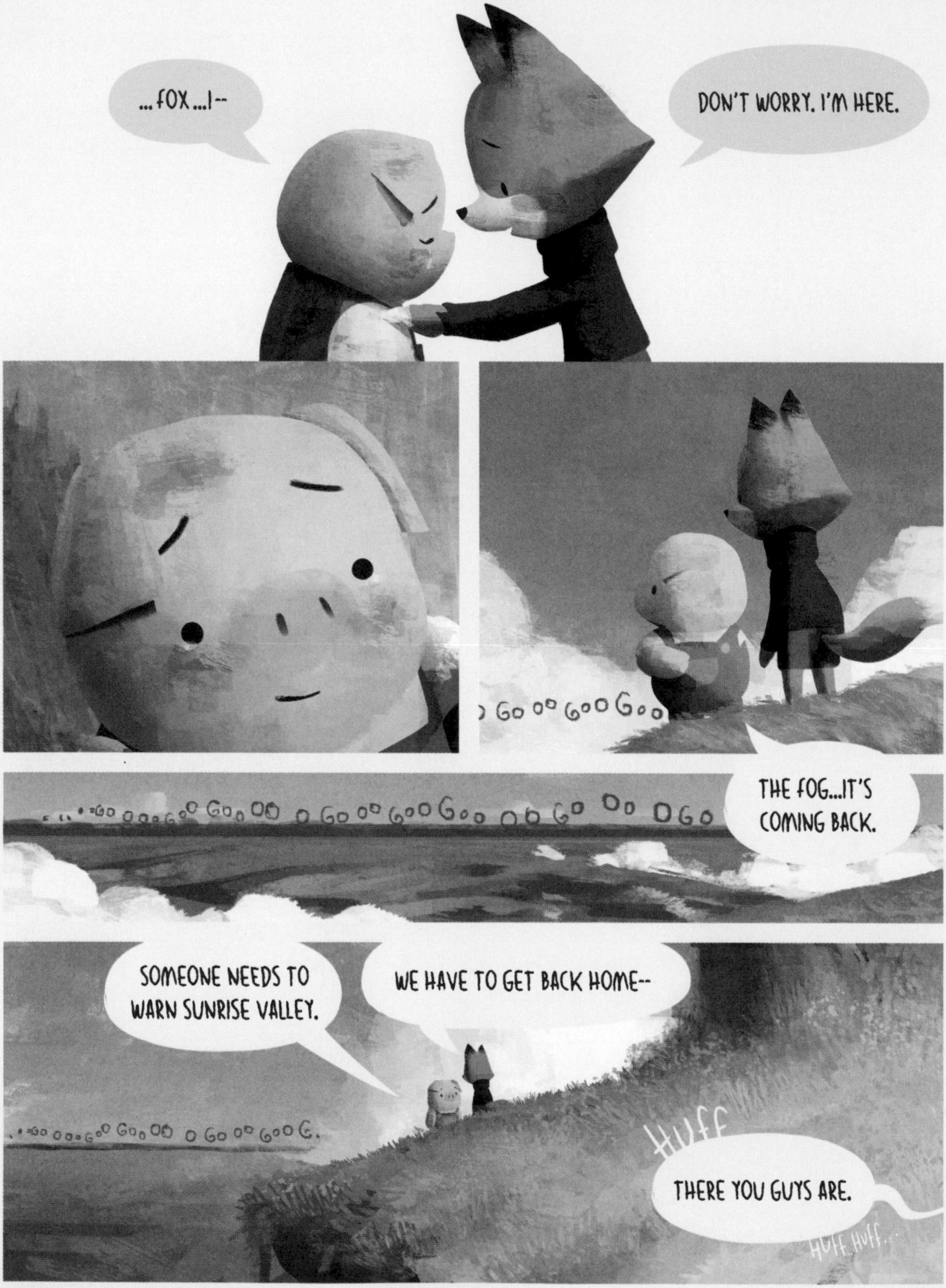

...FOX...I--
DON'T WORRY. I'M HERE.
THE FOG...IT'S COMING BACK.
SOMEONE NEEDS TO WARN SUNRISE VALLEY.
WE HAVE TO GET BACK HOME--
HUFF
THERE YOU GUYS ARE.
HUFF HUFF...

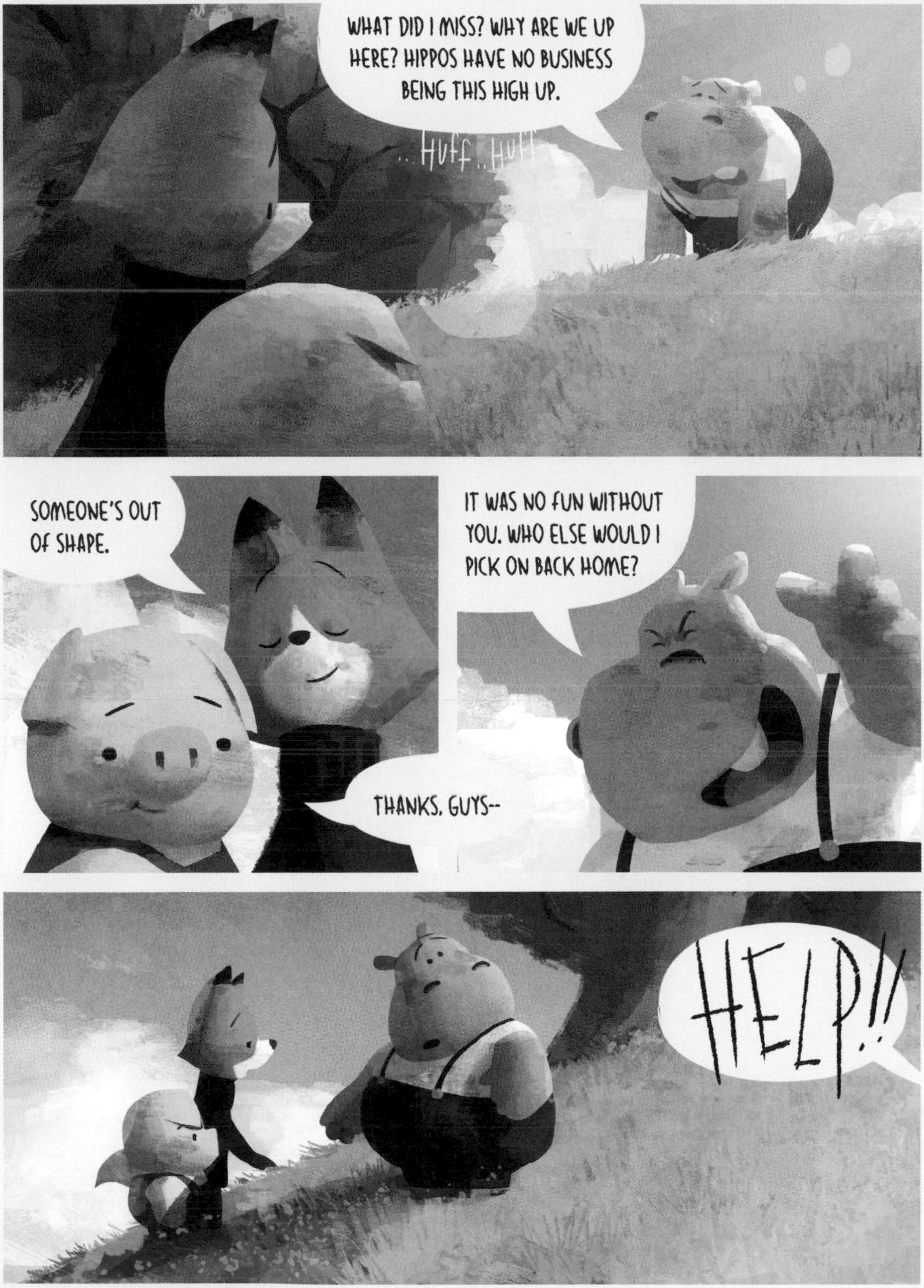
WHAT DID I MISS? WHY ARE WE UP HERE? HIPPOS HAVE NO BUSINESS BEING THIS HIGH UP.
...HUFF...HUFF
SOMEONE'S OUT OF SHAPE.
IT WAS NO FUN WITHOUT YOU. WHO ELSE WOULD I PICK ON BACK HOME?
THANKS, GUYS--
HELP!!

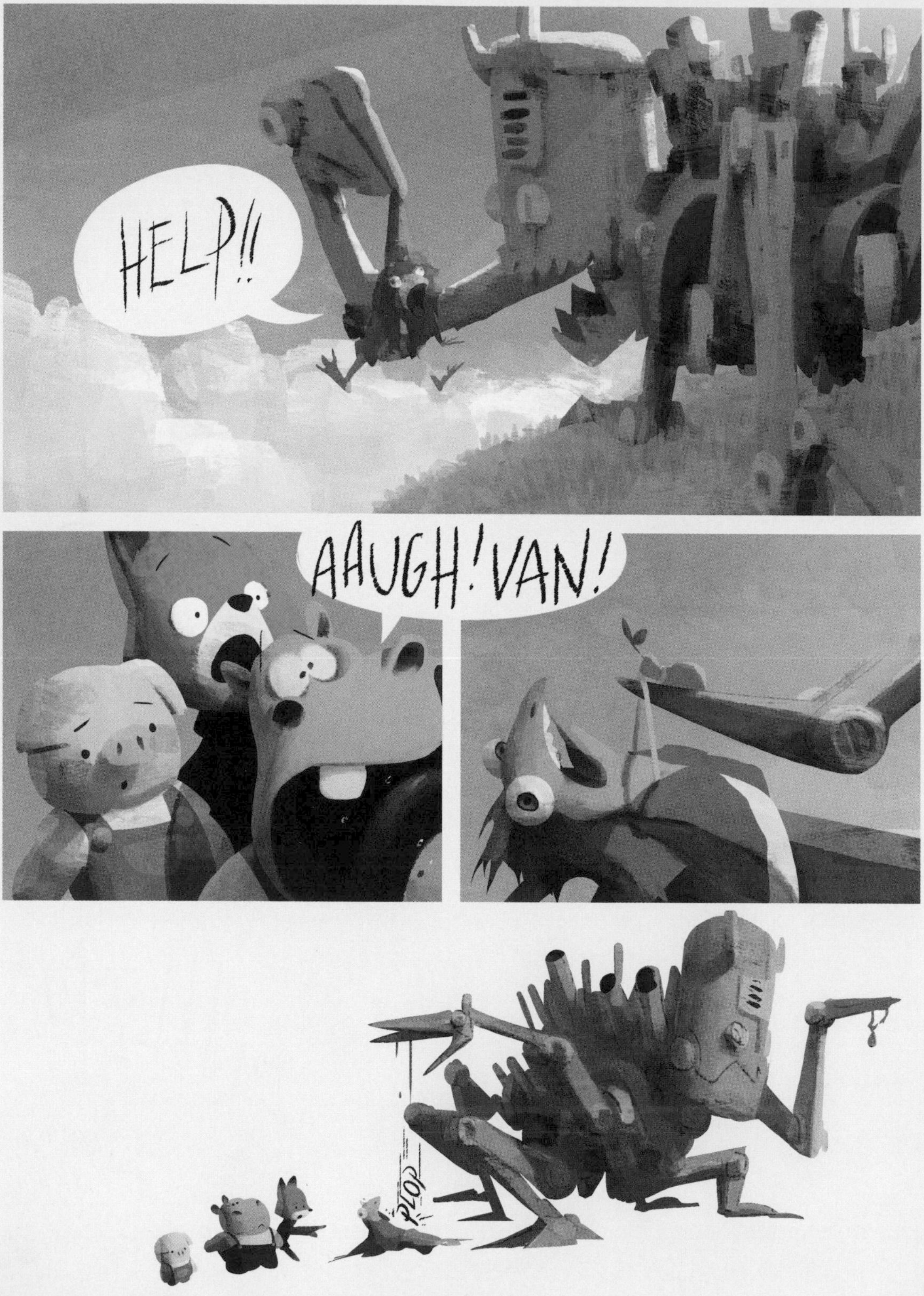
HELP!!
AAUGH! VAN!
PLOP

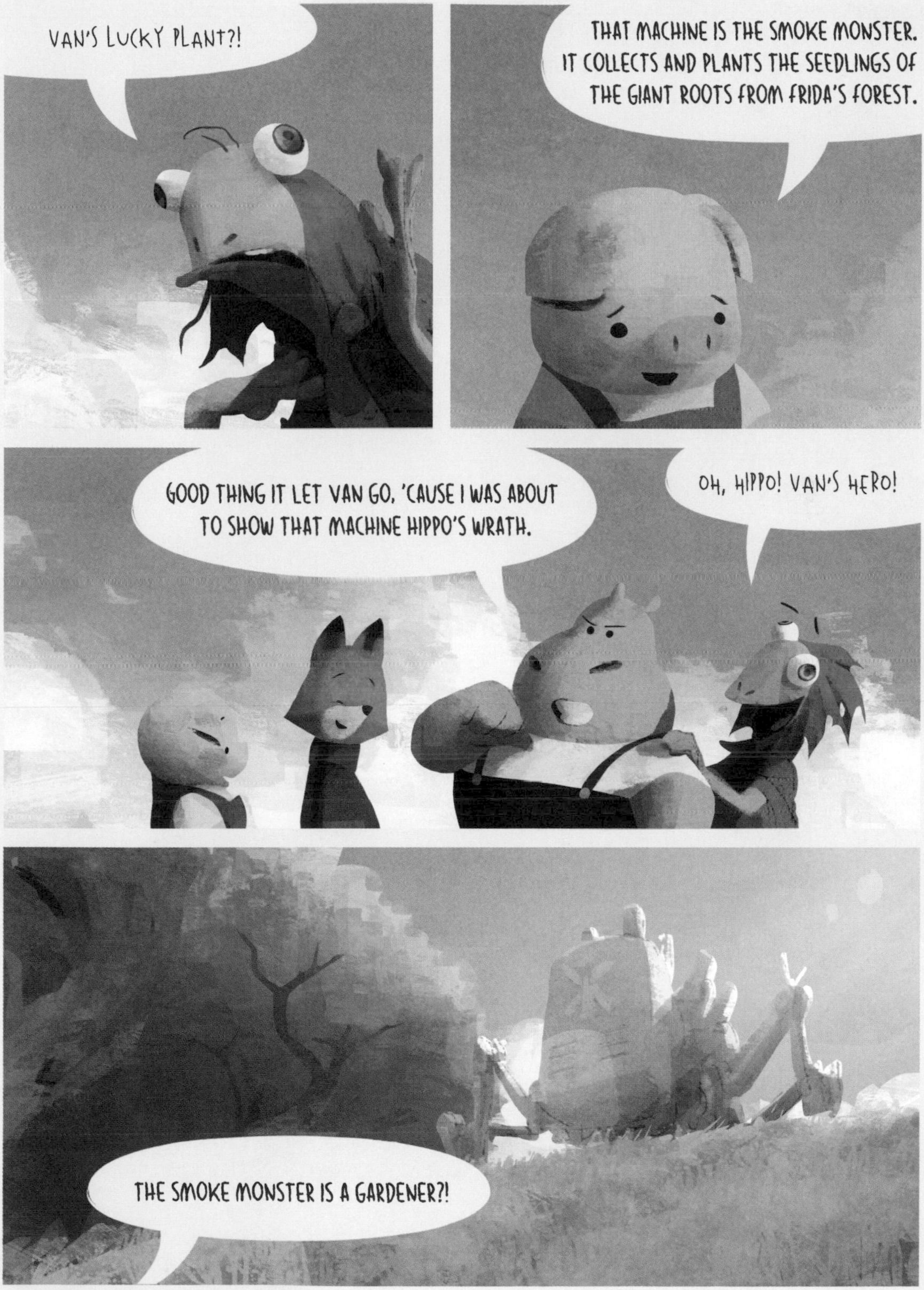
VAN'S LUCKY PLANT?!
THAT MACHINE IS THE SMOKE MONSTER. IT COLLECTS AND PLANTS THE SEEDLINGS OF THE GIANT ROOTS FROM FRIDA'S FOREST.
GOOD THING IT LET VAN GO, 'CAUSE I WAS ABOUT TO SHOW THAT MACHINE HIPPO'S WRATH.
OH, HIPPO! VAN'S HERO!
THE SMOKE MONSTER IS A GARDENER?!

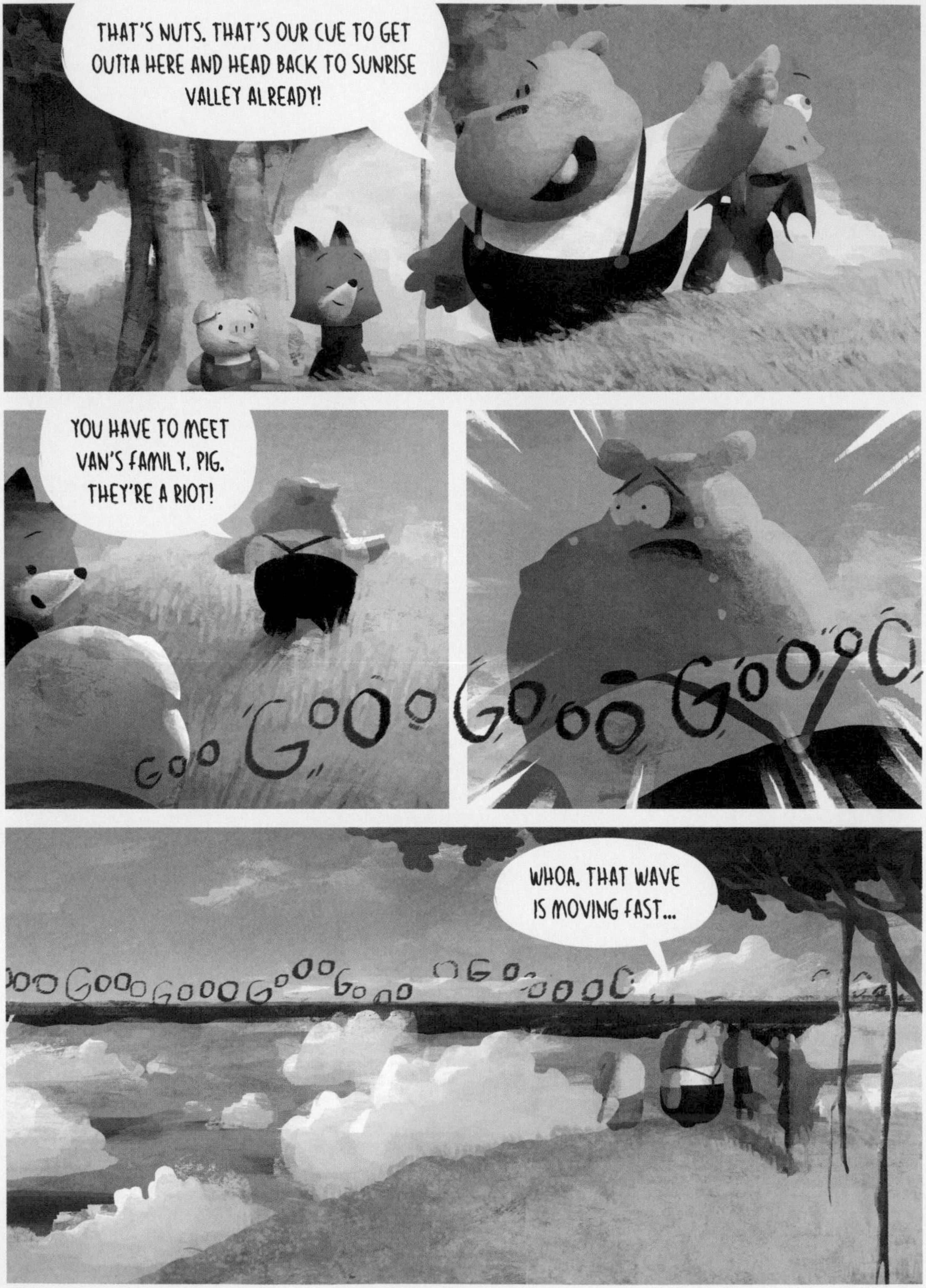
THAT'S NUTS. THAT'S OUR CUE TO GET OUTTA HERE AND HEAD BACK TO SUNRISE VALLEY ALREADY!
YOU HAVE TO MEET VAN'S FAMILY, PIG. THEY'RE A RIOT!
GOO GOOO GOOOO GOOOO
WHOA. THAT WAVE IS MOVING FAST...

CAN WE GET BACK IN TIME?

VAN'S FAMILY SHIP FLY SUPER FAST!

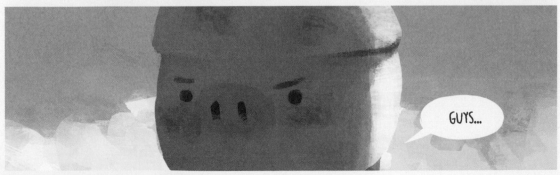

GUYS...

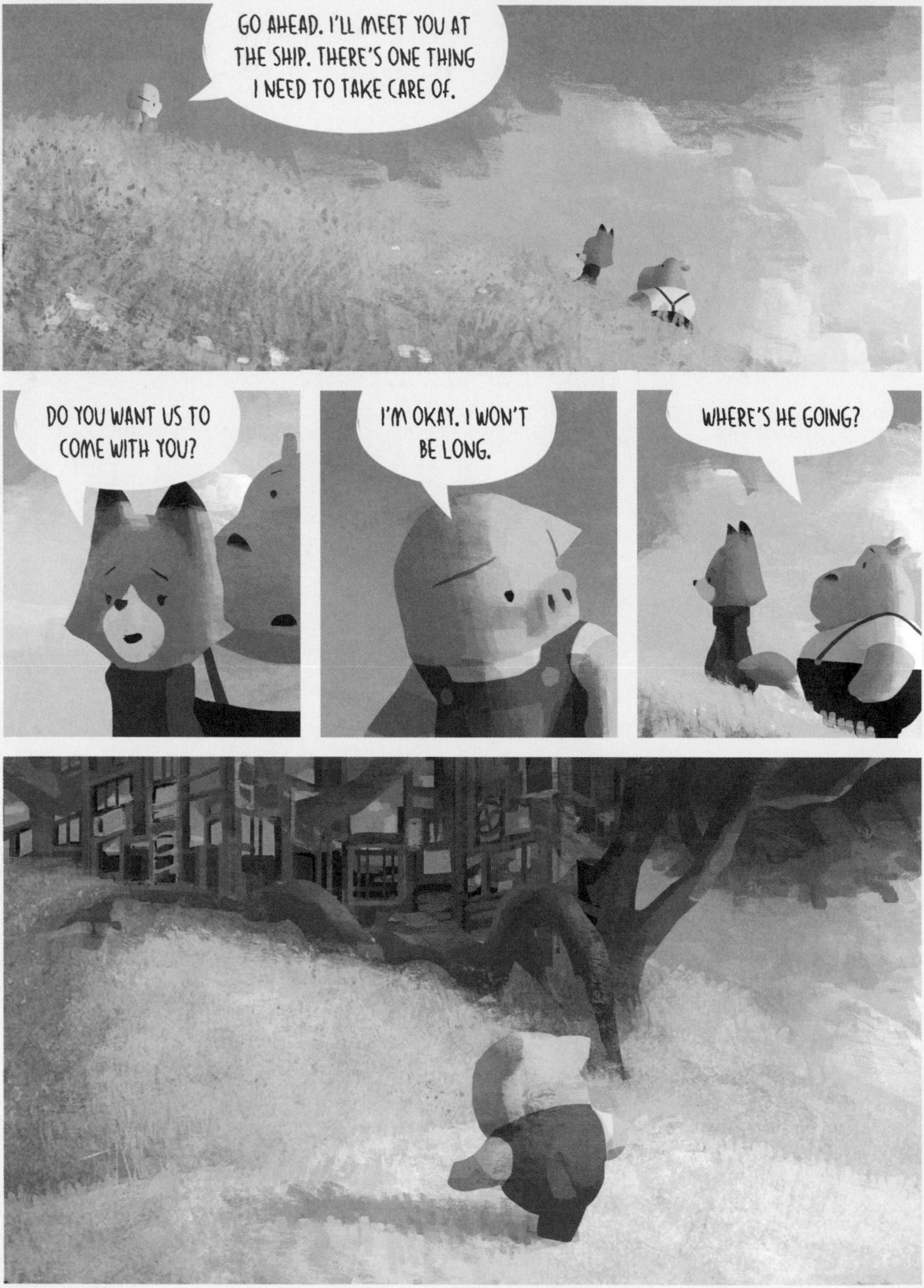
GO AHEAD. I'LL MEET YOU AT THE SHIP. THERE'S ONE THING I NEED TO TAKE CARE OF.
DO YOU WANT US TO COME WITH YOU?
I'M OKAY. I WON'T BE LONG.
WHERE'S HE GOING?

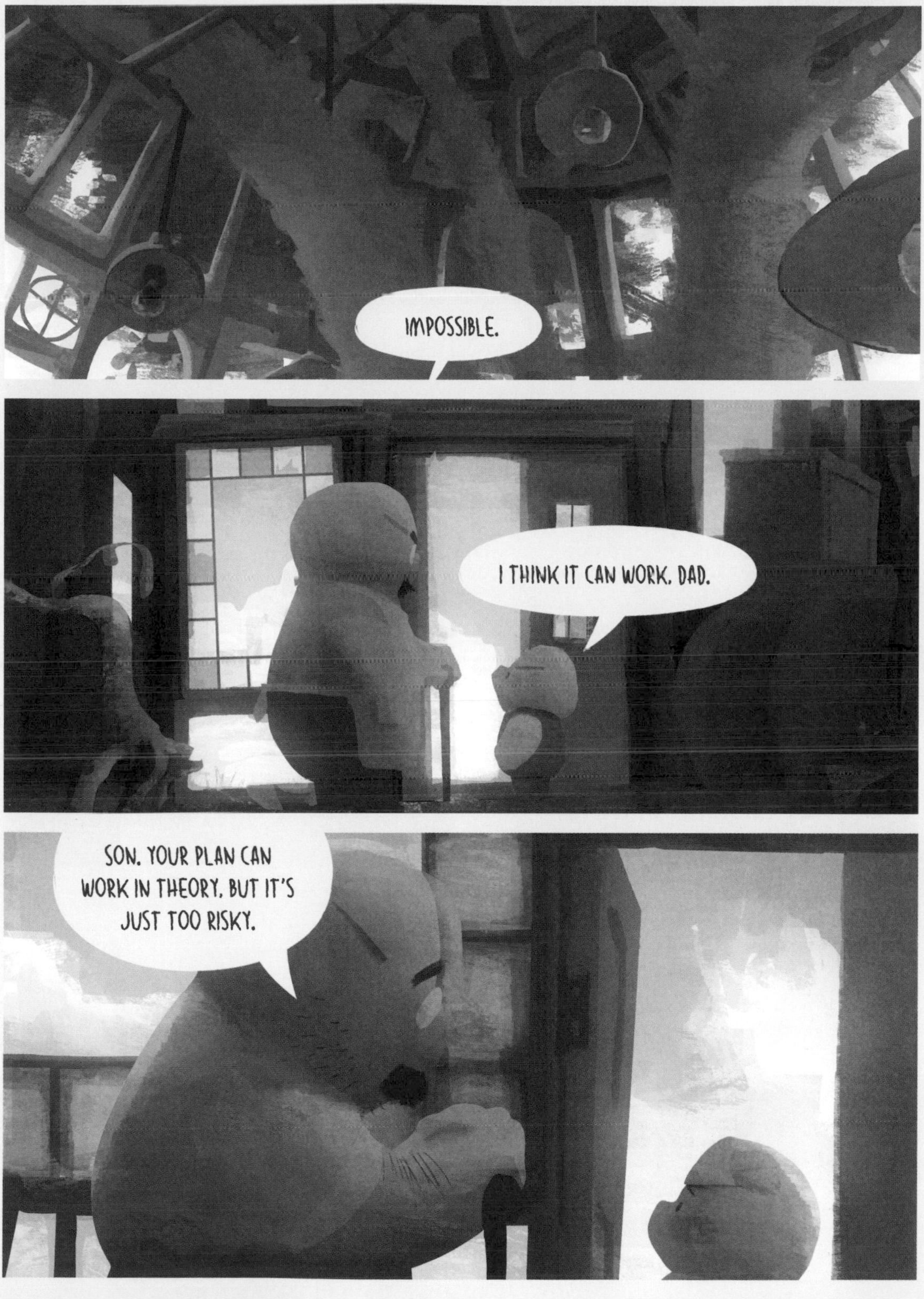
IMPOSSIBLE.
I THINK IT CAN WORK, DAD.
SON, YOUR PLAN CAN WORK IN THEORY, BUT IT'S JUST TOO RISKY.

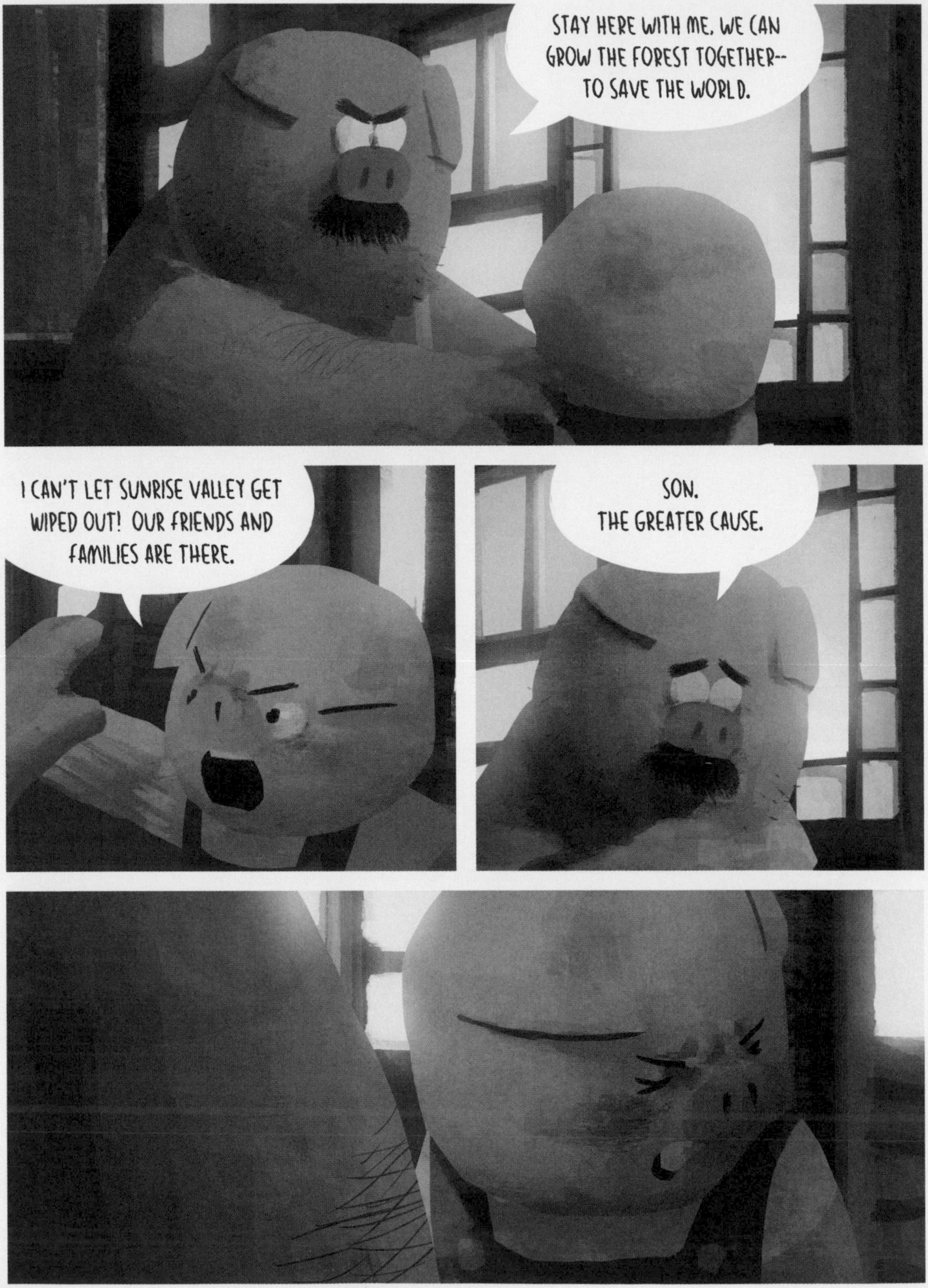
STAY HERE WITH ME. WE CAN GROW THE FOREST TOGETHER-- TO SAVE THE WORLD.
I CAN'T LET SUNRISE VALLEY GET WIPED OUT! OUR FRIENDS AND FAMILIES ARE THERE.
SON. THE GREATER CAUSE.

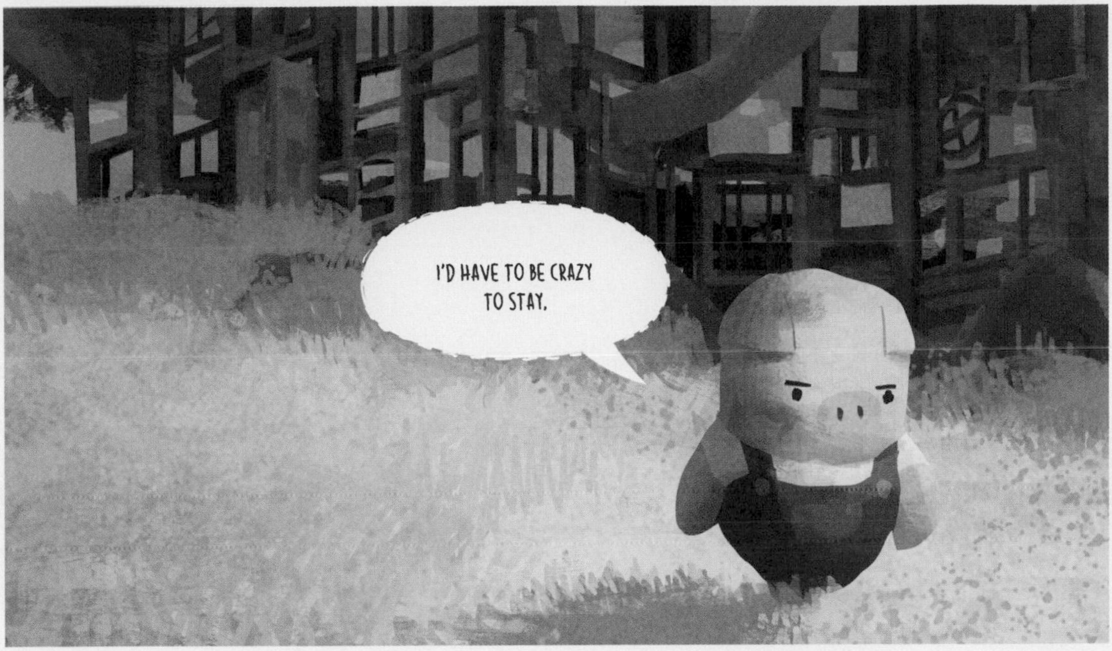
I'D HAVE TO BE CRAZY
TO STAY.

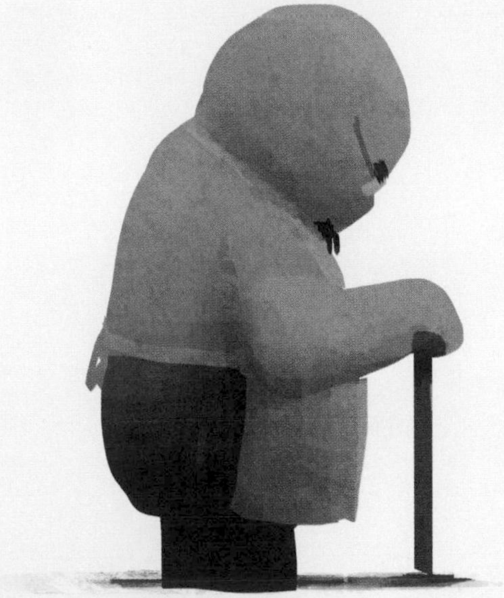

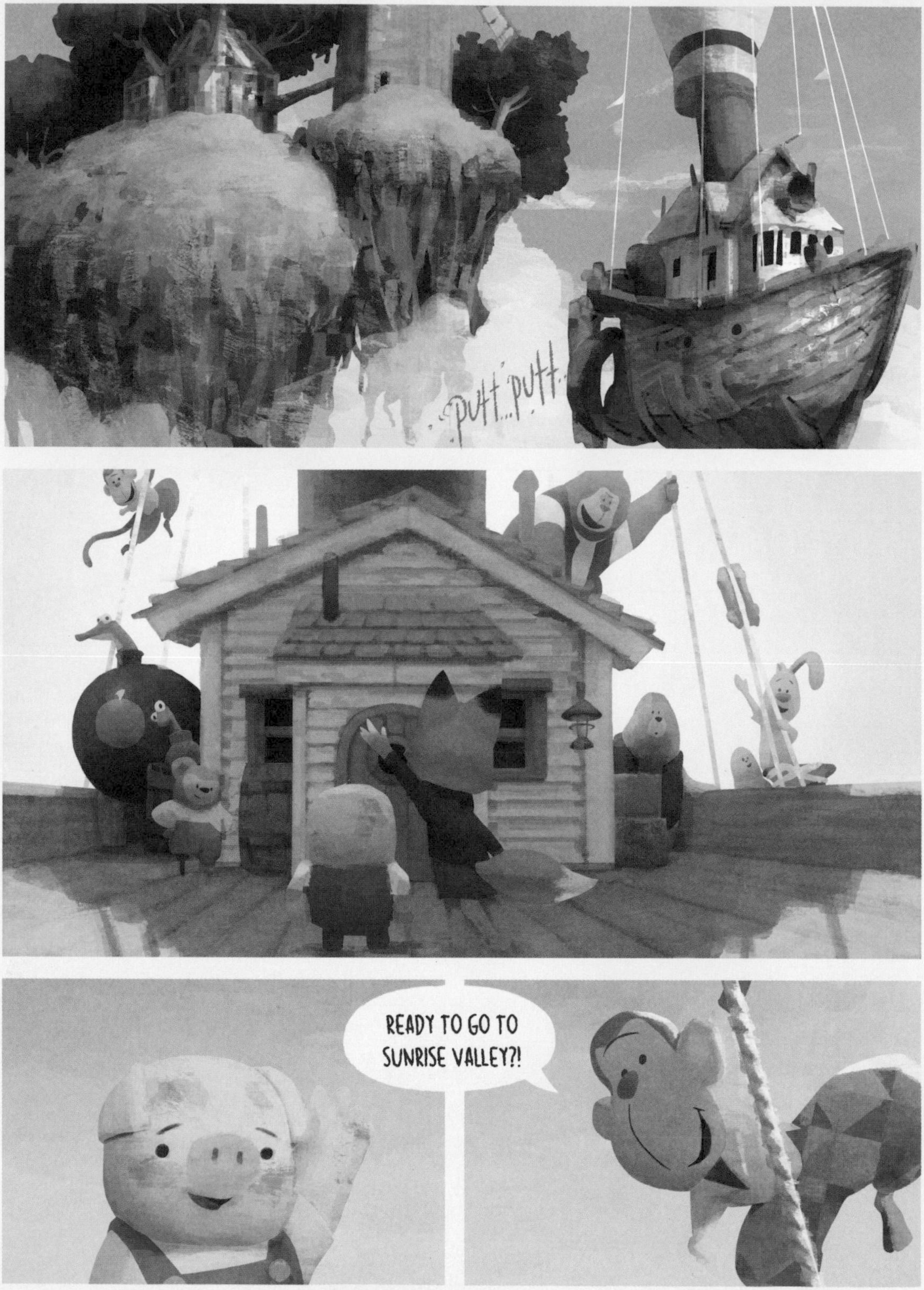
putt...putt...
READY TO GO TO SUNRISE VALLEY?!

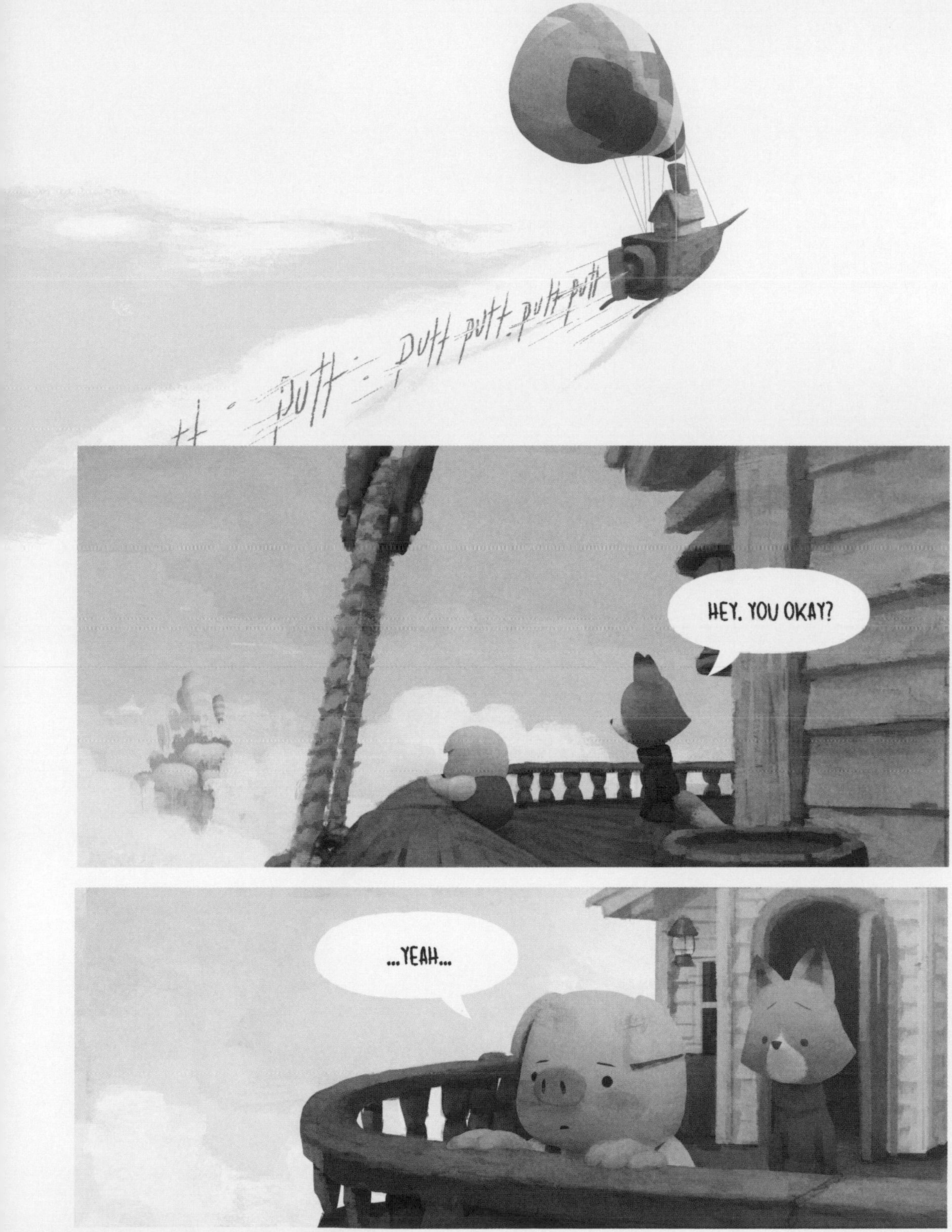

puff puff puff puff puff
HEY. YOU OKAY?
...YEAH...

SEVERAL HOURS LATER...

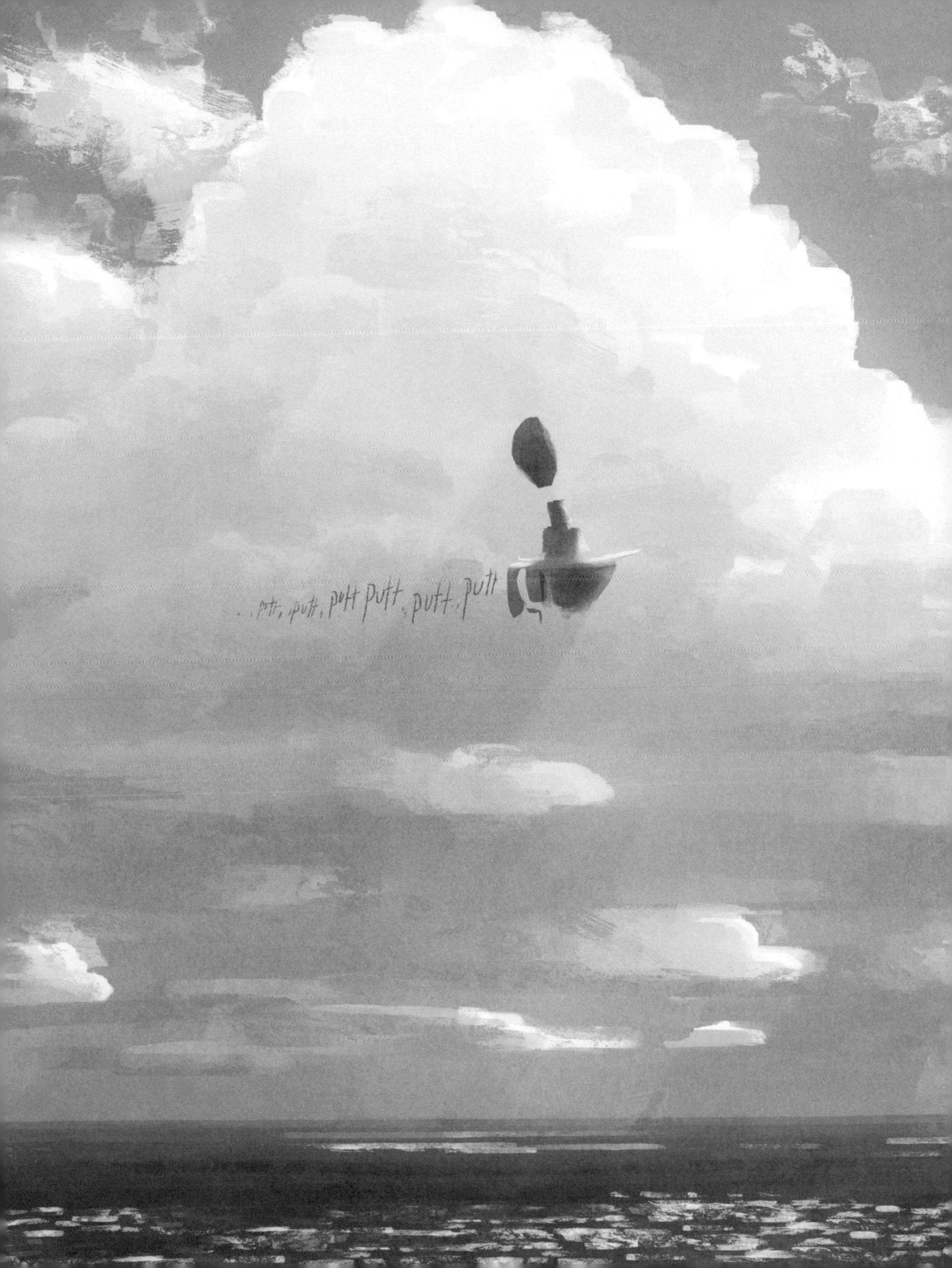
. . putt, putt, putt putt, putt, putt

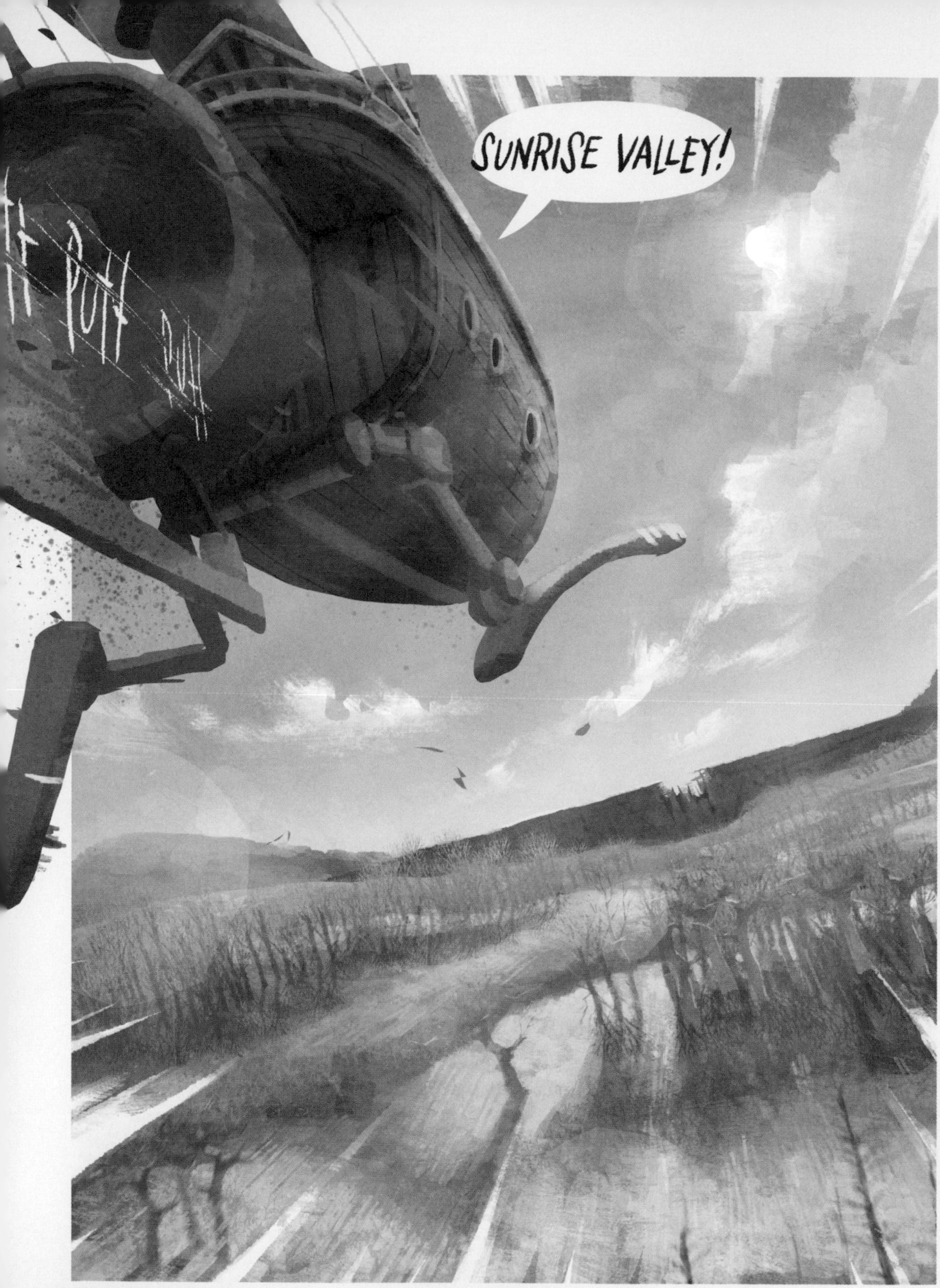
SUNRISE VALLEY!

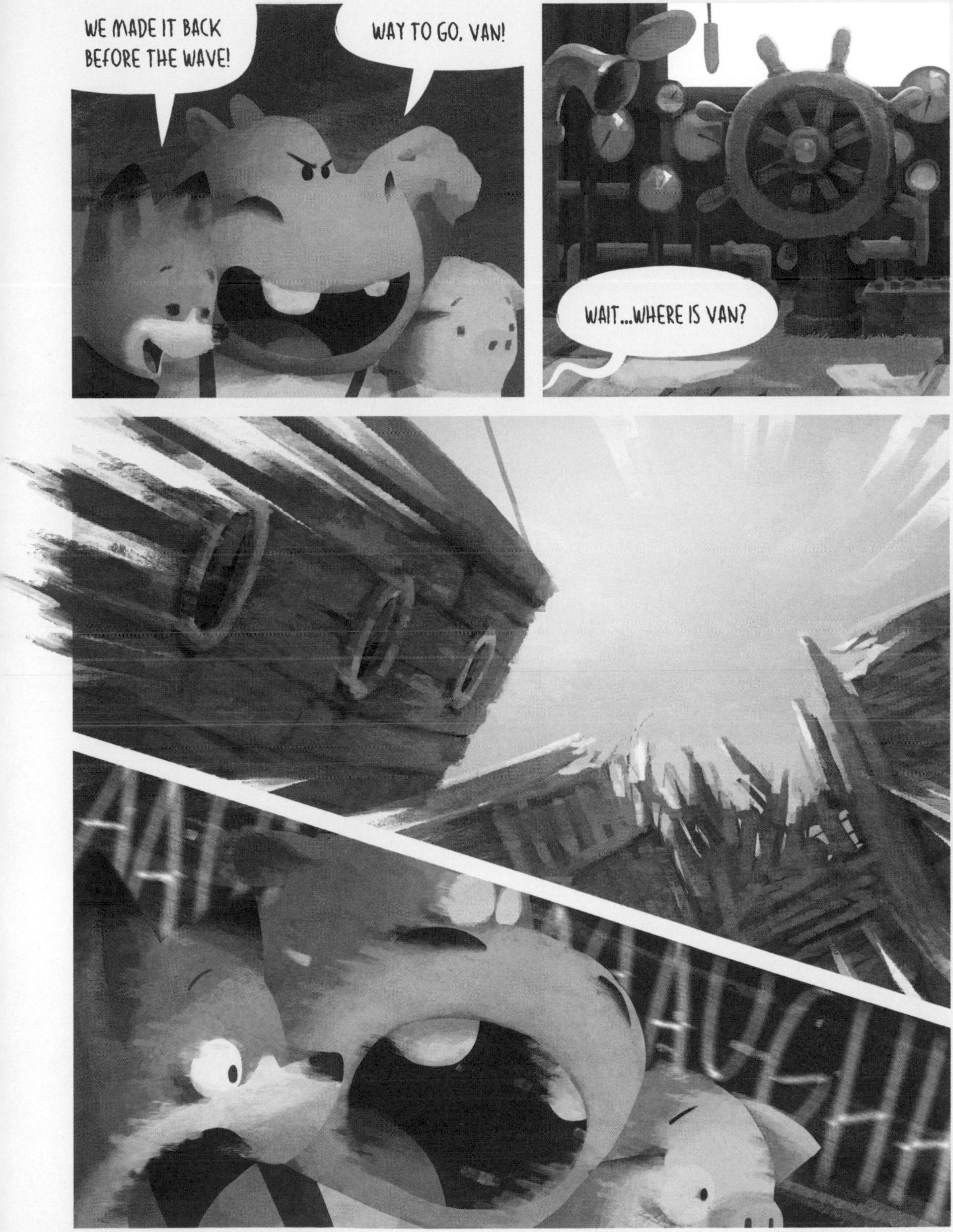
WE MADE IT BACK BEFORE THE WAVE!
WAY TO GO, VAN!
WAIT...WHERE IS VAN?

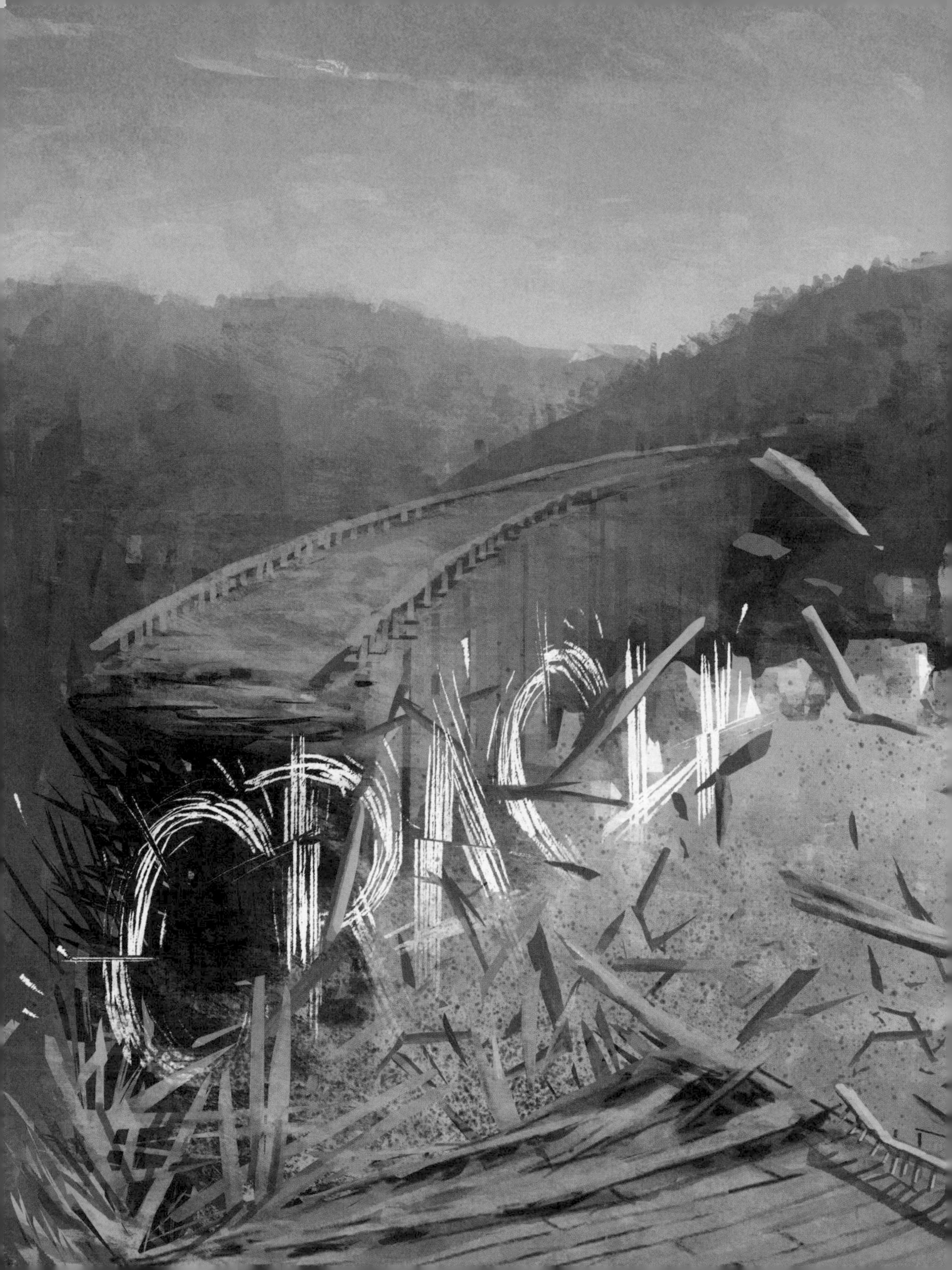
CRACK

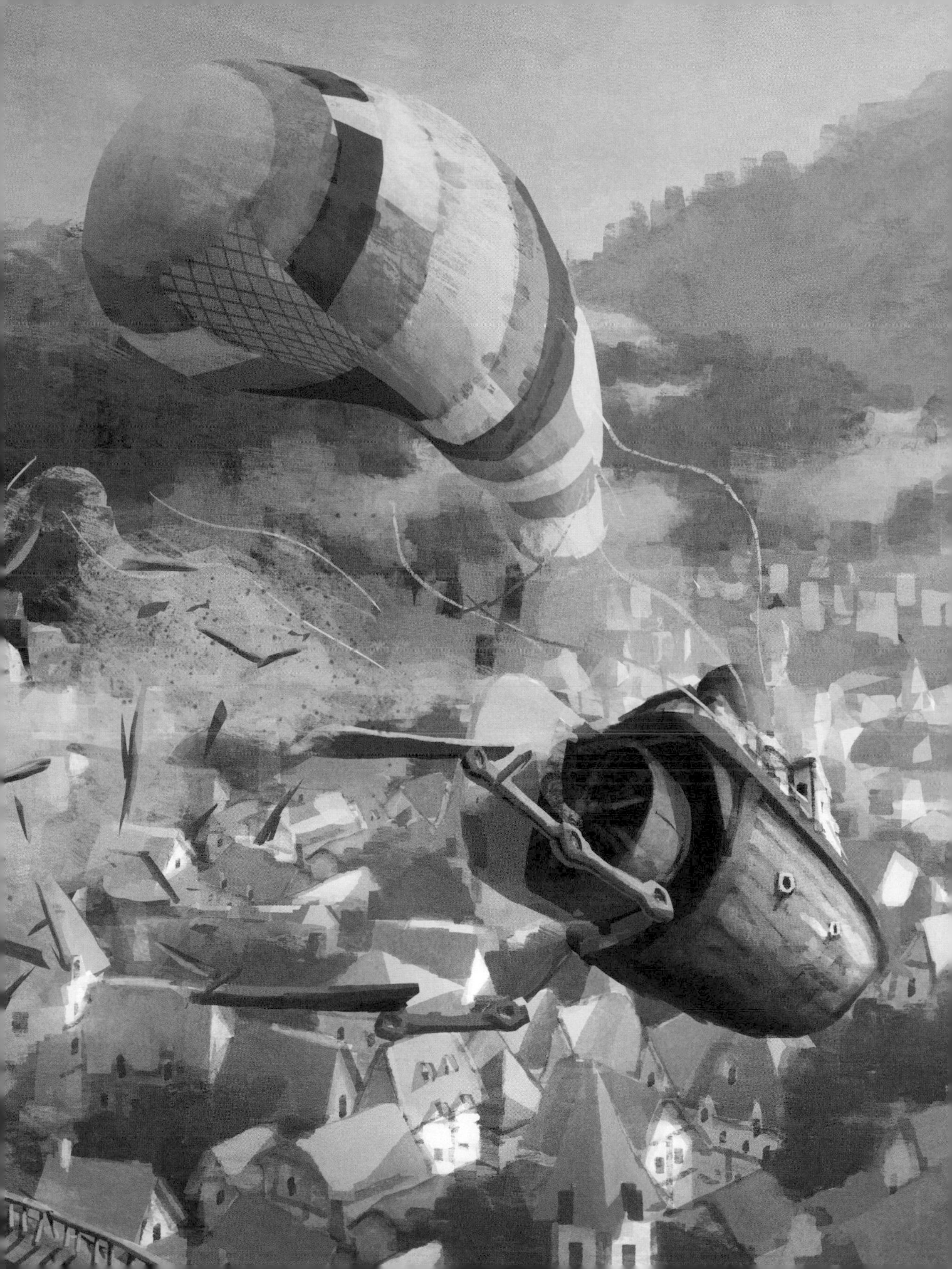

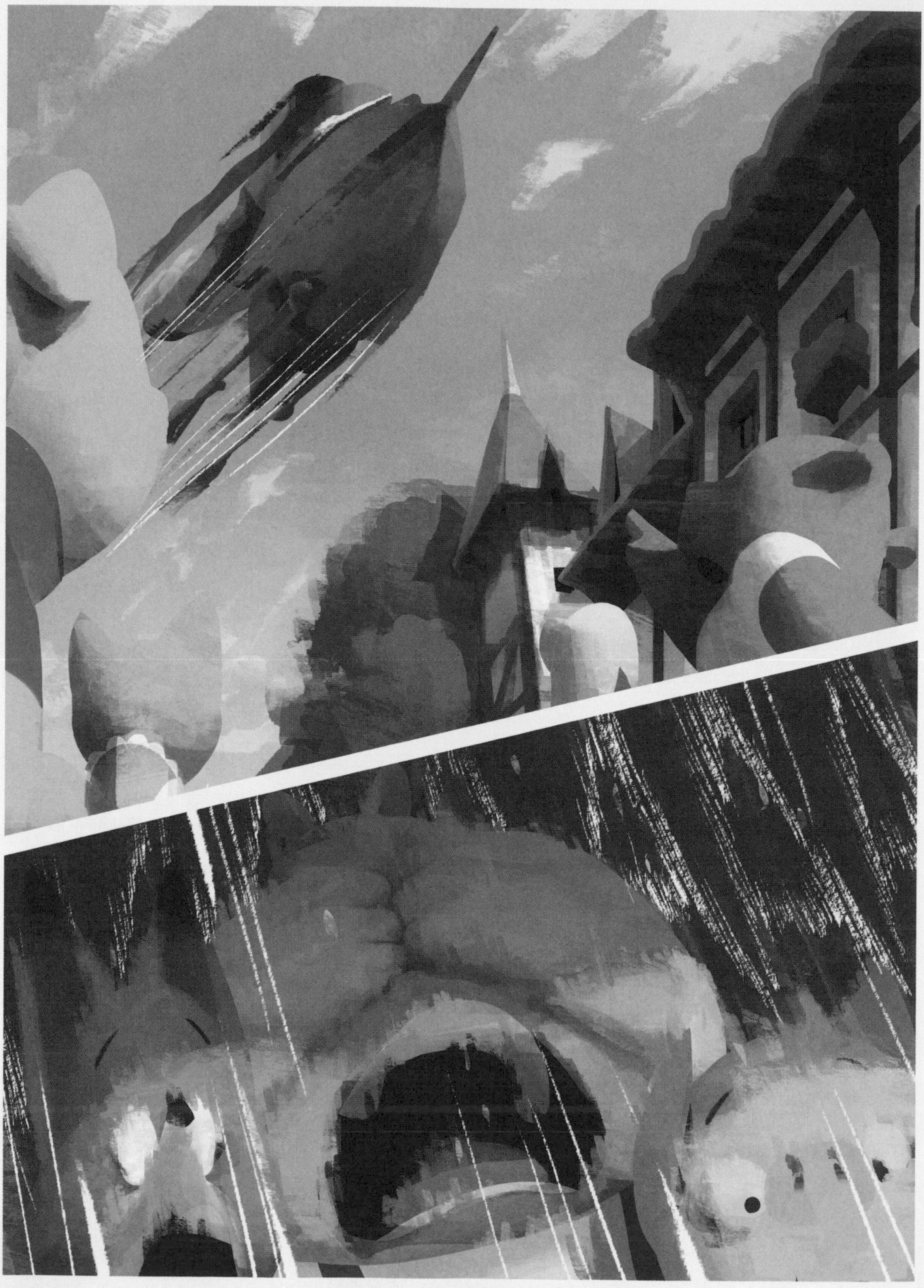

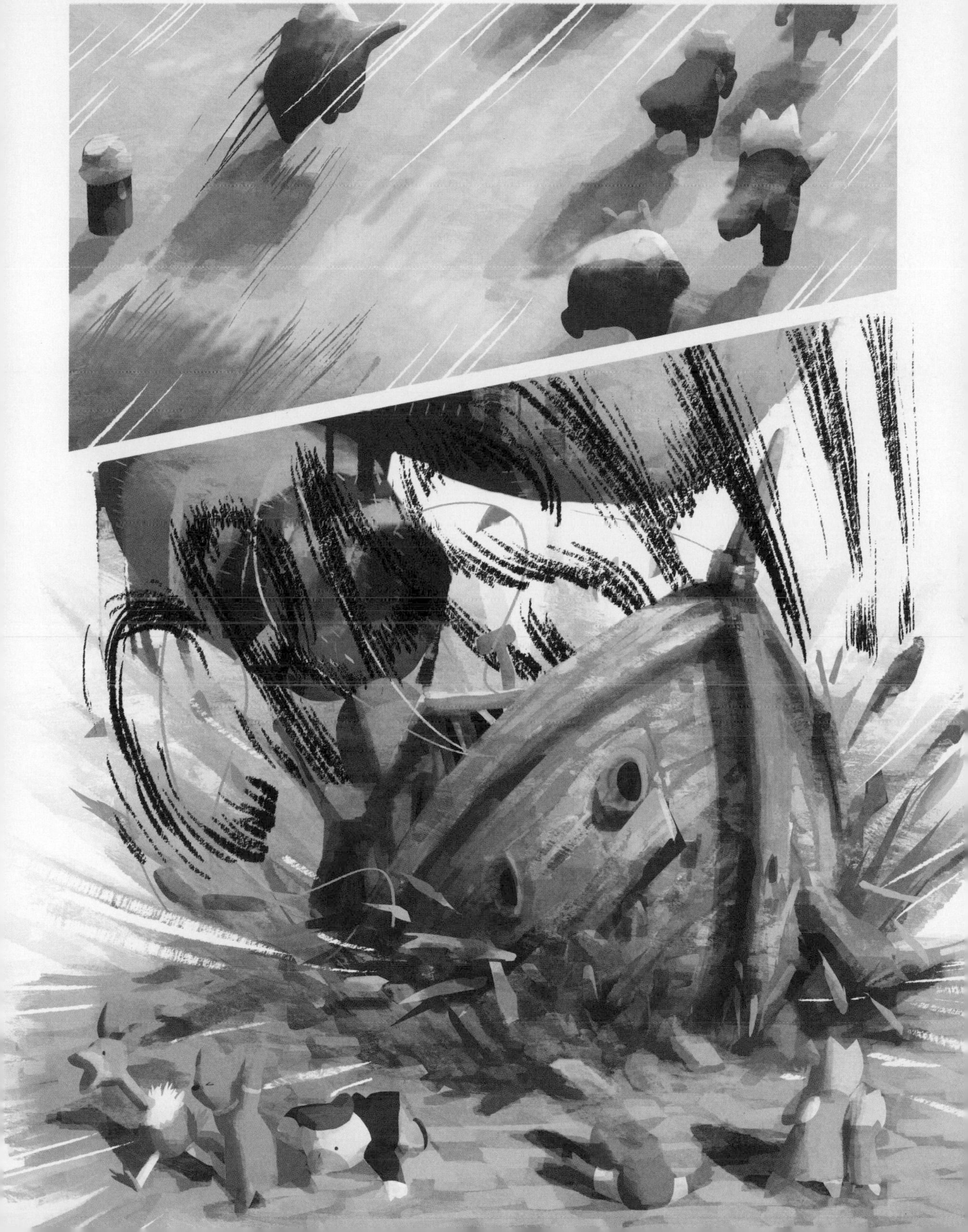

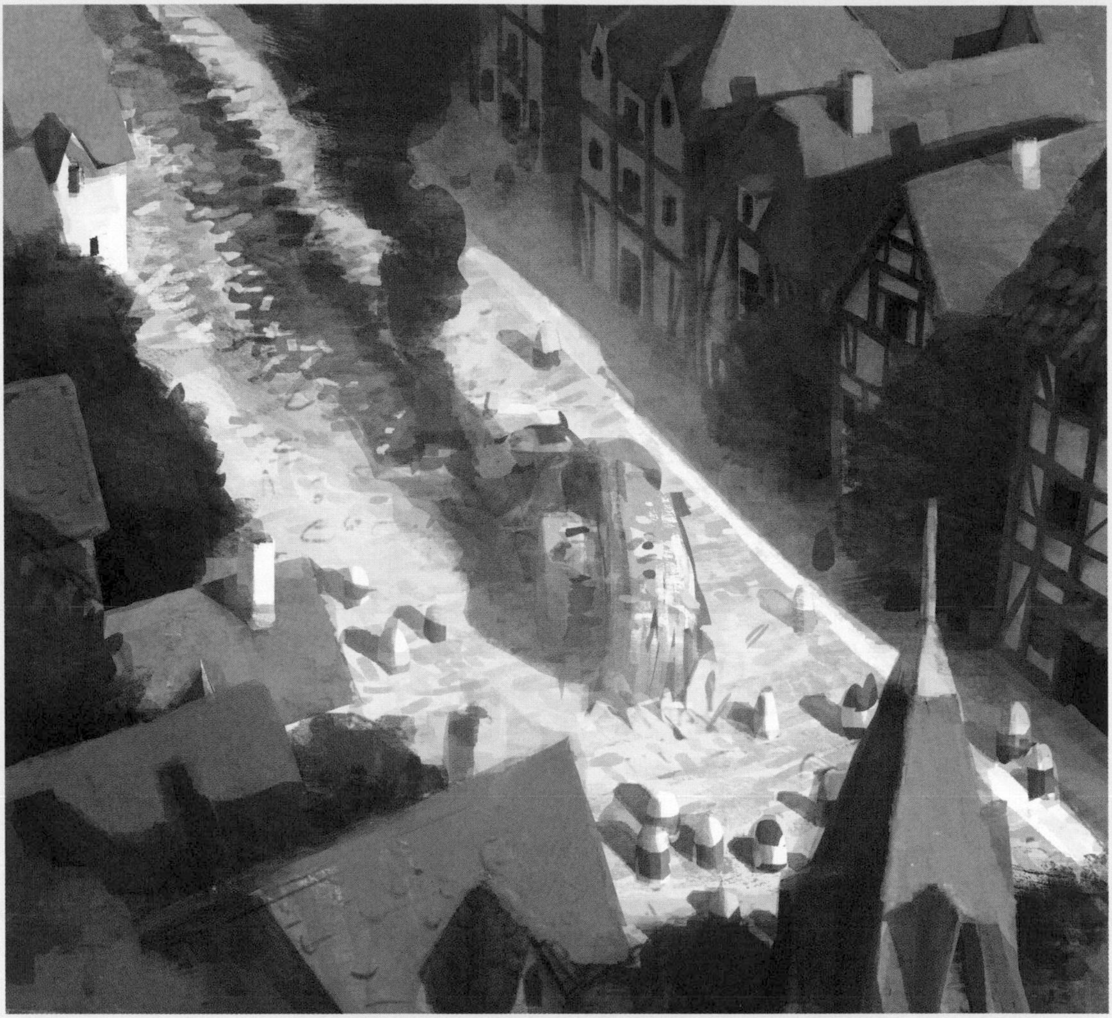

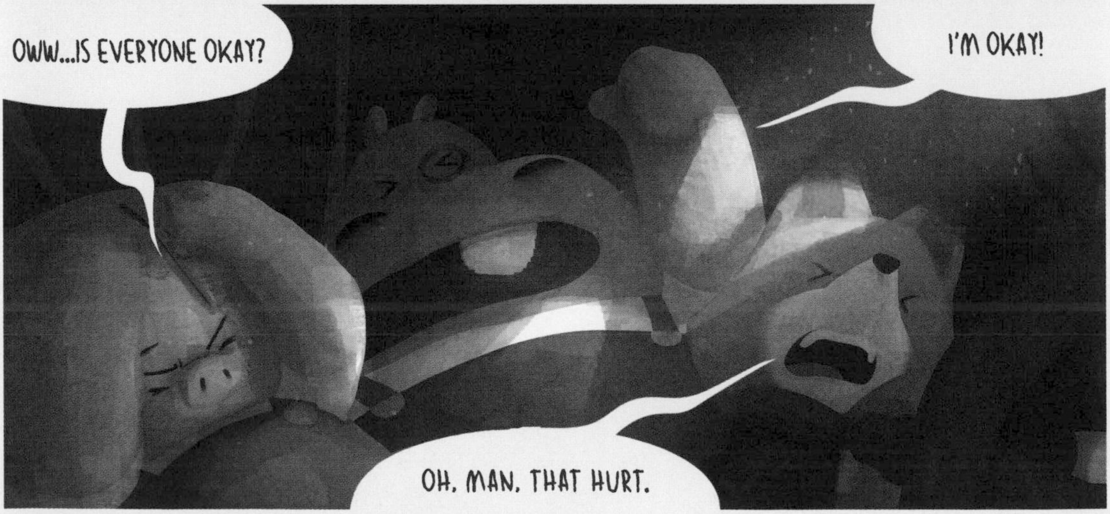
OWW...IS EVERYONE OKAY?
I'M OKAY!
OH, MAN, THAT HURT.

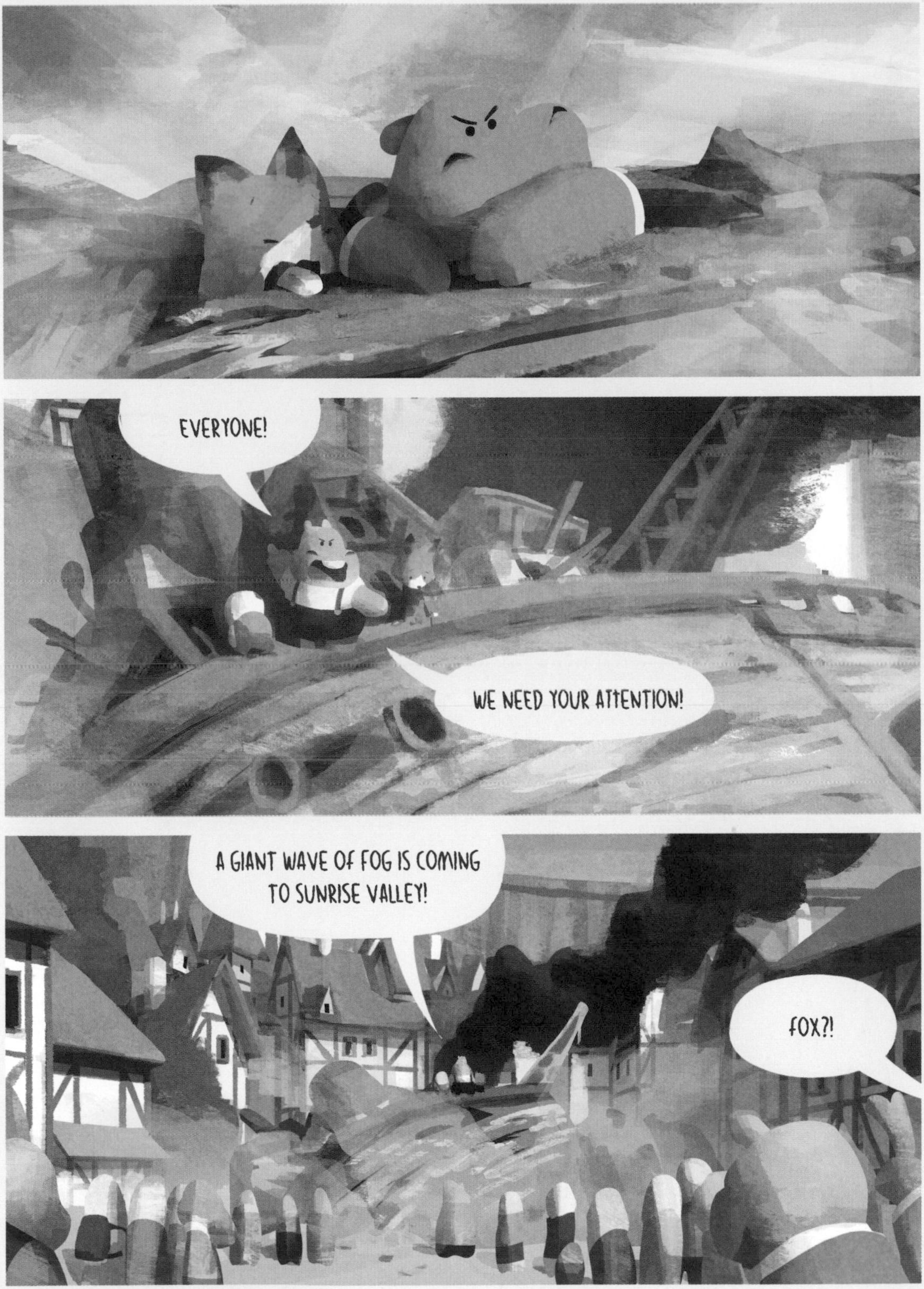
EVERYONE!
WE NEED YOUR ATTENTION!
A GIANT WAVE OF FOG IS COMING TO SUNRISE VALLEY!
FOX?!

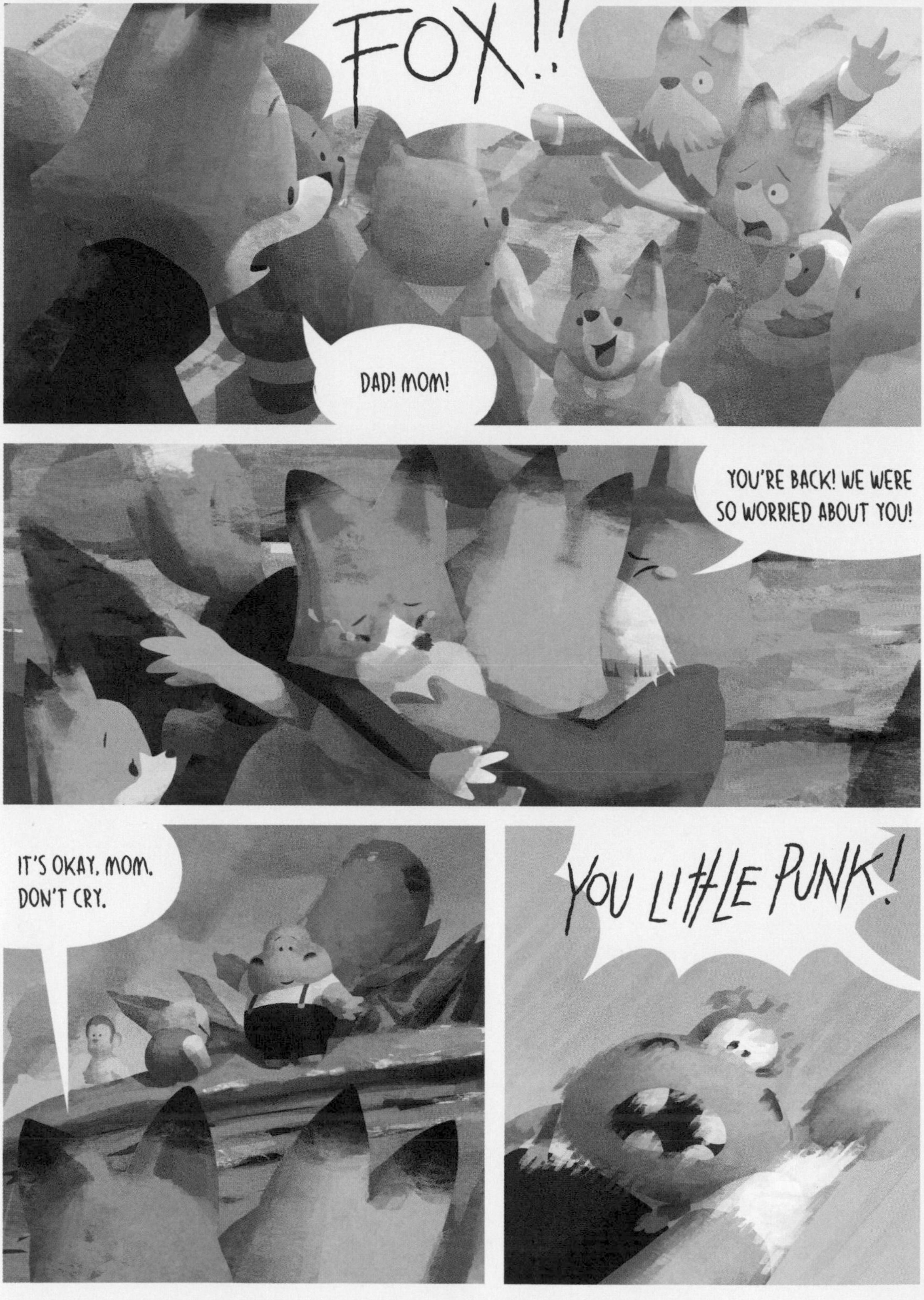
FOX!!
DAD! MOM!
YOU'RE BACK! WE WERE SO WORRIED ABOUT YOU!
IT'S OKAY, MOM. DON'T CRY.
YOU LITTLE PUNK!

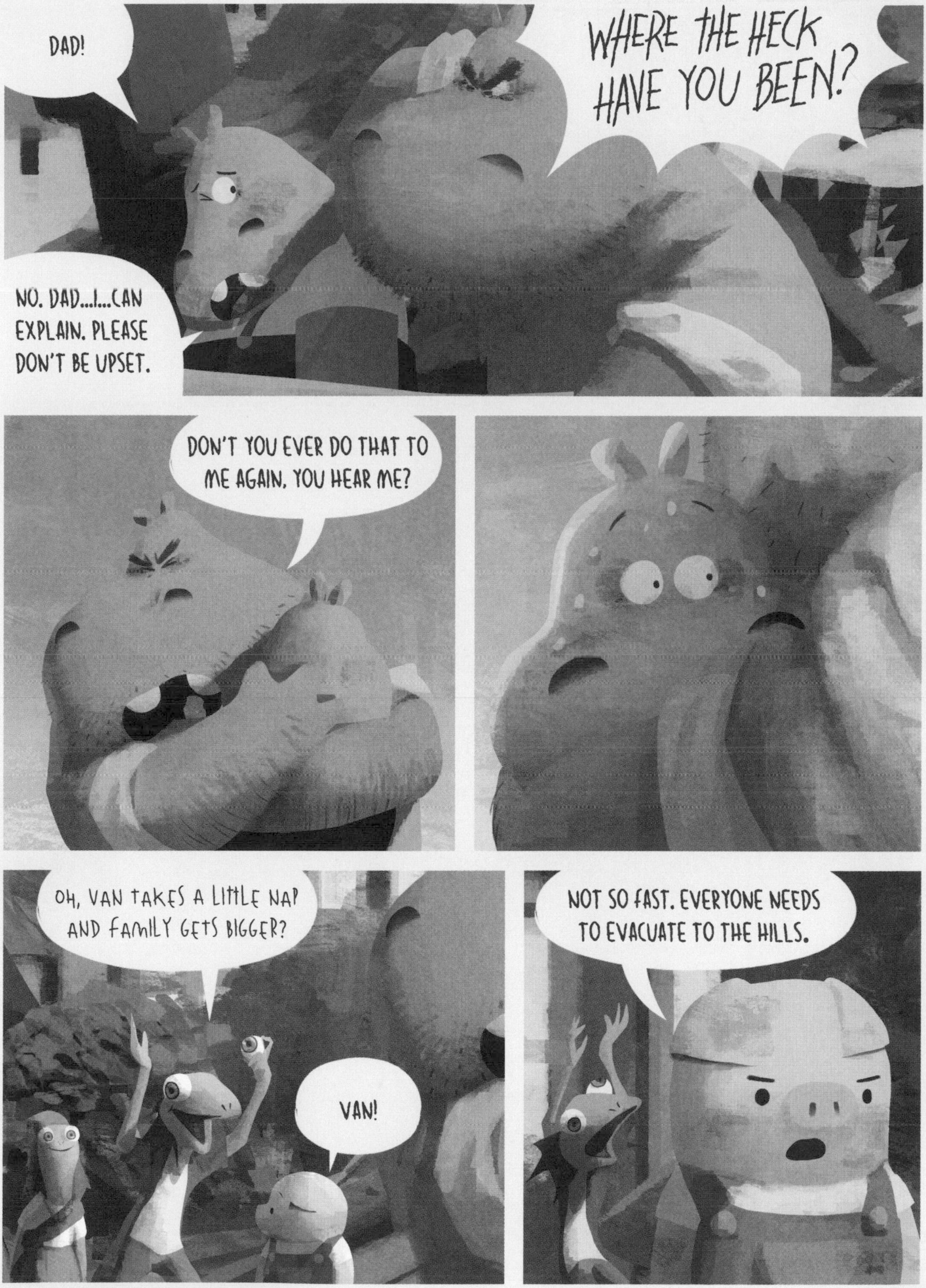
DAD!
WHERE THE HECK HAVE YOU BEEN?
NO. DAD...I...CAN EXPLAIN. PLEASE DON'T BE UPSET.
DON'T YOU EVER DO THAT TO ME AGAIN, YOU HEAR ME?
OH, VAN TAKES A LITTLE NAP AND FAMILY GETS BIGGER?
VAN!
NOT SO FAST. EVERYONE NEEDS TO EVACUATE TO THE HILLS.

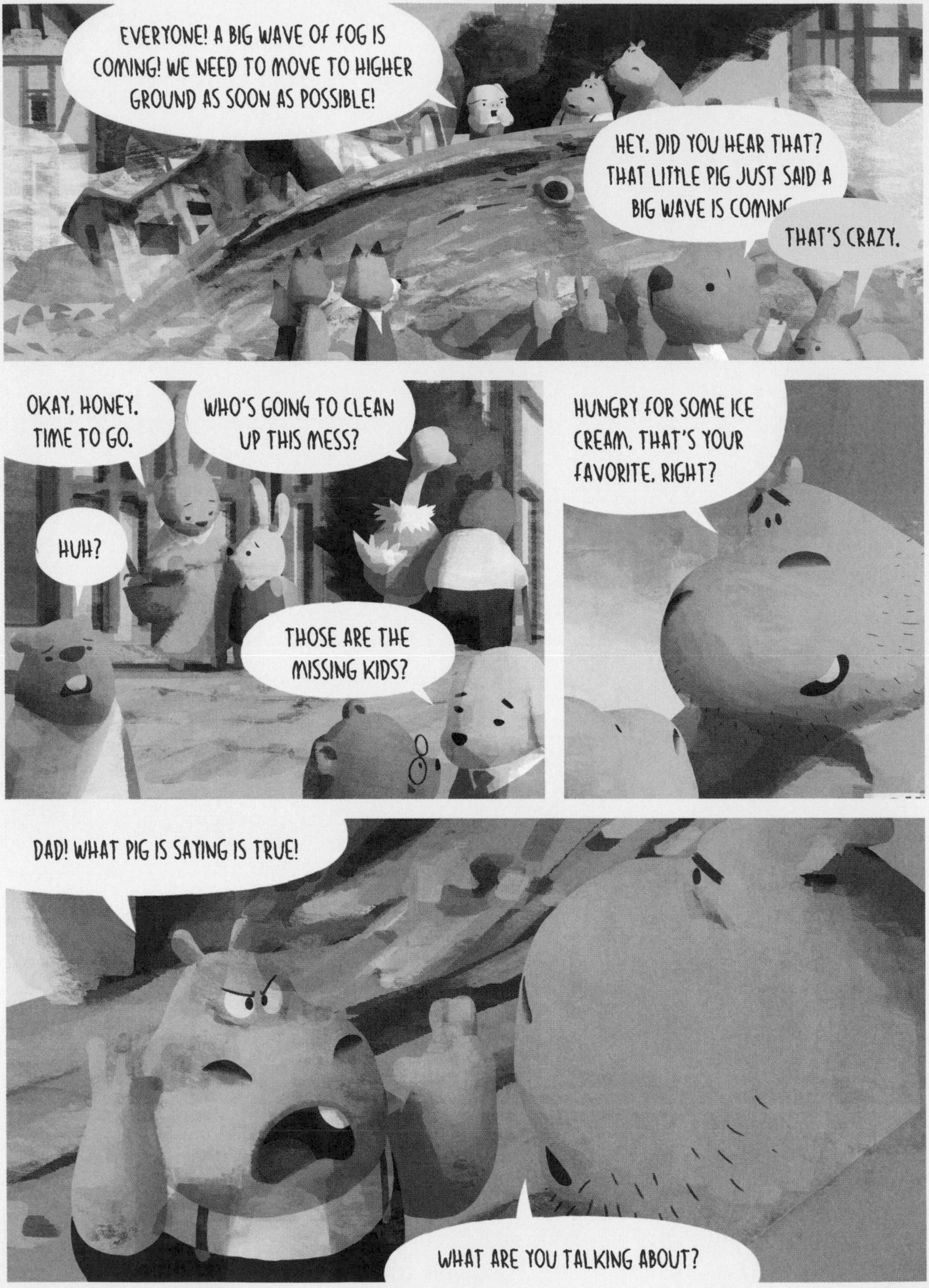
EVERYONE! A BIG WAVE OF FOG IS COMING! WE NEED TO MOVE TO HIGHER GROUND AS SOON AS POSSIBLE!
HEY, DID YOU HEAR THAT? THAT LITTLE PIG JUST SAID A BIG WAVE IS COMIN
THAT'S CRAZY.
OKAY, HONEY. TIME TO GO.
WHO'S GOING TO CLEAN UP THIS MESS?
HUH?
THOSE ARE THE MISSING KIDS?
HUNGRY FOR SOME ICE CREAM. THAT'S YOUR FAVORITE, RIGHT?
DAD! WHAT PIG IS SAYING IS TRUE!
WHAT ARE YOU TALKING ABOUT?

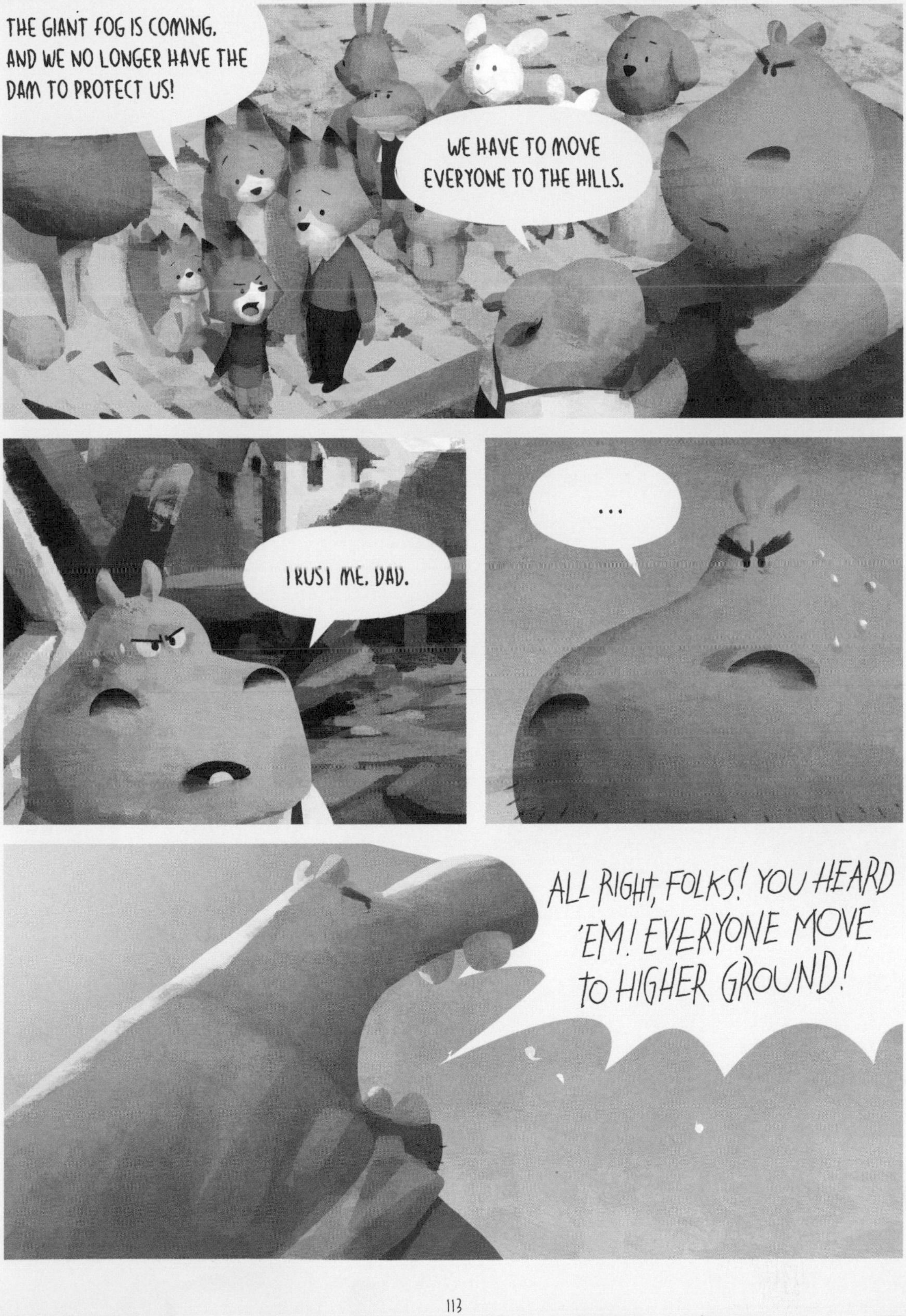
THE GIANT FOG IS COMING. AND WE NO LONGER HAVE THE DAM TO PROTECT US!
WE HAVE TO MOVE EVERYONE TO THE HILLS.
TRUST ME, DAD.
...
ALL RIGHT, FOLKS! YOU HEARD 'EM! EVERYONE MOVE TO HIGHER GROUND!

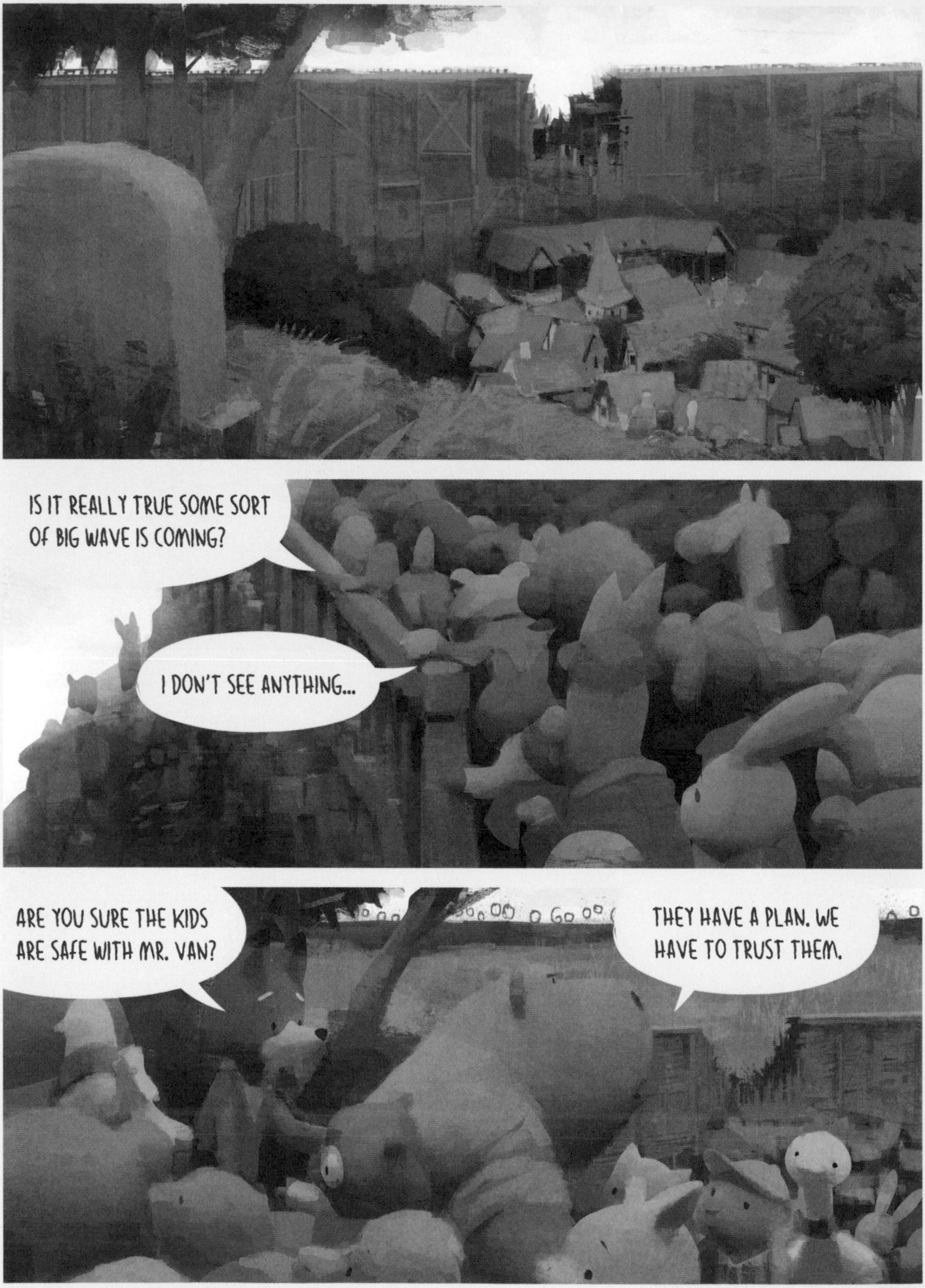
IS IT REALLY TRUE SOME SORT OF BIG WAVE IS COMING?
I DON'T SEE ANYTHING...
ARE YOU SURE THE KIDS ARE SAFE WITH MR. VAN?
THEY HAVE A PLAN. WE HAVE TO TRUST THEM.

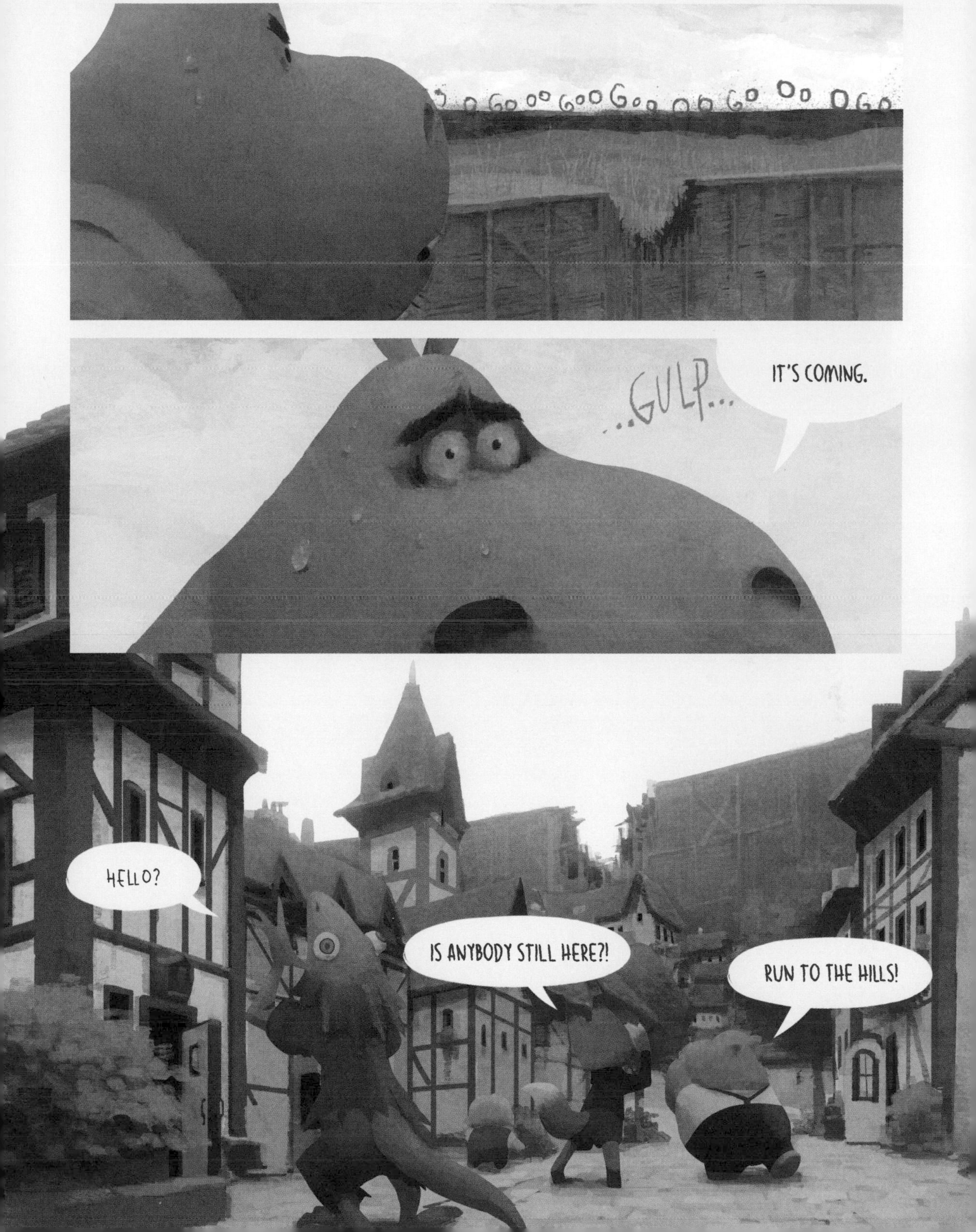

...GULP...
IT'S COMING.
HELLO?
IS ANYBODY STILL HERE?!
RUN TO THE HILLS!

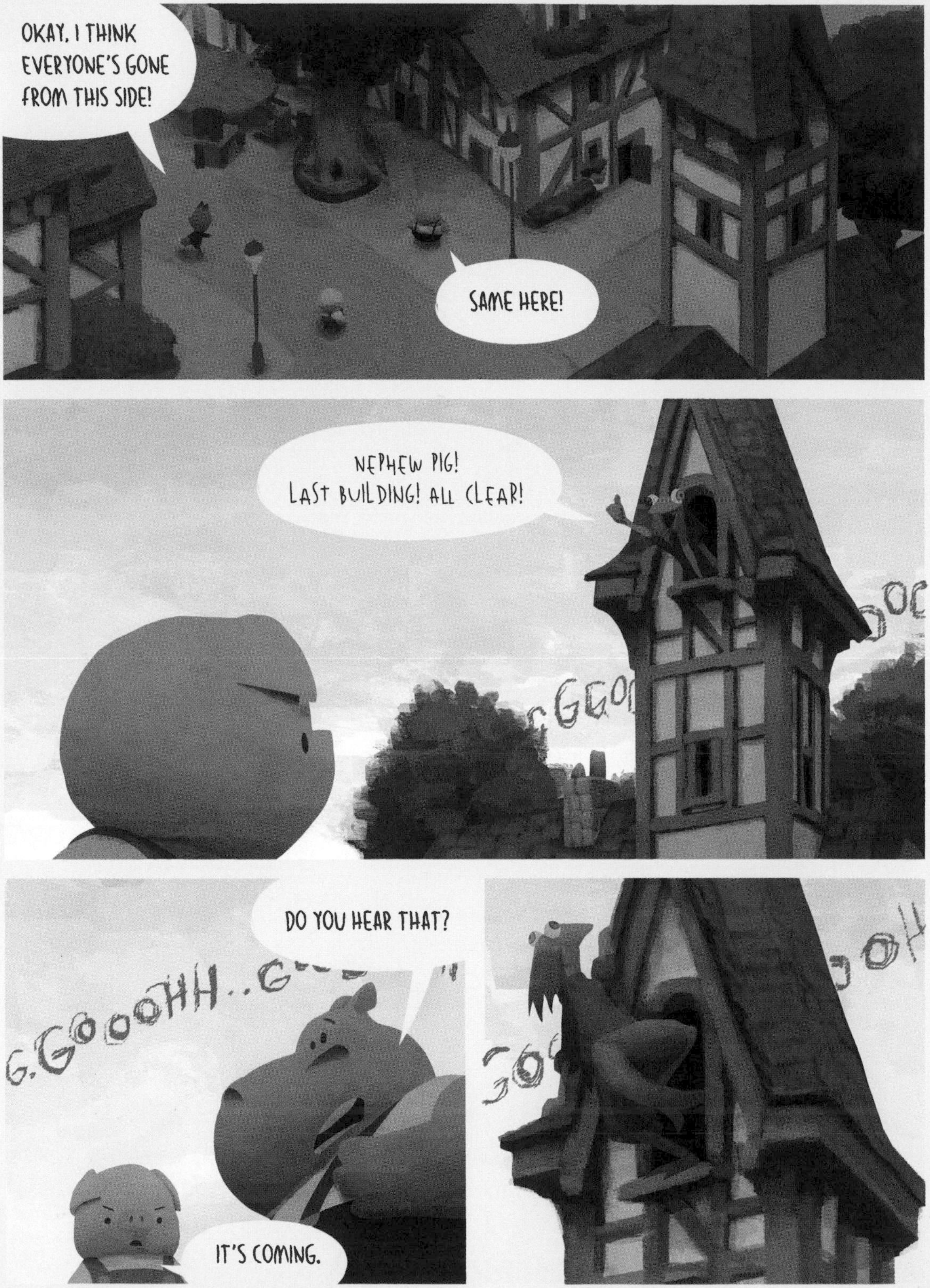
OKAY, I THINK EVERYONE'S GONE FROM THIS SIDE!
SAME HERE!
NEPHEW PIG! LAST BUILDING! ALL CLEAR!
DO YOU HEAR THAT?
G.GOOOOHH..
IT'S COMING.

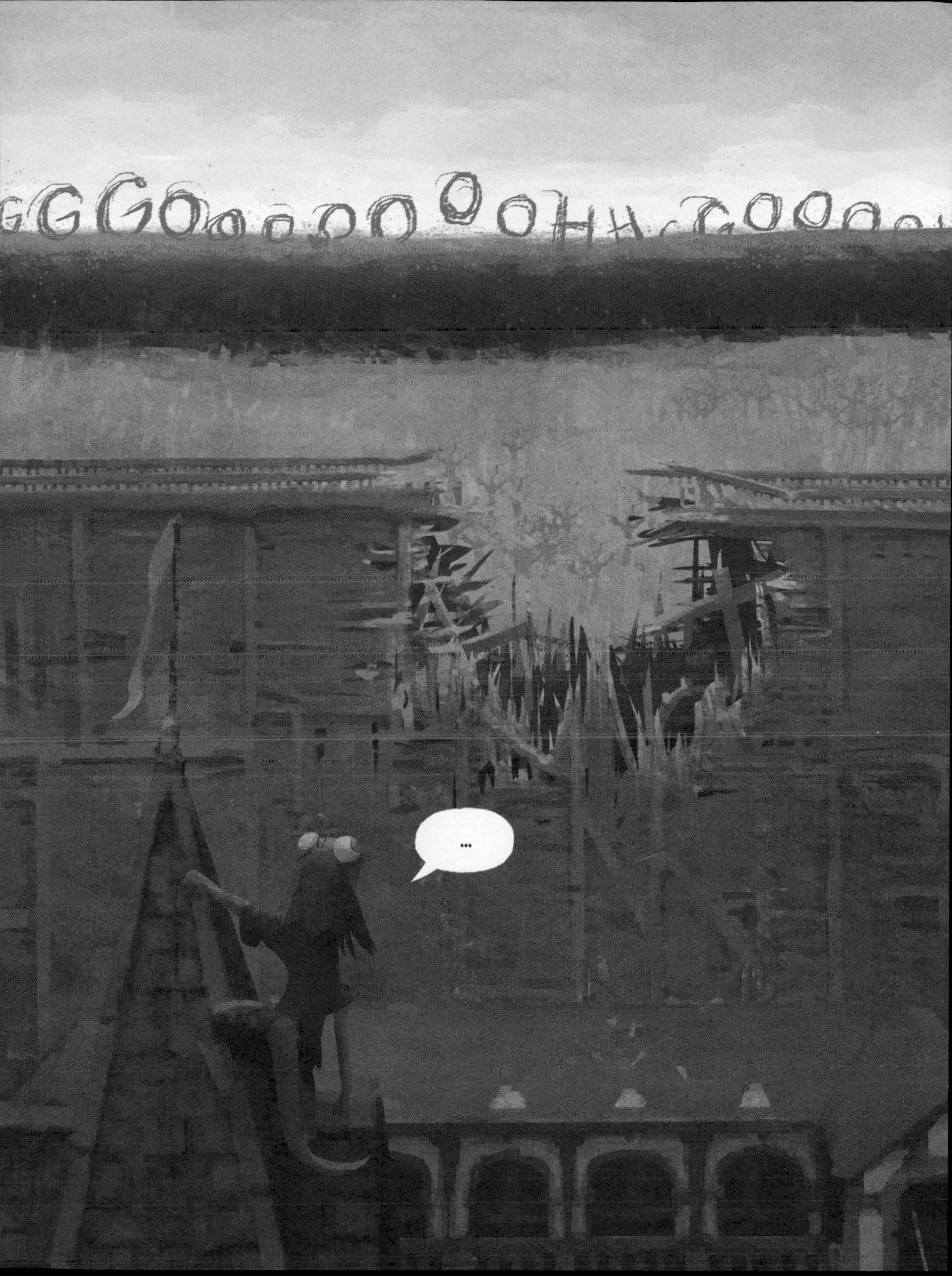
GGGOooooOOOHH GOOoo
...

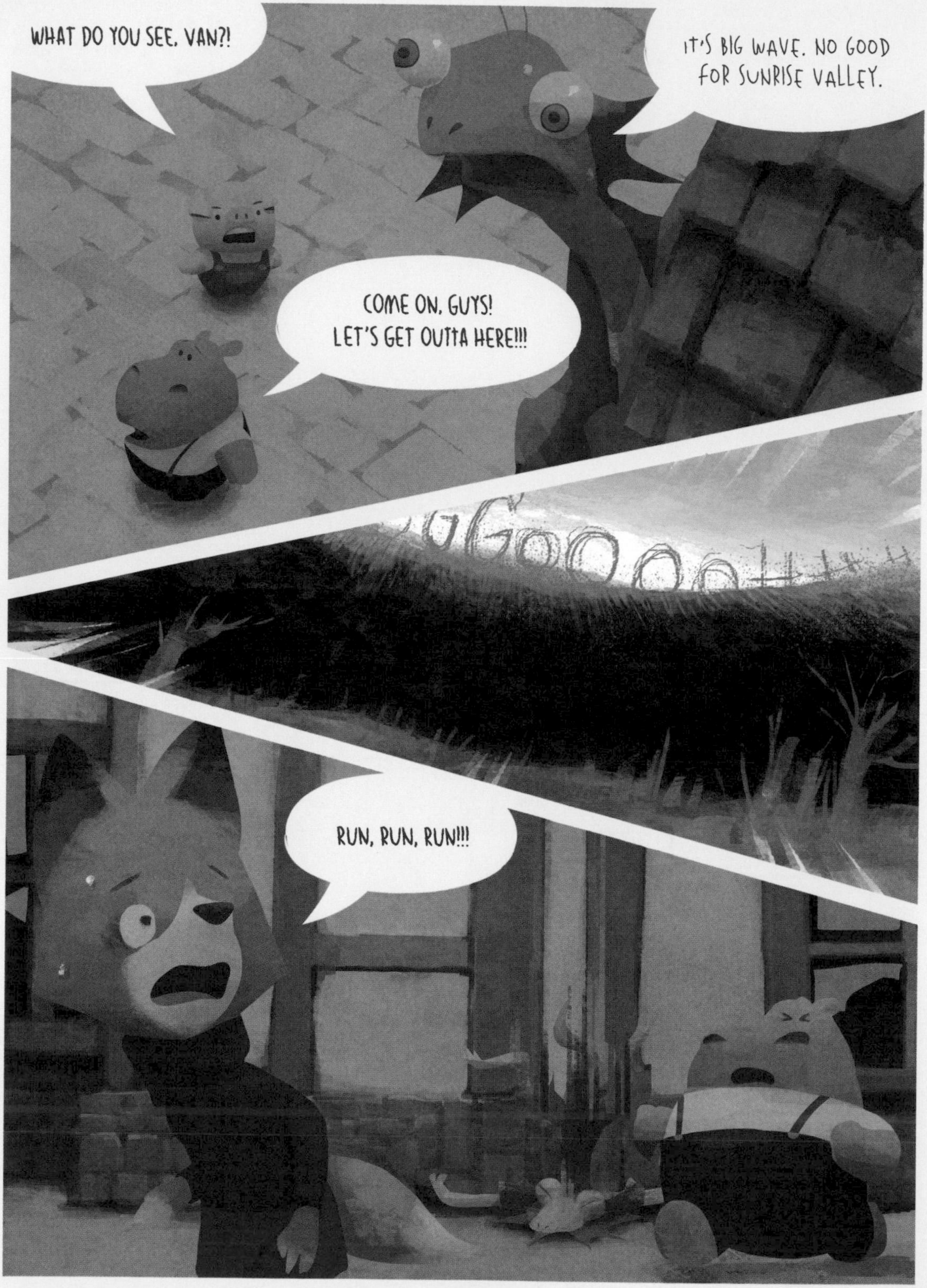
WHAT DO YOU SEE, VAN?!
IT'S BIG WAVE. NO GOOD FOR SUNRISE VALLEY.
COME ON, GUYS! LET'S GET OUTTA HERE!!!
RUN, RUN, RUN!!!

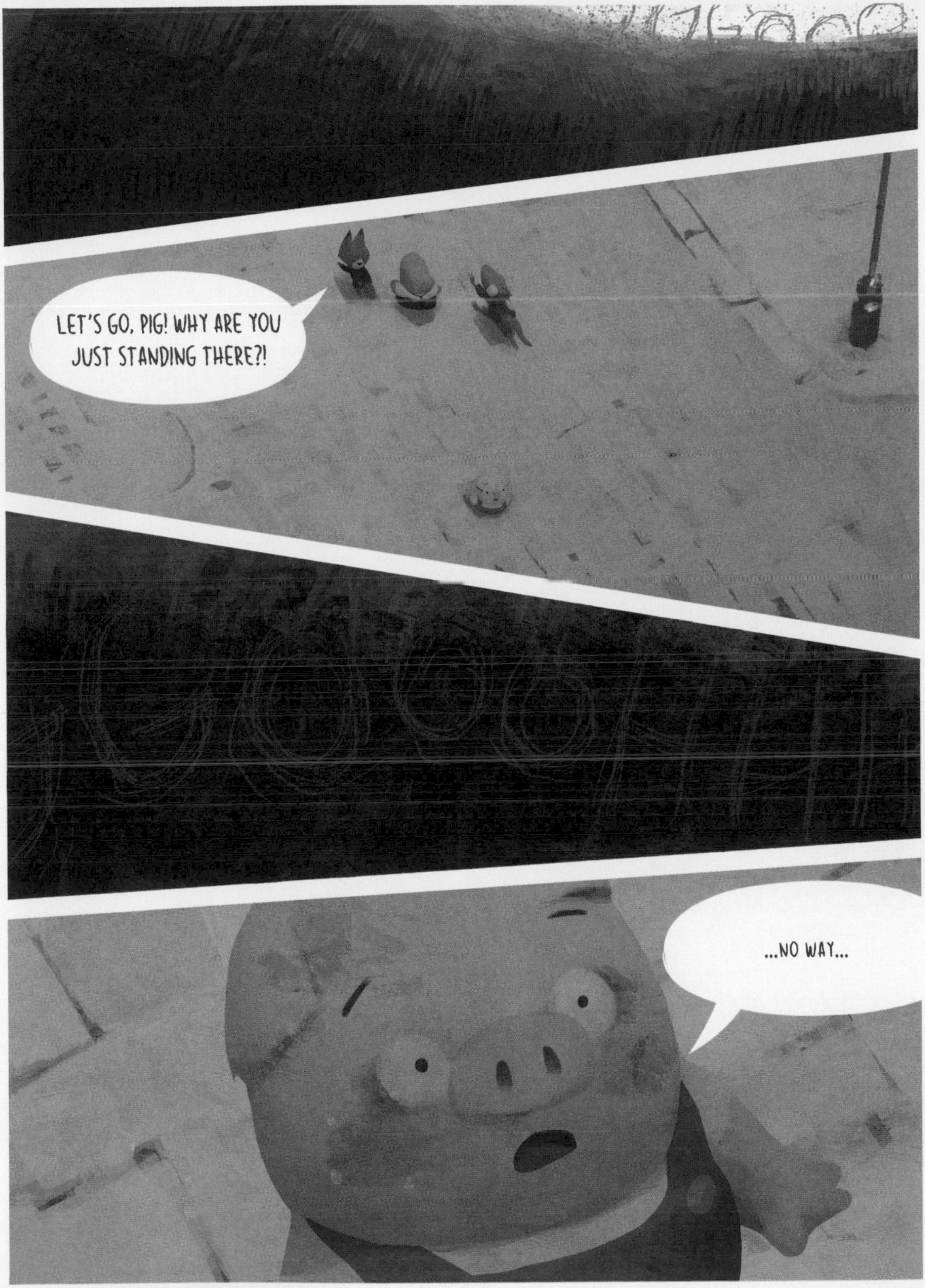
LET'S GO, PIG! WHY ARE YOU JUST STANDING THERE?!
...NO WAY...

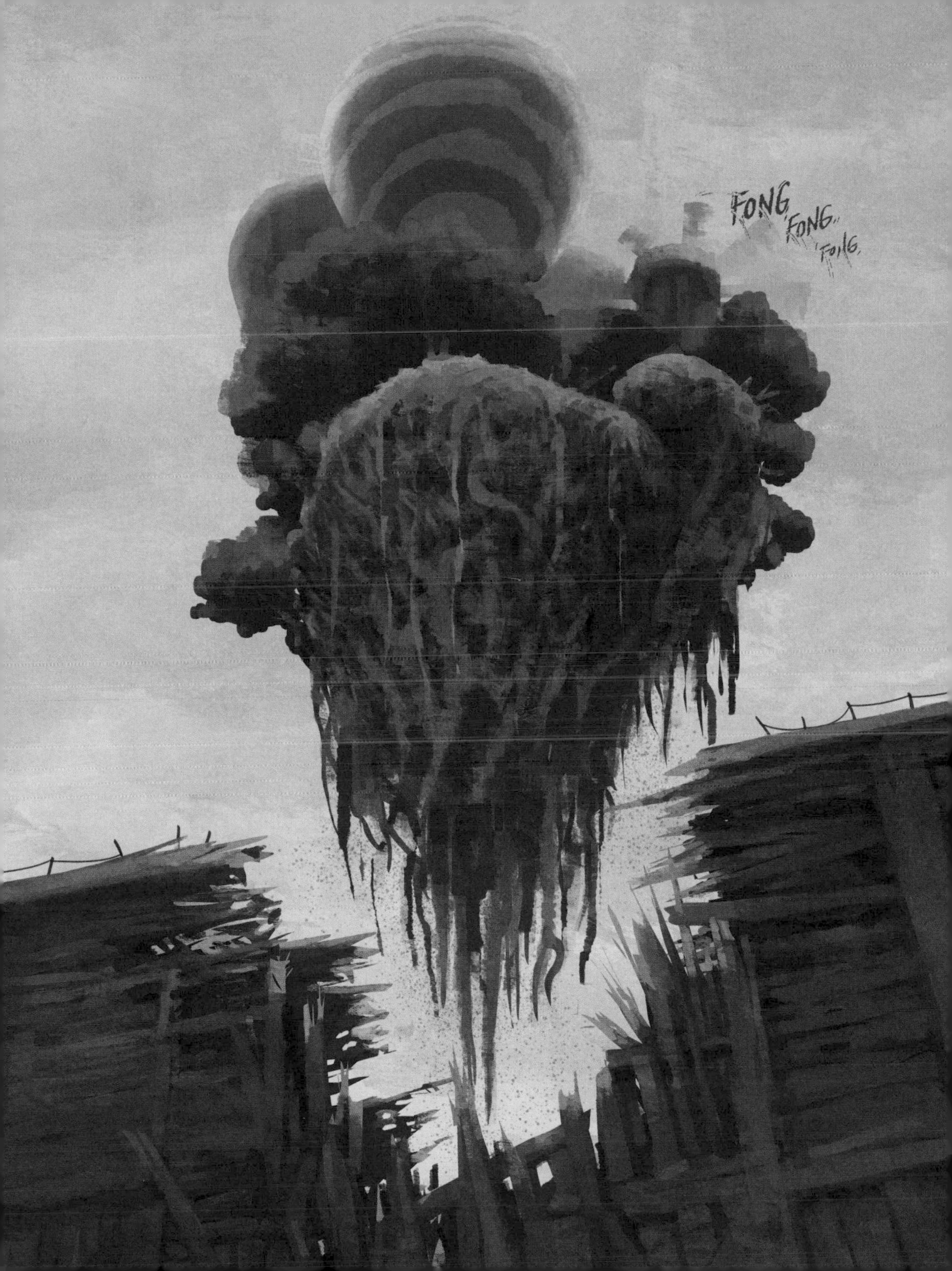
FONG
FONG
FONG

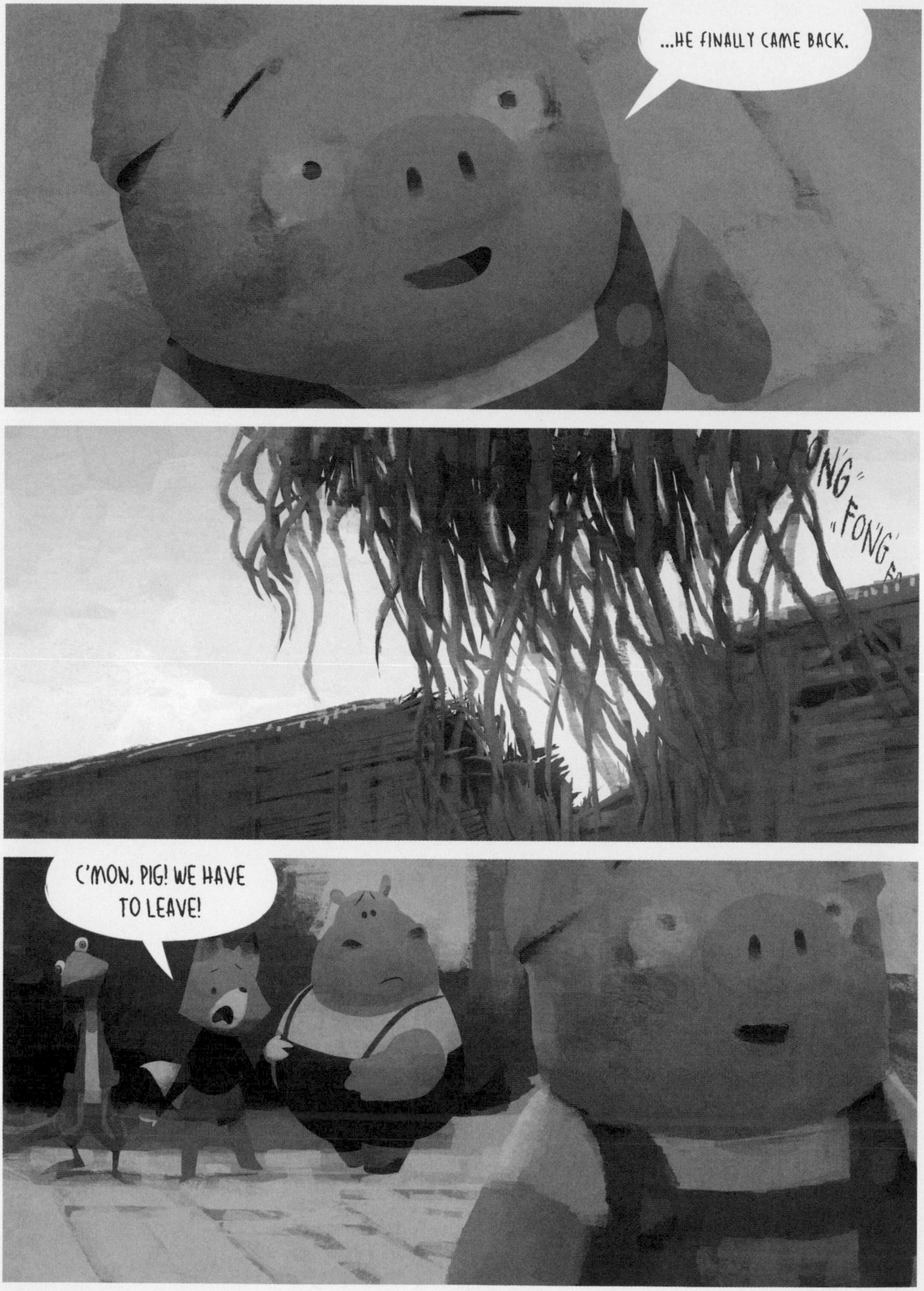
...HE FINALLY CAME BACK.
"FONG"
C'MON, PIG! WE HAVE TO LEAVE!

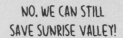

NO. WE CAN STILL SAVE SUNRISE VALLEY!

WHAT?!

WE WILL MAKE A NEW DAM!

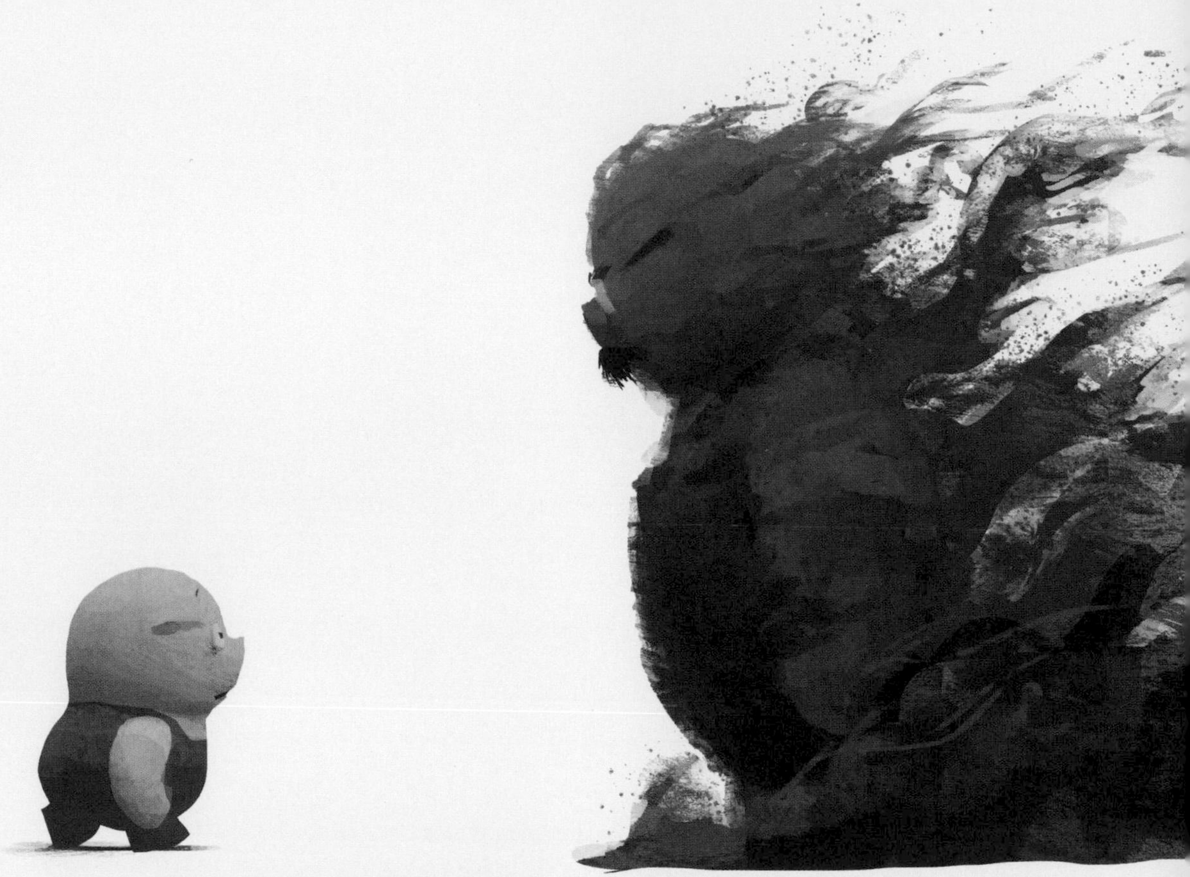

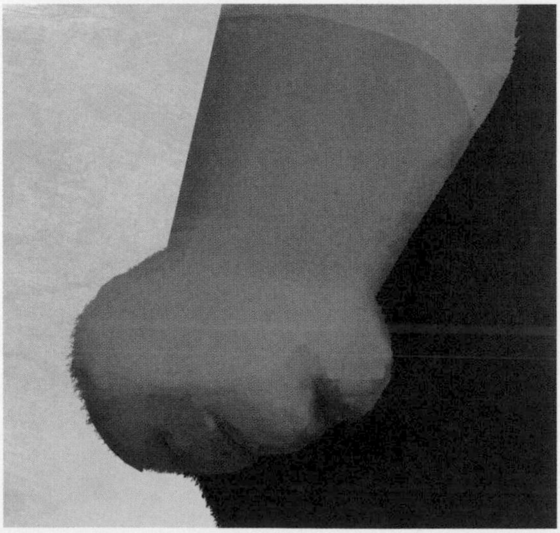

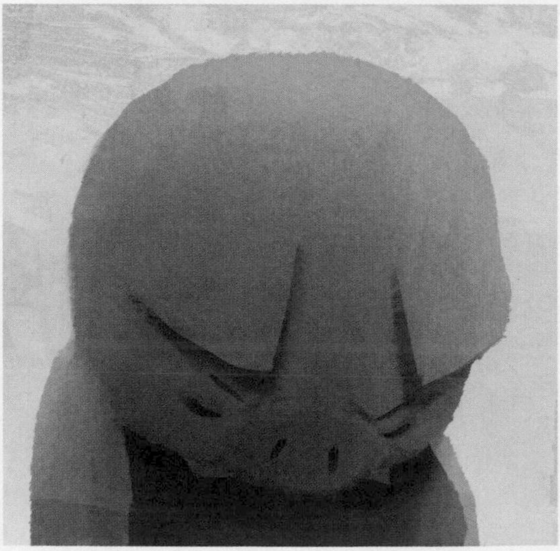

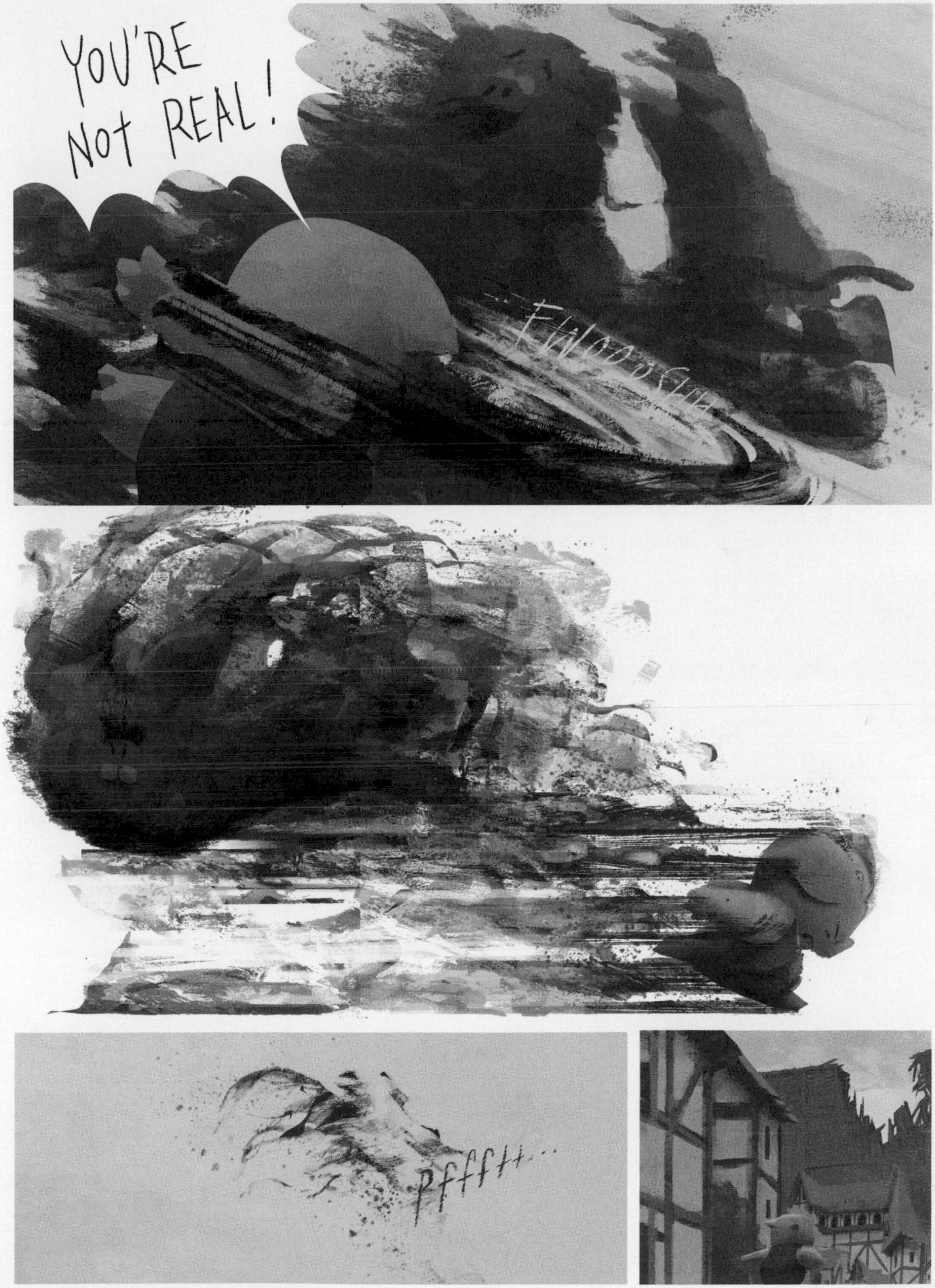
YOU'RE Not REAL!
FWOOOSH
Pffftt...

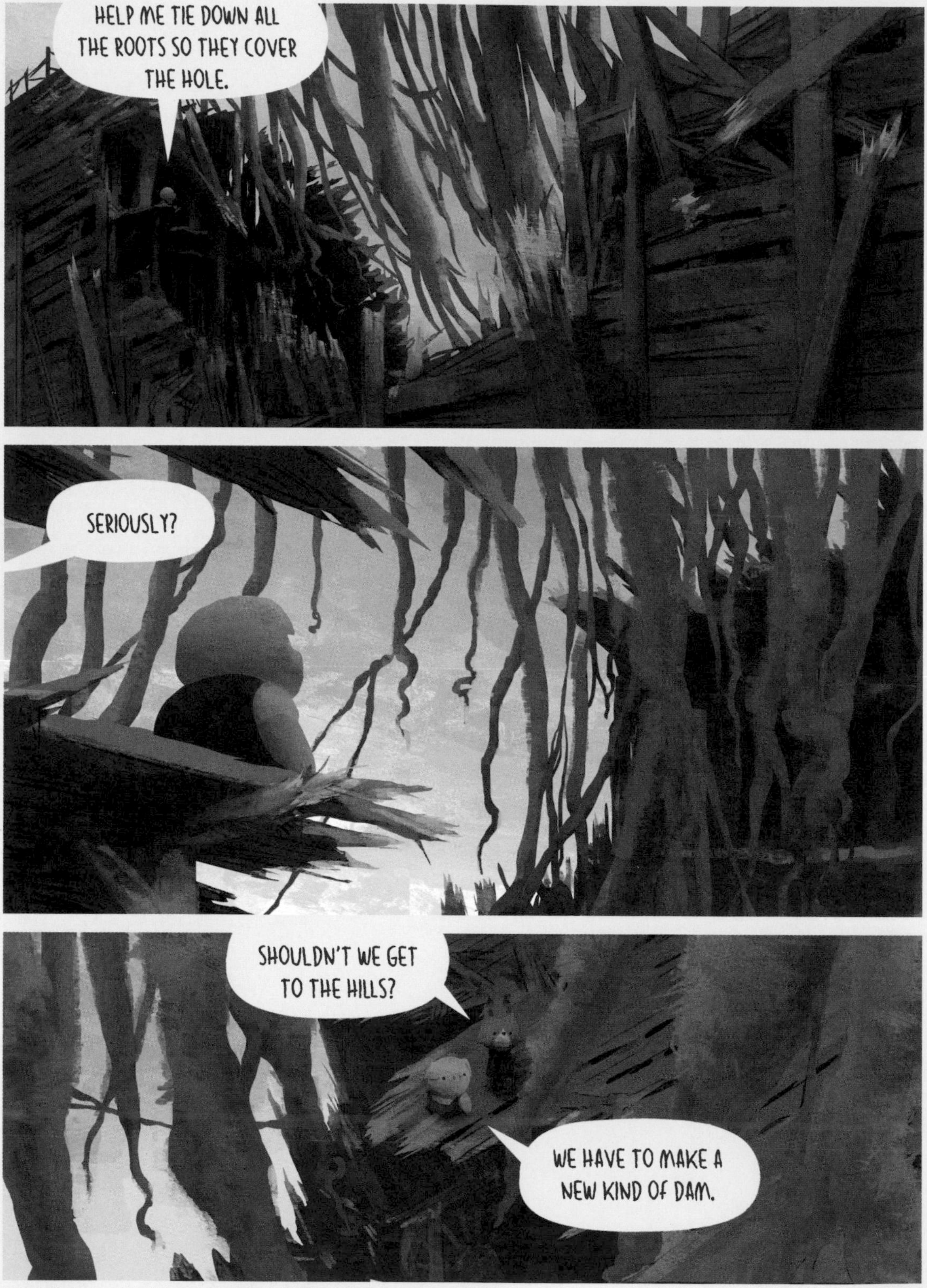
HELP ME TIE DOWN ALL THE ROOTS SO THEY COVER THE HOLE.
SERIOUSLY?
SHOULDN'T WE GET TO THE HILLS?
WE HAVE TO MAKE A NEW KIND OF DAM.

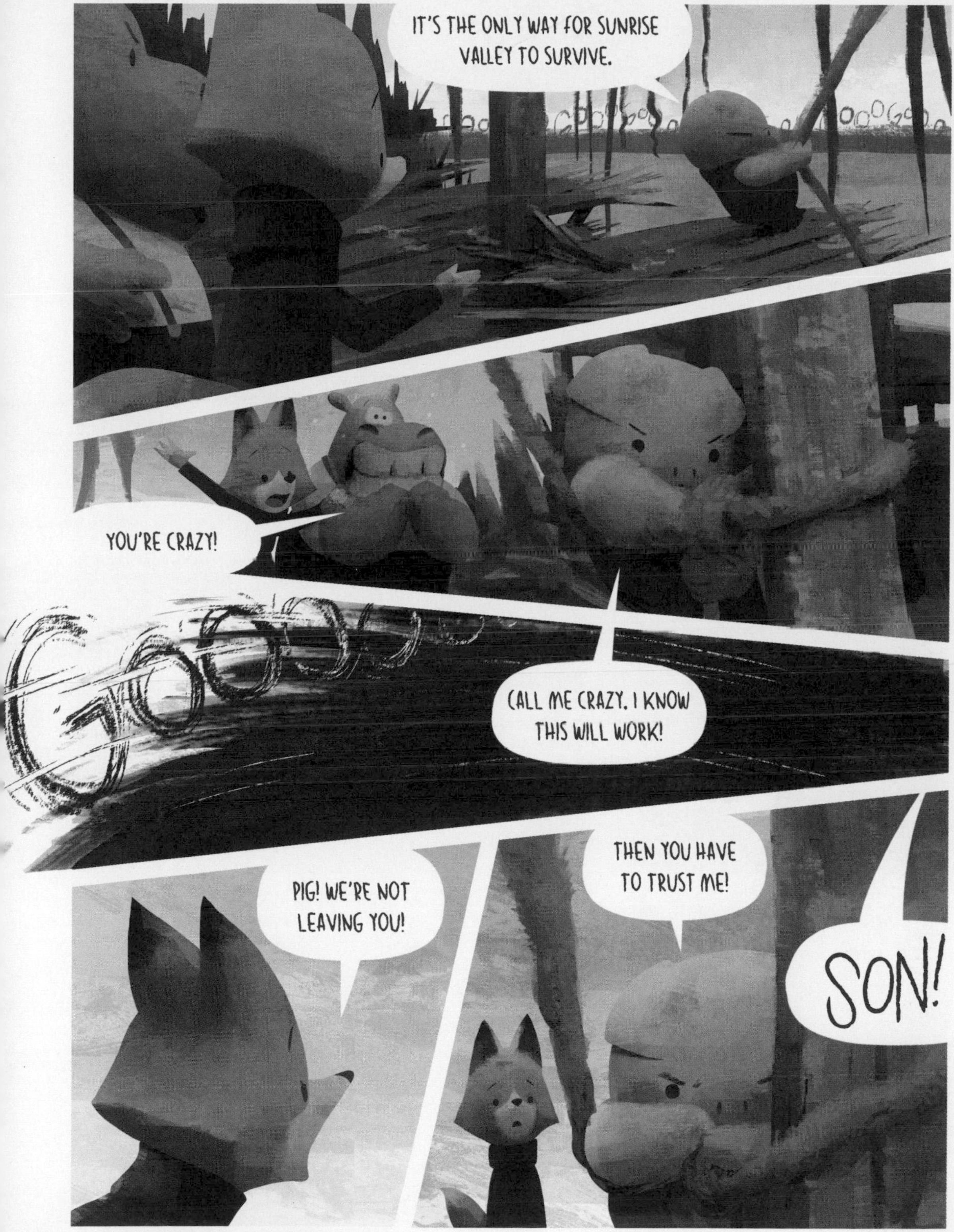
IT'S THE ONLY WAY FOR SUNRISE VALLEY TO SURVIVE.
YOU'RE CRAZY!
CALL ME CRAZY. I KNOW THIS WILL WORK!
PIG! WE'RE NOT LEAVING YOU!
THEN YOU HAVE TO TRUST ME!
SON!

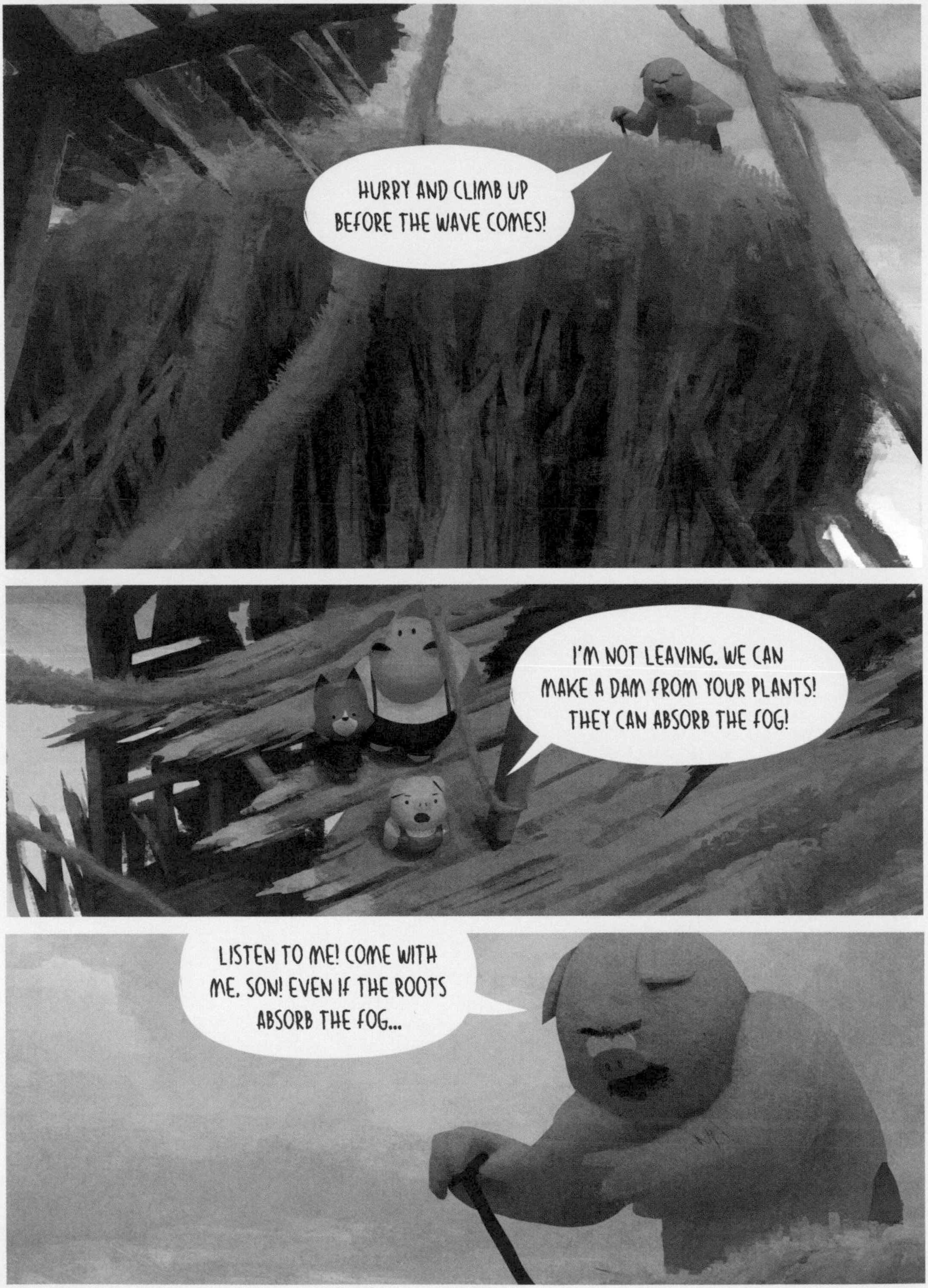
HURRY AND CLIMB UP BEFORE THE WAVE COMES!
I'M NOT LEAVING. WE CAN MAKE A DAM FROM YOUR PLANTS! THEY CAN ABSORB THE FOG!
LISTEN TO ME! COME WITH ME, SON! EVEN IF THE ROOTS ABSORB THE FOG...

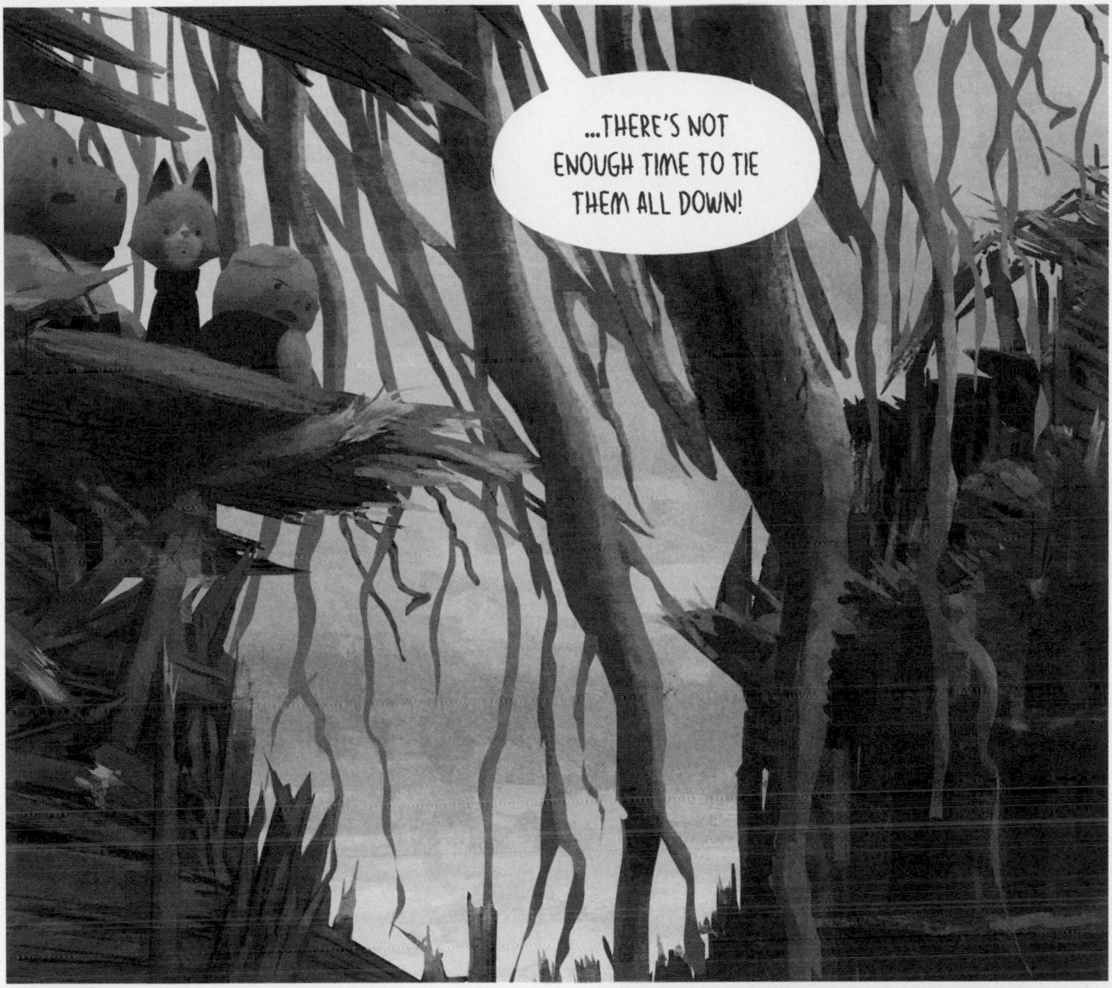
...THERE'S NOT ENOUGH TIME TO TIE THEM ALL DOWN!

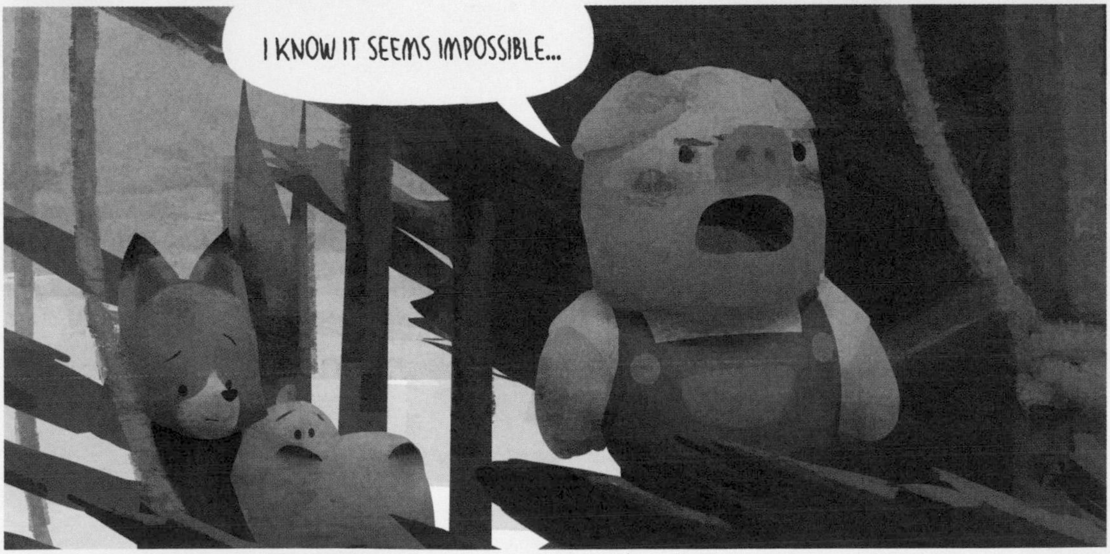
I KNOW IT SEEMS IMPOSSIBLE...

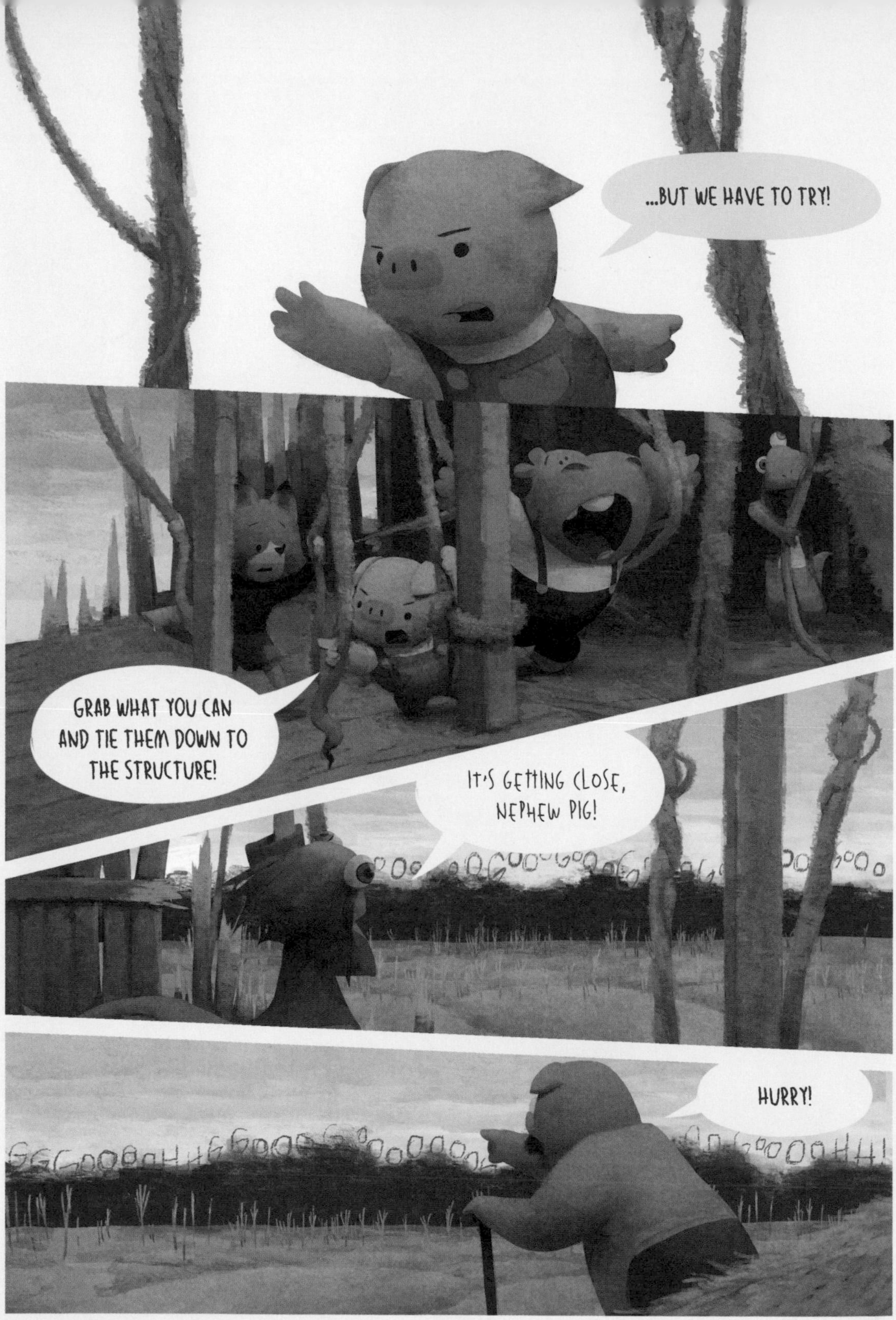
...BUT WE HAVE TO TRY!
GRAB WHAT YOU CAN AND TIE THEM DOWN TO THE STRUCTURE!
IT'S GETTING CLOSE, NEPHEW PIG!
HURRY!

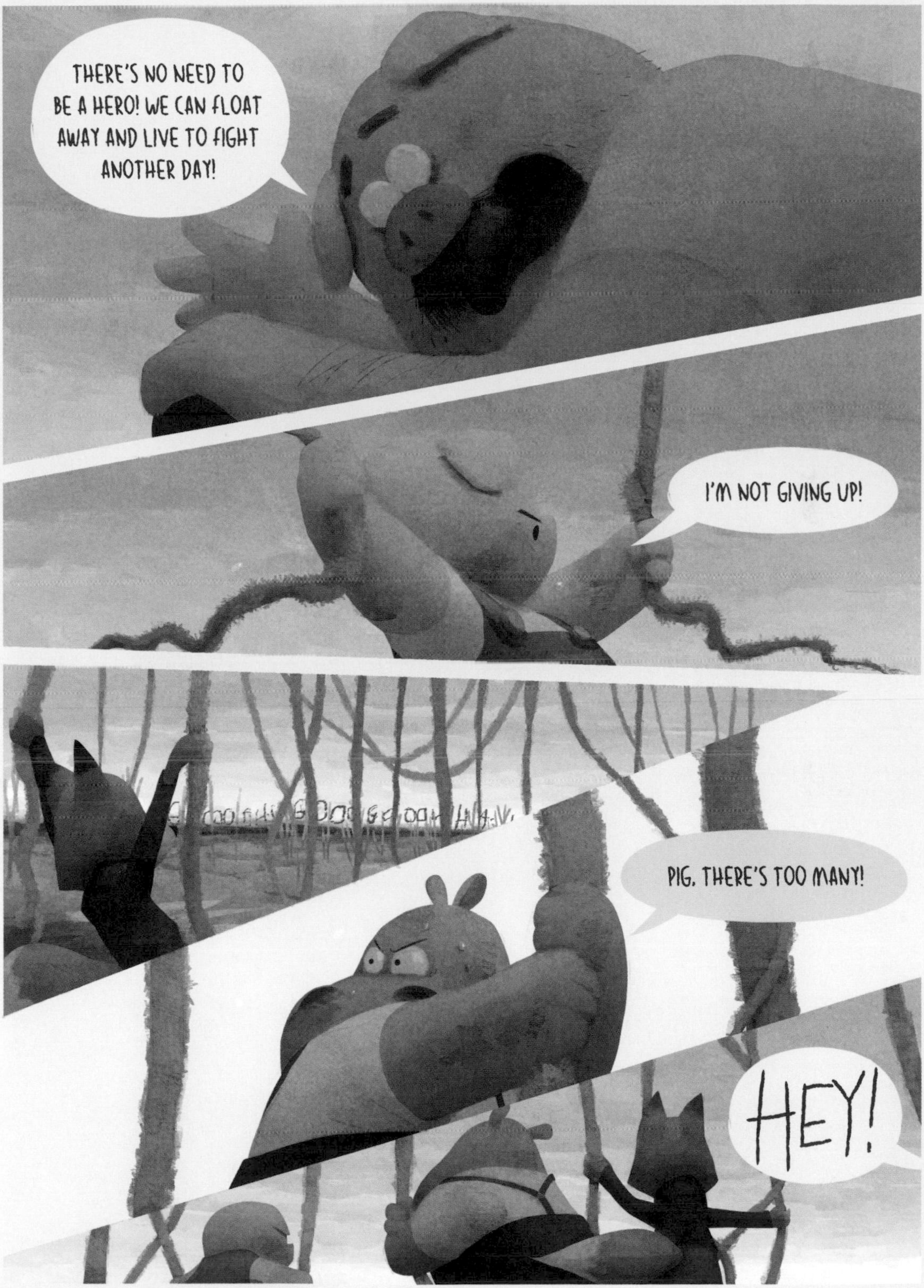
THERE'S NO NEED TO BE A HERO! WE CAN FLOAT AWAY AND LIVE TO FIGHT ANOTHER DAY!
I'M NOT GIVING UP!
PIG. THERE'S TOO MANY!
HEY!

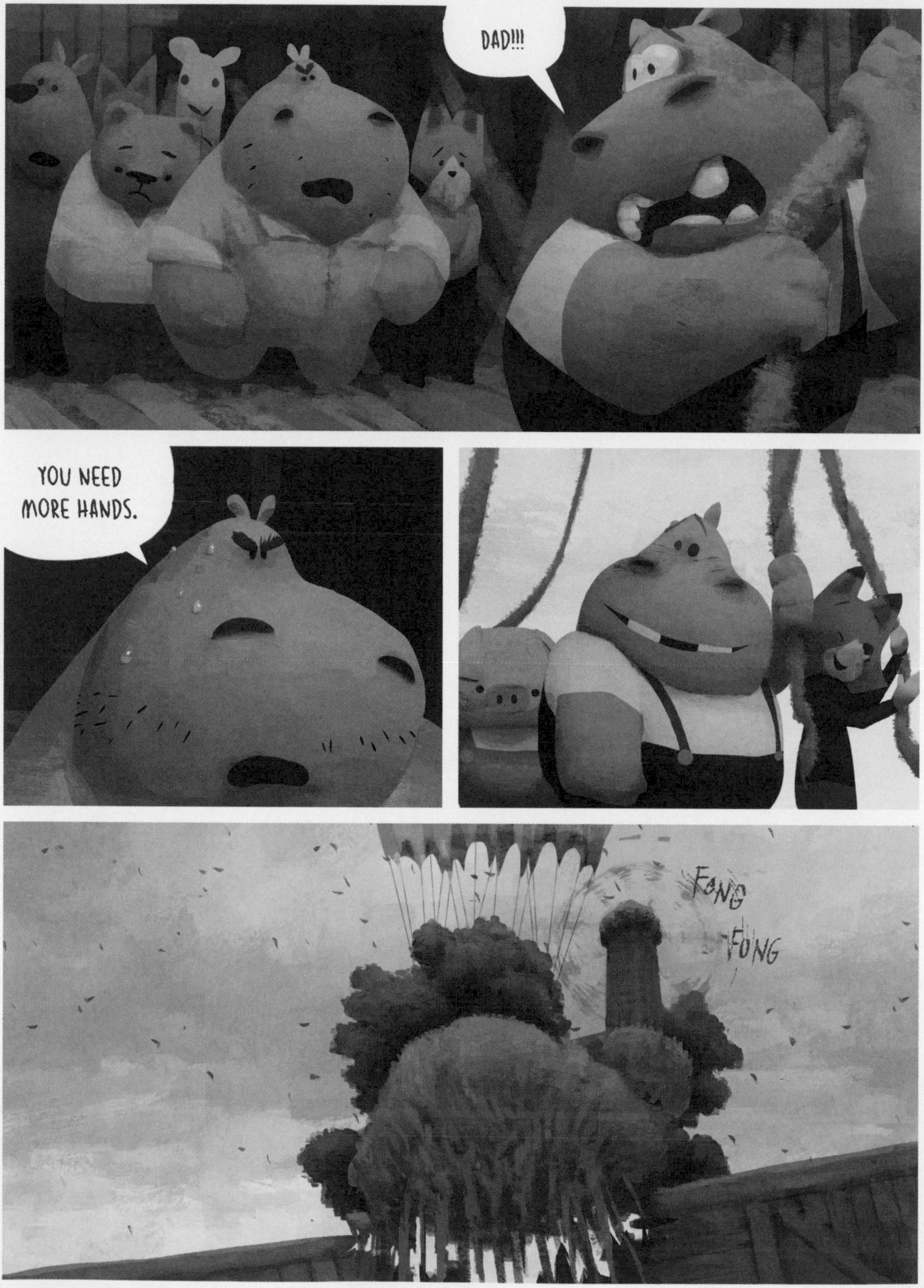
DAD!!!
YOU NEED MORE HANDS.
FONG
FONG

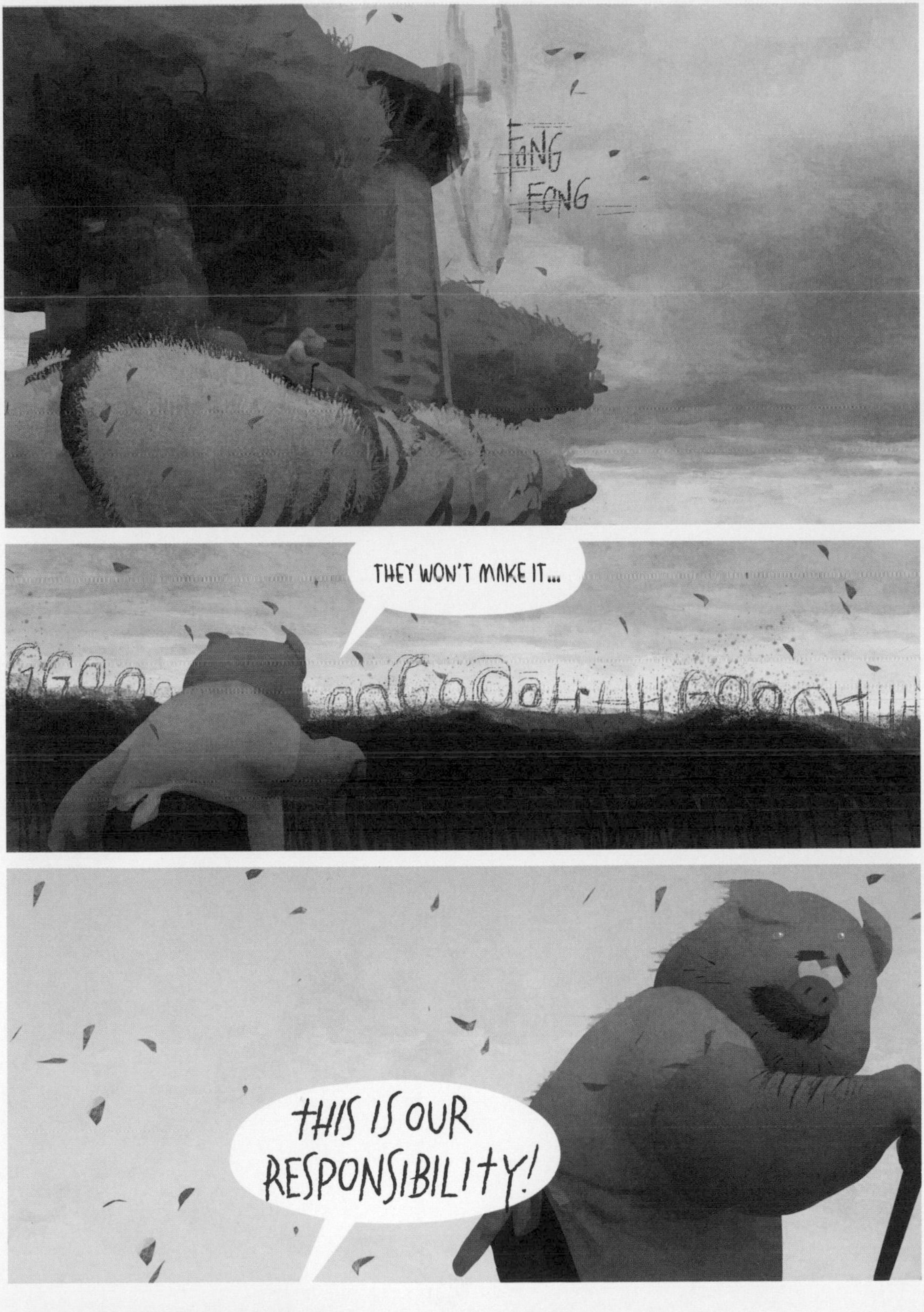
FONG
FONG
THEY WON'T MAKE IT...
THIS IS OUR RESPONSIBILITY!

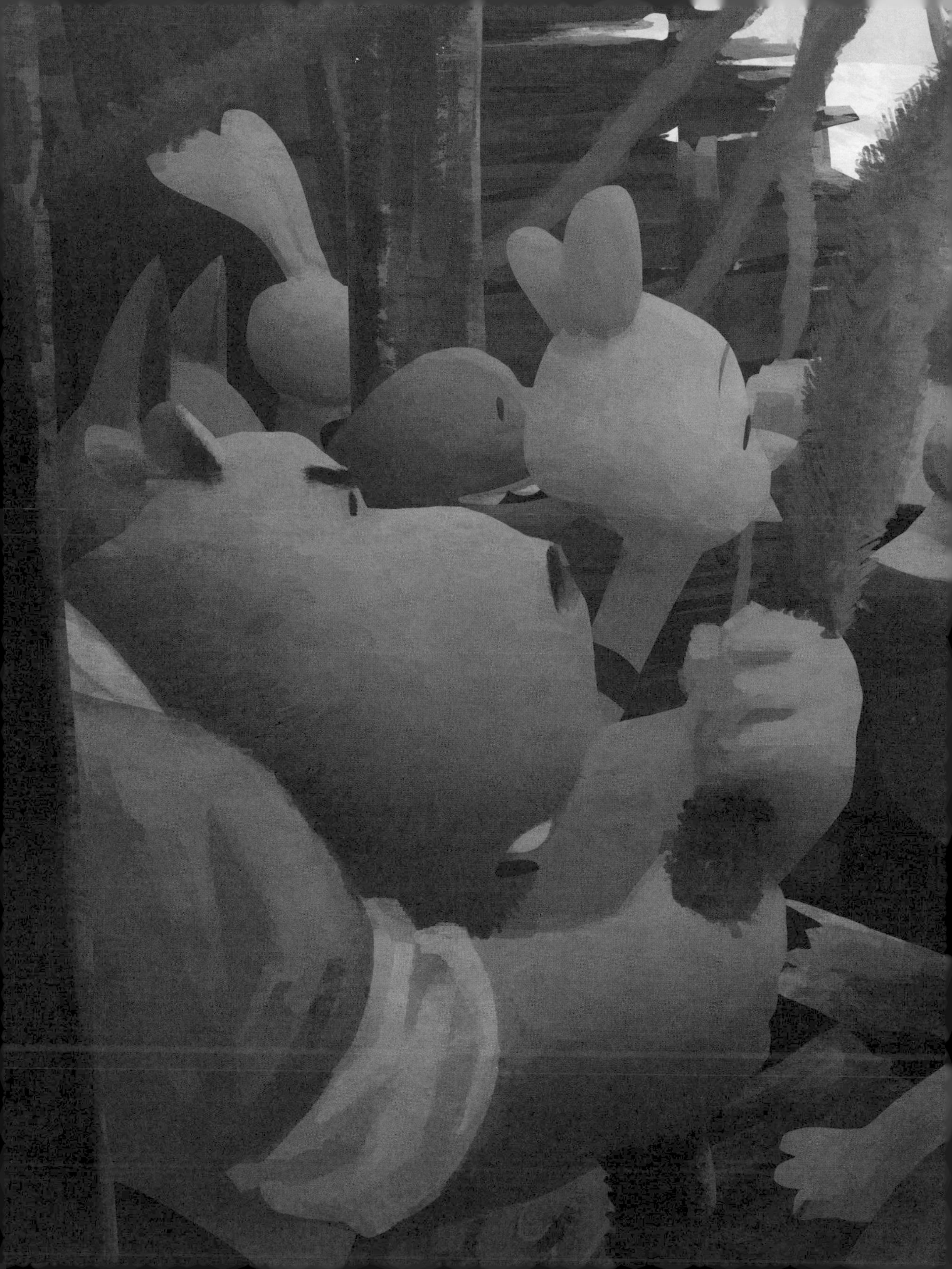

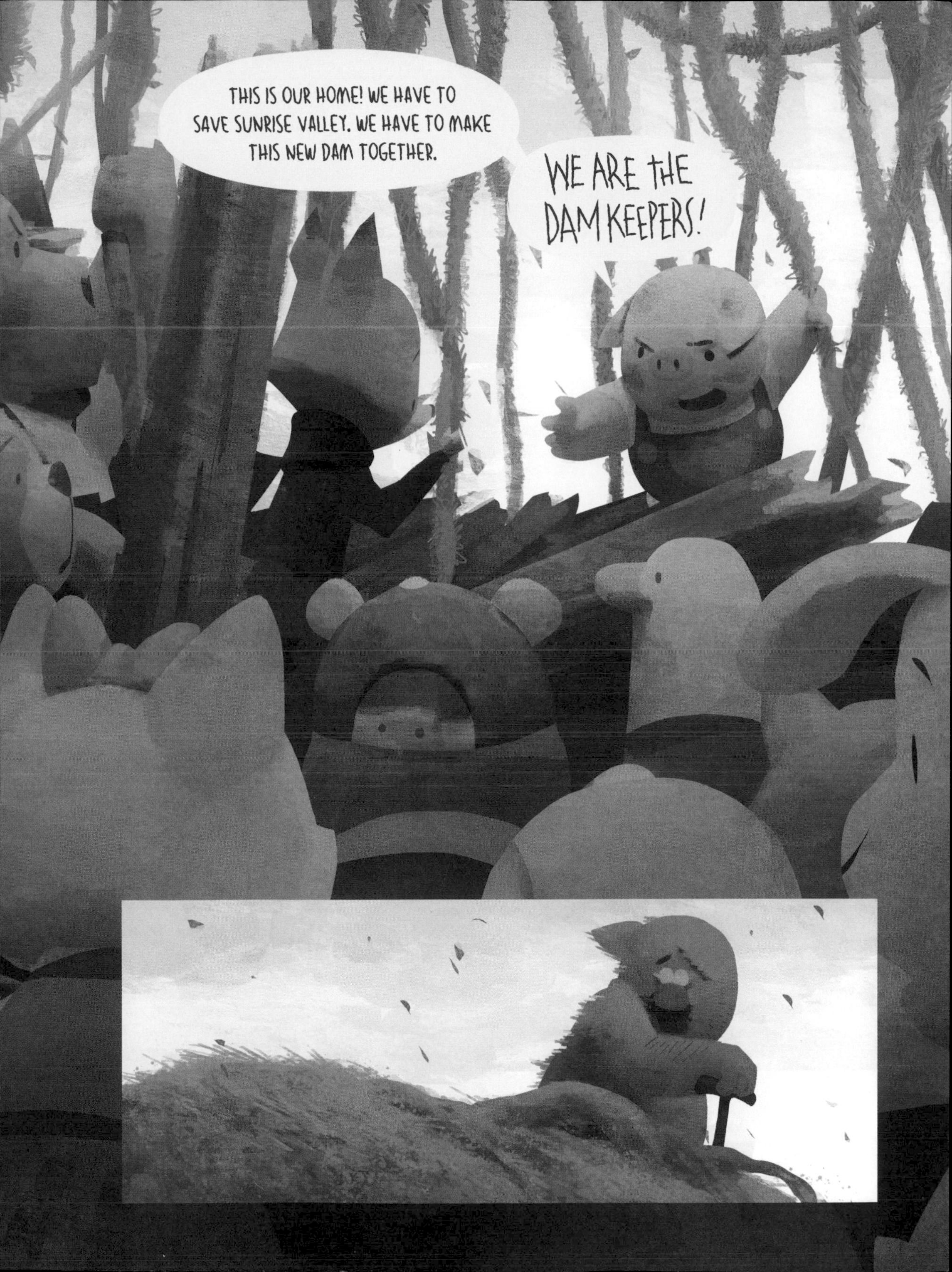
THIS IS OUR HOME! WE HAVE TO SAVE SUNRISE VALLEY. WE HAVE TO MAKE THIS NEW DAM TOGETHER.
WE ARE THE DAM KEEPERS!

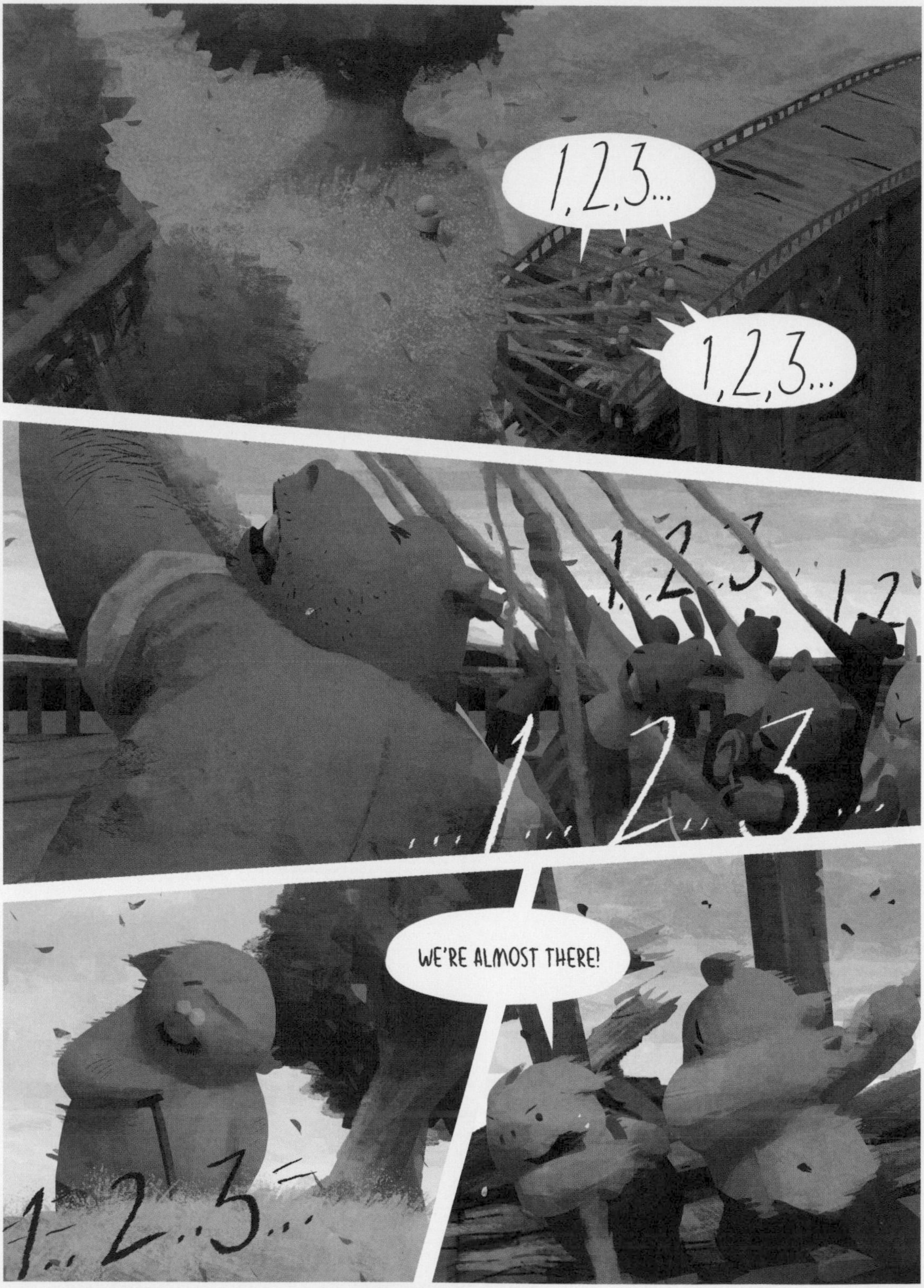
1,2,3...
1,2,3...
1..2..3..
1..2..3...
...1...2...3...
1..2..3...
WE'RE ALMOST THERE!

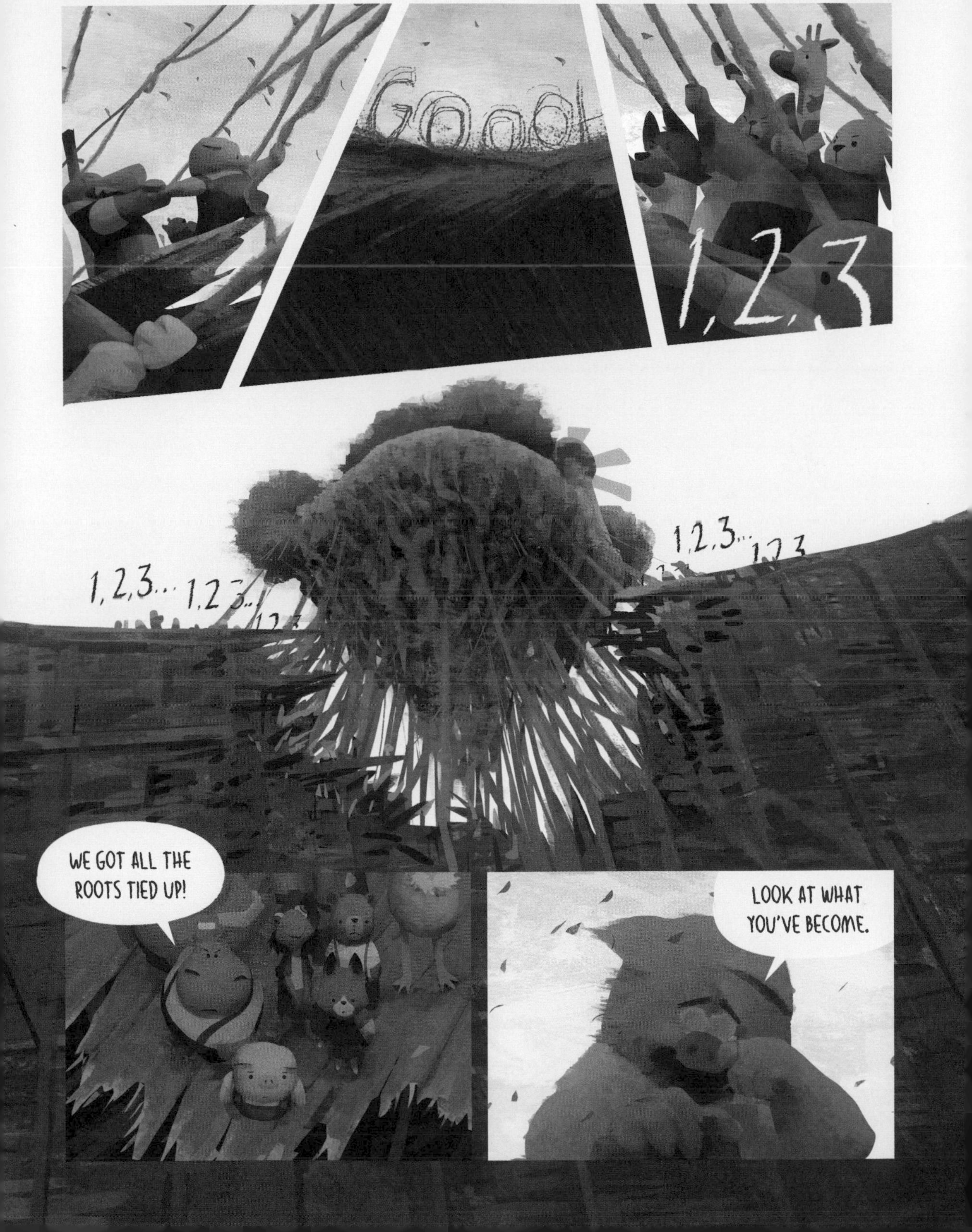
Good
1,2,3
1,2,3... 1,2,3...
1,2,3... 1,2,3
WE GOT ALL THE ROOTS TIED UP!
LOOK AT WHAT YOU'VE BECOME.

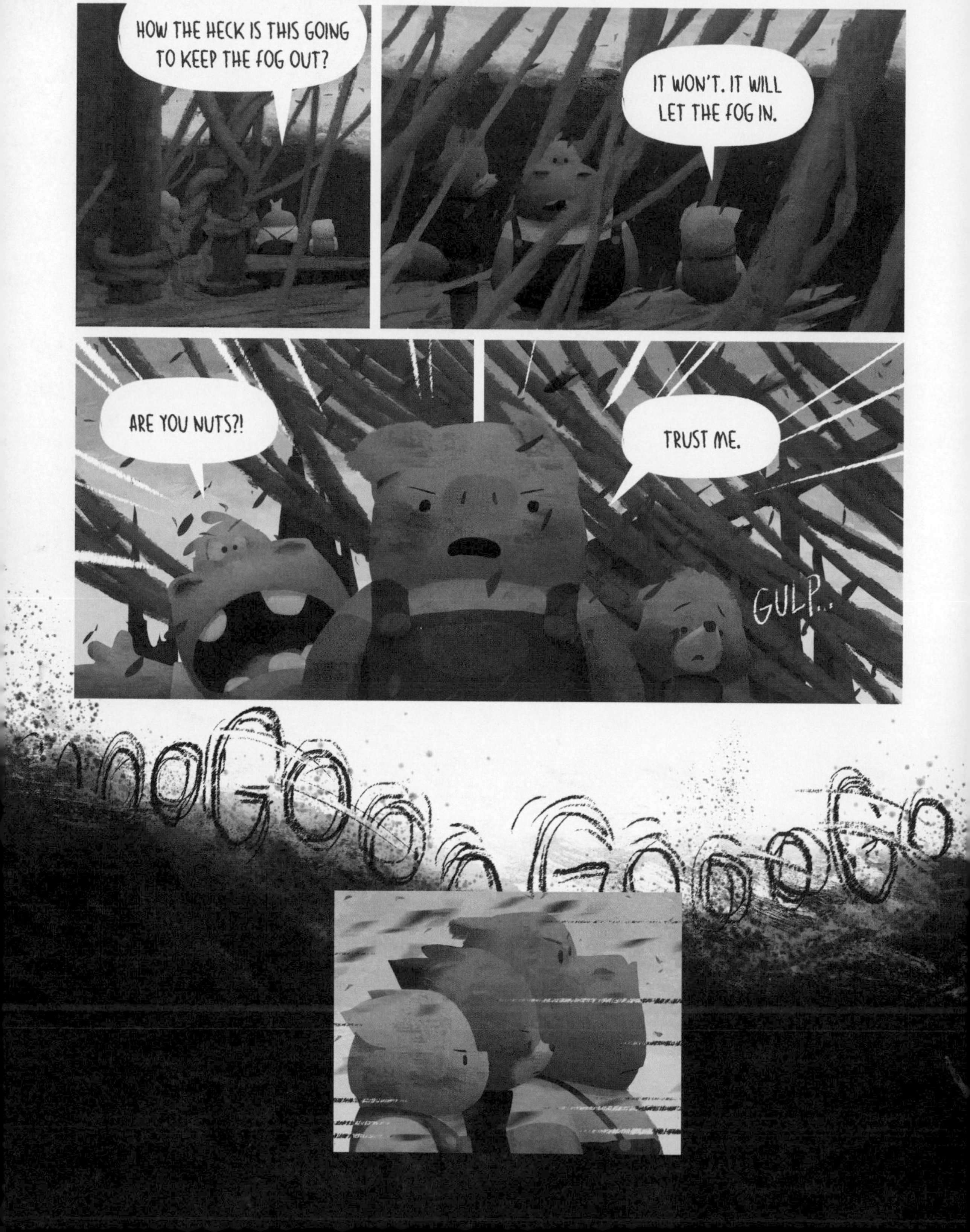
HOW THE HECK IS THIS GOING TO KEEP THE FOG OUT?
IT WON'T. IT WILL LET THE FOG IN.
ARE YOU NUTS?!
TRUST ME.
GULP...

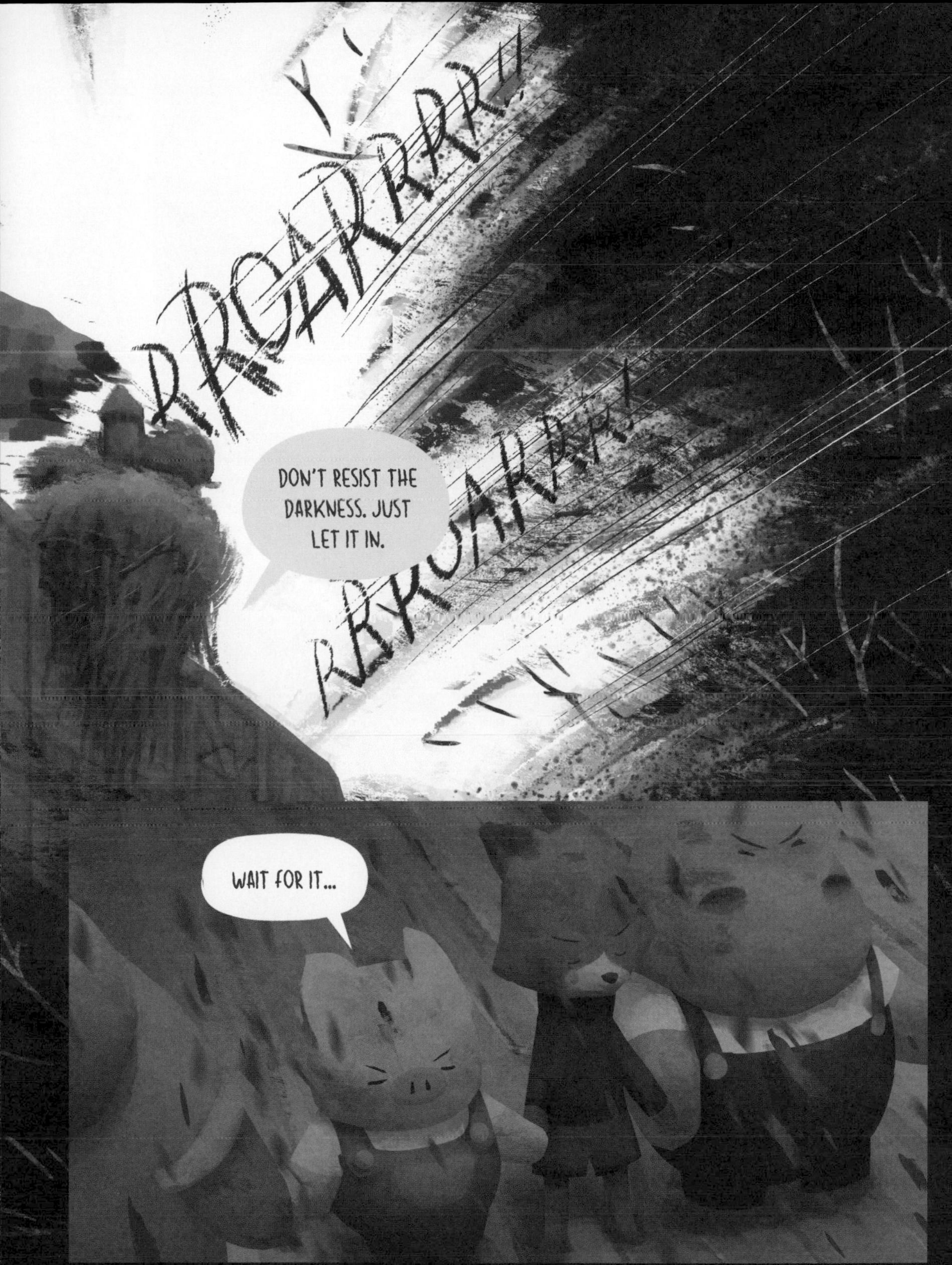
RROARRRR!!
RRROARRR!
DON'T RESIST THE DARKNESS. JUST LET IT IN.
WAIT FOR IT...

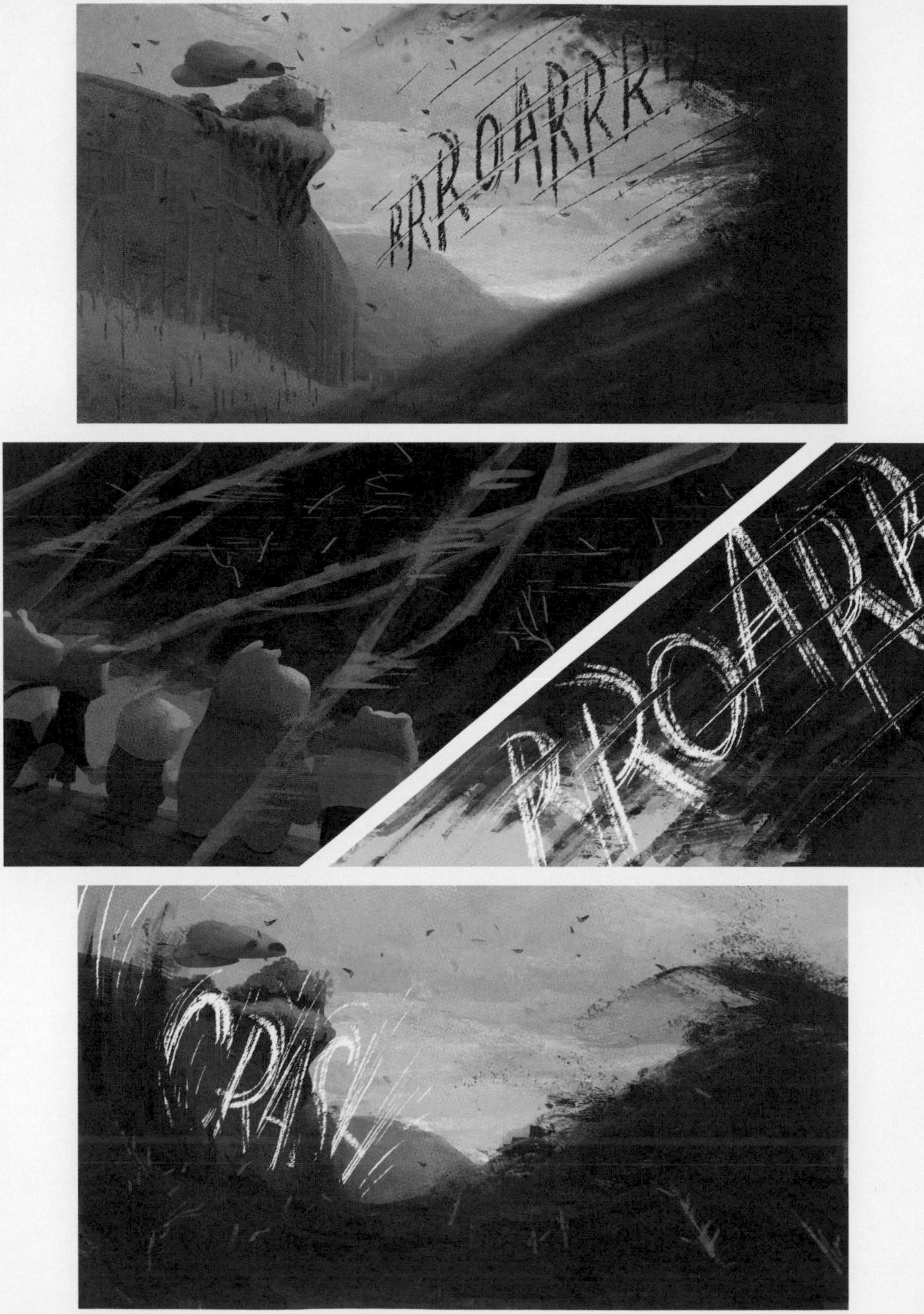
RRROARRK
RROARR
CRACK

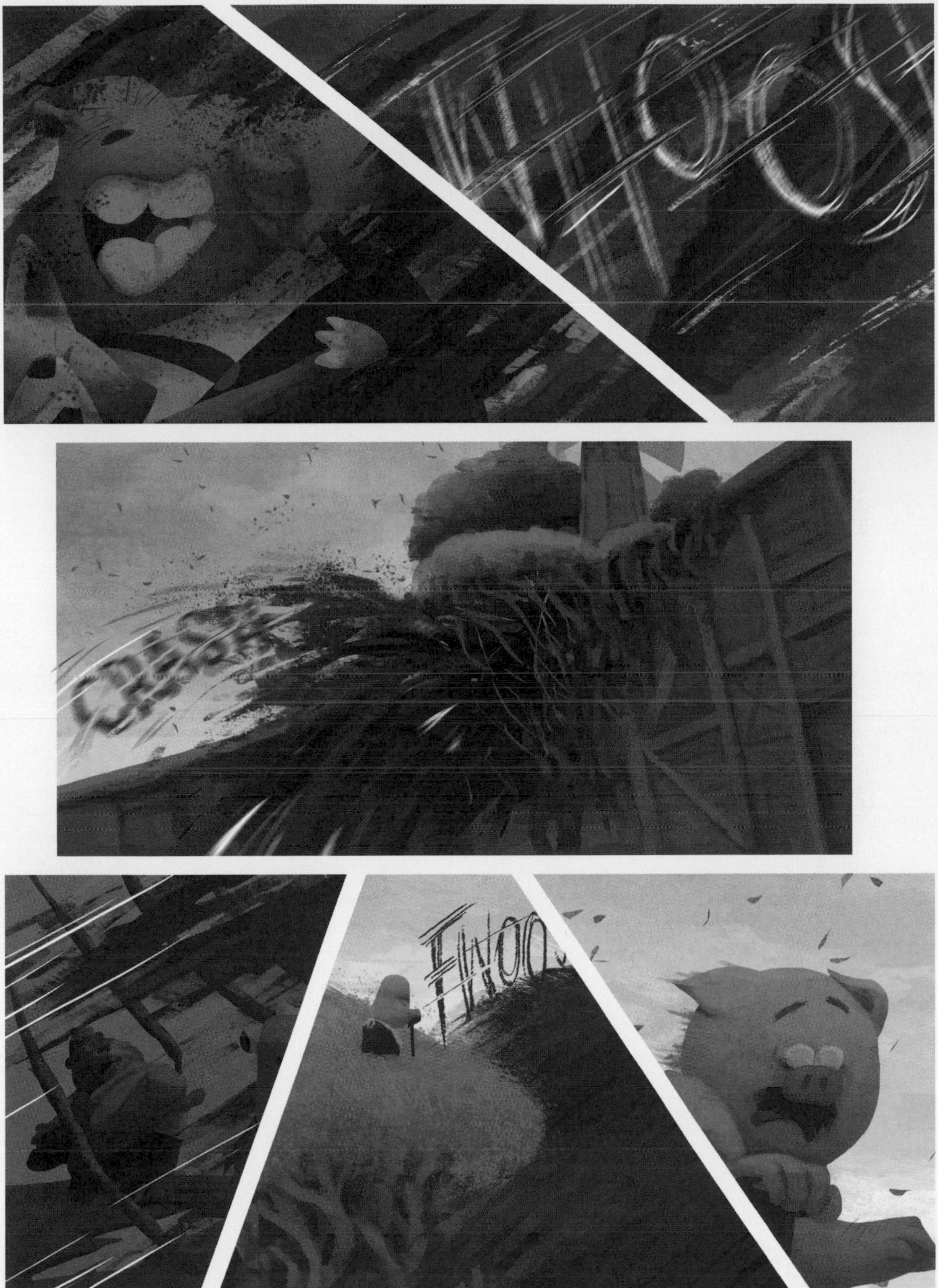
WHOOS
CRASH
FWOO

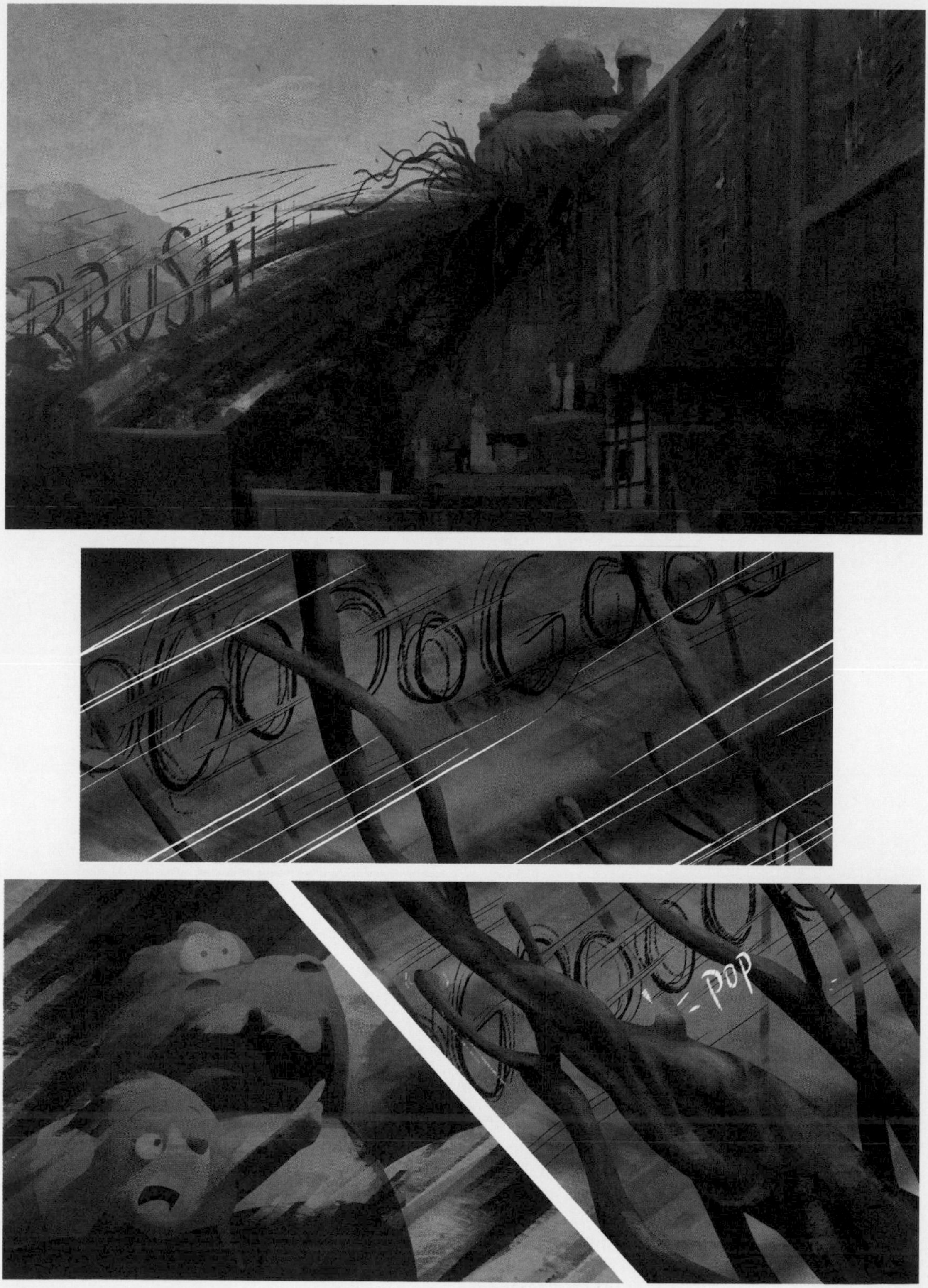
BRUSH
POP

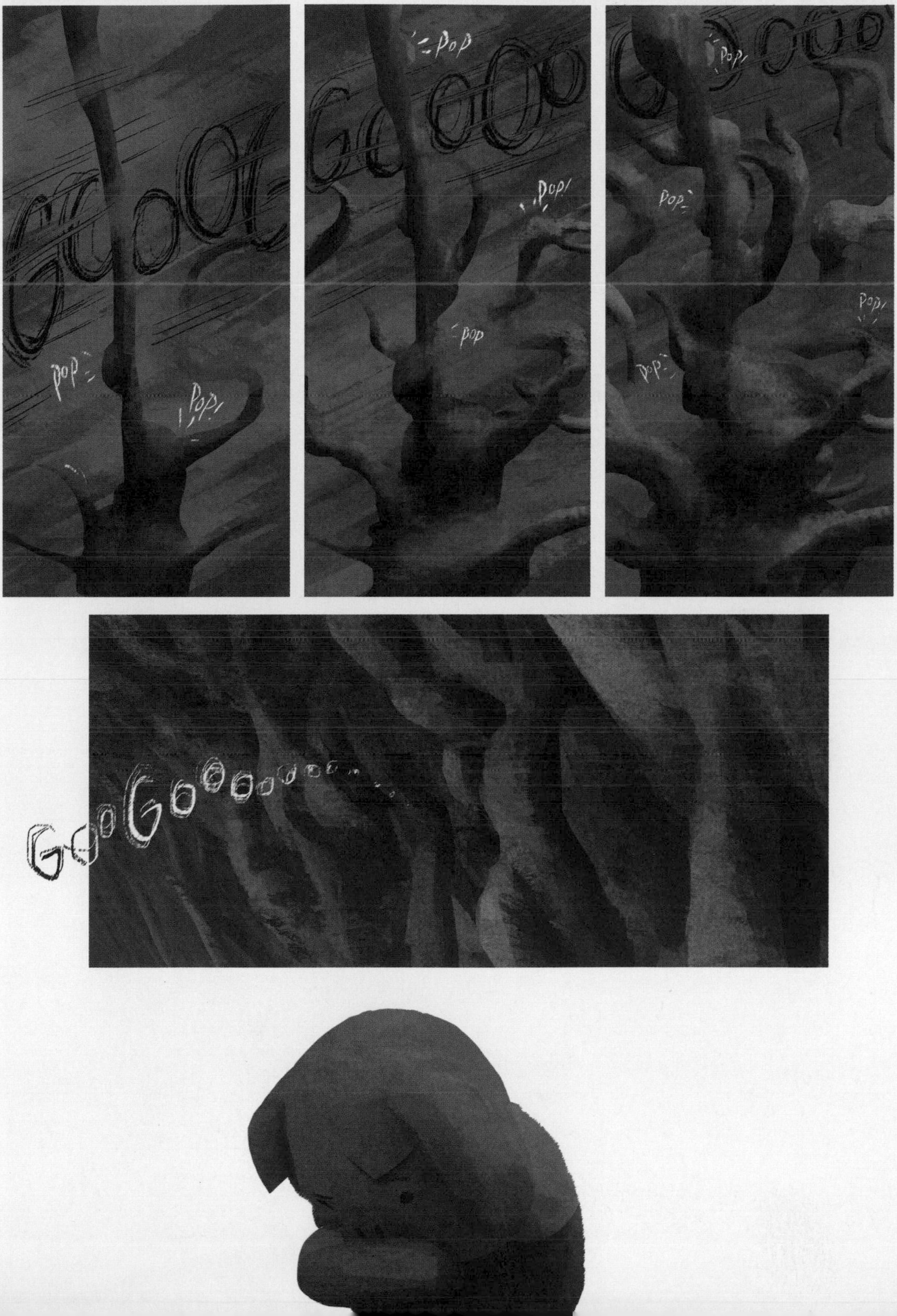

GOOOL
POP
POP!
POP
GOOOOOO
POP!
POP
POP!
GOOOOOO
POP!
POP
POP!
POP
GOOGOOOOOOOOO...

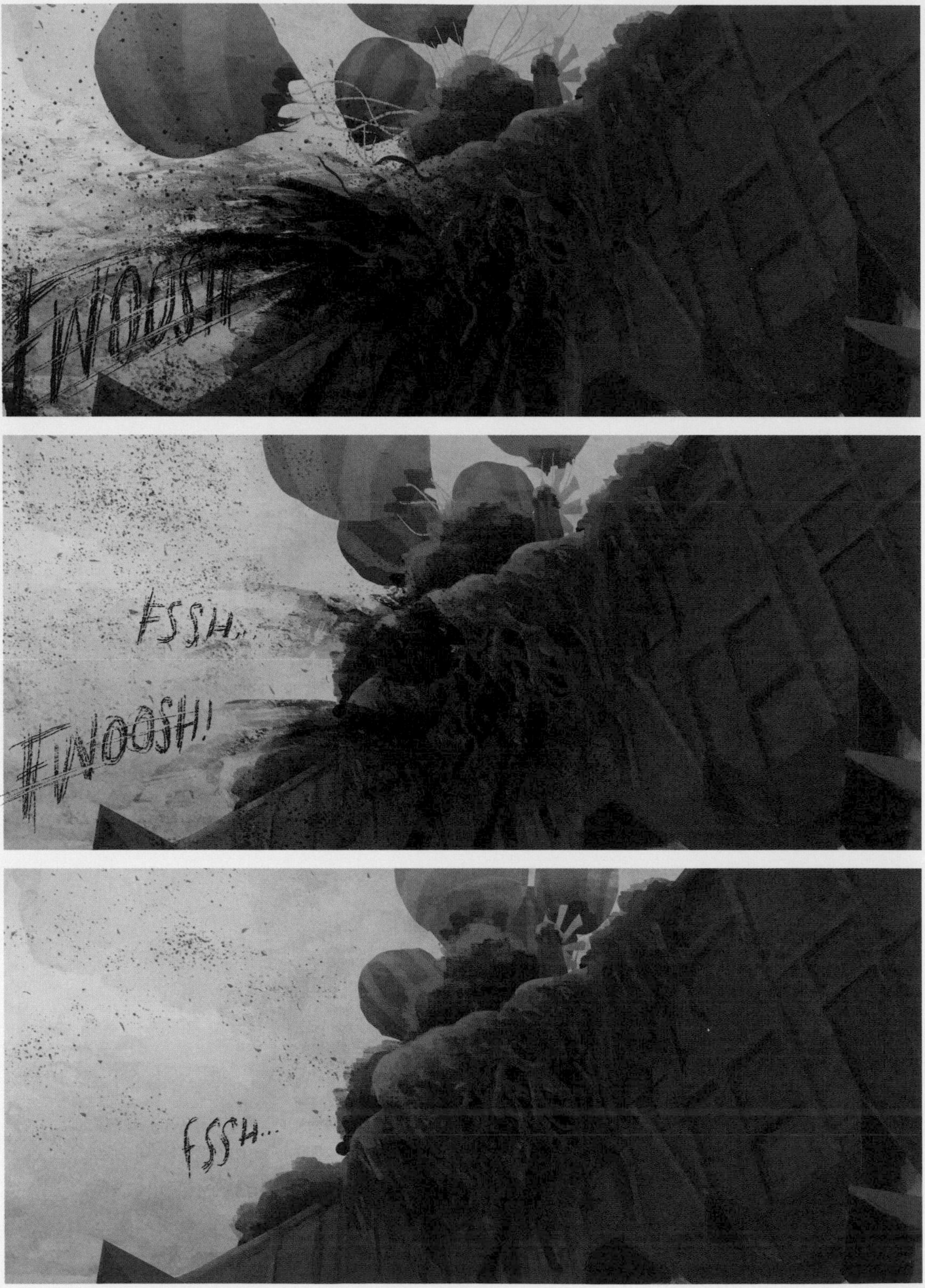
FWOOSH!
FSSH...
FWOOSH!
FSSH...

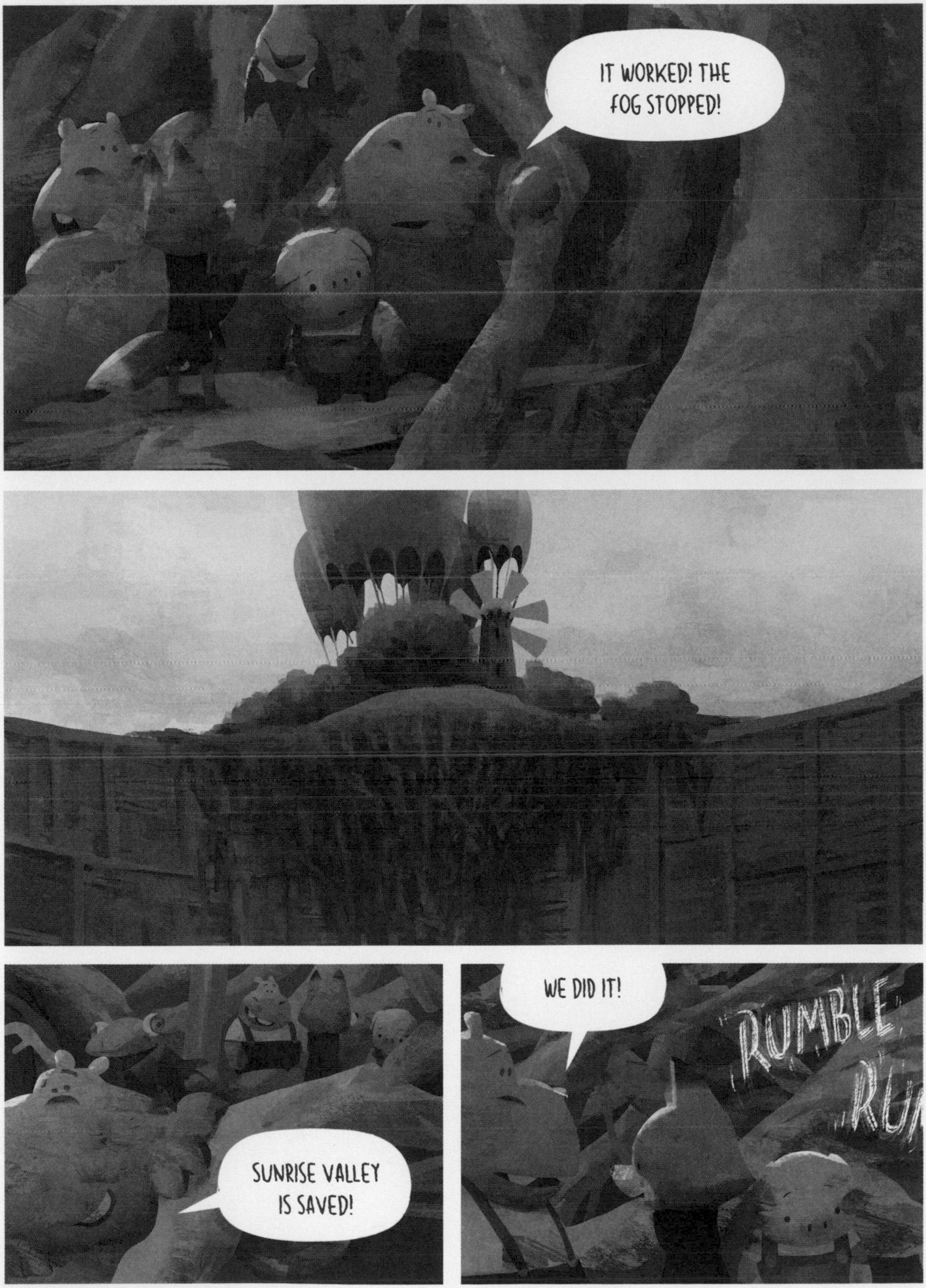
IT WORKED! THE FOG STOPPED!
SUNRISE VALLEY IS SAVED!
WE DID IT!
RUMBLE

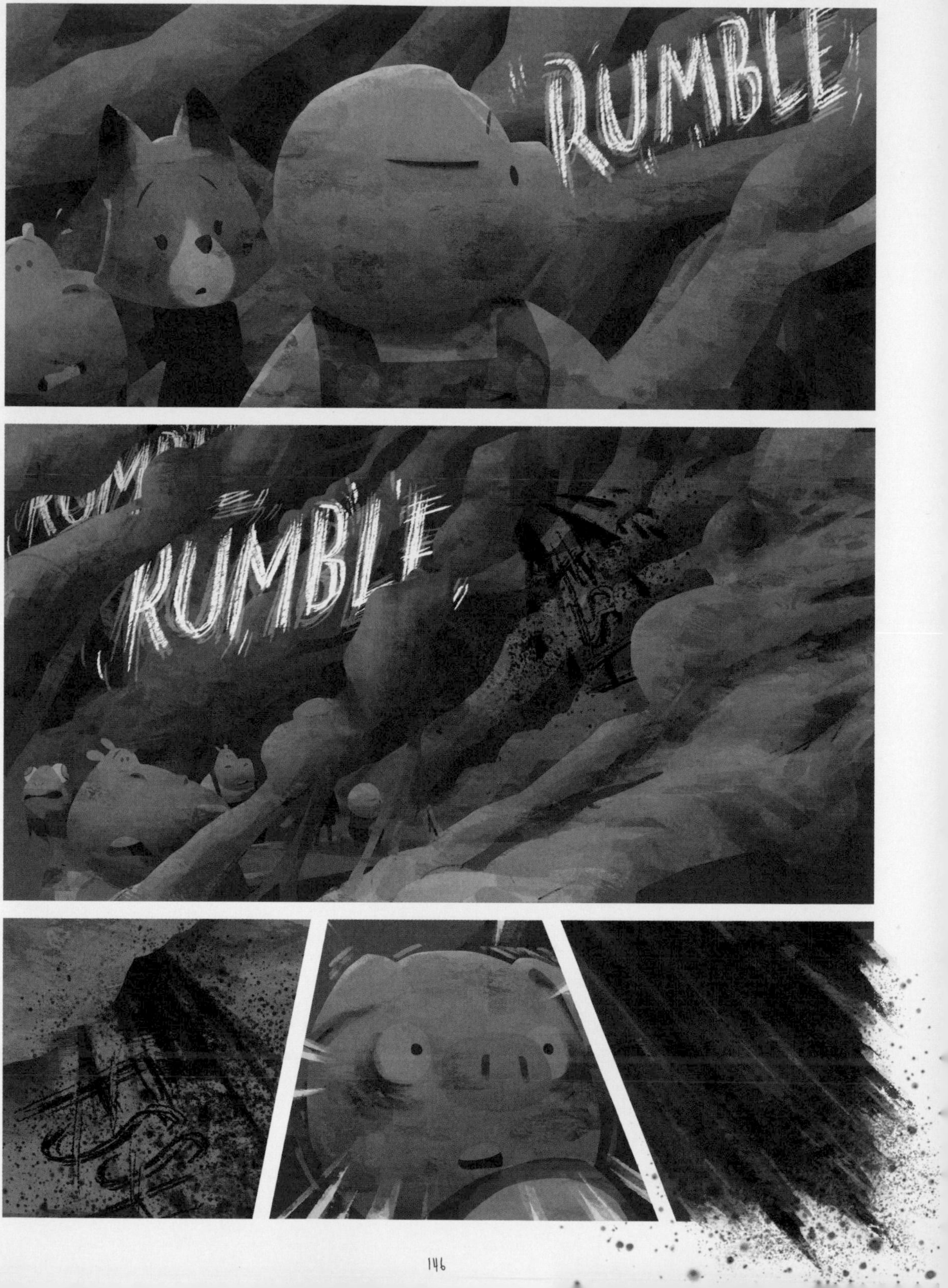
RUMBLE
RUMBLE

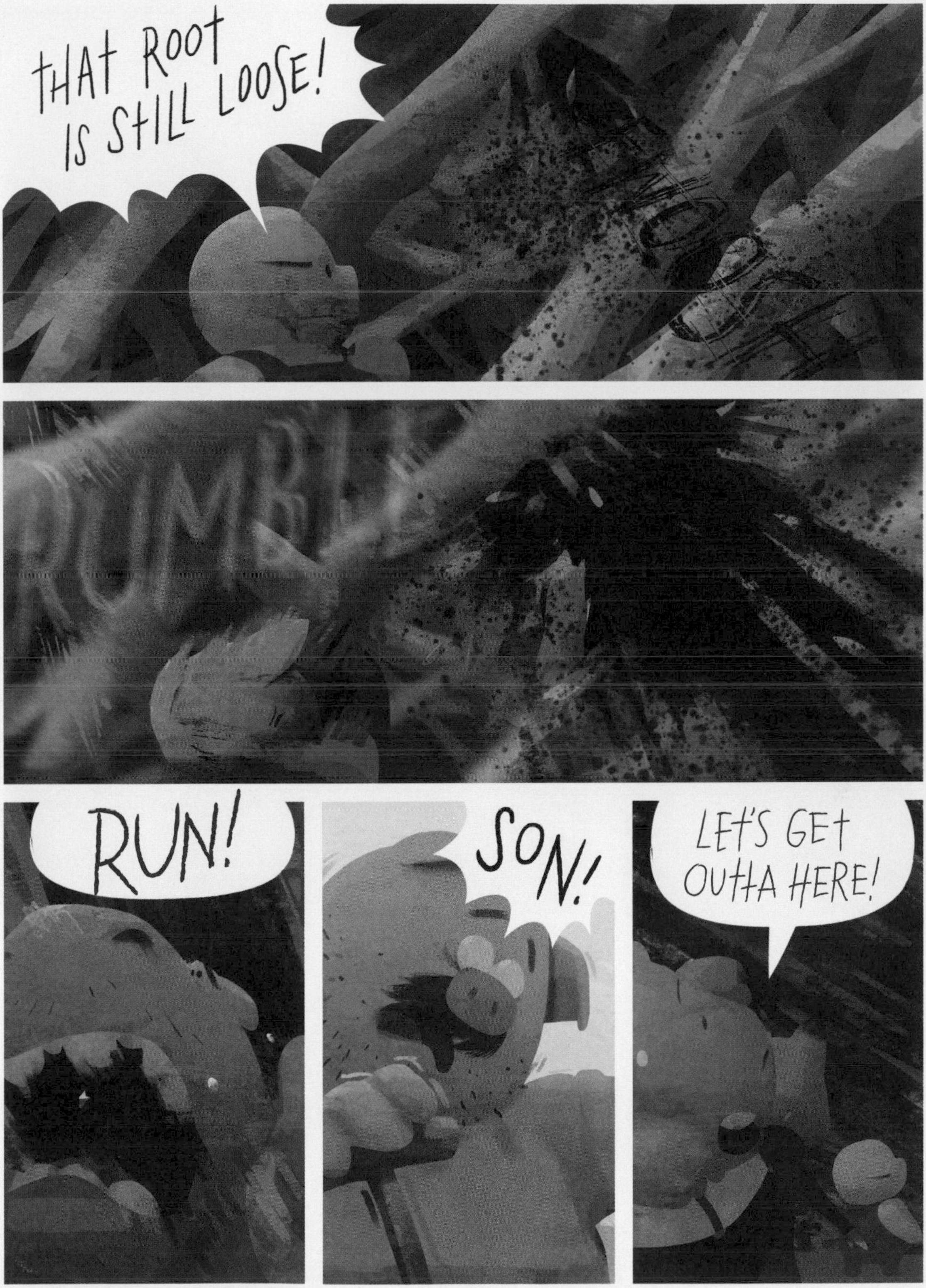
THAT ROOT IS STILL LOOSE!
RUN!
SON!
LET'S GET OUTTA HERE!

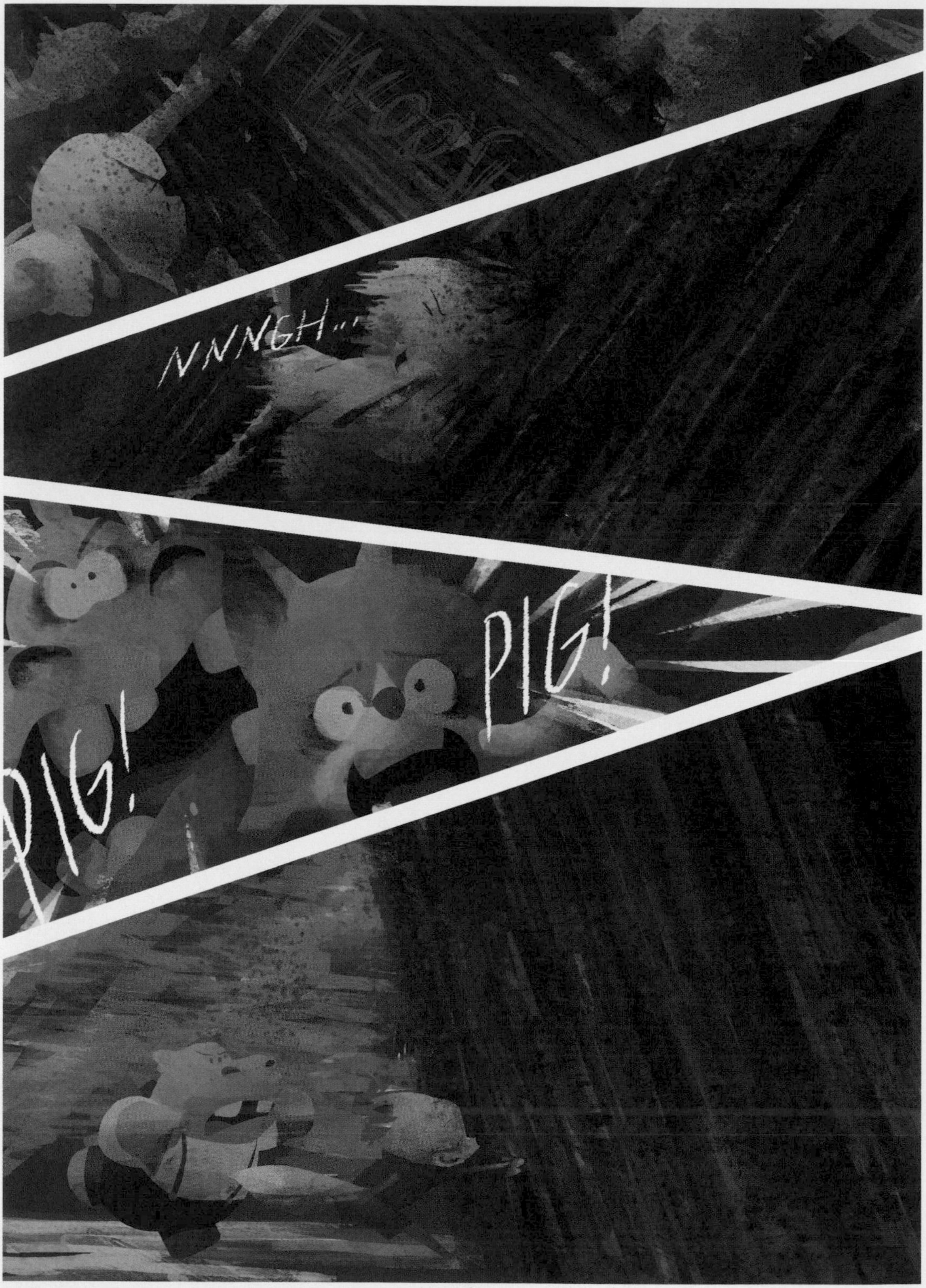
NNNGH...
PIG!
PIG!

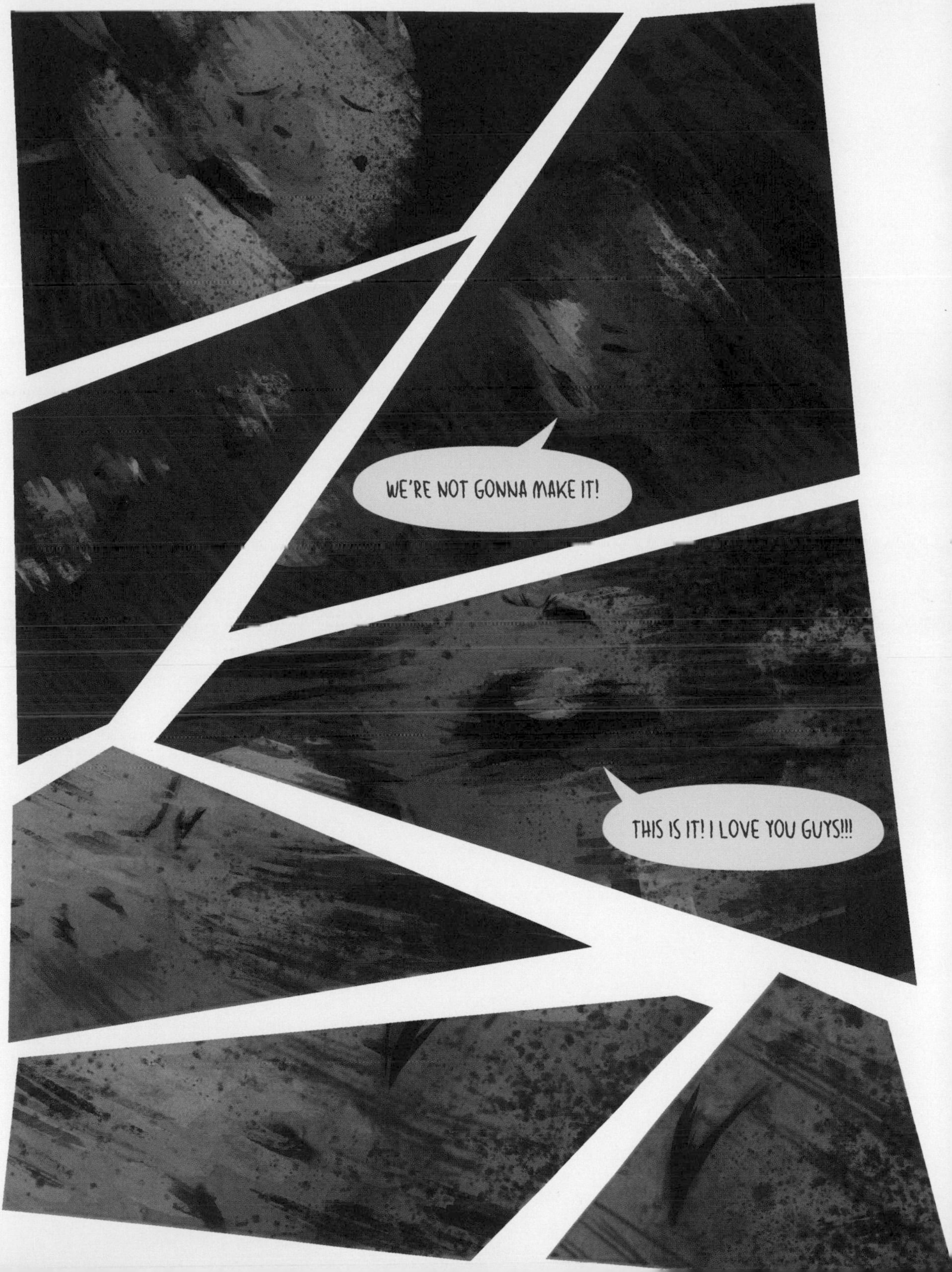
WE'RE NOT GONNA MAKE IT!
THIS IS IT! I LOVE YOU GUYS!!!

FWOOSH

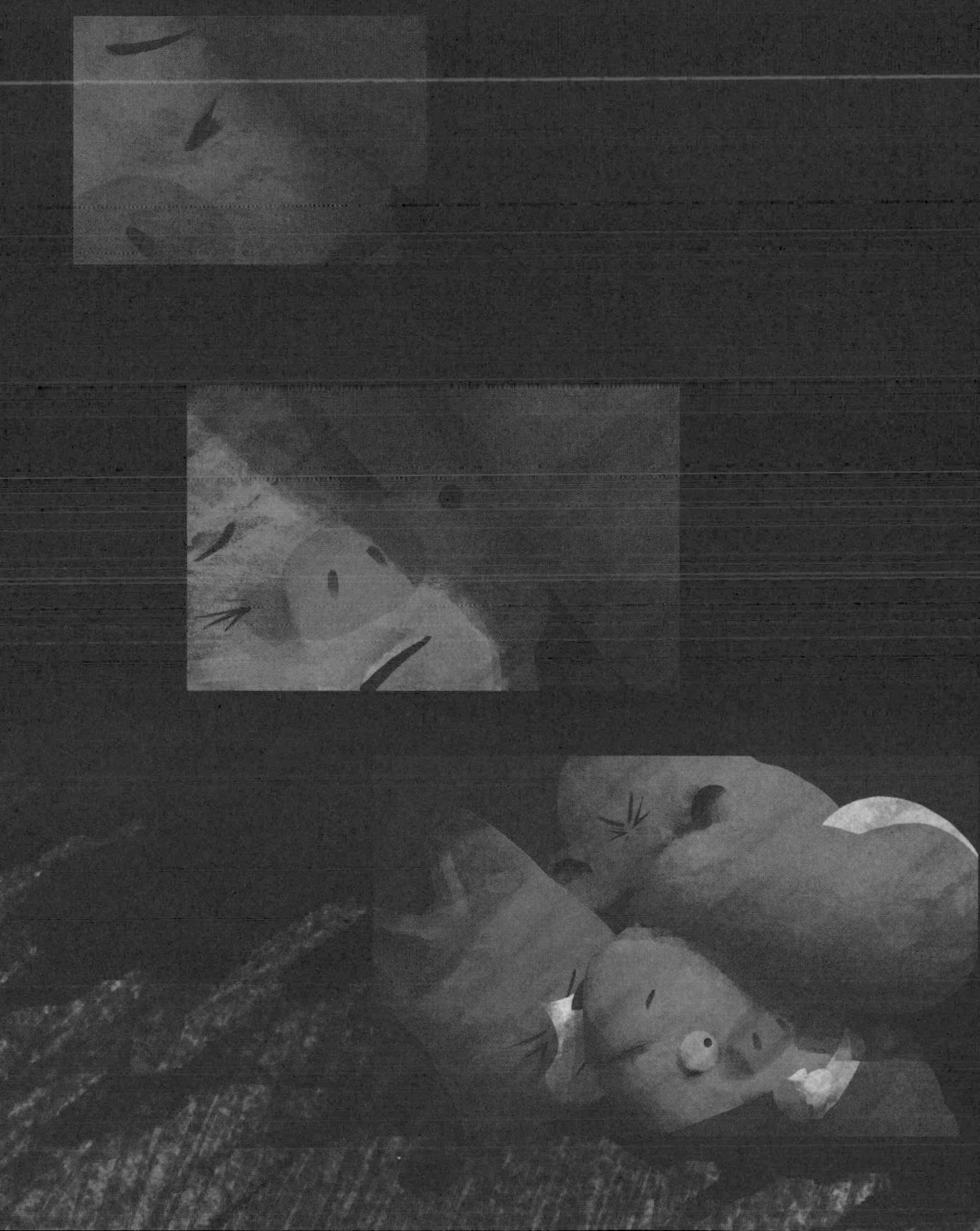

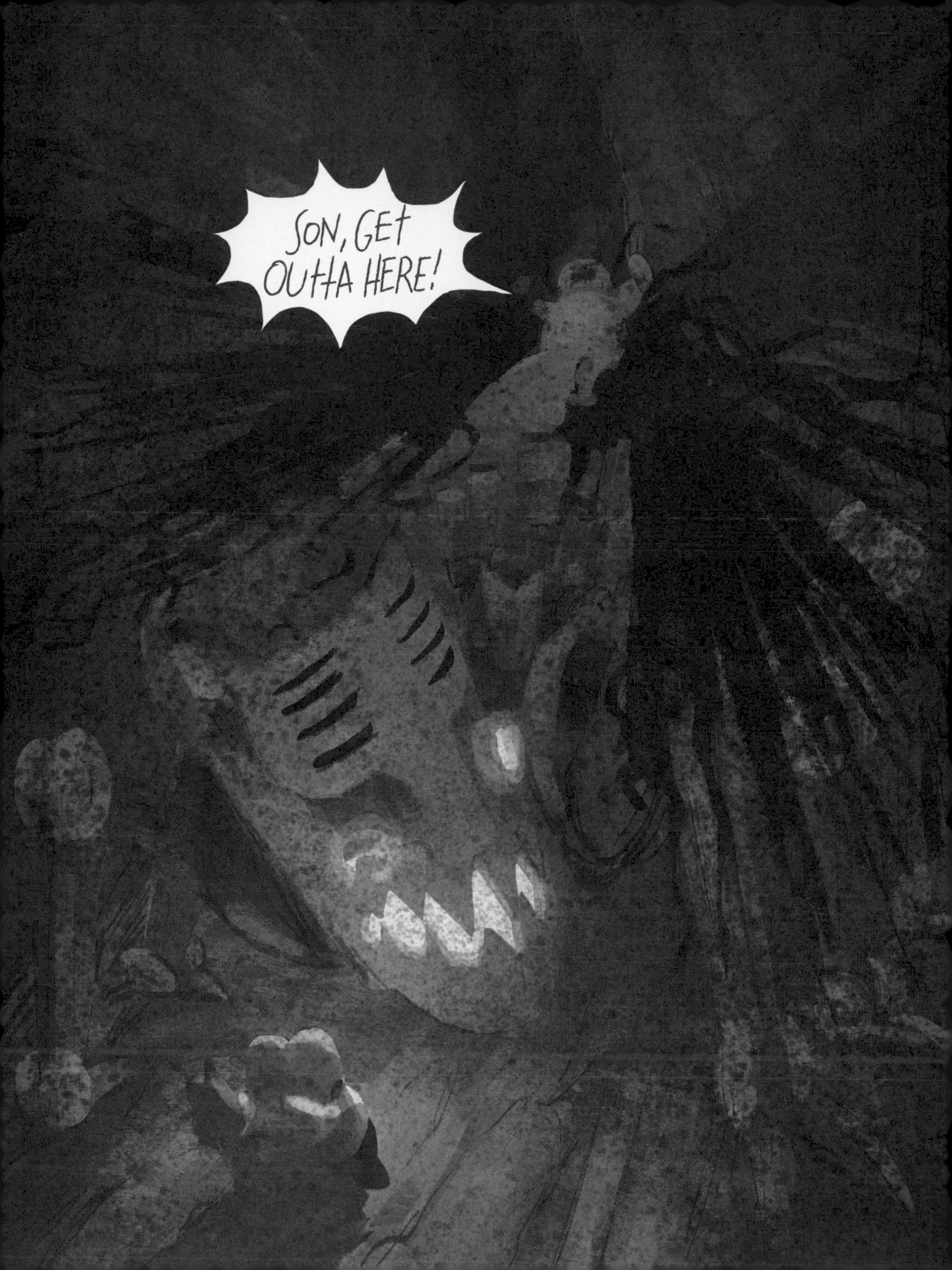
SON, GET OUTTA HERE!

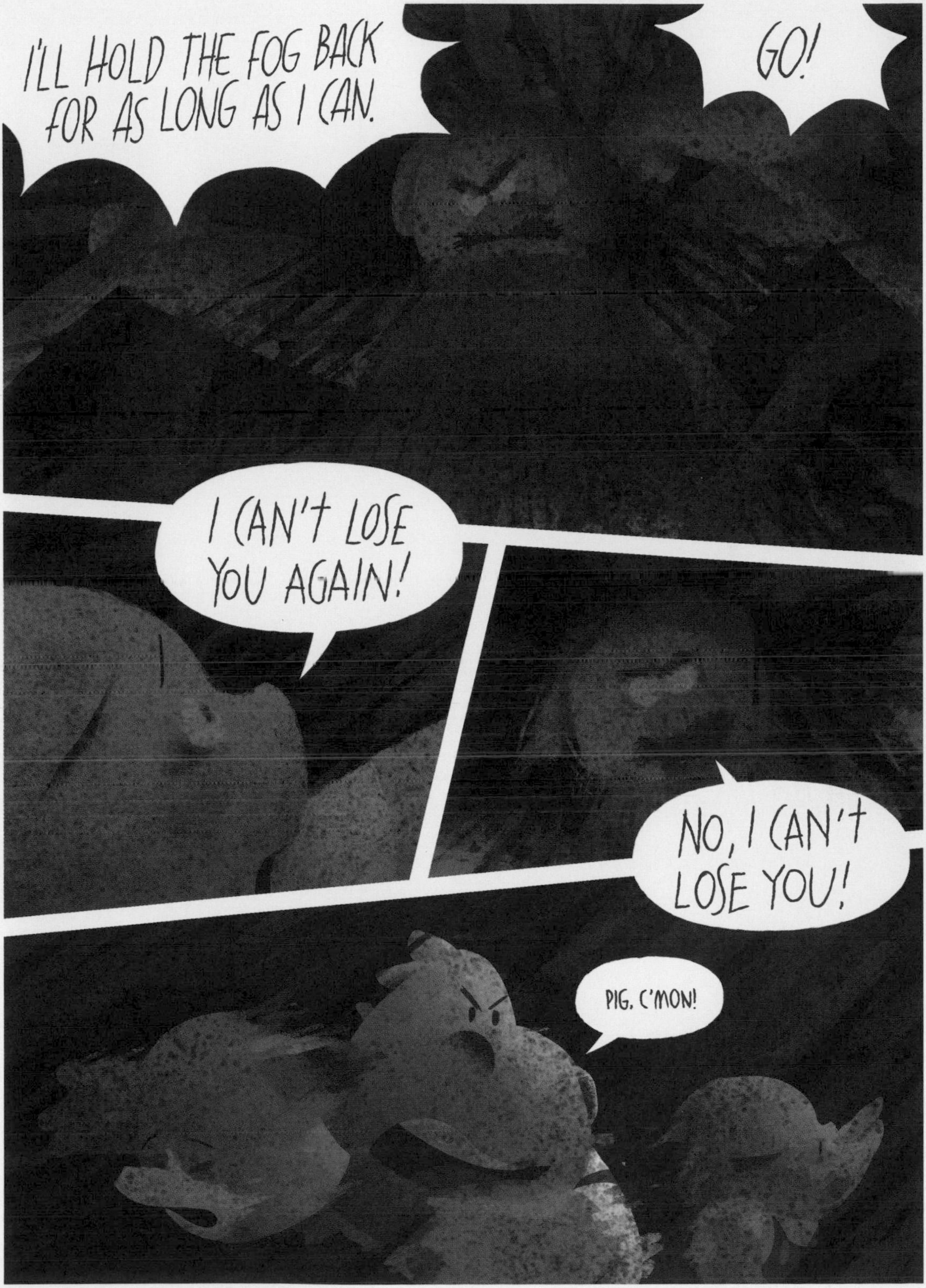
I'LL HOLD THE FOG BACK FOR AS LONG AS I CAN.
GO!
I CAN'T LOSE YOU AGAIN!
NO, I CAN'T LOSE YOU!
PIG. C'MON!

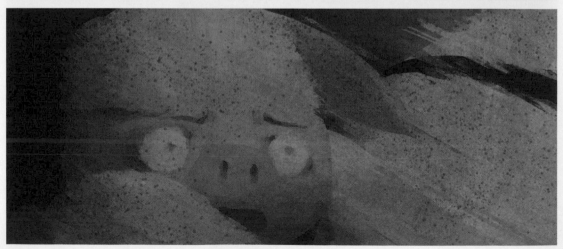

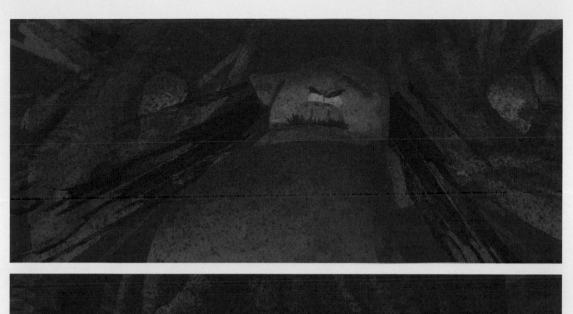

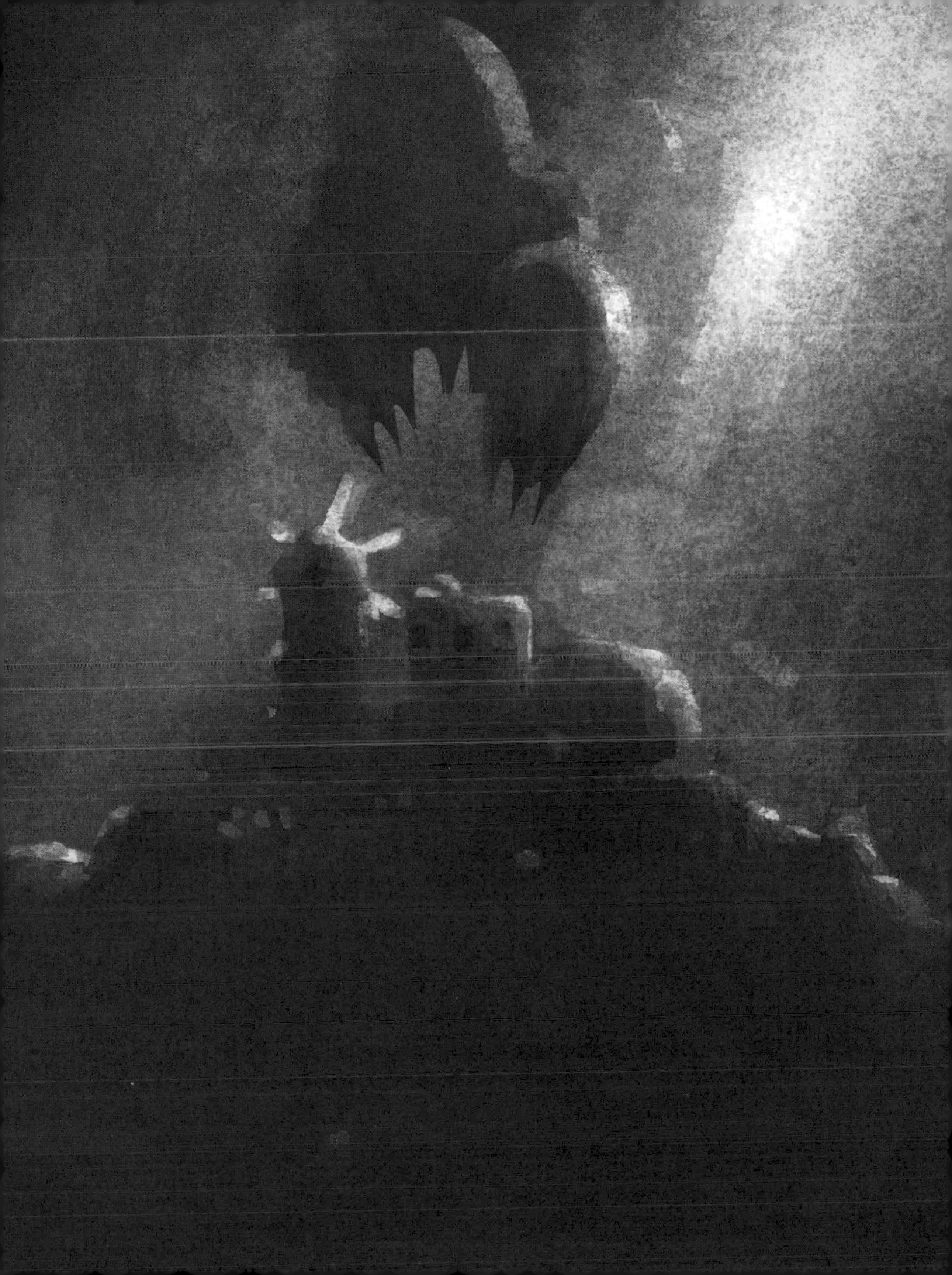

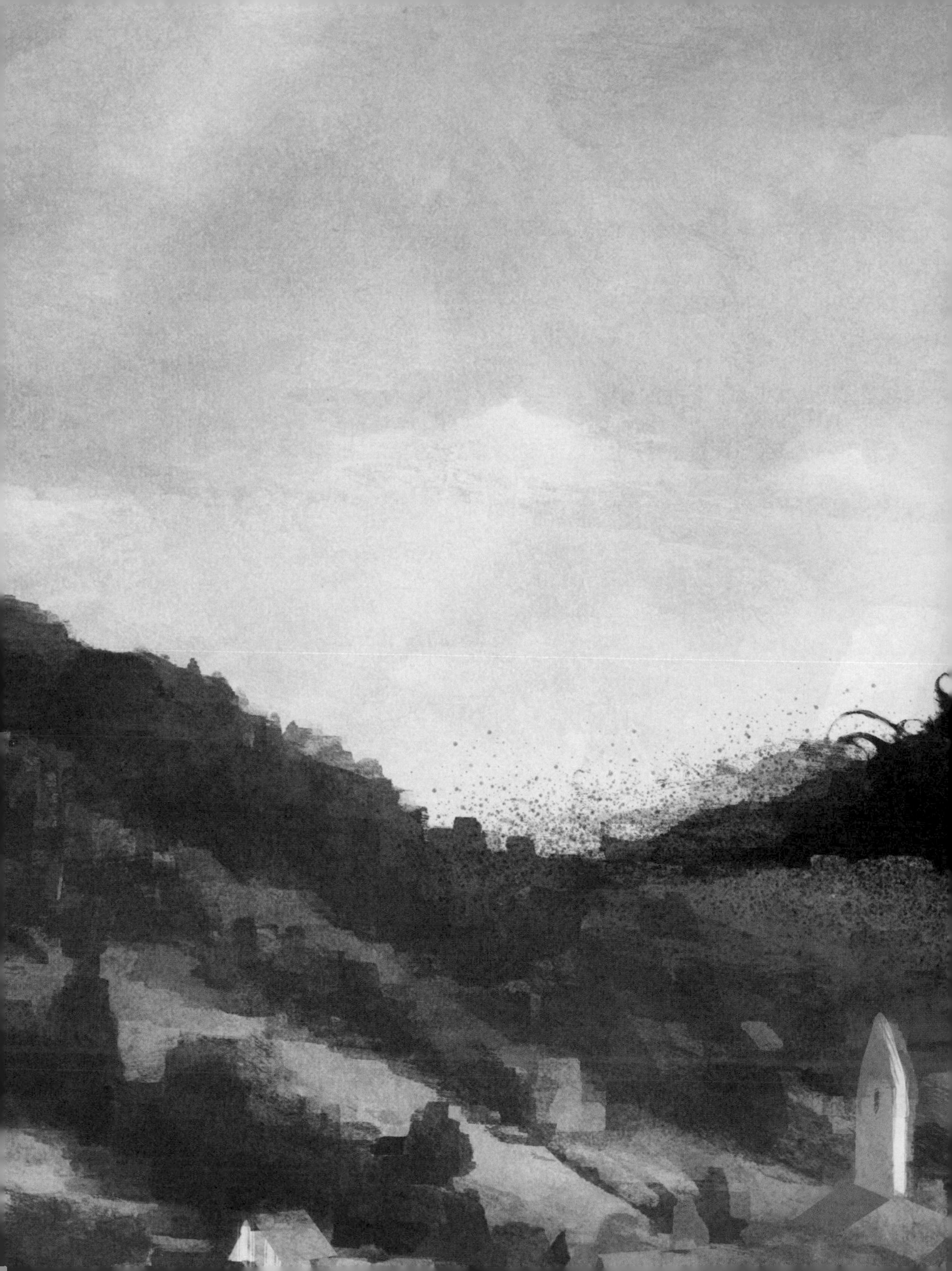

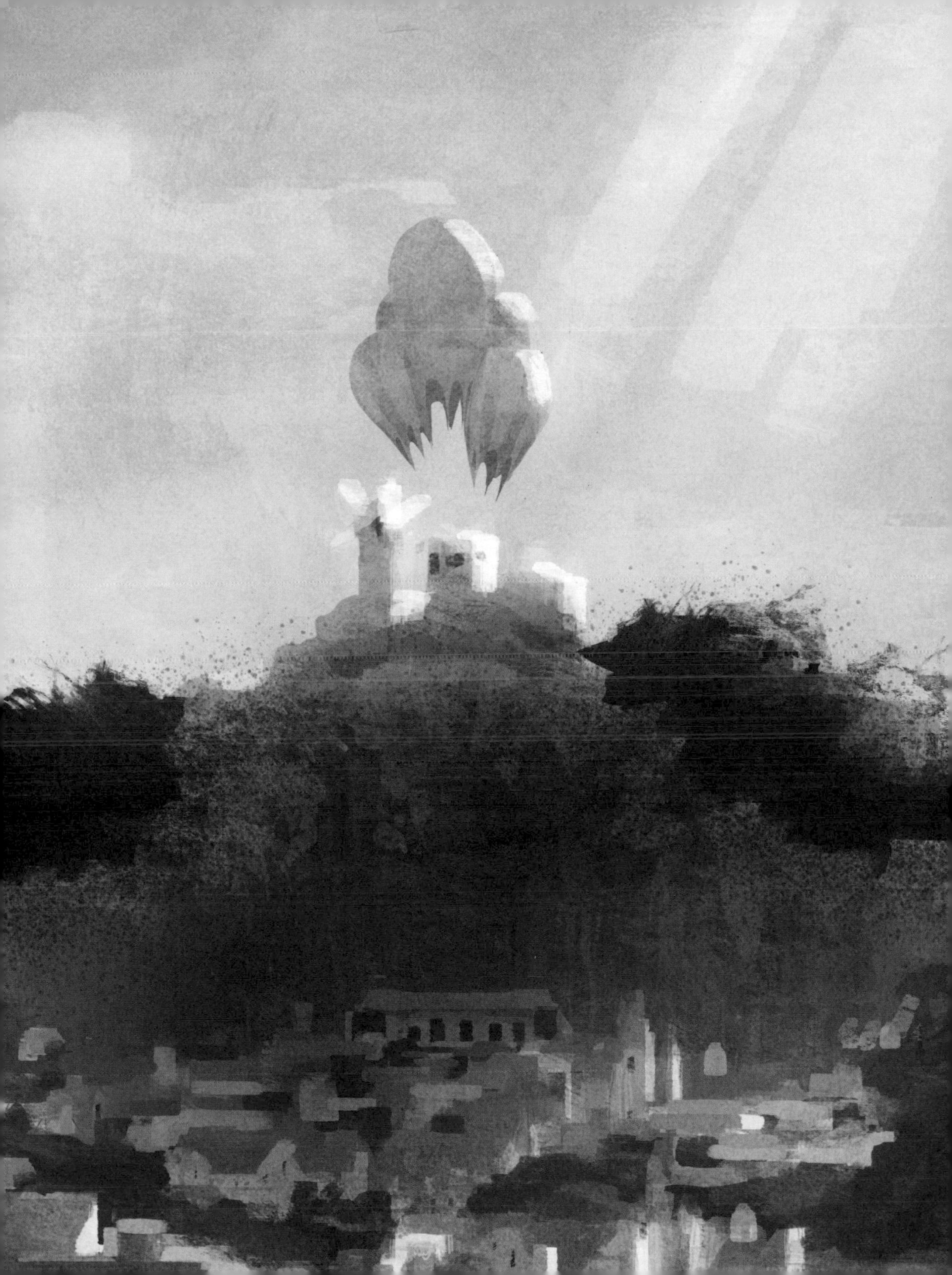

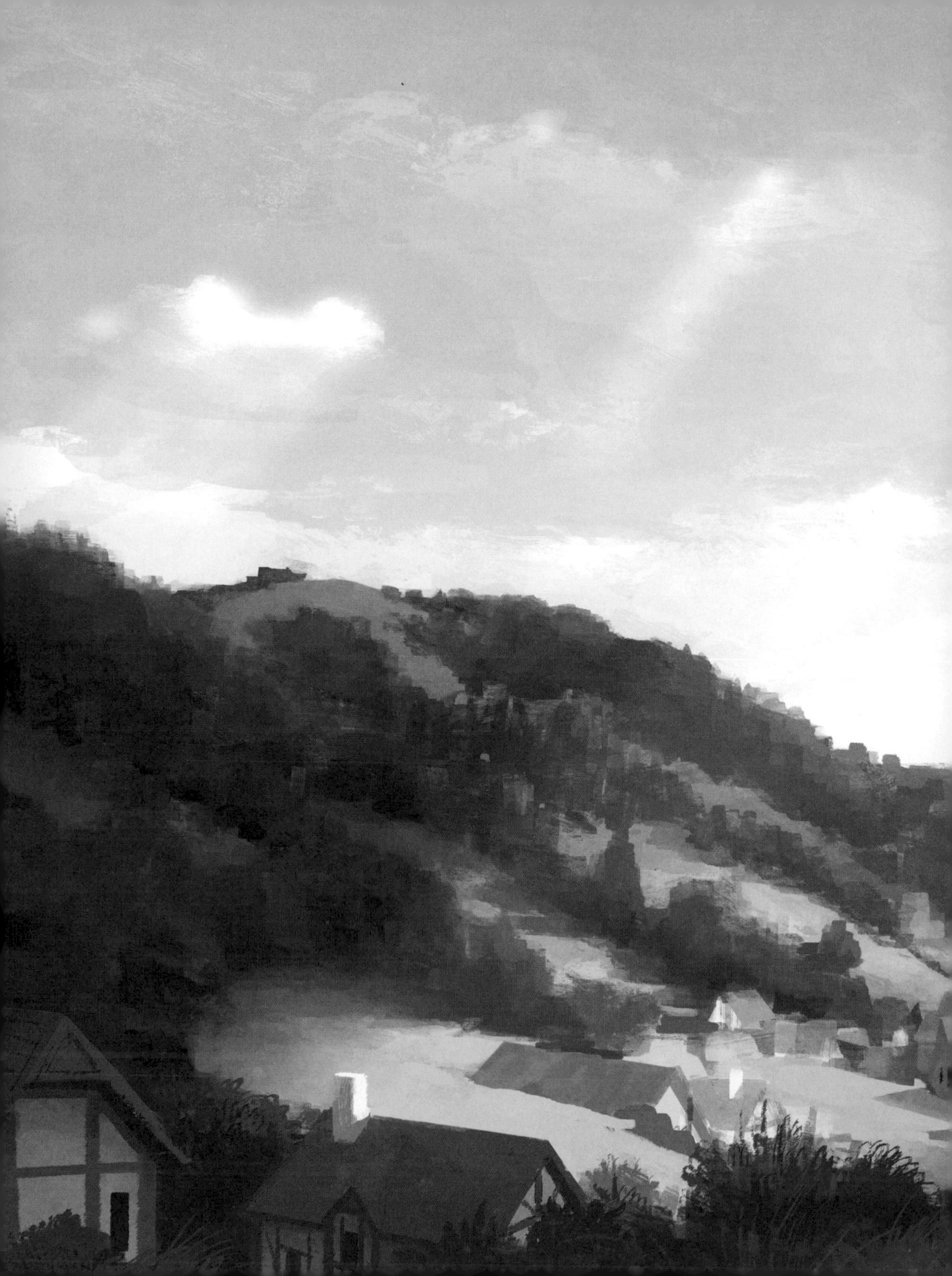

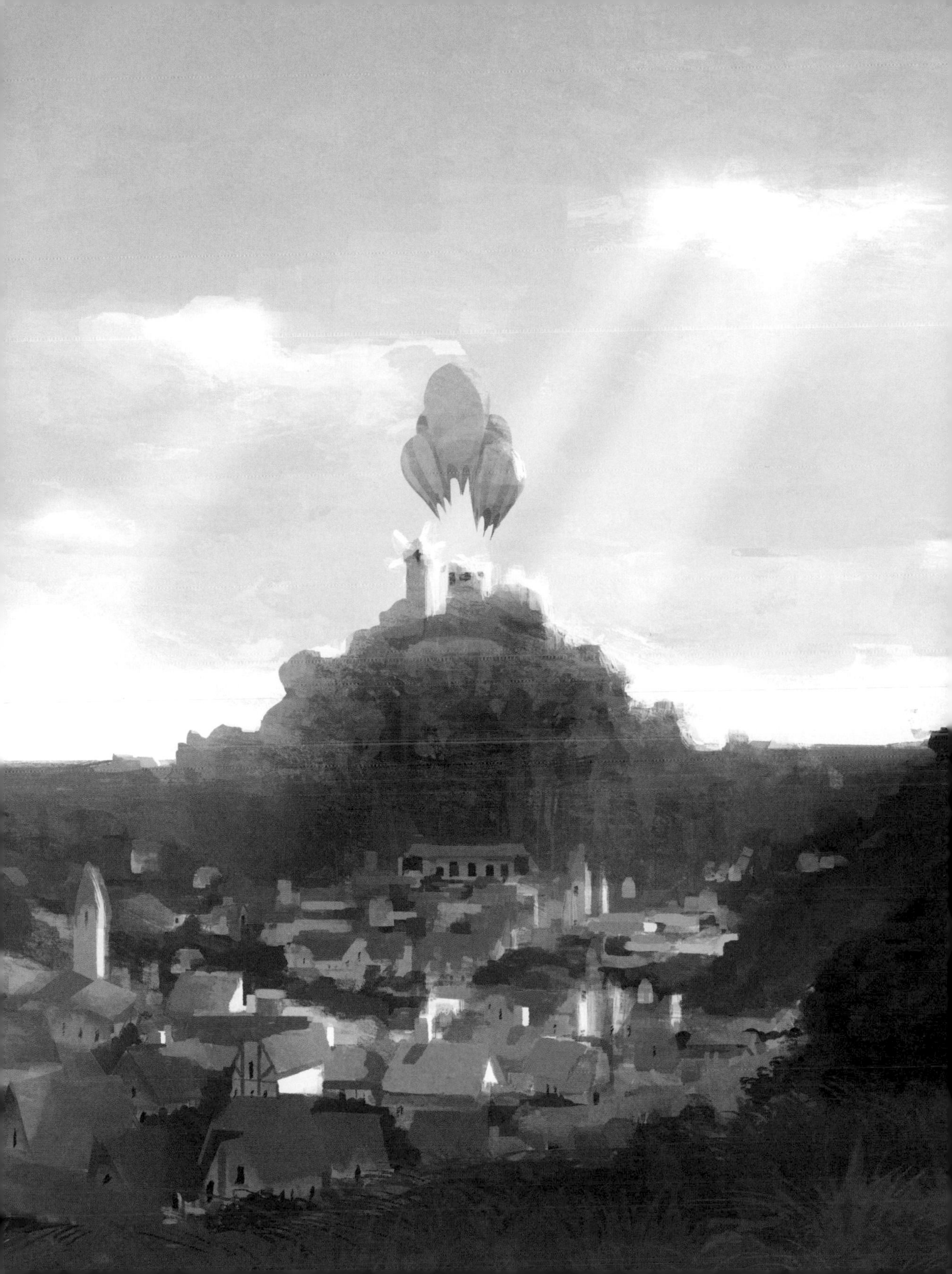

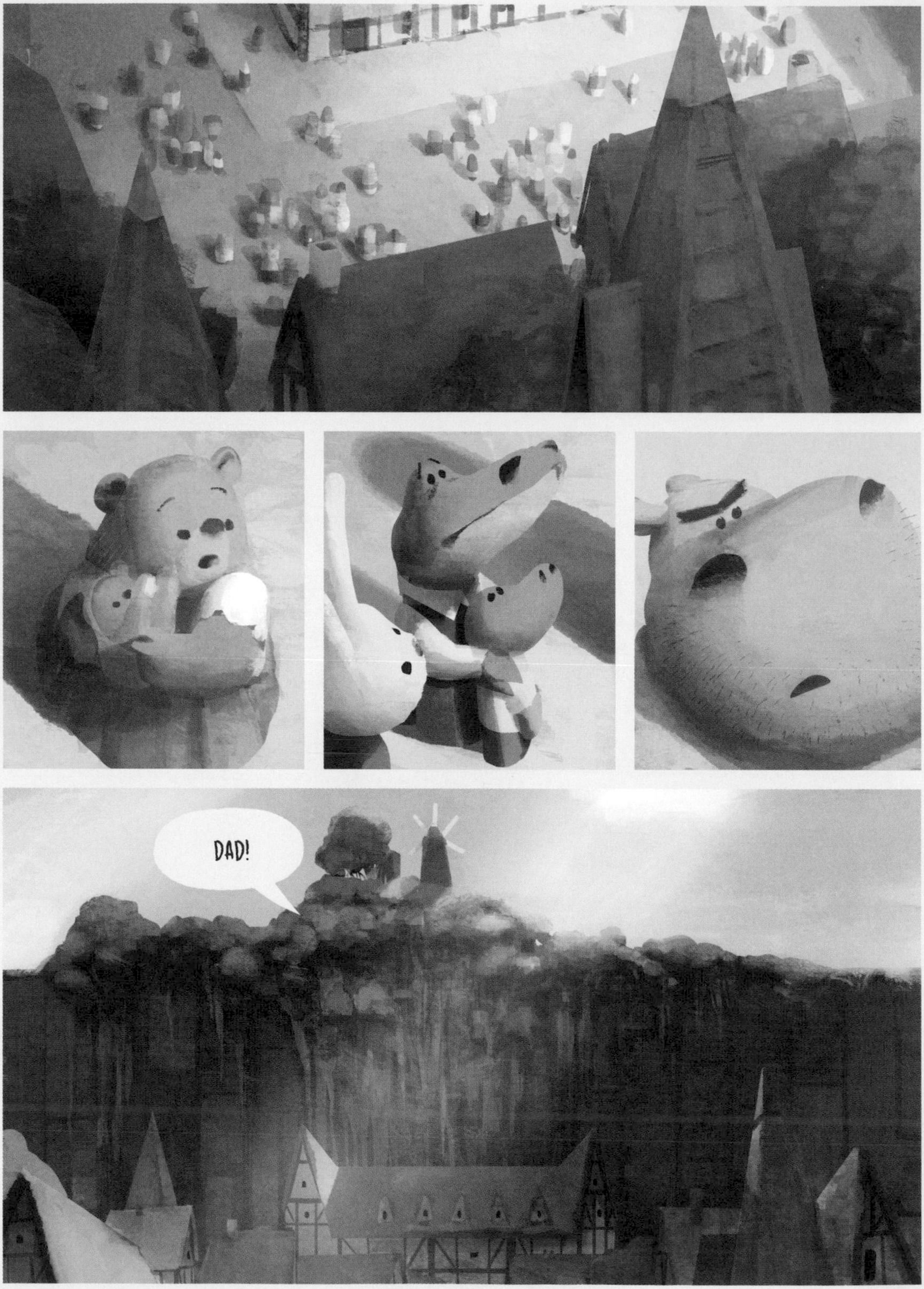
DAD!

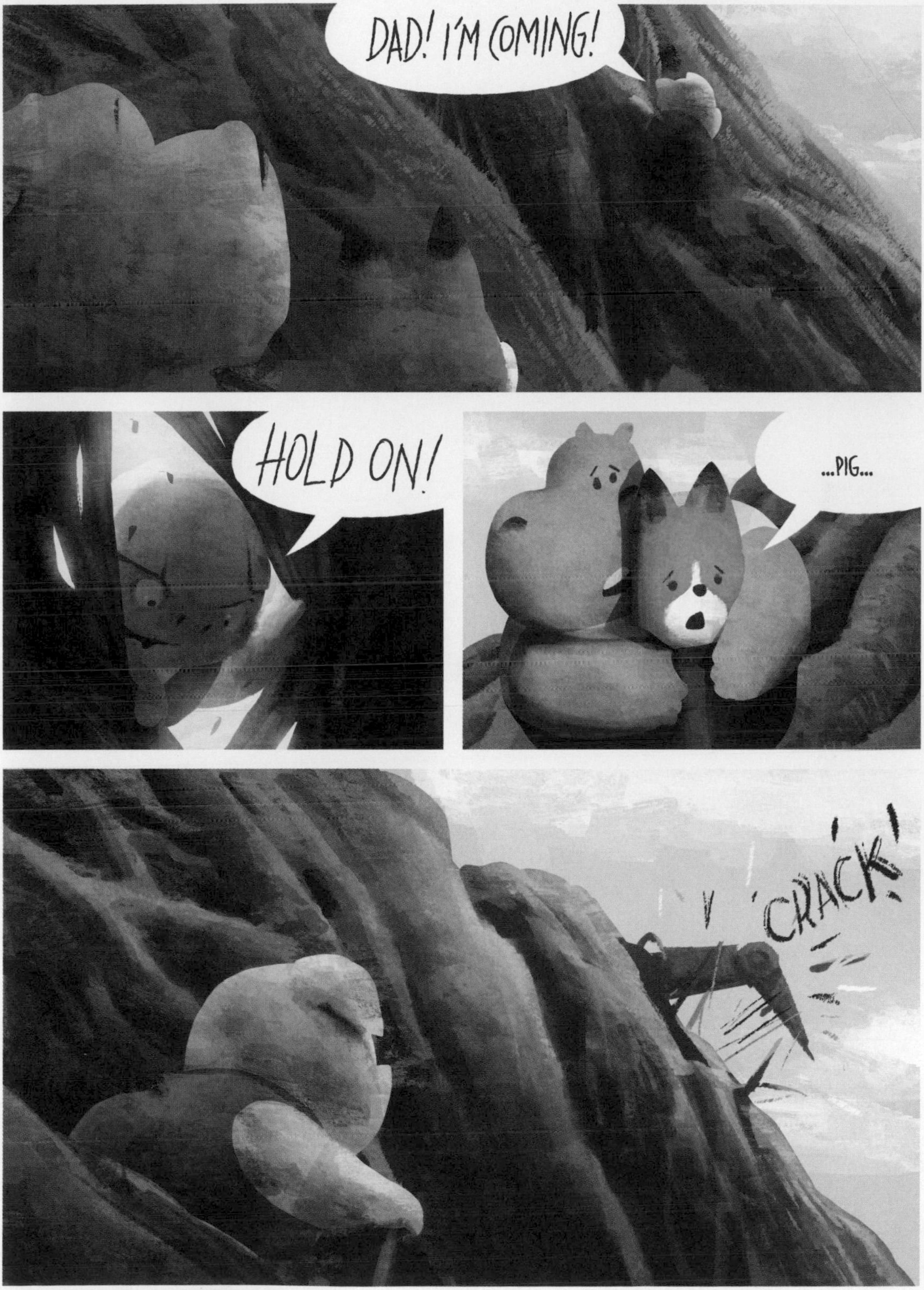
DAD! I'M COMING!
HOLD ON!
...PIG...
CRACK!

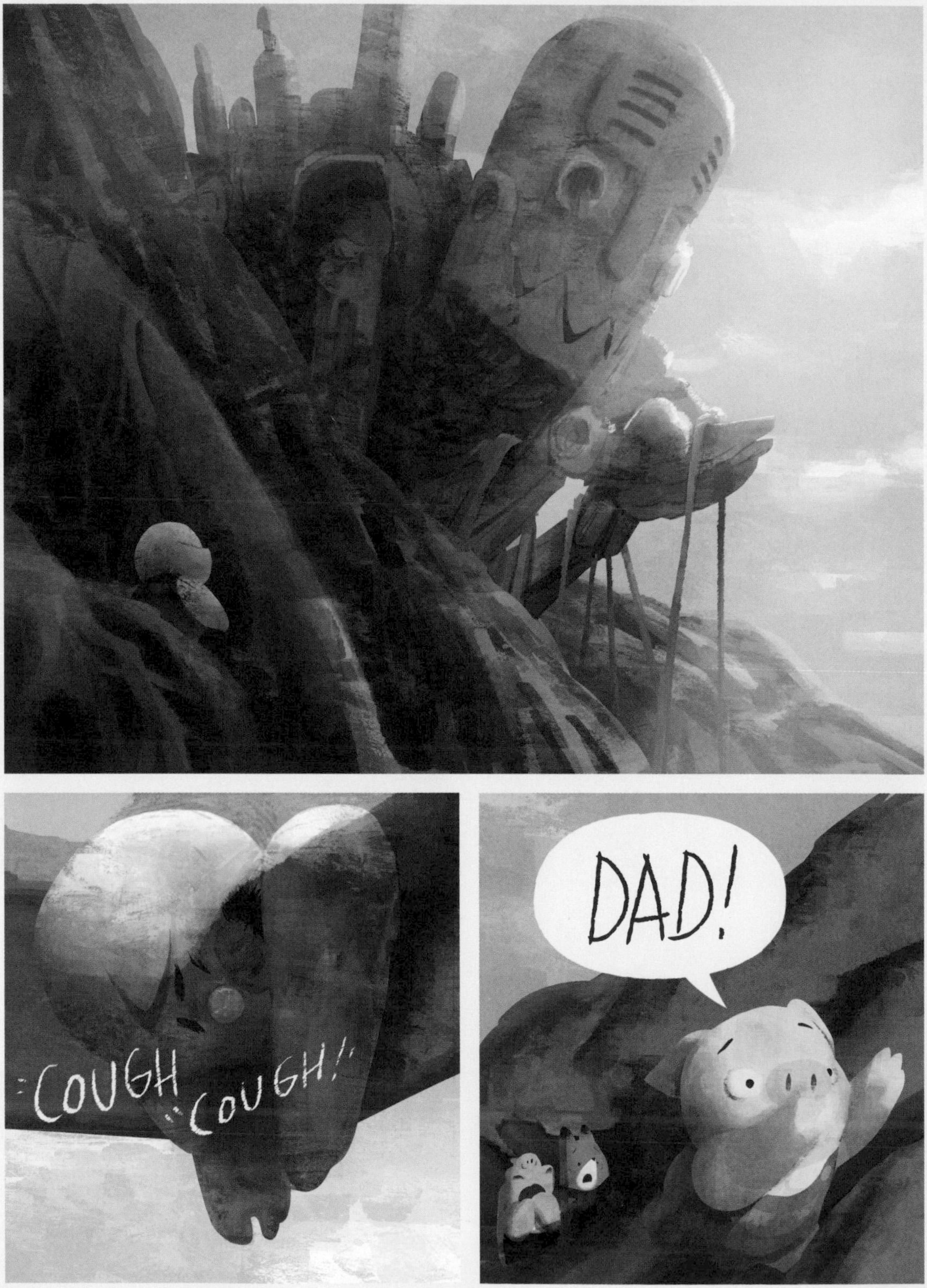
COUGH! COUGH!
DAD!

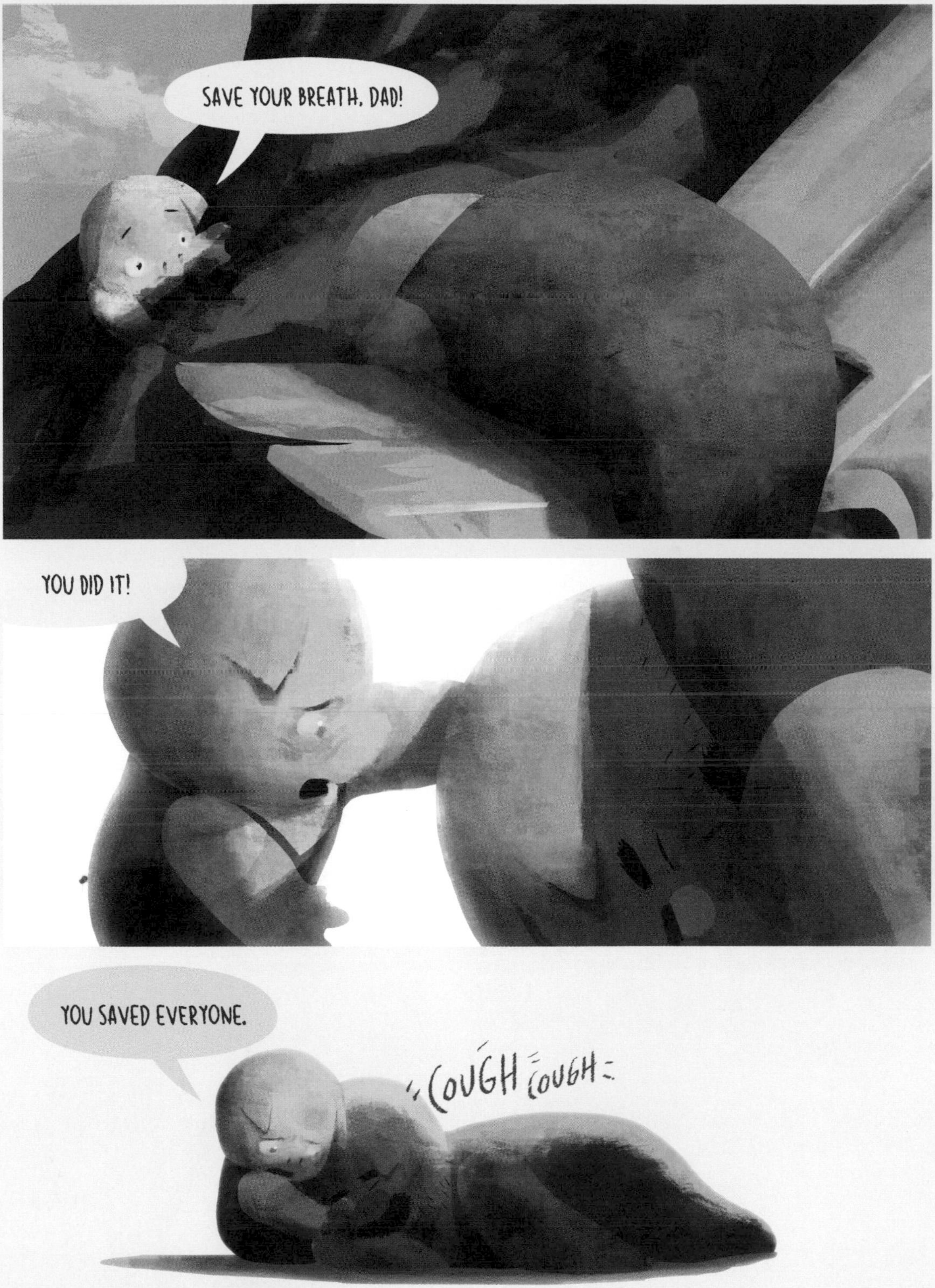
SAVE YOUR BREATH, DAD!
YOU DID IT!
YOU SAVED EVERYONE.
COUGH COUGH

NO, SON...

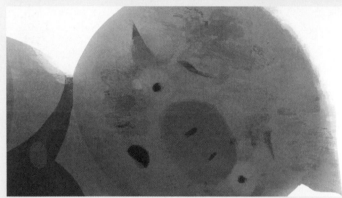

...YOU DID IT.

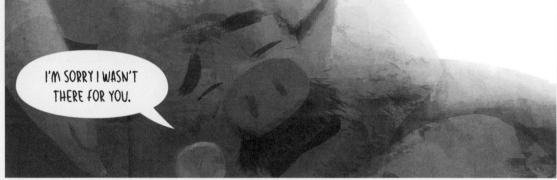

I'M SORRY I WASN'T THERE FOR YOU.

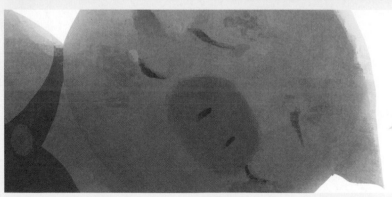

IT'S OKAY.

170

I AM PROUD TO BE YOUR SON.

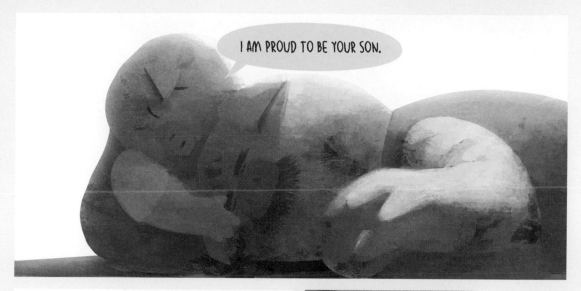

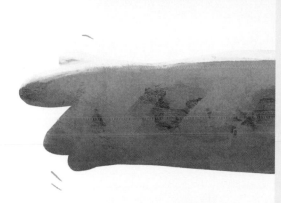

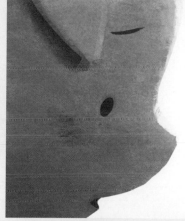

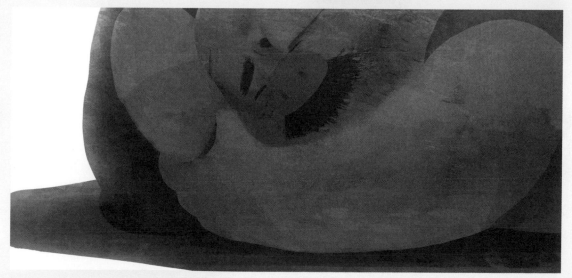

I...I AM...

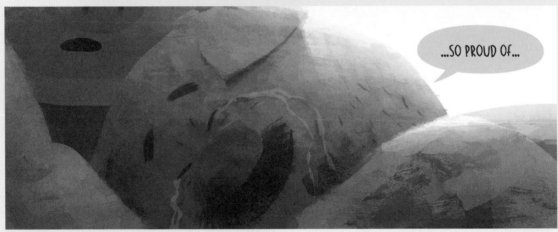

...SO PROUD OF...

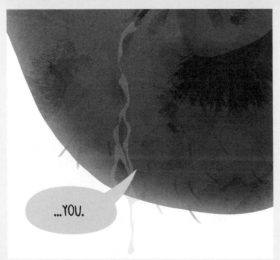

...YOU.

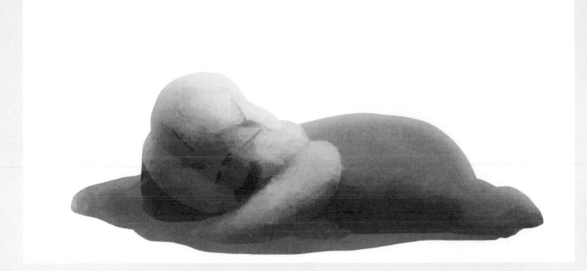

NO...

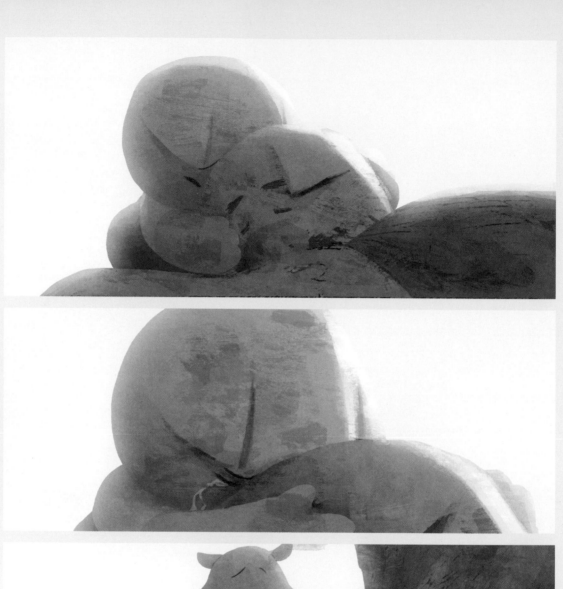

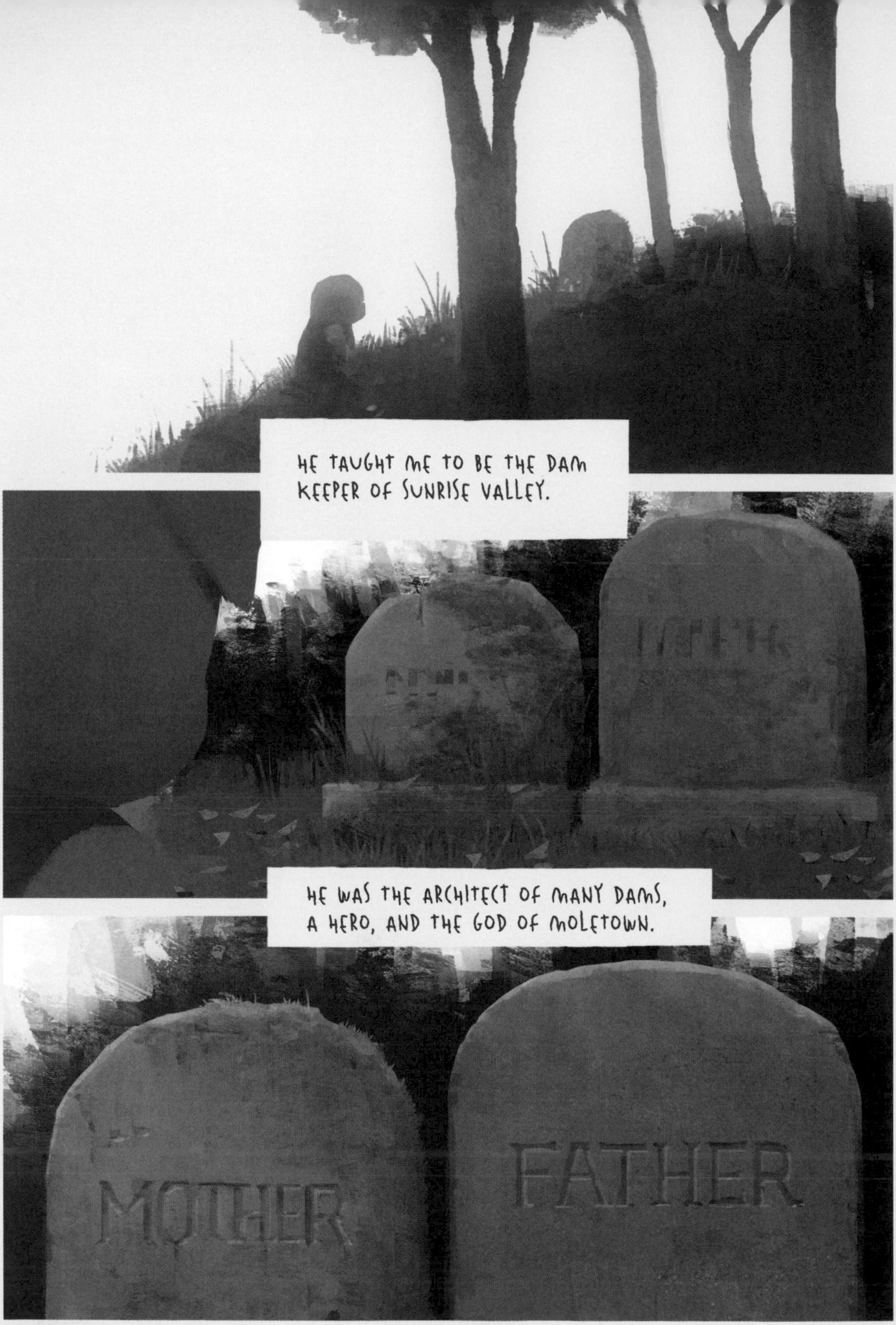
HE TAUGHT ME TO BE THE DAM KEEPER OF SUNRISE VALLEY.
HE WAS THE ARCHITECT OF MANY DAMS, A HERO, AND THE GOD OF MOLETOWN.
MOTHER
FATHER

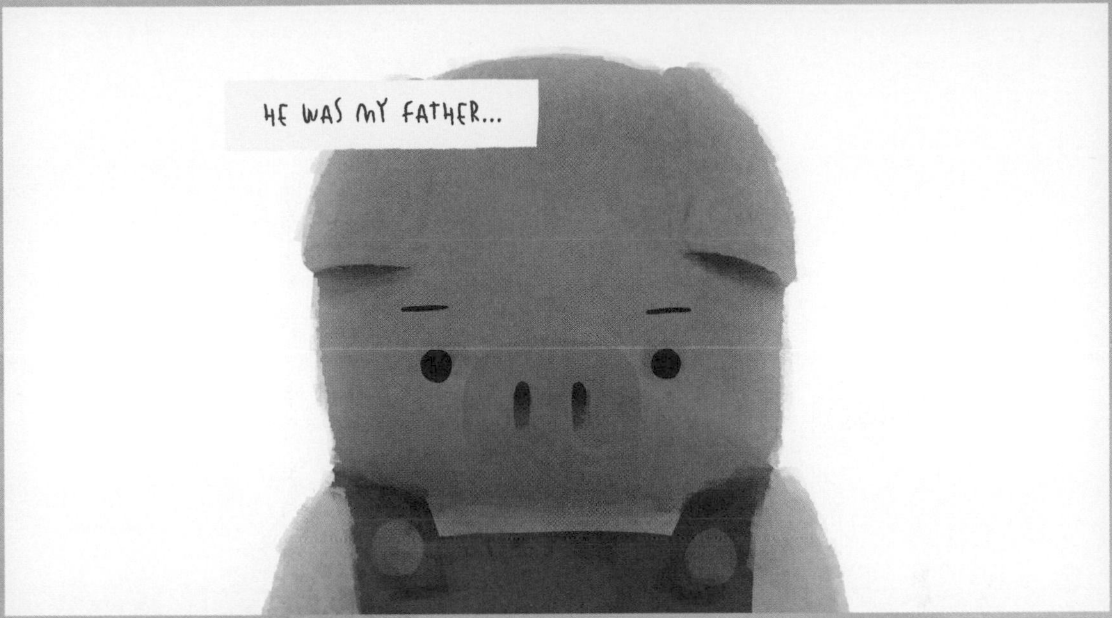
HE WAS MY FATHER...

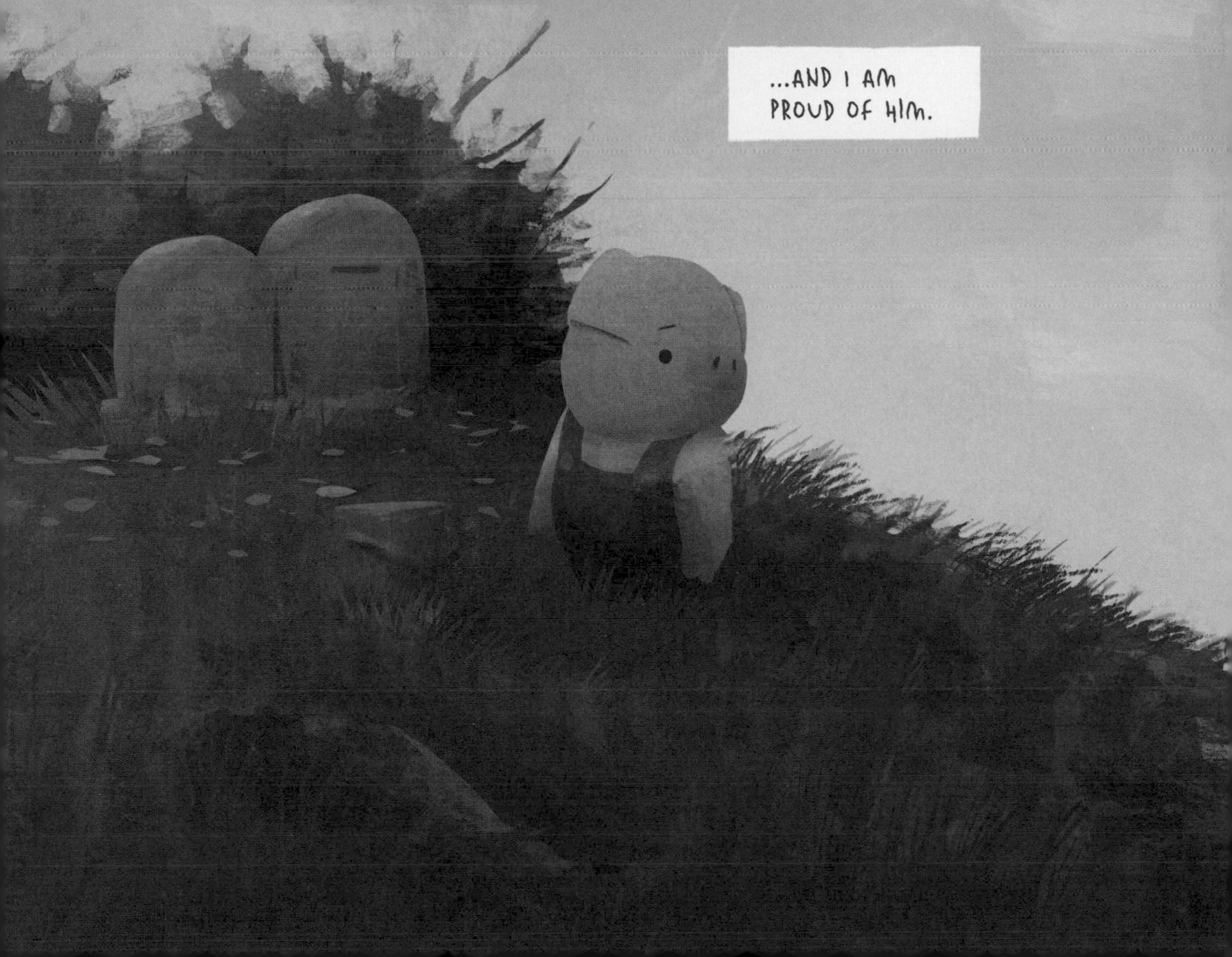
...AND I AM PROUD OF HIM.

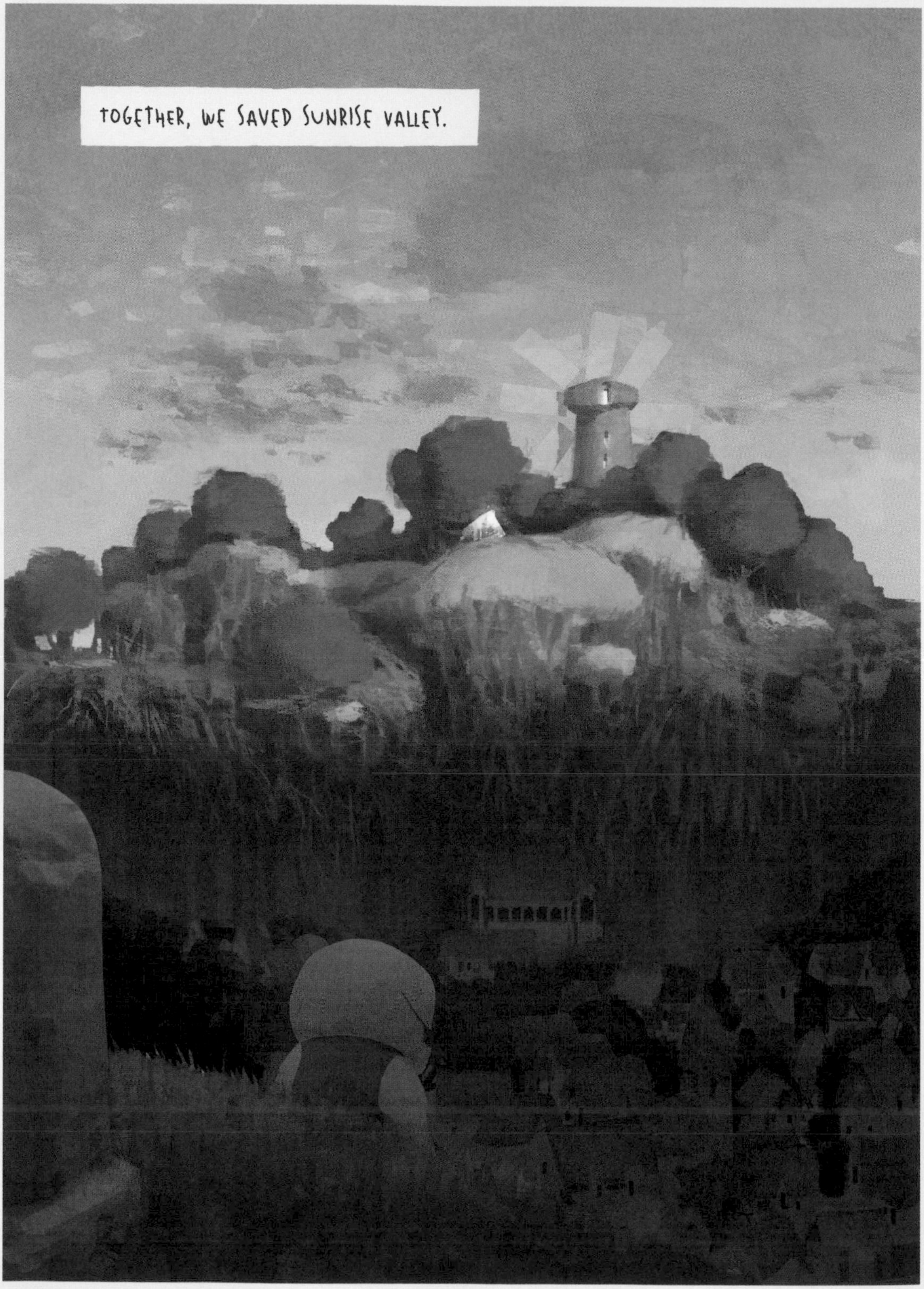
TOGETHER, WE SAVED SUNRISE VALLEY.

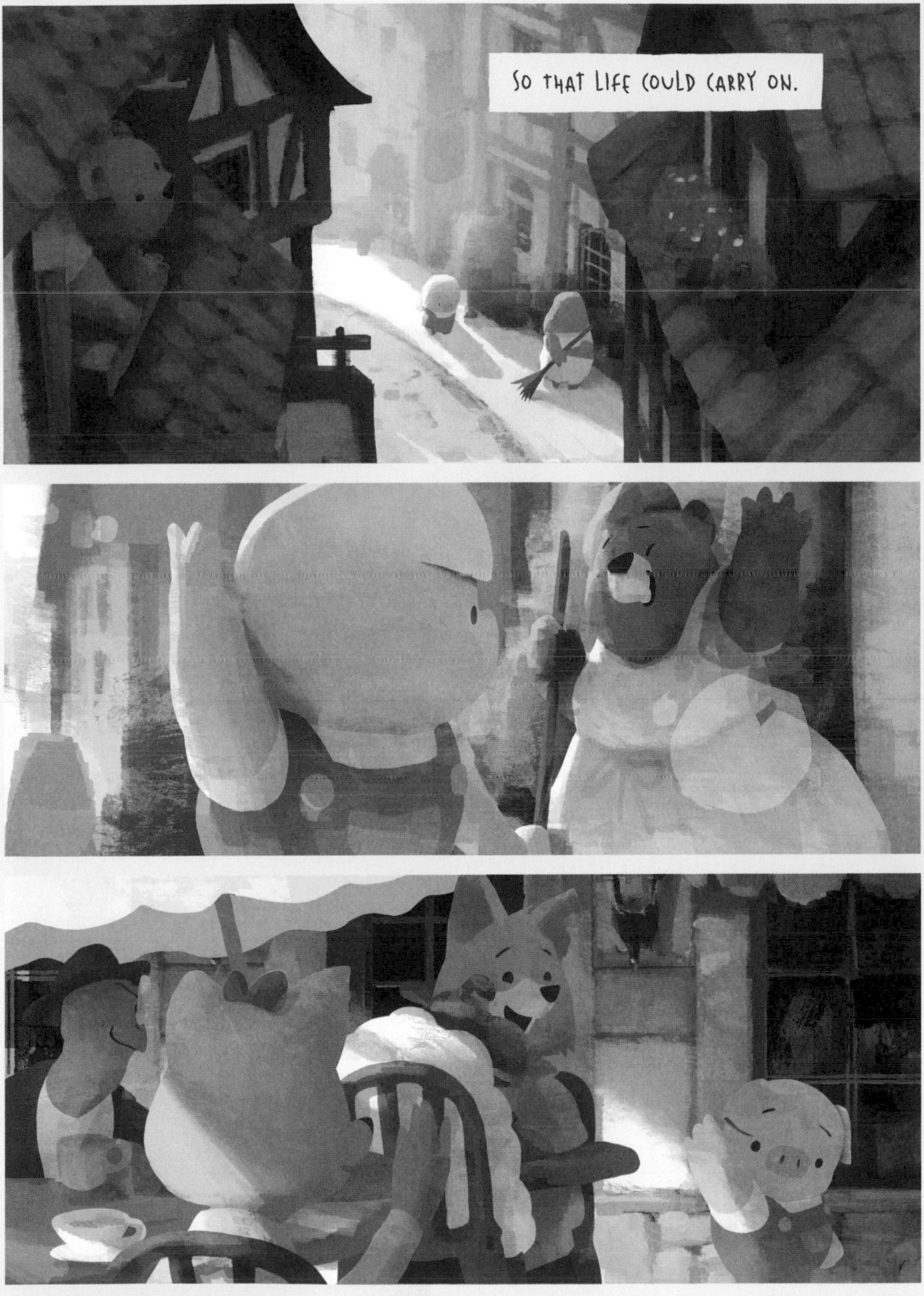
SO THAT LIFE COULD CARRY ON.

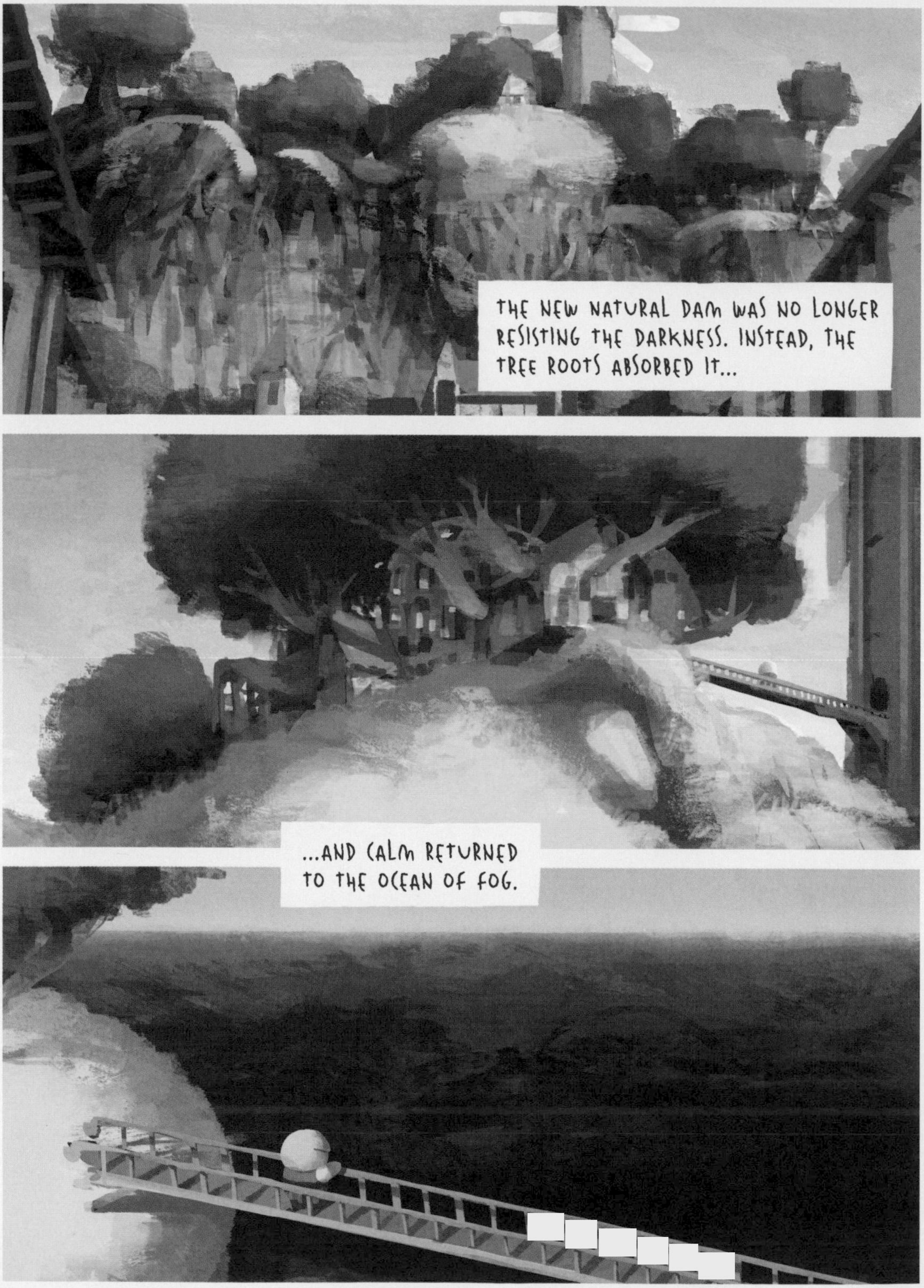
THE NEW NATURAL DAM WAS NO LONGER RESISTING THE DARKNESS. INSTEAD, THE TREE ROOTS ABSORBED IT...
...AND CALM RETURNED TO THE OCEAN OF FOG.

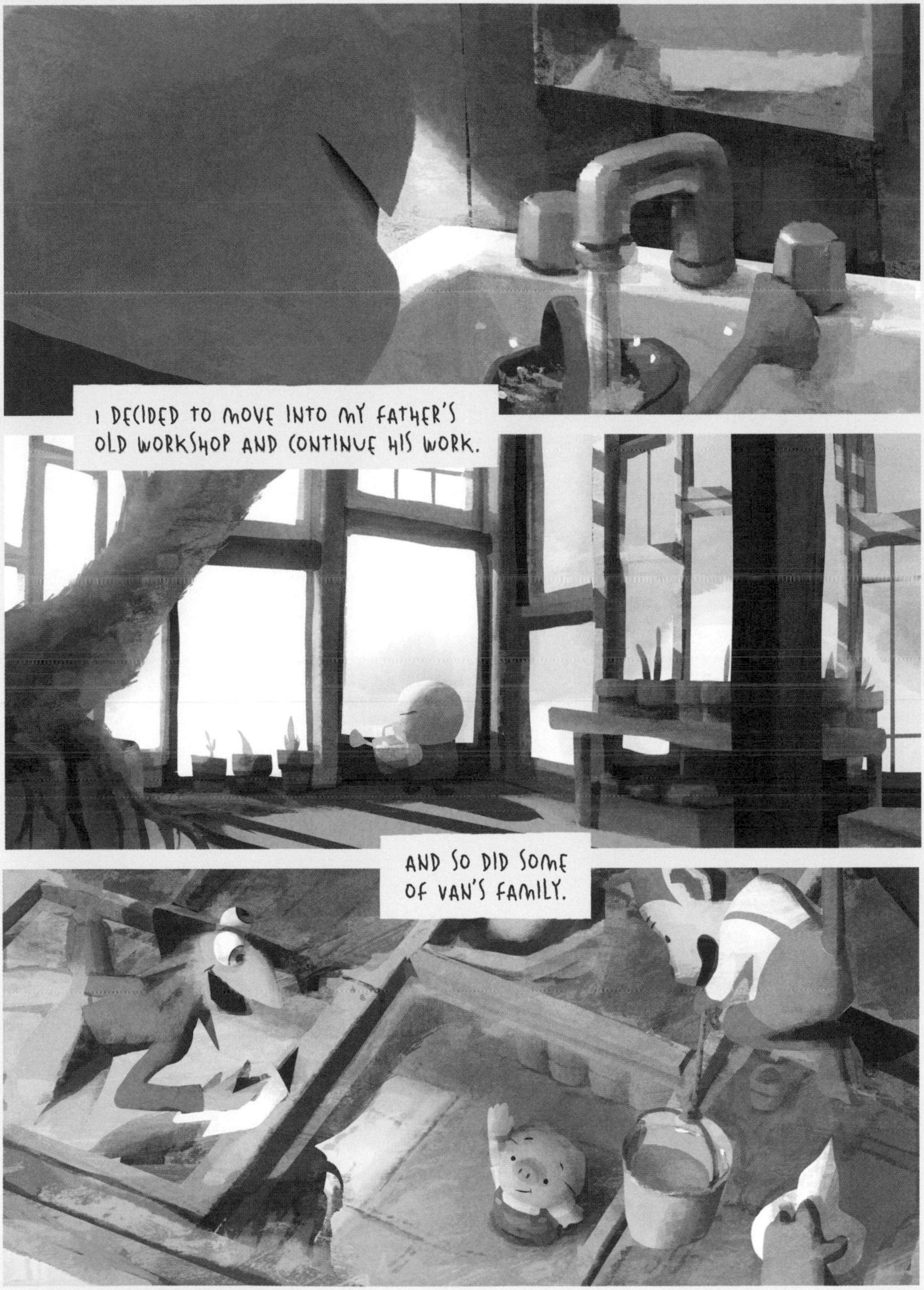
I DECIDED TO MOVE INTO MY FATHER'S OLD WORKSHOP AND CONTINUE HIS WORK.
AND SO DID SOME OF VAN'S FAMILY.

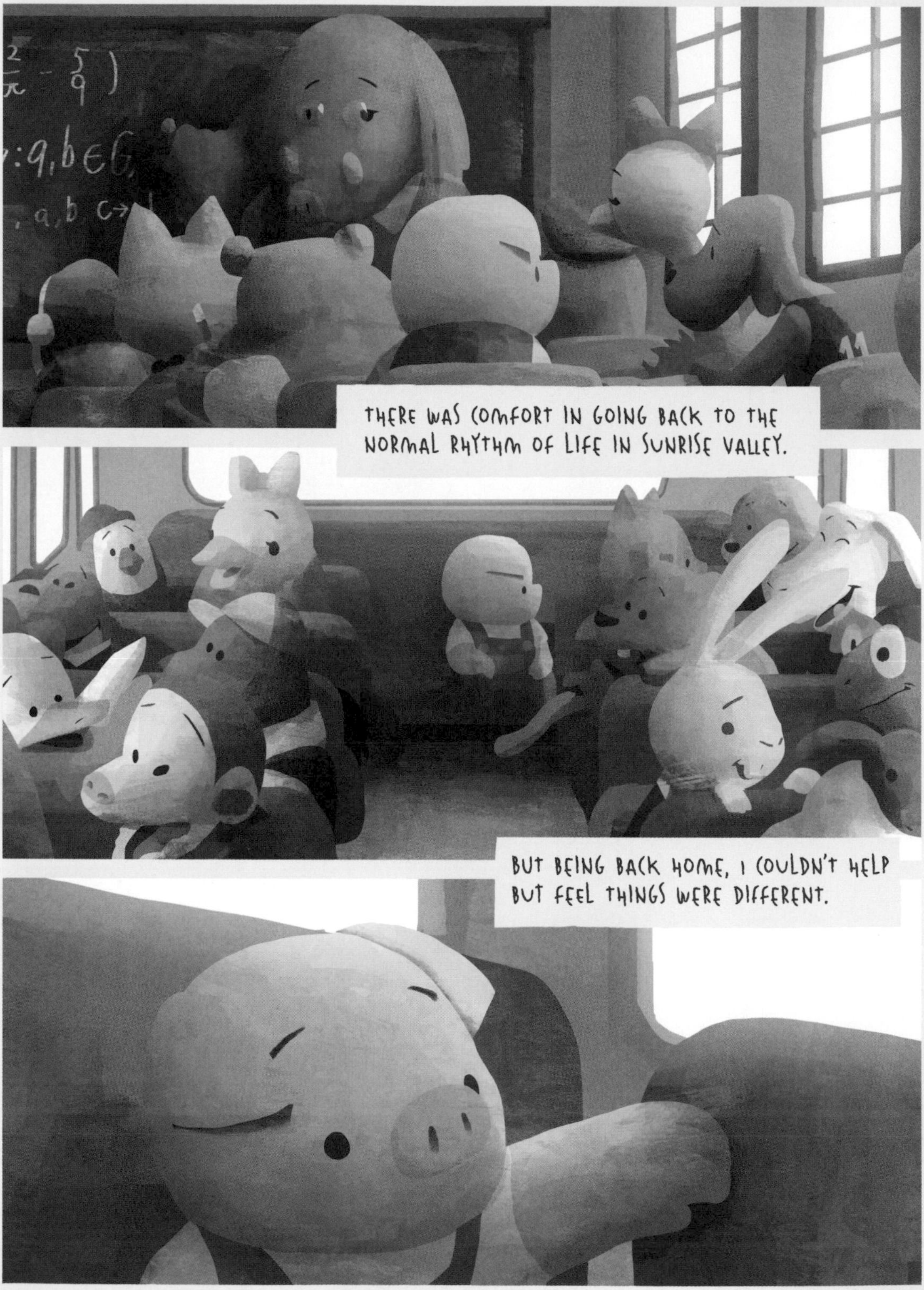
THERE WAS COMFORT IN GOING BACK TO THE NORMAL RHYTHM OF LIFE IN SUNRISE VALLEY.
BUT BEING BACK HOME, I COULDN'T HELP BUT FEEL THINGS WERE DIFFERENT.

THAT SUMMER FOREVER CHANGED THE WAY I SAW THE WORLD.

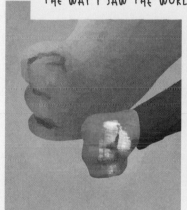

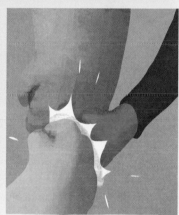

THE WAY I SAW MY FRIENDS.

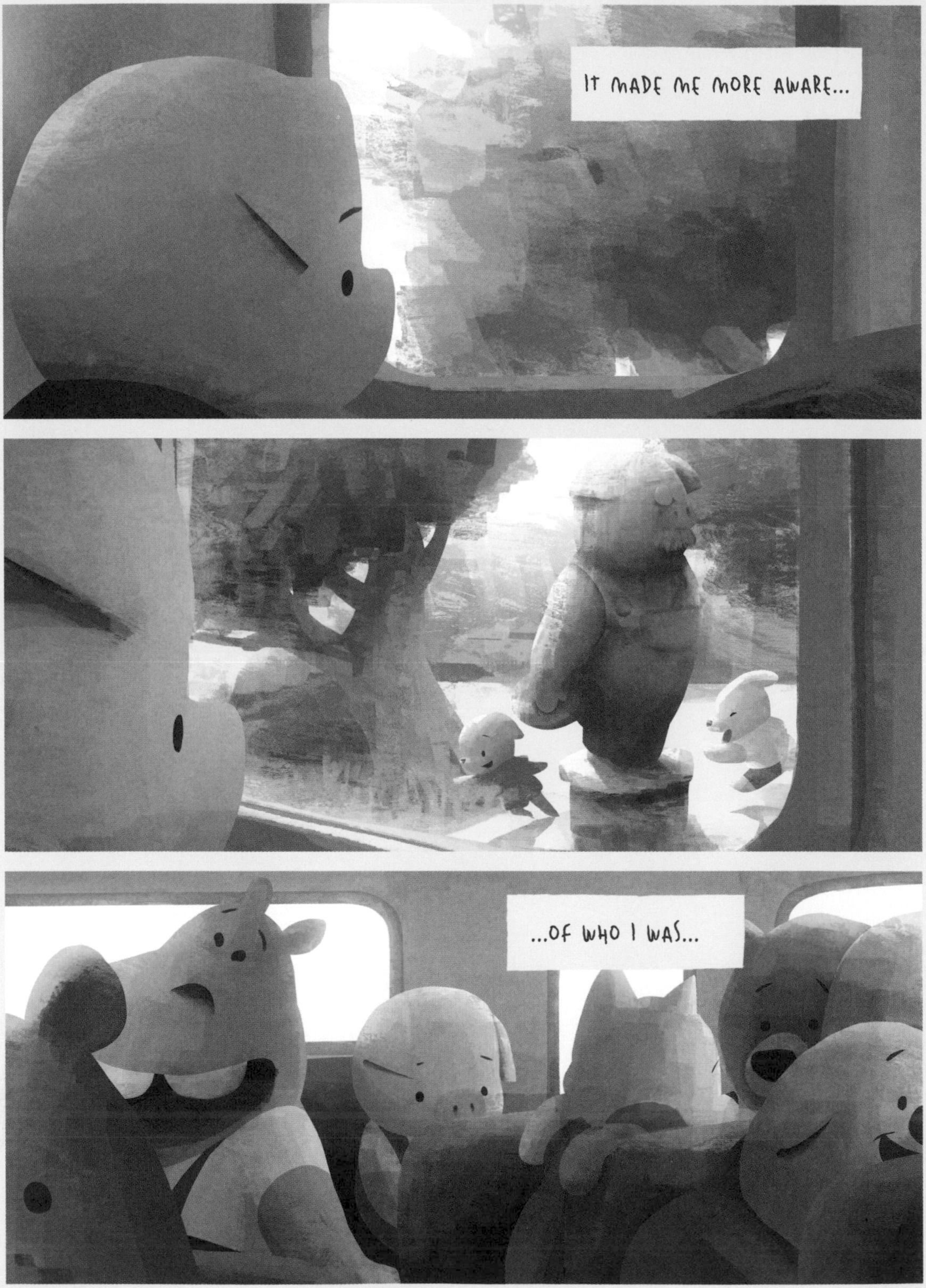

IT MADE ME MORE AWARE...
...OF WHO I WAS...

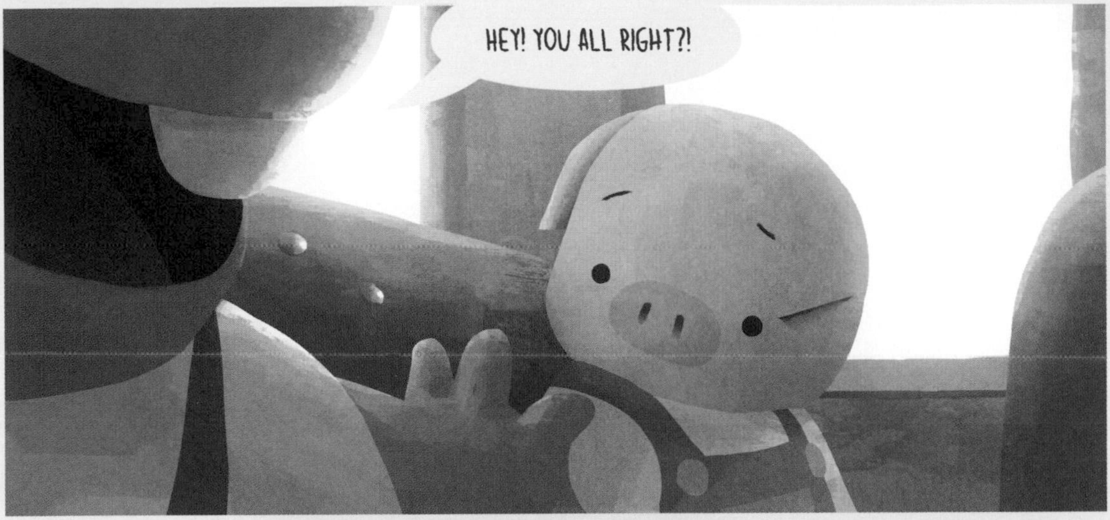
HEY! YOU ALL RIGHT?!

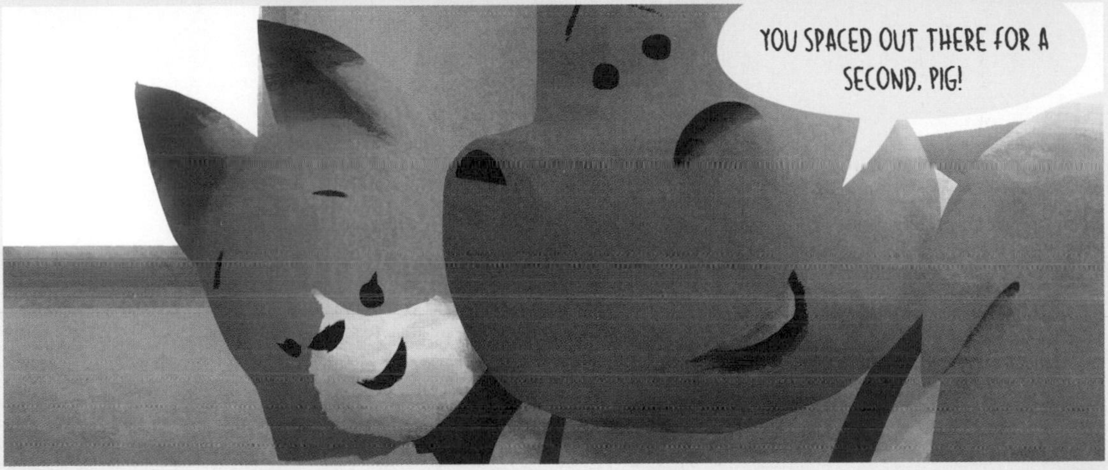
YOU SPACED OUT THERE FOR A SECOND, PIG!

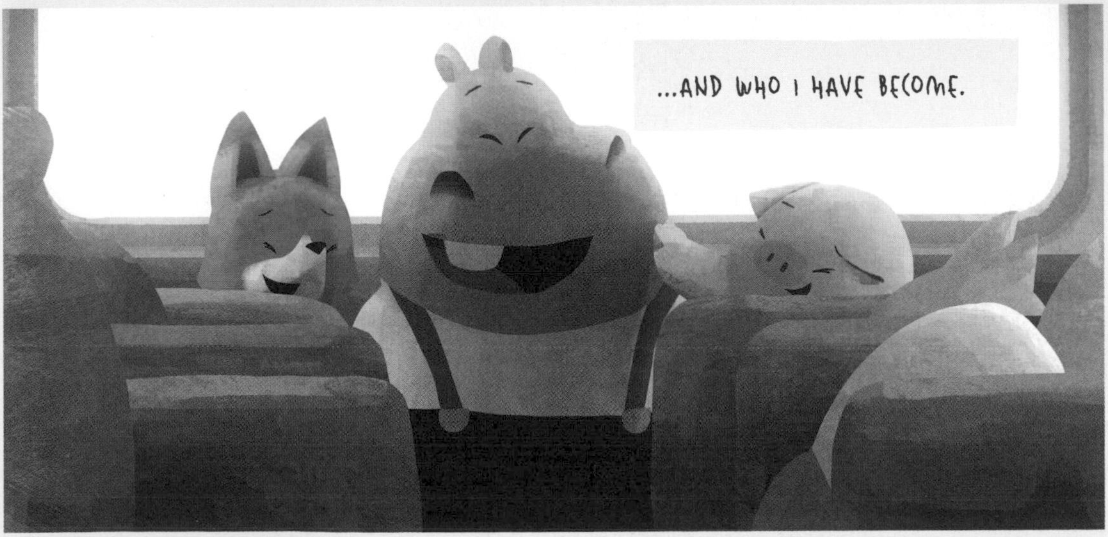
...AND WHO I HAVE BECOME.

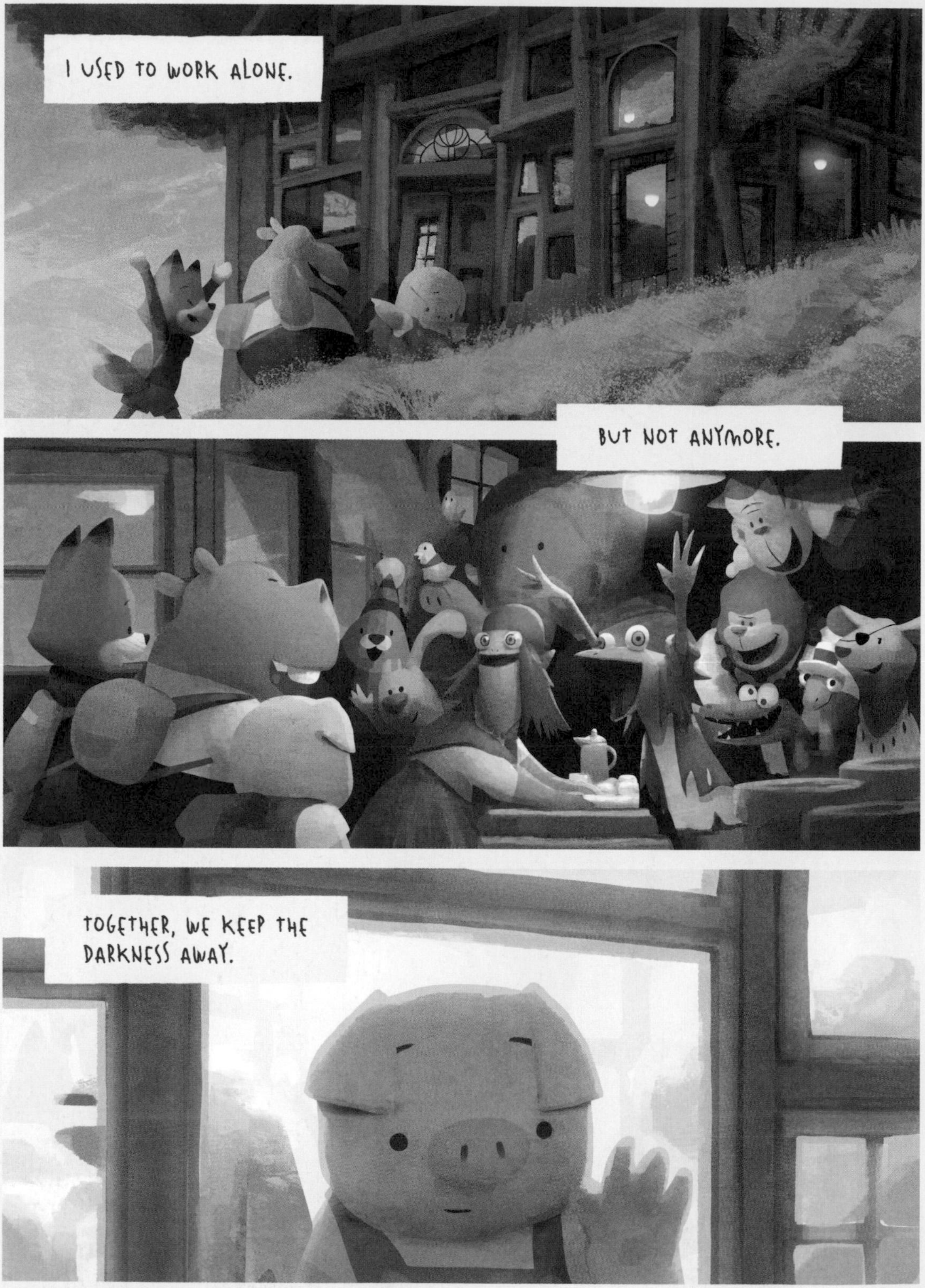
I USED TO WORK ALONE.
BUT NOT ANYMORE.
TOGETHER, WE KEEP THE DARKNESS AWAY.

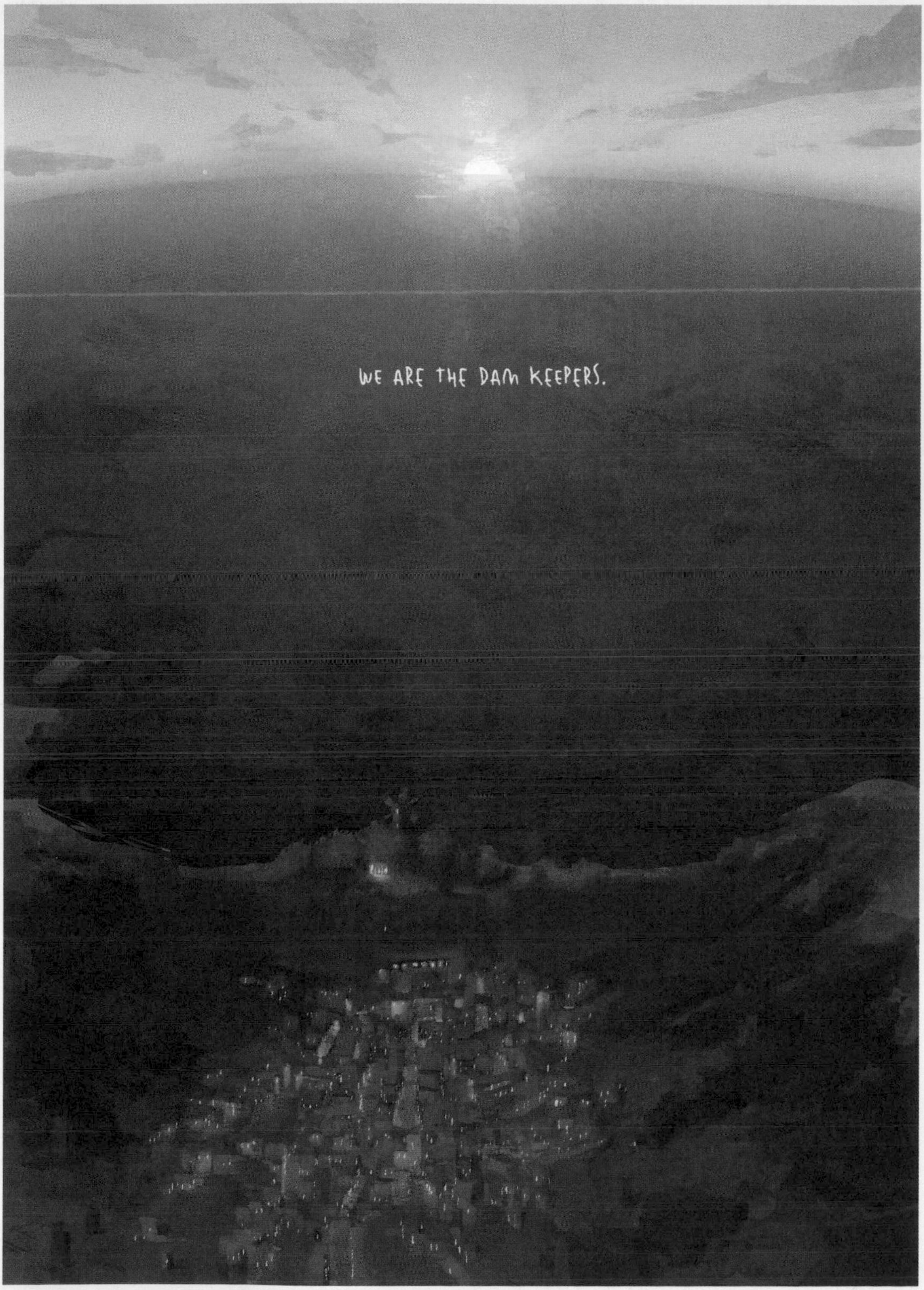
WE ARE THE DAM KEEPERS.

THE END.

APPENDIX

A collection of drawings and sketches for the
construction and layout of various dams, cities,
and workshops created for the preservation of
citizens existing in a world threatened by darkness.

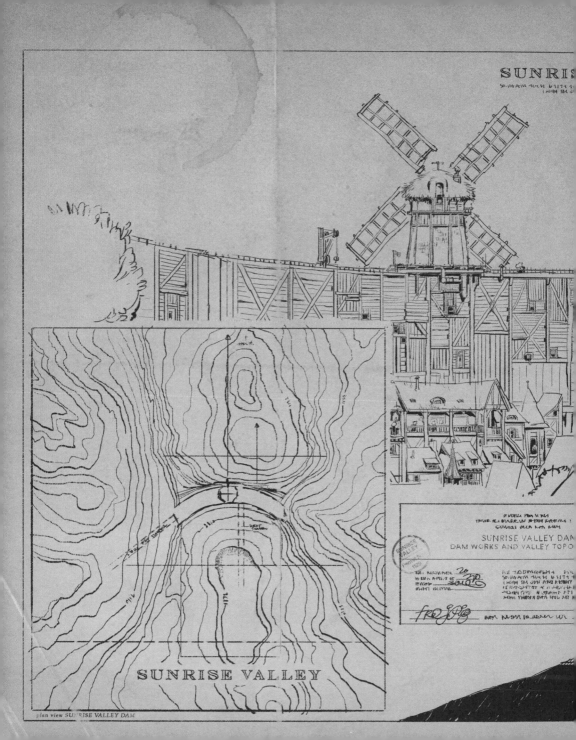

SUNRIS

SUNRISE VALLEY DAM
DAM WORKS AND VALLEY TOPO

SUNRISE VALLEY

plan view SUNRISE VALLEY DAM

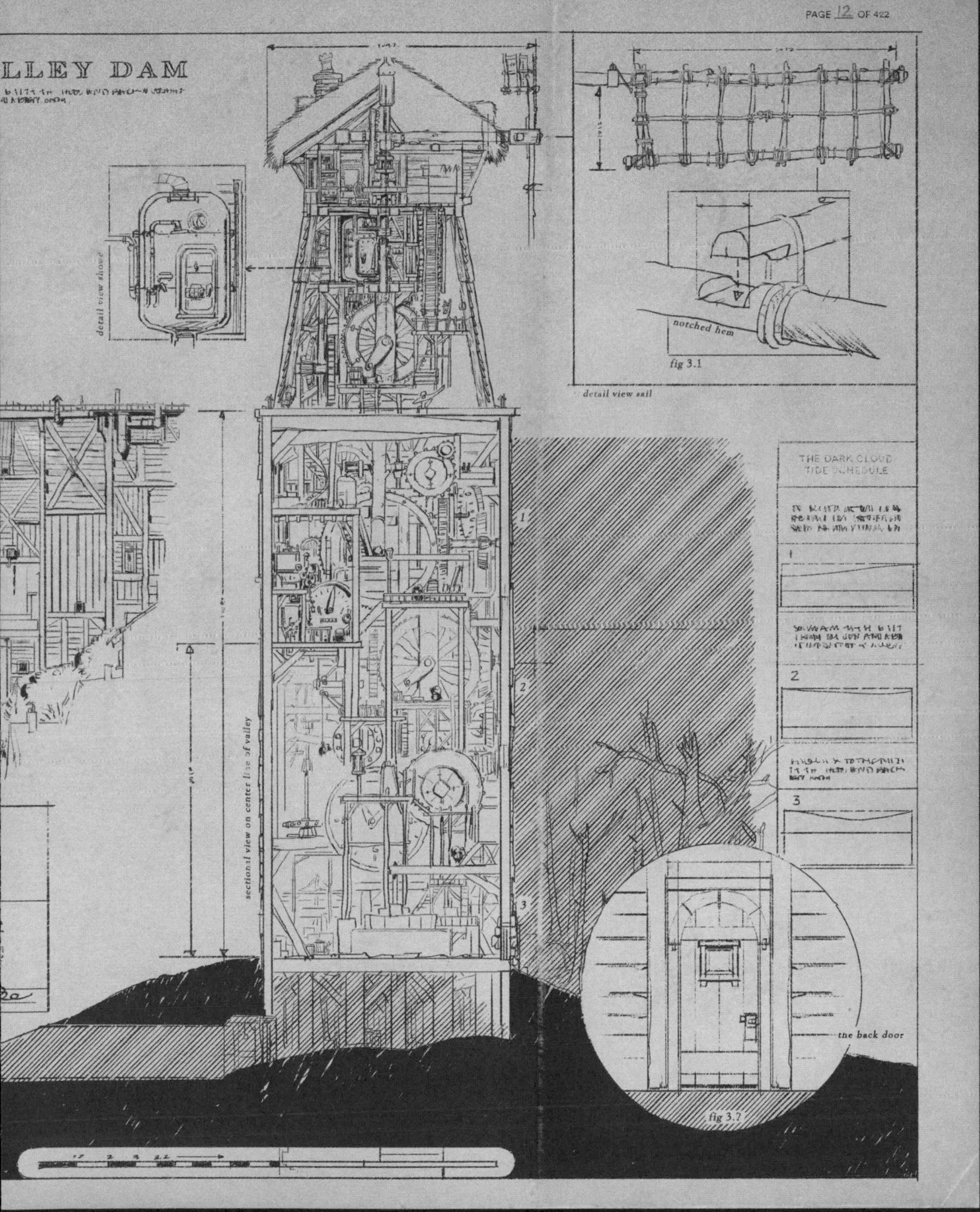
PAGE 12 OF 422
LLEY DAM
detail view above
notched hem
fig 3.1
detail view sail
THE DARK CLOUD
TIDE SCHEDULE
1
2
3
sectional view on center line of valley
the back door
fig 3.2

ARCHITECTURAL PLAN FOR THE DAM OF SUNRISE VALLEY, 12th page of 422-page plan

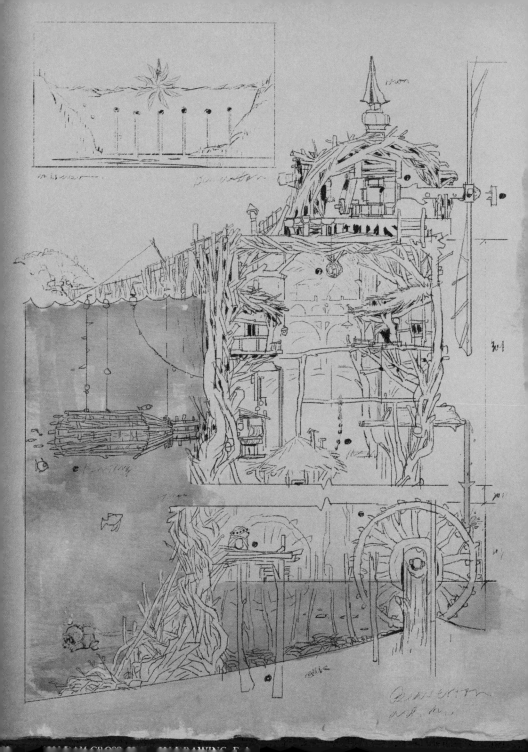

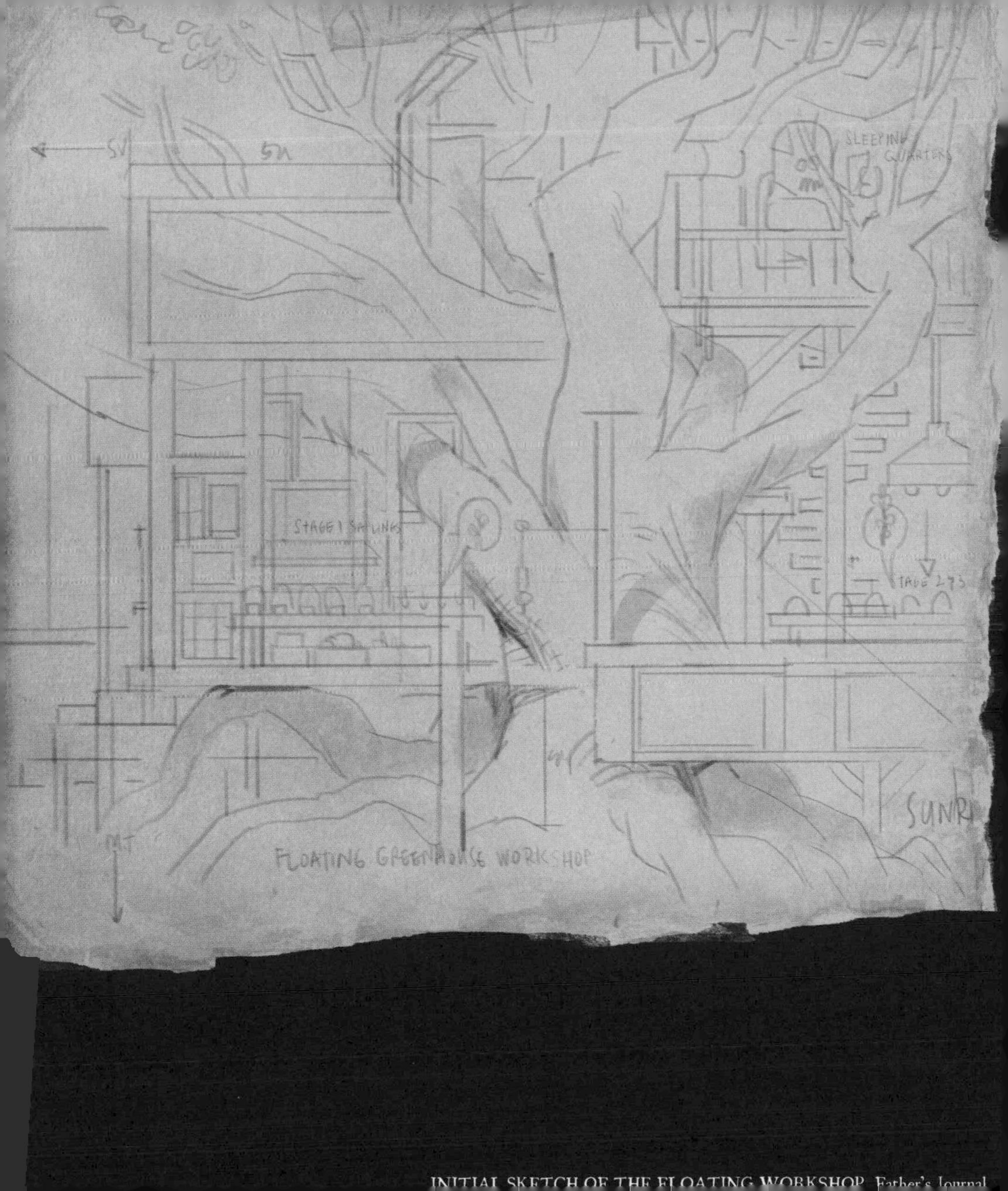
SLEEPING QUARTERS
STAGE 1 SAPLINGS
STAGE 2+3
FLOATING GREENHOUSE WORKSHOP
SUNRI

INITIAL SKETCH OF THE FLOATING WORKSHOP Father's Journal

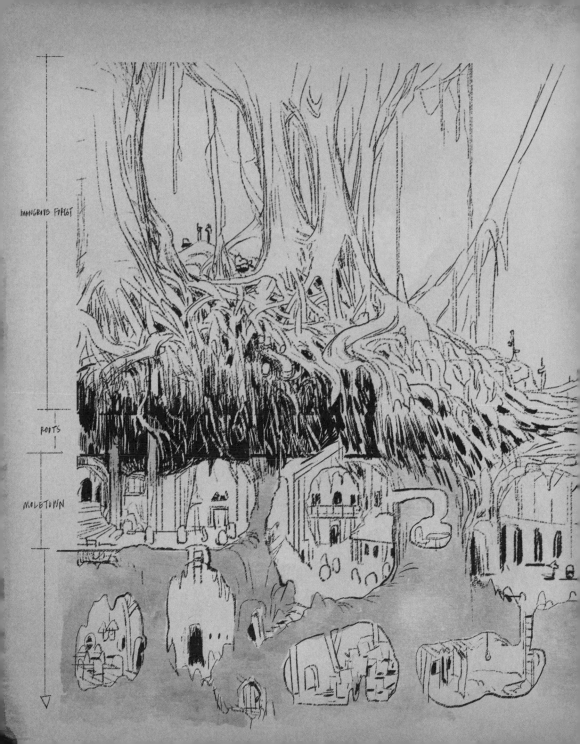

MANGROVE FOREST

ROOTS

MOLETOWN

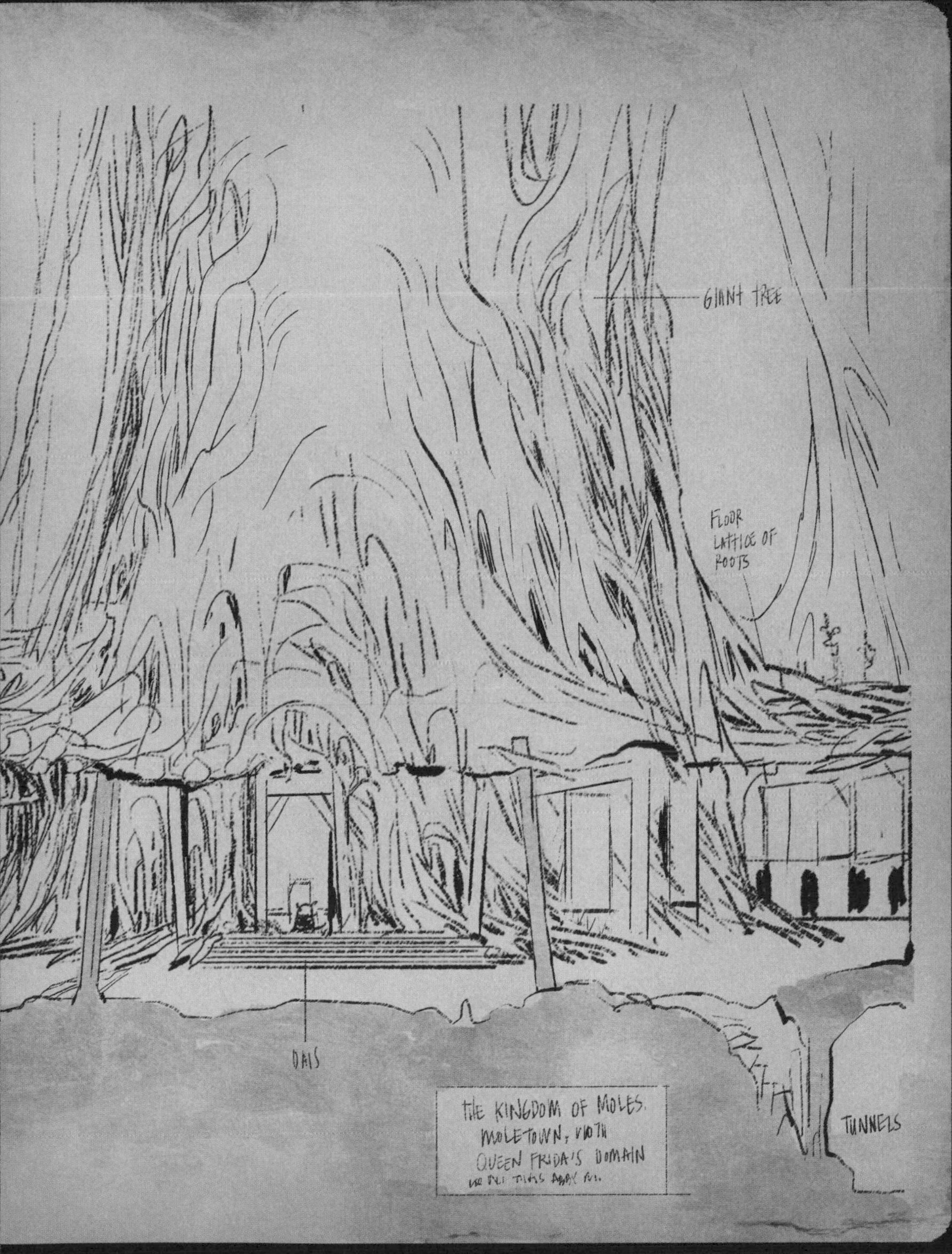
GIANT TREE
FLOOR
LATTICE OF
ROOTS
DAIS
TUNNELS
THE KINGDOM OF MOLES.
MOLETOWN,
QUEEN FRIDA'S DOMAIN

SKETCH OF MOLETOWN, Father's Journal

Thank you to our families and significant others on this journey. Thank you, John Henry Hinkel. A special thanks to Mark Siegel, Robyn Chapman, Andrew Arnold, Tim Stout, and the entire team at First Second and Macmillan Publishers.

And of course, a big thanks to our team at Tonko House.
—Robert & Dice

For Norm Schureman
—RK

First Second

Copyright © 2019 by Tonko House Inc.

Published by First Second
First Second is an imprint of Roaring Brook Press,
a division of Holtzbrinck Publishing Holdings Limited Partnership
120 Broadway, New York, NY 10271

Don't miss your next favorite book from First Second!
For the latest updates, go to firstsecondnewsletter.com and sign up for our e-newsletter.

All rights reserved

Library of Congress Control Number: 2018944053

ISBN: 978-1-62672-456-3

Our books may be purchased in bulk for promotional, educational, or business use.
Please contact your local bookseller or the Macmillan Corporate and Premium Sales Department
at (800) 221-7945 ext. 5442 or by e-mail at MacmillanSpecialMarkets@macmillan.com.

First edition, 2019
Edited by Mark Siegel and Tim Stout
Book design by John Green

Printed in China by RR Donnelley Asia Printing Solutions Ltd., Dongguan City, Guangdong Province

Penciled with Shiyoon Kim's Wet Ink brush and painted with
Tonko House's custom paintbrush in Adobe Photoshop.

1 3 5 7 9 10 8 6 4 2